The Fantastically Underwhelming Epic

of a dead wizard and an average bard

Kian N. Ardalan

D1522556

ISBN: 9798694331210

Cover design by: Rumyana Zarkova

Map design by: FantasyMapsPro on Fiverr

Editing: Anne-Marie Rutella

Library of Congress Control Number: 2018675309

Printed in the United States of America

To my grandfather and grandmother who have spoilt me with their love and support—thank you for believing in me.

Map commissioned by the Wings of Vrania for escort routes and guides

Prologue

Within a bar known only as Lost Dreams, there strummed a bard upon his lute and softened the moods of all present.

Children now filled the space where years before it was just the drunken stupor of the wildly inebriated.

Laughter also filled the area, though that was nothing new, but it no longer had that hint of worry and dread that was being submerged in mead.

The bard strummed his lute once more.

The place was old, but full of charm. It had a scent, the bar, sometimes it was the scent of cinnamon during the colder months, other times it was that of polished wood.

The children aptly complained about the stinking odour of foamy mead which had worked its way into the floorboards from all the times the golden liquid escaped from the rim of its tankards.

With sticky feet and squeaky steps, the inn filled with life.

There was another thing that was different from years before.

Not just that the roads were secure and monsters were kept at bay, nor was it that previously perilous lands were safe to travel.

More than anything else, it was the fact that magic had returned to the world, and Tiria flourished like a blotch of paint upon canvas that blossomed into a full rosy bloom.

Another string was hit at the lute.

"What would you like to hear next?" The children smiled devilishly with restrained anticipation—it was absolutely no secret what they wanted to hear.

Yet their arms sprang up and their hands fluttered as their faces filled with exasperated excitement.

The bard chuckled—it was already obvious.

"The story about Simantiar!" one kid cried out, and all the others nodded in agreement.

The bard ran his finely lithe and dexterous fingers over his curled dirt-brown hair and sighed with exasperation. But he knew how it went, he knew the song and tale that brought most to the town of Haven, and more precisely, to the bar of Lost Dreams.

He resigned himself to his fate and teased the children.

"That tale? Oh, but it's such an old story. Most don't even believe any of it. You don't want to listen to that," the bard playfully groused.

"Yes, we do!" cried one child.

"How about this new one I have been working on? It is about goblins—"

"No! We want to hear about Simantiar!"

The kids chanted together, even old-timers joined in. The bard leaned forward and blew away a curled strand of hair that hung over his defeated expression.

The children chanted the rhyme that all mothers taught so that the fear of a monster would instil good behaviour into their little ones.

"Simantiar, Simantiar,
Never forget his name,
Simantiar, Simantiar,
For he will judge your pain,
Simantiar, Simantiar,
Your happiness is his bane,
Simantiar, Simantiar,
Be good or another child he will gain."

They all laughed cherubically, as if celebrating the defeat of a nonexistent fear.

"So, you want to hear about Simantiar?"

The children rose up in an elated uproar, only quieting down at a placating motion from the bard.

"Fine." He readied his lute and prepared his voice. "Do you think Simantiar strong?"

The children nodded.

"Do you think him wise?"

Again another nod as they leaned in expectantly, each question punctuated with a strike of a cord.

"Do you think him a stoic legend?"

One child had to catch herself lest she planted her face to the ground.

The bard restrained a loving smirk and allowed himself a scratch upon his bristling chin beard.

"Well, Simantiar is none of those things, and all of those things. Get ready to be disappointed, for this is not the kind of story you think it will be. It is one of average people, of unimpressive magic, of pain. It is 'The Fantastically Underwhelming Epic.'"

The children chimed in to finish the rest, "Of a dead wizard and an average bard!"

Chapter 1

"Ow."

"What was that?"

"Nothing." George leaned against the table giving his best smile, a smile that he had practised for many years. A smile that had people give him the benefit of the doubt and girls throw themselves at him. Yet underneath his composure he was anything but calm as he tried hard to silence the skull that chattered away in his bag.

"Well okay, then. Take the third door on the right," the tavern keeper said, wiping down a tankard. George nodded, dropping a few copper coins on the counter and striding up the stairs before the chattering skull forced him to pretend he was a ventriloquist. ﹢

Leaning against the door, George panted in relief, rubbing his cheeks that had turned sore from all the smiling. When he finally felt it was safe and that no one would knock on their door, he rummaged through the bag and pulled out a coughing skull.

"So dusty in there—do you ever clean?" it asked snarkily.

"You're a skeleton, you don't have a throat to cough with." George frowned.

When George had braved the dark and perilous tomb of Simantiar only a year before, he had dodged many a trap from winding paths to false floors, pressure plates just waiting to be set off, and derelict mechanisms too obscure for George's understanding. What worried George most were the curiously placed statues that seemed ready to jump to life at any moment, peering out through lifeless eyes of reflecting gems—of course George permitted himself a treasure or two during his expeditions, including the large oculus gems.

Thus one can't blame George's disappointment for when he found that the wizard, albeit immortal and truly capable of warding off magic, was rather lame.

"What took you so bloody long? Listen, I have an itch, right there on my nose—can you get it for me? I would, but my arms aren't really what they used to be." That. Those were the first words that Simantiar ever spoke to George at their first meeting before bursting into cackling laughter.

George wondered if Simantiar was always that insane, or perhaps the centuries of solitude had driven him mad. Or maybe where his body was immortal, his mind was less so, having gone senile a long time ago.

"Well, maybe it is to get the point across that the great Simantiar shouldn't be the lucky talisman of a bloody bard. Let alone stuffed into a bag."

"Oh, shut it." George tossed the wizard's skull onto a table, the complaints uttered by the skinless, fleshless skull turning into white noise as George undid his boots.

"How about you take me around town, show me where the ladies are at?"

George ignored him. He was trying hard to drown out the skull's voice.

"Oh, come on, you owe me at least that much after dragging me around all day."

"I need to get some rest; we are leaving early tomorrow." George spoke the words quietly. It was true that he had expected a more stoic character when coming across the remains of the Great Wizard, as even finding the tomb had taken him the better part of three years and the lives of several mercenaries. As he contemplated the journey, he had realised that the trials made more and more sense. Each tomb with another puzzle that led to the next, led George on a wild-goose chase until he finally came to the last.

Even the manic cackling of Simantiar couldn't completely drown out the screams. George was secretly appreciative of Simantiar's antics as they were a pleasant distraction.

"Why do you even need to move your jaws to talk?" George asked.

"Haven't you ever heard it's rude to talk with your mouth closed?"

"No?"

"Well, it's a thing. There is such a thing as 'The Skeleton Code.'"

"You're making that up."

"No. I'm not. Skeleton's honour!"

George rolled his eyes. "Fine, I give up." Rising to his feet, George stretched his arms high over his head and wiggled his toes, enjoying that sweet feeling of having them unencumbered by leather boots. *Is this what it is like when women let their breasts breathe?* he pondered, as he sank back into the comforts of a hard and unpleasant bed, yet he didn't complain as it was far better than anything the road had to offer over the past week.

George sighed, the only thing that was missing was someone he could share the covers with. It was a shame he couldn't lure a cute girl to give him company, since Simantiar always made sure that nothing would ever come of the night. The one night George did try, he thought himself smart for gagging the skull, and the plotting wizard played along until George brought a rather striking woman home. That was when George realised that Simantiar spoke through more magical means: the wizard didn't hesitate when it came to making George feel miserable.

"Don't bother with him. I have heard him mess around with women in the sack, not so great. And his athlete's foot? I have never seen a case that severe! And I have lived for a *very* long time." Rather than Simantiar's unsettling accounts, George suspected it was more likely the sight of a talking skeleton that sent her screaming. "Nice girl. When are you going to see her again?" Simantiar mocked, even his skeletal jaw always seemed to be grinning.

Morning finally came, first light breaking into George's room. He groaned, rubbing his eyes and rising with a wide yawn.

"Sleep well?" Simantiar asked.

"No." George didn't bother adding to the comment. He found it hard to sleep with Simantiar constantly talking throughout the night. Even in his dreams he wouldn't find peace as an even more annoying skull berated him, while floating no less.

George played his lute in the tavern, earning himself a few coins before receiving a cut of bread on the house and leaving for the road once more.

"I never did ask you." Simantiar now showing some semblance of seriousness in his voice. "Why did you find me in the first place?"

George stayed silent—he knew that he was going to have to respond eventually. "I need you to unlock something."

"What do you mean?"

"There is a…vault." George sounded almost unsure of himself as he explained, "Its walls are barred with magic that no human can penetrate."

"But an old bag of bones can?"

George didn't reply.

"What will we find inside?"

"A promise."

Chapter 2

"You're messing with me, right?"

"Why?"

"What do you mean 'Why?' It's a bloody book, you asshole." If Simantiar could frown, George was sure he would have. His entire skull was clattering all over the book upon which he rested.

"You dared the perils of my trials for a fairy tale?" Simantiar seemed incredulous, incapable of believing George's words.

"It's not just a book." George closed its pages delicately and stored it away with great care. Even long before he could read the words, the book meant the world to him: to him and another.

Earlier that day, Simantiar had asked George where the vault was located.

"I don't know," the bard had responded.

"What do you mean, you don't know?"

"It means I don't know."

"Well gee, how are we going to find it, then? Wait for a formal invitation? Maybe ask for directions from the town's guard."

"I found you."

"That's because I *wanted* to be found, genius. I left clues. And I can't tell if the fact that it was you out of all people who found me makes me worried for your species, or simply shows how you were the only one stupid enough to actually look."

"Yeah, because finding you wasn't a great disappointment for me either."

"Fine. How do you even know this place is real, then?" And that was when George took out the book and turned it to his page. Simantiar's incredulous look was most likely the result of being shown a children's book, as if it were the most holy of books and told that all the stories are true. The exact page that was being referenced had a gorgeous rendition of golden gates that stood tall and grand. Even though the colour of the page had faded a long time ago, it still carried a wonder to it that filled George with hope.

"Oh god. This is it, isn't it? My punishment. My hell. I am supposed to travel the world endlessly with this idiot looking for a fairy tale." Simantiar lamented, his voice seemingly on the verge of breaking and devoid of hope.

"Believe what you want. I am finding that place and when I do, I will rub you against the seal until you are nothing but dust."

"Do you even know what is inside?"

George shrugged. "The book simply says 'What the heart most desires.'"

Simantiar opened his skeletal jaw and remained silent for several moments to accentuate his disbelief. "That could be a bloody sandwich for all you know!"

George had enough at that point. He didn't care how old the wizard was. He didn't appreciate him shitting on his only dream since he was a child.

Keeping Simantiar quiet at the town's market while buying fruits and other rations proved taxing to George. When they finally left for the road, Simantiar wouldn't stop spinning anticlimactic tales. "The Fantastically Underwhelming Epic of a dead wizard and an average bard—a tale that will make you cry and laugh; an epic tale of woe and shit."

Even Simantiar struggled to come up with new insults over time, becoming quiet only to shout random updates.

"I'm hungry."

"You're dead..."

"I don't know, I'm craving ribs. Luckily, you brought along my own! Mind passing them over?"

"No wonder someone buried you deep in that tomb." When George didn't get a response, he looked over his shoulder to where Simantiar was perched and expected another snarky quip, but he heard only silence.

George wondered if he struck a nerve and considered apologising, but thought it best to hold his tongue.

Most of the trip was done in silence, and it was in the next town over where Simantiar seemed to realise where they were headed, probably due to the standing signpost which said Adna—Last Refuge Before The Forest of The Dead.

"Oh, how curious—your travel destination coincidentally also takes us along to where the Forest of the Dead resides?" Simantiar said after George had paid and entered a new room.

"Yes."

"Well, that is such a funny coincidence! Where are we headed?" Simantiar asked, though George knew that Simantiar already knew the answer.

"The Forest of the Dead."

A moment of rare quiet before Simantiar finally said, "Well, how about this? Let's not."

"We have to go through there, anyway. And we will look for a sword for hire in the morning."

"A boy like you should be frolicking with several girls he believes to be his true love till the next is found! You are too young to go into a place named Forest of the Dead."

"I am at my sixteenth spring, I think I am old enough."

"Well, what about me?! You wouldn't dare take a thousand-year-old man on such a dangerous trip."

George rolled his eyes.

"Look, I am old enough, and I have seen things. Just two years ago I followed the trails of one of your tombs and barely escaped with my life— my guide sure as hell didn't."

"What killed him? Don't tell me, don't tell me." Simantiar gave a long drone of a sound as if trying to evoke some precognitive ability. "Darts from the walls! Oh, a rolling boulder! Oh, oh, oh—poisonous gas!"

"Me," George corrected.

Simantiar suddenly got very silent.

"I have grown up, I have seen things, I have matured. Trust me, I am not some clueless boy."

Silence filled the space between them. George sighed in defeat; perhaps he had gone too far?

"Have you ever considered why these places have such terrifying names? Why not, 'Forest of the Rainbows' or, 'Forest of the Friendly Puppies' or, 'Nice Place?'" Simantiar rambled.

"Good night, Simantiar." George gave himself to the rough and hard comfort of his bed.

The skull gave a sigh of his own. "Good night." George looked over to Simantiar perched upon the small round tea table, expecting more quips and insults and general tirades...nothing. George went to sleep that night, without any distractions or being woken by relentless talking. The skull was...curious. A sombre stillness to him, his constant rambling perhaps more than just nonsensical... George wondered if it was perhaps even pathological. All that George knew for sure was that Simantiar's own memory was as complete and cohesive as his own skeletal body.

Morning came and George was already about looking for their ticket through the forest. The tavern they stayed at was called Equinox. It was an incredibly fitting name, and as a bard, George desperately wanted to know about its origin. After all, this was the last refuge before wandering into the rather perilous woods.

George remembered the very first time when he approached a mercenary—how his voice broke and his knees trembled. George leaned against a wall and observed the men: there weren't many. Most of them either had gotten bored waiting for an employer and instead drowned themselves in their ale while a third-rate bard played simple melodies out of tune; few others seemed to want to entertain the idea of being hired by a young boy. George finally chose one, and though they all looked as if the sight of a small boy would cause them to be annoyed, at least this one seemed bored enough to humour the idea of employment.

"Are you for hire?" George asked a man who carried a thick and foreboding air to him, his back hunched with a leather hide fastened about his shoulders and torso. The man seemed to be in an awful mood already, but all swords for hire seemed like they were about to kill the first thing that gave them an excuse, or at least that was George's impression. This one held a mug of ale in his hand as he sat at the tavern bar, drinking away at the contents as if whatever joy or comfort it once provided was long ago.

"Move along, kid, this isn't a game," spoke the man with a deep and rustic voice, eyes glued to the contents of his mug, as if somewhere under its surface was something he had lost.

"I can pay." George reached into his pocket and pulled out two gold coins. The mercenary finally turned to George, eying him up and down with the eyes of a raven. George could more clearly now see the man's features—a diagonal scar ran across his face, and deep brown eyes that seemed more feral than human thanks to the brambles he would have called eyebrows. The man scratched his black stubble.

"How does a kid like you have coin like that?"

"Don't worry, I earned it. So, are you up for hire or not?" The mercenary chuckled, and George could feel a restless skull trying to get his attention from within the bag.

"Not now," George whispered to his bag, yet Simantiar became even more frantic.

The mercenary finally stood up, towering over George. "You are not very bright, are you, boy?"

George finally understood as he took a step back. Simantiar wasn't trying to embarrass him, he was trying to warn him. How foolish it was for him to display gold like that so far out.

"How about I take some of that gold off your hands?"

George was about to turn away, when he noticed two more burly men stand with scarred and battle-forged bodies.

The one on the left was truly bigger, as if he had giant's blood running through him. A bald scalp and a nose that seemed to have been started on, but the artist gave up halfway when realising that the entire thing was a hopeless eyesore. The one on the right was as hefty as a man could be, with well-built forearms and a thick pitch-black beard that covered the lower half of his face.

"Come on, let's go outside so we can talk some more," said the raven-eyed man with false courtesy.

George scanned the room for help, but found that, though not crowded, everyone was already engaged in some way or another and too deep into their tankards to heed any call for help.

"Fine. Let me just finish my drink." George looked around to the nearest table and took what seemed to be an abandoned tankard. George suppressed the rising bile at the thought of drinking down the ale of another man and refused to consider how long the tankard had been sitting there or what kind of man it belonged to. The lingering warmth and froth of the ale didn't help. George gulped it all down, its liquid running rivers down his chin as the dour-eyed man stood patiently.

In one flash of a moment George swung the tankard, smashing it across the man's head and bolting before any of them could realise what just happened.

"Get him!" George heard someone call from behind as he vaulted over the bar table.

With the entrance to the tavern barred by drunken folk, George ran through the back, coming across a rather large innkeeper who shouted unheard complaints at him.

Bursting through the door, George didn't slow his advantage, a few chickens flying by his path with surprised squawks. George grabbed one and managed to stay on his feet. He turned to toss the chicken into the face of his pursuers before continuing to flee down turns and bends within the small town of Adna just before the embrace of the wild.

"Got you!" The first mercenary turned the corner, grabbing George by the arm and slamming him against the wall. In spite of the blood which ran down the man's scalp, the grin he sported suggested he was more than fine. Well, as fine as a deranged lunatic can be.

George looked everywhere for a clue, for a way to escape; he survived far more dangerous situations before. He'd like to think it was mostly due to some peculiar cunning, but more often than not, it was just rather preposterous luck.

There. Within the inconsequential routine of strolling bystanders and labouring workers, George saw a glint of steel betray his absolution.

"You!" Even with his back pressed against a wall and callused fists clutching his garments, George stared not at the three mercenaries that were about to beat him to a pulp, but at another mercenary leaning against the opposite building.

The man looked over at George and his three oppressors with great disinterest, seeming almost annoyed for being involved.

"What do you want, kid?" The question was asked harshly.

"I hire you as my bodyguard." The three aggressors seemed more than just shocked; they were about to beat him up and take all he had to offer, and there he was completely ignoring them only to ask for another's services.

"I don't come cheap. I doubt a runt like you can afford me."

"Why do you think these guys want to beat me up so bad?"

The man smiled; George wasn't sure if it was for the promise of gold or if he liked his courage. Nonetheless, the swordsman unsheathed one of his blades with great confidence and moved towards his new employer's attackers.

George nurtured his wounded confidence as he trailed behind his hired guard, Kendrith, towards the entrance of the forest. Considering how, for all his statements about being grown and knowledgeable, George hadn't considered the foolishness in flaunting his gold. He surely also didn't wish to mention that more often than not, the lives he had taken were by pure luck and chance rather than some great feat of combat.

"Are you sure we can trust him?"

"Shhhhh!" Every time Simantiar tried to lower his voice, George seemed to shush him even louder.

"Did you say something?" Their new hired guard turned around to eye his employer. Where George's first choice held the stalking eyes of a raven, this man held the eyes of a wolf.

"Nothing." George put on his best innocuous smile, as Kendrith turned his gaze back onto the road.

George's smile died on his lips. Other than his incomprehensible luck and cunning, his smile was his greatest weapon. A smile that displayed some faux innocence, as if he were too young to understand concepts such as lying and deceit.

He was no longer in the city, no longer among the heart of civilisation. His smile would do little to ward off whatever horrors awaited them at the forest, let alone hardened folk like Kendrith.

"I have to pee," George stated, and as expected, Kendrith groaned.

"Again? If the size of your bladder and your lack of beard are anything to go by, your prick must be a damned sorry thing," Kendrith spoke the words coldly and without any humour, but it didn't matter, George could hear the snickering that came from his bag.

George slammed a hand against the bag, gratified by a muffled "ow" that reached only his own ears.

"Sorry. Best go now before we enter the forest."

"I am guessing you want to go alone again?"

George nodded.

"It really must be small if you don't want me to see it." Simantiar's cackle grew even louder at that. George didn't hesitate, running off behind a lonesome tree and an equally lonely boulder with such haste as to remove Simantiar from earshot.

"Be quiet," George whispered harshly as he placed Simantiar onto the ground.

"You know what? Never mind. I like the guy."

"Of course you do, he's an asshole."

"Says the guy travelling the world looking for a fairy tale."

"Whatever. Look. Just be quiet. Forget the gold. Do you know how much someone would pay if they found a talking skull like you? Let alone the fact when they realise who you truly are. Magic may be a rarity nowadays and very scarce, but it doesn't change the fact that you'd be worth a fortune."

George wasn't sure, but he imagined the silent stare that the skull gave him was to express his understanding. "You're right, I will try to be more careful."

George nodded.

"Besides, it sounds like Kendrith will be doing my job for me for a while," the skull mused.

"For such a tiny dick, you do piss out a stream, don't you?" George heard Kendrith call from afar.

"Pleeeeease, can we keep him?" Simantiar begged as George groaned, stuffing the skull back into the bag.

It didn't take long until the two reached the edge of the forest, and the sun had already begun its slow descent a few hours before.

"Is this the Forest of the Dead?" George asked as they stepped into the cover of trees. It still seemed rather peaceful.

"No. Not yet, but we are at the edges. We will be there at nightfall."

"Did he say nightfall?"

George slammed a hand against his satchel to silence Simantiar. Kendrith stopped in his tracks and turned around.

"I-I sometimes speak in third person..."

Kendrith returned his eyes to the path before him, George was unsure if his hire believed him.

"Yes, we will be arriving at nightfall," Kendrith answered the question.

"Is it safe?"

"As safe as the Forest of the Dead can be."

Kendrith and George truly did arrive at nightfall. They gathered wood for a fire to cook three rabbits which Kendrith captured. The unfortunate critters never saw Kendrith's throwing knife strike true.

The fire warmed them, wood snapping and burning to the heat. The two quietly bit away at the tough muscle of rabbit flesh.

"Thank you for saving me back there at the town," George said.

"Stop."

"Stop what?"

"This." Kendrith pointed at the space between them. "We aren't friends. You hired me to take you through the forest safely and towards the next town over. We will part ways after. And that will be the end of it. Making friendships at the cost of professionalism costs lives." Kendrith punctuated his willingness to start a rapport by tearing off a piece of chewy meat from the rabbit. "I know, I've tried."

George went silent. Kendrith was right. He felt alone and far from home. The closest thing he had to a friend was a talking immortal skull that berated him at every turn. So, he let it be, only the cracking of fire to fill the void. But there was a peculiar aura to Kendrith that George took note of and understood—Kendrith wasn't harsh, he was a professional. George was to be delivered to the final destination in one piece; emotions could get in the way of that. It seeded a hurt in George that he had come across often enough—he longed for that kind of stoic strength, a silent courage that helped him protect what mattered. Though it was a little too late for him.

A snap. George turned around with a start, seeing the large shadowy figure of some anthropomorphic monster that skulked several feet from their camp, roaming aimlessly within the darkness. George couldn't tell for certain, but the hunched beasts seemed to tower in at six feet or more.

"Kendrith," George whispered harshly at the mercenary.

"What?" The swordsman didn't take George's lowered voice as enough reason to remain quiet. George simply pointed over his shoulder at the creature's outline.

"Don't worry about them," Kendrith said, returning to his rabbit that was almost bare bones.

"What do you mean? What are they?"

"They don't have a name. Out here, we just call them husks. They aren't interested in you or me. If you leave it be, it will leave you be." None of what Kendrith said in his stoic confidence rubbed off on George. He was still scared shitless.

The night droned on and Kendrith advised they find some sleep as he threw some more wood into the fire to keep the flames from dying. George had played a little bit on his lute, and it had earned him a smile from Kendrith. George hated the fact that Kendrith's approval meant so much to him.

Kendrith and George talked still despite Kendrith's words from earlier. Perhaps the lute opened the man up, or perhaps it was the fact that he saw George as a young boy in an unknown territory that warranted a little distraction.

"Why do you want to get to Haven?" Kendrith asked. "Family there?" The flames of the fire crackled between them, with lingering shadows of wandering husks roaming in the background.

"Haven?" George inquired with a frown.

Kendrith's eyes widened. "You aren't going to the next town over?" George rapped his fingers against the wooden hull of his lute.

George knew of the neighbouring lands. The valley that Kendrith and him were wandering through was one of the most dangerous and peculiar areas of the entire continent of Lenaren. With the strongest concentration of lingering magic and known territories too dangerous to explore. George had only said he wanted to get through the forest, never anything about his final destination. Kendrith must have assumed that Haven was his goal.

"You don't have to tell me," Kendrith said. "Everyone has their own reasons for doing what they do."

"No, it's fine. I can tell—"

"Shhh."

George frowned. "No really, it's fine. I am—"

Kendrith suddenly looked up, his gaze turning from placidity into one of deadly focus.

"What is it?" George asked, finally realising that there was something else that caught Kendrith's attention.

"I don't recall there being this many husks..." Kendrith said, standing up. If George found himself uncomfortable before Kendrith's words of confidence, he definitely found himself shitting up a storm now.

The bard looked around and found the skulking figures had come closer and closer to the camp and in bigger numbers. With the faint aid of the camplight, George could make out more of their unnerving features.

Long black arms which reached the floor, wired with muscle, and lithe. Fingers split into three. Defined shoulders to hold the weight of their appendages and their black chests giving off a shine as if polished. They stepped into the light, numbering closer to six. George could clearly see their faces, or rather just their mouths. Circular maws with row upon row of teeth lined back-to-back like that of a worm.

"Get up," Kendrith said through gritted teeth. His long black hair was tied into a ponytail so that it wouldn't get in his way as he unsheathed his blade. This one gleamed with not the familiar glint of steel, but rather the polish of silver.

"I thought you said they don't come after the likes of us?" George reminded Kendrith, standing back-to-back, as if the monsters would suddenly realise this and excuse themselves.

"They don't...unless..." Kendrith suddenly turned around and grabbed George's bag from him. Ignoring the sudden "hey," Kendrith rummaged through it, the rattling of bones colliding against each other.

The husks snarled like the hiss of a snake played in reverse, drawing closer with outstretched arms and taloned fingers, only a few feet away. Kendrith withdrew a skull from within.

"Well, this is awkward," Simantiar said, as the husks suddenly snarled with what could only be described as a deep hunger.

Chapter 3

Kendrith stammered, "I-but-what?"

The husks approached slowly, long prehensile tongues like that of an anteater shooting out to taste what George imagined was the lingering taste of whatever was drawing them in.

"Simantiar the Immortal, The Great, The Spectacular—pleasure to make your acquaintance," said Simantiar as the husks leaned in for the upheld skull as if he were being served on a silver platter. One could barely hear his introduction over the hungry snarls of the languid creatures.

Kendrith broke free from his trance, his shoulder reeling back for a toss.

"No-no-no-no!" George and Simantiar mutually retorted with shared panic as George waved his hands.

"They are after the magic! I can't take on this many of them!" Kendrith said.

"I need him!" George's words were filled with pleading desperation and equal threat. Kendrith scanned the boy, and whatever it was that he found made him relent.

"Fine!" Kendrith turned around with the skull in hand near one of the husks that towered over him. It reached for the mercenary, its boneless maw widening and stretching to devour Kendrith and Simantiar whole. George thought the beasts to be two to three heads taller, but as they straightened their backs, George withheld a squeal when realising that the husks stood at more than double his own height. The husk's three fingers, as long and lithe as the branches of withered trees, reached out for them.

Kendrith didn't try to go through the monster, for surely he would have been killed in an instant. Instead, he raised Simantiar in his hands, taking advantage of the attention he was drawing.

"What are you—" Simantiar's query was cut short, replaced by a long and surprised cry as he suddenly flew into the air. The gaze of the husks followed, their large circular mouths rippling open and shut with saliva the consistency of syrup stretching to the floor and glazing George's shoulder.

"Now!" With the husks distracted, trailing the arc in which Simantiar was flying (and screaming) Kendrith took George's hand and they shoved their way past an opening. The rough and reptilelike skin rubbed against George and made him ready to bring up what was left of the rabbits he had eaten that day.

With an outstretched arm and unparalleled acuity, Kendrith caught Simantiar on his return landing with such precision as if guided by strings.

"I think I'm going to hurl," Simantiar said woozily.

Kendrith didn't slow his pace, running faster and faster as George struggled to keep pace.

"What about our supplies?" George asked, panting as they distanced themselves farther and farther from the light of their camp and into the darkness of an aptly named forest.

"We will circle back. We just have to lose them first," explained Kendrith, as George assumed that Kendrith intentionally slowed his pace to ensure his charge could keep up.

The shrill undulating cry that came from behind made ants crawl up George's spine.

"Oh lord, if I ever make it through here again, I will never turn people I don't like into sheep. I will stop giving people false directions and spouting nonsensical riddles as words of wisdom. I will even stop making fun of George—just save me!" Simantiar prayed.

George tried to run as quickly as he could, but the night made such an endeavour dangerous. Barely able to see before him, George had to strain himself to not trip over tree roots or run into branches with just the lingering shine of the night sky to poorly illuminate the forest floor.

"Why didn't you tell me that magic lured the beasts in?" George asked, dodging under a branch that quite nearly could have knocked him upside the face.

"Oh? Should I have also asked if you were smuggling a talking skull? Perhaps your bloody piss trail is also magical!"

George didn't have anything to say; it was true, the chances of anyone having any magic on them in this day and age were close to zero, let alone a no-name bard. Most relics of a bygone age would now be found in the royal gallery of some ostentatious king rather than in the sorry bag of a young minstrel.

A husk emerged from the right, reaching out with its gnarled fingers. For a moment, it had looked like a still and unmoving tree blending in with the night.

In flash, Kendrith's blade severed its hand—black ichor trailed the air as its monstrous and gnarly appendage plopped to the floor. The beast gave no shrill sound of pain, but rather leaned in hungrily. Kendrith and George continued to run. More and more husks emerged from the sidelines, drawn in by the promise of food.

A loud echoing cry of ravenous hunger came from behind. George looked over his shoulder and found that he preferred it when the husks were walking on their spindly legs, and even that was a terrifying sight, but watching how they scuttled on their elongated limbs of coiled, springlike muscle made the creatures seem like some nightmare-infused spider.

"They are catching up!"

"Fuck!" George had hoped that Kendrith had the answers, but even he seemed unsure of what to do.

The husks just wanted Simantiar, to feed on his endless reserves of magic. No. George didn't brave the dangers of the old world simply to feed the ravenous monsters.

That was when it hit George. They wanted magic, but that didn't mean they had to feed Simantiar to them, at least not his skull.

"What are you doing?" Kendrith asked as he saw George reach into the bag.

"Feeding them." George reached into his bag and took a handful of Simantiar's bones to throw in the way of the husks. They screamed with glee at the clatter of enamel as if it were a dinner bell. Another scream joined the choir—not one of joy but rather one of sorrow.

"No! You monster!" Simantiar wailed. "I swear, if that was my good hand, you're going to be the one 'taking me to town' from now on! And I don't mean that in the literal sense!"

The husks gave up on their chase and the trio returned to their camp in silence save for their heavy breathing; even Simantiar wasn't rapidly firing any more quips.

"We are definitely going to have to raise the price of my fee," Kendrith finally said, looking at the boy, panting as calculating eyes considered things.

"Fine," George groused before collapsing in front of the comfort of their crackling campfire.

"What is the story behind that skull anyway?" Kendrith asked.

George remained quiet, his knees drawn up to his chest and his face turned to the darkness of the woods.

"If I wanted to take him from you, I already would have."

George looked up to Kendrith, considering his response.

George saw the man in a new light within the glow of their humble campfire. Still, Kendrith carried the sharp gaze of a wary wolf, but underneath the fringe of his long black hair and short stubble, there was a human that began to show himself; Kendrith had the look of a man who had experienced many things, things that had made him equally as callous as he was humble, as cautious as he was understanding. Compassion was simply something he could not afford in his line of work, at least not before he knew the person in question.

George turned to the skull that now sat on a small cut of stone. Simantiar was quiet, a rarity that carried with it respect. George knew that the skull wanted to know more about the boy as well. The promise. The story behind the golden vault. The story behind the book. But the time for that would come.

Until then, George simply settled for explaining who Simantiar was.

He told Kendrith everything: how he had come across a map that noted the remains of a legendary wizard from the old world where magic once flowed as abundantly as the sea was filled with water, of a fractured tale that told of a great war which caused Simantiar to become nothing more than immortal bones and the well of magic to be drained. Of course, Kendrith already knew about all this—everyone did within their world of Tiria. Though none really cared for it, they were tales of a time long gone and did little for anyone who wasn't a scholar.

But George told of how he followed the vague and broken tales and found the thread which led to the first of Simantiar's tombs.

"Wait. I know about you. You're kidding, right? *The* Simantiar?" Kendrith's incredulous look was the first expression that broke his austere domineer, making him seem more than just a mercenary with killer eyes.

"In the flesh; I'd give you an autograph, but you know," Simantiar joked.

Instead, Kendrith burst out laughing.

"What's so funny?" Simantiar asked as if insulted.

"Simantiar, Simantiar,
Never forget his name,
Simantiar, Simantiar,
For he will judge your pain,
Simantiar, Simantiar,
Your happiness is his bane,
Simantiar, Simantiar,
Be good or another child he will gain."

Kendrith was delirious with laughter, and Simantiar opened his jaw wide, "Is that how people remember me?" he asked George, and the boy just shrugged awkwardly, unsure of what to say.

"Great, so I'm a folktale looking for a fairy tale—this just keeps getting better and better."

Kendrith suddenly stopped laughing. "What do you mean?" he asked.

George and Simantiar exchanged hesitant glances.

"Doesn't matter. What matters is that Simantiar used to be a very powerful wizard before our idea of him changed from the old world. He isn't as powerful as he once was, but he can work wonders on a lot."

"Well, okay, I'll bite. Show me a magic trick," Kendrith said.

George and Simantiar sat there in silence.

"Well?" Kendrith prodded.

"I can't do any spells," Simantiar admitted.

Kendrith looked perplexed. "I thought you said you were a wizard?"

"And I am, but I don't remember much, and whatever power I had in my past life I don't have anymore."

"I don't get it. So, what's the point? And why do you need him?" Kendrith asked George.

George wasn't sure he could trust Kendrith. "It's getting late. We should go to bed," was all he said before resigning himself to the comforts of sleep.

"They must have come through here." The man rubbed his thumb and pointer finger together as he inspected the remains of the campfire. The sun had long since begun its rise and morning chased away the shadows of the forest. "They couldn't have gotten far."

The man rose and scratched his stubble.

"What's the plan, Gaven?" Hank asked. Gaven turned to his compatriot, staring with raven black eyes.

"We keep going. Find the kid. Take his gold. And kill that cocky merc as well." Gaven said, still finding the memory of being toyed with gnawing at him. The embarrassment fuelled his anger, and he was certain that he would have his revenge even if they had to go deep into the Forest of the Dead.

"Boss, you may want to see this," the other comrade said, returning to the camp after doing a perimeter check.

Gaven trusted Salo. His meaty figure did little to help his rather unappealing face and bald scalp. And as far as smarts go, he wasn't the brightest. But he had a nose for things. Literally. His nose could be a miniature mountain from its size and peaked bridge. But he also just had an intuitive sense which would put women to shame.

They followed Salo to a clearing that didn't seem to hold anything of particular note, but then Gaven looked closer…and still he found nothing.

"What is it?" he asked Salo.

"Bones."

"I see that, dipshit. What about 'em?"

"Husks."

Gaven's eyes widened. Perhaps Salo wasn't so stupid, after all. He bent over and realised that it was true. The bones weren't new, not by any means. They seemed too brown and looked almost as if they would snap with just the slightest effort. But they were dripping wet, coated with some form of thick saliva typical with husks. Circular bite marks marked the broken pieces and whatever bone marrow there had been was drained.

Gaven picked it up, inspecting it with gloved hands as viscous saliva stretched to the floor in a sheen of sticky drool.

"Gaven, your necklace," Hank suddenly said, frowning as he looked at Gaven. Gaven's necklace had slipped out of his collar. Gaven lifted the pendant to his eyes, an azure teardrop-sized gem reflecting sunlight.

"What about it?"

"It seems kind of…fainter than usual."

Gaven considered that it was true, his gem didn't seem as bright.

"Alight," Gaven spoke the magic word, expecting the gem to turn on with luminescent light.

Salo noticed this. "Boss, why no light?"

"I don't know, Salo." Gaven tried to hide his irritation.

He shook the necklace and spoke the command word, but the gem wouldn't shine.

A thought brightened inside Gaven, as if the command took form within instead of without.

"Hank, give me the ether stone."

Hank frantically rummaged through his bag.

"Quickly."

Hank finally pulled out a scintillating gem that would fit inside the grip of a fully grown man.

Pointing the rock towards the bone, even with most of its contents drained by the husks, the gem brightened, glowing brighter and brighter till it suddenly forced the trio to cover their eyes and listen to the outstretched rock crack.

Gaven suddenly pulled the gem away, as the chirping of spring birds filled the canopy of trees and forest life returned to its own version of normal.

Gaven panted, excited at what he had just discovered.

"What was that?" Hank asked as Gaven pointed the gem towards his own necklace, but it did not shine the way the bone caused it to, in fact, it didn't shine at all.

"Damn it! Did the bone break the gem? You know how difficult it is to get a magic tracking crystal?" Hank complained.

But Gaven just smiled.

"You don't get it—it's not that the bone broke the crystal, but rather that it sucked the crystal dry." Gaven tore off the teardrop necklace and discarded it with little care.

His chest heaved, and his mind raced. He pointed the crystal at the bone again, and it shone with a whisper that promised such unimaginable riches.

"The bone cancels out magic...it drains it...and judging by the remnants of the bones here, I bet that boy has several more!"

Gaven turned to his boys and rose to his feet with such avarice in his eyes. "Boys, we are going to be *rich*!"

"How much farther?"

"As far as we need to go."

"But my feet are getting tired."

"You see, if it was George who was complaining about the trek then I would understand, *but not a legless skull*!" Kendrith retorted, his usual stoic calm lost under a sea of frustration.

"That, my good friend, is discrimination," Simantiar challenged

"I preferred it when you were hiding," Kendrith said.

"You've got it lucky. I have to deal with him every day," George said. Kendrith's and George's relationship had improved. Though going from professionally distant to bouts of conversation wasn't a grave improvement.

"Are we going to be seeing more husks?" George asked. He was under no disillusion about his age. Only sixteen years old with no beard to show, short, and carrying thin arms. His hair was curly and tousled, and a sweet dirty-brown colour. The entire ensemble made him a treat for women that didn't know how easy he found it to slither. But out in the Forest of the Dead and beyond where life took a darker turn, he felt even younger. George knew of the perplexing way he shifted between confidence and timidness, sometimes seeming far younger than he actually was. He didn't want Kendrith to see him as a child. For one reason or another, be it the fact that Kendrith was the first soul George had seen in a long time or some other unknown variable, he found he wanted Kendrith's approval, and that sickened him.

He wanted to impress Kendrith, and so stayed wary of asking stupid questions. After much deliberation and many crunching leaves and many more passing trees, he finally decided that asking about the husks would not be a stupid question.

"No. They wander the outskirts of the forest, foraging for magical sources or soft leaks. They suck it from trees or other sources. As you can imagine, being killed by a husk is exceedingly rare as they keep their distance from humans."

"So, why don't they live farther into the forest?"

"Because there are worse things than husks." Kendrith answered.

George gulped.

For a time, it seemed as if all they did was walk great distances. Kendrith spotted the occasional forest critter to kill or fruits to gather. "Enjoy it while it lasts, the deeper we go, the less of these bunnies we will see."

George nodded—he didn't need an explanation as to why.

Kendrith stared up through the canopy of trees and squinted at the peeking light.

"Let's take a break."

"Thank Vrania," Simantiar said, earning a scowl from Kendrith.

"I will be over there," George said.

"Don't wander too far."

George hesitated, then nodded. Was Kendrith being protective? Or did he just not want his charge to pass and forgo on his payment? George allowed himself to believe it was the former.

Chapter 4

Simantiar looked at the departing George. He had never left his side, for no one could be trusted to simply not steal a talking skull. The days since he had been taken from the tomb seemed so strange, like a living dream.

"Mommy?" Simantiar mused as George left.

With the boy no longer there to be made fun of, he turned instead to the merc.

"So. Kendrith, huh? Your parents must have wanted you to be the protagonist of the story."

The merc froze for a second as he sorted his belongings. But then he pretended to not have heard the pointless small talk of a talking skull, and returned to his task.

"So the silent brooding type? Cool, cool. You must get a lot of girls."

Silence.

"We have a lot in common, you know? You're an asshole, I'm an asshole. We both like making fun of George."

Still nothing.

"It's like talking to a brick wall. I think I'd prefer the husks."

"That can be arranged," Kendrith finally said with a more than complacent smile.

"...I want George back..."

Several minutes had gone by and George still had not returned. "We should go check on the boy." Kendrith picked up the skull and walked in the direction where George had previously disappeared.

"Hey! You don't manhandle me! Put me down, I am Simantiar!"

Kendrith completely ignored the cries.

Originally unable to tell where the boy was, Kendrith suddenly stumbled onto George who sat leaning against a tree with a book set on his lap. The page was turned to a gorgeous rendition of golden gates.

"What you got there?" Kendrith asked.

George suddenly shut the book closed and jumped to his feet, his bag hanging loosely by his elbow and the book now hidden behind him.

Kendrith suddenly got very serious, and Simantiar's own mood darkened as he saw George's defensive stance, as if Kendrith had just walked in on something very, very private. Simantiar hadn't considered how much that book must have meant to him, and only then did he consider his foolishness. It was a fairy tale to Simantiar, nothing more and nothing less, but obviously its contents meant so much more to George that he would be willing to risk his life for it.

Kendrith didn't feel attacked, or at least he didn't seem that way. "It's all right, kid. Everyone has something to hide, something to be protective of. I can respect that." And then he departed, leaving George behind with teary eyes and pursed lips as if ready to strike.

"I can tell you, you know?" Simantiar said to Kendrith.

"No. If it's none of my business, it's none of my business. If George feels it important to tell me, then he will. I wasn't hired to become friends with him."

Kendrith seemed so distant, so professional in his stature all of a sudden.

George returned eventually, sitting by the two and hugging his closed book in contemplative silence. His eyes were red and puffy as he stared down at Kendrith threateningly, like a wounded dog might look at a helping human.

Kendrith on the other hand, seemed languid in his posture, leaning against a tree and plucking a berry from a bramble with no eye trailing towards George.

Simantiar on the other hand, sat between the two on a little low jutting rock of his own.

"Wow, the awkwardness is actually killing me, and I'm immortal," Simantiar said.

Kendrith looked to the book, and then to the canopy of the trees. "Listen, either you want to tell me what you have there and get it over with, or you don't and I can finish taking you to the end of the path."

George didn't seem to take note of what Kendrith had said until his arms slackened and his tightly knit expression softened.

"Sorry. I just realised I must have been glaring at you. I was just thinking."

"That was you *thinking?* My god, never before did I find the term 'if looks could kill' so relatable as I did in the past ten minutes," said Simantiar.

"It's not that the book is a secret, but it is very important to me…and you did catch me off guard."

"Where are you going, kid?" Kendrith asked.

George seemed to consider his next words wisely and instead of saying anything, he allowed the pages to speak for him as he opened the book to a previous page:

"In a time as old as tomorrow
and as new as yesterday,
there lay the golden gates.
Tucked under dipping mountains,
hung over rising lakes,
there stands the golden gate.
Let the man of stone be your guide,
but don't let it take a bite.
If you find the golden gates,
know that the builders made the vault,
and their souls made the lock.
Magic be its seal,
'to want' be its zeal.
A prison it is to be,
of wishes and dreams aplenty.
So open thy door of longing
to find that which you always have been wanting."

"I think I understand," Kendrith said, if he had any queries about the authenticity of the passage, he didn't voice them. "You are following the landmarks in the poem to where you believe the golden vault is hidden," he stated.

"That was the stupidest thing I have ever—*eeerahhhhh*—" Simantiar gave off a long cry as Kendrith tossed him carelessly several feet away, having him land in a cushion of leaves.

George said nothing for a while. "I don't remember my parents growing up. It was just my sister and me. We had to steal food, and hide in run-down homes. We fled from an orphanage and squatted in some ruined home. But one thing we always had with us was this book. We couldn't read the pages at the time, but it didn't matter. We loved the picture of the golden gates." George ran his fingers over the faded colours wistfully. "We made a promise to each other that we would find the vault. It kept us going for so long."

"What happened to her?" Kendrith asked.

"She died."

Chapter 5

"This is a big forest," said George. The air had thickened the longer they travelled. The trees were stacked closer together and the land shifted from the typical fringes of forest trees to something more unhinged.

"The name is a misnomer—it is not 'just' a forest."

"What do you mean?"

Kendrith turned to George. "Let's take a break," Kendrith said, using his backpack as a seat while George simply sat on his rear. Kendrith eyed Simantiar silently, staring at him for a long time.

"What? Do I have something between my teeth?" the wizard asked.

"Simantiar, you are old, right? Like, really old?"

"Well, gee, aren't you a charmer? Yes. I am really old. Though people tell me that I don't look a day over a hundred."

Kendrith rolled his eyes and George tried to hold back a snicker. "How come there is so much about the world you don't seem to know. I mean, you say you were a renowned wizard. But you seemed clueless about the husks?"

George realised that Kendrith had a point. He also wanted to know why.

"It's true. I don't remember anything about husks. Though I do know about the Forest of the Dead. Yet, I believe it has drastically changed since my time. My memories are fragmented for a good part. Being stuck in a tomb for millennia with no contact with the outside world made me forget a lot about the past."

Kendrith nodded. "I guessed as much." The man took a stick, kicked away the bundle of leaves to reveal a patch of dirt, and began to draw in it.

"My knowledge on this is based on what I was taught as a chil—" Kendrith caught himself, pausing halfway through his sketch. He sighed, whatever he let slip was too late to hide now. "…Child. And also at the guild."

"Guild?" George asked.

"I am not like those drifters from the town before. They try to find unknowing individuals to drag into the woods and kill them before taking their belongings." Kendrith pulled open his cloak to reveal a golden pin of folded and overlapping wings that formed a V shape.

"I'm part of the guild in the next city over, The Wings of Vrania. I'm a hunter." He closed the cloak.

"Vrania? As in the god? I never knew he had wings."

Kendrith seemed to almost guffaw.

"He's not just a god, and of course he had wings!"

George was taken aback by the sudden spurt of passion with which Kendrith tackled the topic.

"I'm sorry, I never learnt any of this as a child. Didn't really have someone to teach me."

Kendrith cleared his throat as if to get rid of the sudden flux of emotion. "During the origins of Tiria, the world was split and darkness reigned manifest as a torrent of fiends sewn together by darkness. Vrania wielded his sword, also known as the sword of Vrania against these monsters."

"What kind of sword?" George asked, finding he was being drawn in by Kendrith's own enthusiasm for the tale.

"It was one forged by Ivaldi himself, the dwarf god who plucked a blue star from the heavens and brandished a sword so powerful it cut through darkness itself and birthed light. Legend has it that the sword is wonderfully crafted with old sigils etched into its fuller."

"A fuller?" George interrupted.

Kendrith caught himself. "Ah yes, the middle dent that runs from sword guard to tip. The sword glows a bright blue hue that demands reverence, but only for those it deems worthy. The pommel is that of a crescent moon and the simple guard is anything but simple."

"Wow, you seem to know quite a bit about the sword."

Kendrith suddenly bowed his head as if caught in something embarrassing.

"Just something I was fascinated with since I was a child."

George pondered for a moment. "How do you know if you are worthy?" George asked.

Kendrith shrugged. "It's just a tale. The chances that the sword exists are unlikely. My mother spoke about it quite often. I would imagine that any who carry the blade will be worthy from then on. The mere prestige that would come with that is awe inspiring."

"Do you think you'd be worthy?" George asked.

Kendrith seemed taken aback by that. "I hope to be some day." The man suddenly grabbed at his chest at a pendant hidden underneath his shirt.

George nodded, trying to change the subject.

"If you are from the guild, why didn't you arrest those men in that case?" George asked.

"Why? Do I look like a guard? Plus, I had no evidence that they were about to murder you. Do you expect me to kill anyone who looks fishy?" Kendrith returned to his callous self.

"So, why so hesitant about mentioning your childhood? Bad uncle? I totally get it," Simantiar mocked.

"Not quite. I was stationed at Adna to await such individuals and follow them into the woods. If they seemed like they were about to murder innocent travellers, I was to capture and deliver them to the town's guard. But if approached, I could also take on a new benefactor. In your case, I could also just afford to beat them up."

Continuing to draw, Kendrith formed a large circle which verged on being an oval with five lines coming from the corners to meet at the middle. The lines never touched however, instead, another smaller circle formed at the very centre.

"It's not an exact representation, but it will do. We were originally here where we found the husks." Kendrith pointed at the second biggest portion of his map. "This is the entrance to the forest from the town of Adna. It is also the safest place."

"The forest is a lot bigger than I thought," George said.

Kendrith nodded. "From what I understand, after magic began to bleed from this world, there were certain spots which were less affected such as the Forest of the Dead and the uncharted lands beyond. It is like an endless well that attracts the inexplicable. Much of the magic is incapable of being harnessed, and besides, a lot of our knowledge on how to use magic was lost with the old world. That being said, the unstable magic resulted in many aberrations thriving in these locations and the forest expanded and changed into more of a jungle. It is why husks roam this place—they can feed on the magic."

"So, why is it still called Forest of the Dead?" George asked.

Kendrith laughed. Was it a stupid question? George felt like a child again, feeling as if he had just embarrassed himself.

"To be honest, from what we understand, the forest never was that much of a threat in the old world. It was only after the coincidental and sudden mutation of the magical essence that it became unstable and uncontainable. It corrupted anything it wanted to with unforeseeable consequences. The reason why we call it Forest of the Dead is because it's good for business."

"But how come I remember it as the same name?" asked Simantiar.

Kendrith shrugged. "No idea, that is just what the scarce amount of sources tell us."

"So, what about the other locations?" George asked.

"This is the swamp. We will be trying to stay away from here." Kendrith pointed at the eastern portion of the land. It was smaller with squiggly drawn borders. "It is the home of ghastly Hobbers. They are short and not much of a threat alone, but their numbers make up for that. Green and slimy with large frog-like eyes that move independently from each other. Bumps marking their skin and greasy black hair that grow in patches. They use rather crude tools, but should they find us—well, let's just say that we are the bunnies in this analogy."

George repressed his gulp, which seemed to have found its way through Simantiar's nonexistent throat anyway.

Kendrith continued to point at the other sections to explain the design. The western part of his map was notorious for being home to vindictive and indiscriminate ghosts. Wraiths and shadows, banshees and the undead, rumours of ghastly fiends with a seething jealousy for all who lived.

The other location wasn't notable for any particular creatures, but was host to many monsters. Werewolves to wendigos, goblins to kobolds, pit devils to abhorrent abominations without a name. Even the occasional ghoul wandering the lands.

"This one will be the trickiest. It is home to wood nymphs and other guardians of the forest. They fight off the abominations, but uphold the equilibrium of their world. They provide free passage through their woods for any mortal who doesn't ravage the forest for its resources. But for all that do, the sylvan as they are called, come to make an example of you."

"Kill you?" asked Simantiar. "Doesn't seem very nature-y."

Kendrith shook his head. "They turn you into a tree, whereby you are forced to replace and become one with the nature you sought to harm."

"I know of 'if you can't beat them join them,' but I don't think this is that."

"And this one?" George asked, pointing at the centre.

Kendrith hesitated, and George hesitantly withdrew his finger as if even touching the drawn circle was a poor choice. The boy could see the worry in Kendrith's eyes.

"Never go there. No matter what happens."

"Why?"

"We don't know what roams at the centre, but whatever it is, it can't be good. We have sent expedition teams through there, the best of the best. Paladins. Alchemists. Renowned warriors. The lucky ones were found dead. We found their corpses hung in the most unimaginably terrifying ways. Their limbs contorted to take the form of standing altars or statues. Decapitated heads forced to perform unsightly acts on other bodies. The unlucky ones returned to us delirious and mad, their flesh branded and their skin mutilated, as if used as nightmarish tools for evil artistic expression.

"They rambled nonsensical things about the shadow of the forest. Of the 'truth'—whatever that means. Some said the monster was a centipede, others a hawk, or simply a shifting cloud of darkness. They were all made a mockery of." A bead of sweat slid from Kendrith's brow as he seemed to recall the horrifying memories he had witnessed.

George drew himself away as Kendrith noticed his fear.

"Sorry. Just, whatever happens, stay away from the centre."

George nodded.

The rest of the trip would take them a few days of travel. Kendrith wanted to stick to the western path, through the ends of the forest entrance and onto the spectral ghosts. "I would rather wrestle a lich than be stuck with Hobbers," Kendrith had said.

George began to notice how seldom they heard the singing of birds now. And it had been a long time since they found a rabbit or even a deer that leapt through the woods. The air of the forest got thicker the deeper they went, and he felt as if even the trees lived in constant fright—unable to grow limbs and flee the woods forever, forced to curse their existence in silence.

It was as the entrance of the forest was nearing its end, and they heard the first wail of some unknown horror pierce the canopies, that George knew they were almost at the plane of ghosts.

"Boss, let's turn back."

"Stop being such a pussy." Though Gaven said those words, it took a considerable amount of restraint to hold back his fear. He only had to make the trip through the Forest of the Dead four times, and even that was four too many. He preferred the path through the swamp, finding he had a knack for outsmarting the Hobbers. But he was clueless when it came to the plane of ghosts.

"Damn it," he cursed under his breath. Gaven knew that Kendrith was a professional, with a belt of potions and items made to fend off the supernatural.

"Come on," he said. Gaven could tell Hank was nervous though he tried to hide it, while Salo attempted no such thing. Salo looked quite comical as a grown and burly man who shook in his boots; looking no different from an overgrown quivering child.

But it was too late for them to turn back down, the promise of stolen riches and an opportunity to get rid of their pitiful lives egged Gaven and his friends on.

Chapter 6

"Sim."

The young boy turned to his mother sitting upon a bench, a tall and straight-postured man stood next to her. She seemed serene within the extravagant garden, an addition that complemented the stone walk and babbling brook. There was a small pond in which fish swam within their little world and looked to the sky where giants stared down at them.

The water that the boy had raised from the pond was constructed into an exact replica of the great magical temple of Eindeiheid where students learned the mystic arts. Timmy tried to bite the construct, his canine snout struggling to decide between gurgling up water and biting it down, and let loose a frustrated bark.

Soon enough the masterpiece collapsed back into the pond as the boy's concentration broke.

Sim ran to his mother and tackled her with a hug, Timmy running alongside him. As Simantiar longed for his mother's attention Timmy seemed to long for his.

"Did you see it?" The boy asked in a lisp, a baby tooth missing.

The mother chuckled. "Yes, yes I did." She stroked the boy's hair.

"That was quite incredible, Simantiar. Even apprentices struggle to show that level of control and focus when it comes to the micromanagement of magic." The man had a thick, groomed beard in contrast to his bald head—as if all the hair that was supposed to cover his scalp had gotten lost and found its way to his chin instead. He was draped in an exuberant and fashionable black robe with faint impressions forming into obscure patterns that informed of his status as a master mage.

Sim retreated behind his mother.

"It's okay," his mother said, laughing before kissing her son on the head. "This man is a good friend of mine, and of your father's. His name is Mylor and he is the headmaster of Eindeiheid," she said reassuringly, stroking Simantiar's back.

Simantiar's reservation suddenly vanished to be replaced by unrepressed awe.

"Are you sure you don't wish to pursue other methods for your therapy?" the man asked, continuing some conversation from earlier with Simantiar's mother.

"Really, it's fine," she said, massaging her thigh absent-mindedly.

Leaning out from behind his mother's legs, Simantiar summoned the courage to speak. "Are you going to be my teacher?"

The man laughed.

"Sim!" Simantiar's mother retorted.

"It's quite all right, Giselle." The man turned his attention to Simantiar with a friendly and trusting smile, the contours of his black stubbly beard spreading to reveal a loving smile. He carried a certain earthy musk to him that spoke of experience and confidence, but also of warmth and protection—Simantiar imagined that his father would have a similar scent to him.

"I don't see why not. Your mother tells me you are quite gifted when it comes to magic."

Simantiar retreated behind his mother, clutching at her dress.

"He is a little shy."

Mylor gave his own bemused chuckle. "Not just him." The man reached behind his back and as if from a hidden pouch, brought forth a boy not much older than Sim.

"Sim, this is Usellyes—he will be your friend." The world closed in on the two. Where Sim had blond hair with blue eyes that made him seem akin to royalty, the boy had piercing brown eyes that warded caution and tousled black hair.

"Where did you find him?" The mother asked.

"On the streets."

"So, who is paying for his tuition?" The mother frowned.

"The board will cover it. His magical aptitude is second perhaps to only your son."

Sim didn't hear the rest of the conversation; instead, Sim found himself lost in the reflection of Usellyes's eyes, and felt Usellyes share that impression. Just like fish that swam within their little world, in that very moment, there existed just the two boys known as Simantiar and Usellyes.

Simantiar didn't dream. He had no need to. Left as nothing but a skull with a bag of old bones, he would simply stare out into the eternal night for hours, his mind becoming stagnant and still. He watched how the flames of the campfire danced on the backs of Kendrith and George.

His memories were fragmented, much of them gone and some of them returning.

He remembered a battle, a great one just before he was entombed.

He just recalled the vague memory of a boy, the blank face of his mother, though he was sure she was beautiful. And the fateful meeting between him and another child. Usellyes. Even after so many years the name still seemed to cling to the old wizard, a ringing familiarity like a childhood memory thought forgotten, only to return as an echo of a reminder.

Kendrith and George believed that Simantiar's incessant talking was the product of an eccentric personality. It wasn't. It was so that he could keep the memories locked away. Brief memories flashed in his spiritual mind. Battle that would make his spiritual heart tighten. He could still hear the destruction ringing in his spiritual ears. Even in faux death he could not escape the torment.

And so he talked relentlessly, hoping that the constant hum of his annoying voice would keep the sound of war at bay, and keep his mind distracted from the repressed memories.

It was during nighttime when Kendrith and George were permitted the comforts of sleep that Simantiar found the hardest. In the silence of night, as spirits moaned their damnation all around them and the flames of the campfire cracked and flickered: it was then that Simantiar's past came to haunt him without reservation.

Morning finally came and during the day, George used their breaks to read from the book. Never would he put it down, always handling it with utmost care. It seemed like a form of mantra, a ritual to maintain his resolve, and remind him why he was doing what he was doing.

Simantiar gave up at one point and decided that some of the stories could be a good distraction.

"Kendrith, you've got to come and hear this!" Simantiar called to Kendrith's back as he was setting up camp. Kendrith simply scowled.

"No, seriously! It is about a wise duck that is all knowing! Who came up with this stuff?" Simantiar howled with laughter.

George flushed, closed the book, and departed.

The outer areas of the spectral plane didn't have many interesting sights. A thin fog simply drifted through the land. The trees seemed thinner, weathered with age. They did not see any spirits yet, but heard long and pained howls echo through the forest. They were saddening cries that came from a creature that was lost a long, long time ago.

"We are getting closer—be wary."

George nodded.

The first sign of danger did not come from a skeletal body or a spirit or a banshee or any other spectral being. It came from a sudden arrow that suddenly pierced the tree in front of Kendrith.

It took Kendrith a second to register that they weren't being attacked by spectres like he had expected, but rather by humans. "Hide!" Kendrith barked desperately as a second arrow whirred through the trees, piercing him in the shoulder. The merc cried out in surprise and pain.

"Kendrith!" George called in alarm.

"I said *hide*!" he barked again, not waiting until George understood the meaning of the word. He grabbed the boy with his good hand and pulled him behind a tree, just in time to avoid the flight of another arrow.

Kendrith panted heavily, adrenaline pumping through his body, his muscles flexed and body tightened. This was his job; his body bore scars as trophies from many other times when death darkened his door. He may not know how to be friendly, or courteous, but at that very moment, his body knew exactly what it needed to do.

"What are you doing?" George asked as he watched Kendrith grab hold of the arrow shaft, the merc's cheeks expanding with each puffing breath. Until Kendrith snapped the shaft of the arrow, letting loose a cry of pain.

"I think I'm going to hurl," said a queasy Simantiar.

"Take it out!" George said regarding the tipped end.

"Only if I want to bleed to death," said Kendrith, clutching his shoulder.

The mercenary leaned over the corner of the tree, snapping right back behind cover as an arrow soared past.

"Come on out! If you surrender quietly, we won't kill you," shouted a voice from within the fog.

Kendrith simply shook his head to George, and the boy nodded. He was no fool, at least of that Kendrith was certain.

Kendrith cursed his carelessness, how could he have let his guard down? He knew he should have expected the enemy to come chasing after them. His focus on wild ghosts is what distracted him from the threat of another factor. He made a mental note for if there was to be a next time.

"What do you want?" shouted Kendrith back.

"The boy and his bag of bones." Kendrith and George exchanged looks—they were in danger.

"Wait—what are you—" Kendrith grabbed Simantiar from George's shoulder and held him just past their cover.

"What do you see?" Kendrith asked.

"Well—uh. Three guys. It's hard to tell from the fog, but there is one several feet back and two guys approaching. They both have drawn their swords."

Kendrith nodded, handing the skull back to the boy and drawing his own steel with a resounding and satisfying ring. His silver blade was still in its sheath.

George stared at Kendrith's shoulder, and the mercenary noticed. "Don't worry about me, I have dealt with worse," he reassured the boy, though he wasn't so sure if it was the truth.

"Hold Simantiar out a bit. Tell me when they are just behind the tree."

Simantiar's sudden stillness showed his understanding.

Kendrith drew a couple of throwing knives from his belt.

"They're circling around the tree."

"How many are there?" Kendrith asked.

"Three, two in the front and the man with the bow waiting in the distance."

"Are they the same men from Adna?"

"Hard to tell seeing as I was stuck in a bag during that time."

"Is there a large hefty one and a little simple perhaps, with a broken nose and bald scalp?"

Simantiar takes a moment. "Yes."

"It's them," George affirmed.

"Can you tell which one is more of a threat?" Kendrith pressed.

"The one on the left is bigger, he seems far stronger—"

"No. That's not what I meant. Which one seems like they will *be* more of a threat?"

Simantiar looked again, and he seemed to have understood Kendrith's intent.

"The one on the right. He seems like more of a threat. The one on the left looks like he's about to let one loose in his pants."

Kendrith nodded.

"When I tell you to run, you run. Follow the direction we have been going. Run until the fog has hidden us, but you can still hear the sound of combat."

George nodded. He didn't want to leave, but he trusted Kendrith.

Kendrith waited until the sound of crushing leaves became clearer and clearer.

"Now!"

In the blink of an eye Kendrith turned the corner, not turning to fight the smaller man on the right, but the terrified one on the left.

The rush of the moment claimed Kendrith. His charge, George, all but fading from his mind. It was just the dance of battle now. Do or die. His mind would go quiet and the flow of blades would guide his limbs. His eyes held no compassion or contempt, no love or hate. Just the piercing black eyes of a wolf that leapt with bared fangs.

The larger man cried out with a start, the pitch fluctuating. His fear gave form to Kendrith's attack. Was it a ghost? A skeleton? Aberration? Lich? It didn't matter—in that moment Kendrith's sudden speed made him seem like a demon.

It caught the larger man off guard, causing him to stumble back, leaving his body wide open.

Kendrith used the moment to his advantage. He whipped his wrist, snapping a dagger in the direction of the man on the right while raising his sword against the man before him.

Agony flared through Kendrith's shoulder as he brought down his blade, slashing across the man's chest. *Fuck,* Kendrith's shoulder hampered the strength of his swing, along with the man's burly chest and the retreating fall, it caused the cut to be shallow. Still, he had done enough. The man was delirious with fear, not seeing a man before him, but a monster.

As the man scampered away on his rear, Kendrith jumped to the other, blades clashing. If one had to describe Kendrith's movements, it would be akin to a snake. His arms whipped and slithered, his body building momentum for a strike from unexpected angles. Feints, parries, thrusts.

"The beating I gave you wasn't enough?" Kendrith taunted.

The man chuckled. "What can I say? I'm a sore loser."

Kendrith's footwork was masterful. Left. Right. Blade whirring from the flick of his wrist and snapping like a whip to the man's ribs. What the scarred man lacked in grace, he more than made up for in brutality and power. Where Kendrith tried to deceive with great finesse, the man tried to deceive by kicking up dirt into Kendrith's eyes.

The adrenaline began to subside, and the dance of blades began to wane as the flaring pain of Kendrith's shoulder made itself known. It was good of Kendrith to bring down the number of combatants to one, but his movements were limited. He was forced to stay in the same area, holding his opponent between himself and the archer.

I think I bought enough time, Kendrith decided. In one swift movement he kicked the man just above his right knee, bringing him off balance. Kendrith's blade rose from a vertical heave, ready to bring it crashing down, but the scarred man received it with his own raised sword. Blade clashed against blade and propelled the man backwards.

Kendrith cursed silently, falling back behind the cover of a tree just in time to avoid the flight of another arrow. He lost his chance, but it didn't matter—George must have gotten some distance. He ran to catch up with the boy and the bag of bones.

"After them!" the men called from behind.

"Psst." Kendrith heard from within the mists and turned panting towards it. He tried to ignore the pain that came from his shoulder as he followed the voice to a decrepit and lonely tree that stood at the edge of a short drop. Under the slope he recognised George.

The boy put a finger to his lips and motioned for Kendrith to come over with restrained urgency.

Kendrith first assumed the boy was telling him to be quiet to hide from their aggressors until the boy pointed in the general direction behind him, and Kendrith's eyes widened.

Kendrith knew that most monsters found within those parts were identifiable and classifiable. A skeleton was just a reanimated corpse. Same with a zombie. A ghost, just a spectral creature.

But there were some aberrations within the accursed lands that took form not through common means. Every single one of them was different. Taking shapes and forms dependent on their source. Like a malevolent black hole that centred at a heart and drew in everything else to coalesce into something of pure untainted evil.

Kendrith couldn't exactly make out the figure from the thickening fog, but he saw that it towered as tall as any spire. Limbs and other indistinguishable contents dropped from it like rain sliding off cheeks. Its body was large and round, and it stumbled slowly through the dead lands with a trail of limbs left behind it.

As Kendrith was processing what he witnessed before him, he heard the sudden feet of their pursuers. They had lost their advantage.

The men turned around the corner. No more arrows, just three men with swords in hand.

Kendrith did not engage, he did not move. He simply mimicked George and placed a finger to his lips, pointing in the direction of the aberrant.

All three sets of their eyes widened in understanding, all of them incredibly still like bunnies hiding in their burrows. The only thing that could be heard was the sudden audible quake of the monster's footsteps.

And so they waited there in silence for a lifetime, none of them risking the sound of battle or running from their cover.

In that one moment, George, Kendrith, and Simantiar had far greater worries than bandits. So, they all silently agreed to a ceasefire until the insidious force left.

Chapter 7

Kendrith gently squeezed the extraction into the vial. His eyes were level with the glass tap of the alchemist set.

With timid doubt in his young eyes, he raised the vial to his grandfather.

Kendrith's grandfather was a prime example of ruthless discipline and indomitable strength. His beard had long since greyed and hung down to his bulky chest. Scars marked him as if he were a tiger in human form and his muscles seemed about ready to explode.

The man didn't say anything. He simply took the vial from the young boy and eyed it with scrutiny. After a few contemplative hums, he handed the vial back. "Drink it," he said.

The boy's eyes lit up. "So, I did it correctly?"

"No. That is why you must drink it."

The young boy suddenly became frightened as he took the vial with hesitation. "What will happen?" he asked.

"Slight discomfort if you are lucky, or pain for days if you are not."

The young Kendrith eyed the roiling purple mixture in his hands.

"When you are out in the wild, such a concoction can be the difference between life and death. You can't afford to make such mistakes. You need to learn through pain and your body will be your best teacher. Now, drink up," Kendrith's grandfather said with crossed arms and watched as Kendrith took the vial to his lips. It took only a few seconds for the boy to grimace and groan with pain, then a few more to fall to the floor in a fetal position and clutch his stomach. The cry he bellowed told of incomprehensible pain.

"What are you doing?" George whispered to Kendrith as he removed a vial from his pocket. The mixture in his hands roiled a soft sandy brown. He turned to where the raven-eyed drifter and his accomplices squatted, waiting impatiently for their hunt to resume.

"This is an enhancement potion. It will greatly strengthen my reaction time and speed, while numbing the pain in my shoulder. It will last for only a few minutes though. I will buy you more time—remember to run when you get the chance."

George gave no sign that he understood, but Kendrith trusted the boy.

Kendrith eyed the vial in his hands for a moment, his thoughts going back to his very first concoction, to his grandfather, thinking about how far he had gotten. He wondered how he had ended up in this situation. And so he chased away the thoughts with the entire contents of the vial.

His pupils dilated. His heart palpitated. Power coursed through him like endless rolling floods.

The aberrant had cleared enough of a distance where he felt confident they were safe. He relied on the bandits' inexperience to think that the stomping quake of the footsteps was a sign that they still weren't in the clear.

Kendrith seized it; where before his movements were like a striking snake, they now seemed almost feline; an agile nimble fluidity that was barely human.

He rose to his feet, running up the side of the slanted earth and leaping with blade in hand.

Kendrith handled his sword with great finesse. Like the undulated motion of a flowing river, he now moved it as if it were no heavier than cutlery. Careening through the battle. Blade. Blade. Feint. Switch grip.

He juggled the three aggressors with ease, toying with them. Where one blade struck the other, he was already in position to parry the next.

He almost returned to his trance. Forgetting where they were. Forgetting the reason for why he fought. Lost in the melody of clashing steel and dancing blades.

All of it broke as soon as he heard the terrified voice of George return from behind him. "Run!"

They stopped their fighting, turning around to see the boy running, not away from them, but towards them. It dawned on Kendrith that if whatever was out there made him return to the danger of bandits who wanted to kill and rob him, then it must have been for good reason.

But it was too late. The creature that burst forth stood tall at eight feet, scuttling through the uneven and dead ground.

Its entire body was formed from discarded bones held together with flesh and sinew. Bones upon bones piled upon each other to form four spindly legs to carry it while scythe-like arms were held out before it. Its face also resembled that of a praying mantis with mandibles formed by fingers and attached to one another by sinew. It cried out with shrill glee at the prospect of new prey.

"A hollower!" called out the raven-eyed man. So, he had some understanding of the forest.

The creature covered the distance in a flash, scythe-like arms swiping through the air.

Kendrith rolled away. A hollower he could take on. Their size and form usually meant that they did have exploitable weaknesses. Yet, it dawned on him that he couldn't have asked for a better distraction.

The hollower shuffled on its four spindly legs back and forth, swiping and missing the raven-eyed man.

"Now! Run!" Kendrith barked at George, fleeing while the bandits were preoccupied. Even the large frightened one lost himself in his fear, charging with a roar.

"They're getting away!" one shouted from behind.

"Hank! After them!"

As George and Kendrith fled through the trees, they heard and felt the sudden flight of an arrow pass by several feet.

"Keep going!" Kendrith shouted. They could now hear the passing of a river that drew ever closer. Kendrith knew where they were going, but they had no other choice. The path behind them was blocked by a hollower and three murderous bandits. Even if Kendrith could take one of them down, the aftereffect from his potion would have him be easy pickings—leaving him slow and drained.

George cried out as another arrow flew past his head, having him duck.

"Faster!" Kendrith cried out.

They could now see the river that passed by them just beyond the trees.

An arrow flew past George's ear. The boy bent over as he stumbled, catching his foot in the root of a tree and falling forward toward the river. His bag opened, and Simantiar along with a few of his bones fell out.

"Simantiar!" George cried, reaching out as if it'd make a difference. The skull continued to roll down the slope, claimed by the flowing river and drifting off into the distance.

"Come on, nothing we can do," Kendrith said, picking George up and pushing him forward.

"We have to find Simantiar!" George bellowed.

"Not if we die ourselves."

Kendrith pulled George away, falling behind a tree and assessing their options. Kendrith could already feel the effects of the potion waning and panic rising like bile in his throat.

"Why are we stopping?" George asked.

"We are approaching the centre."

"I thought you said—"

"I know what I said!" Kendrith snapped. "But there is nowhere else to run—if we keep running the border they will catch us." A nauseous wave washed over him.

Should they run through the men and take their chances? No. It wasn't likely that they would survive. Was the centre a better option? Should they keep running the border? Kendrith cursed silently.

"Come on out. Don't make this more difficult than it has to be," the one named Hank called out into the forest.

"Kendrith," George said. "Kendrith!" A little louder this time to grab his attention.

"What?" he snarled, a little more on edge than he wished.

"Is the centre magical?" George asked.

"What do you mean?"

"From what you described, the centre seems to be magical in design, right?"

Kendrith nodded, unsure of what George had in mind.

George reached into his bag and pulled out a handful of bones. "I have a plan."

George and Kendrith clutched the bones of Simantiar tightly as they continued to flee the flight of arrows. When they arrived at a thin bend at the river, Kendrith sprinted ahead, leaping the distance and landing on the other side.

"Your hand!" Kendrith shouted. George looked at Kendrith's outstretched arm. He hoped that the man's trust was not misplaced, and that George's madness would reward them. Whatever concoction Kendrith had taken made his feats inhuman, but George met the challenge. Running back for a running jump, he sprinted just as an arrow failed him—he couldn't afford to go back. His feet left the ground as he soared through the air, the ravines below skimming the tip of his shoe just before Kendrith caught him and pulled him to the other side. They both collapsed, panting heavily.

Arrows flew after them, as the two rose and worked their way into the centre. The archer lowered his bow and the arrows stopped coming

"We can stop. We don't have to pass through the centre anymore," George said hopefully, thinking that the men were too scared to get to the border, if at all.

"We are already at the centre."

George didn't notice it at first, but he looked closer. The surrounding trees still seemed decrepit and ghastly, but they didn't seem aged or weathered like in the spectral lands. The air was thick and nauseating, and George found the weight pressing down on his chest.

"Plus, we can't stay here. If the men can track us like this, we are stuck. We can't give them time to regroup and come up with a plan. We need to press our advantage."

George noticed the display of confidence, but also couldn't help taking note of Kendrith's widened eyes as he scanned every shadow and every branch.

"You know, it has long been theorised that whatever is taking place here is a spell from the old world—we are putting that to the test now, aren't we?" He looked down to the bones of Simantiar and clenched them tightly.

"We need to find Simantiar," George said.

"We will. We need to get out alive first. Simantiar is as much my responsibility as you are. And if we do get out of this alive, I owe that nuisance a great thank you."

The fog thinned while the trees thickened—thick and twisted, with jagged or even curled branches that reached for the sky and connived to block out the sun, their interlocking leaves an uncomfortable dark green that bordered almost on some ichor-like tinge.

The trees within the spectral lands felt lonely and woeful to George. He had felt sorrow for them, yet within the centre he felt unwelcome. Where the trees of the spectral lands had no limbs to flee, he was glad the trees before him had none to strike with.

"Hold the bones tightly, and whatever happens, don't leave my side," Kendrith said, drawing his sword.

George took notice of Kendrith's fatigued state, but made sure not to mention anything. Better to give Kendrith the impression that he was seen as strong and comforting, rather than as a liability.

"Uh, Kendrith?"

The mercenary turned around to George and noticed the sudden blue glow within his palms. He looked down at his own hands and noticed the blue light which tried to escape his fist.

"Be ready and stay behind me," Kendrith said with his sword up before him and the light held above his head—a low wince of pain at the motion.

"Do you hear that?" George asked. It sounded like grains of sand brushing against a metal shield, a soft foreboding whisper that promised a creeping death.

"Yes," Kendrith said through gritted teeth, readying himself for what was to come.

Something about the place, about their surroundings, about their situation made George feel as if he were no longer alive, as if his body had collapsed at the border of the entry and just his spirit wandered into that accursed place of death.

"I want you..." What a terrible, accursed voice it was that spoke from out of the seam of some nightmare. The words rang in George's skull like an echo, a soft seductive ring that filled him with terrible fear.

"Please tell me you heard that?" George said.

"It's coming."

What horror it was that became manifest—a sudden black cloud that drifted, or scuttled, or flew, or ran across the land came straight for them.

Chapter 8

The madness came at them with terrifying speed, a tumultuous thing that seemed to shift and morph into an array of shapes.

It suddenly twisted and spun around the two in a blur. The blue light of Simantiar's bones flared bright in response. Kendrith could feel the warmth of blazing magic as it kept the darkness at bay, a bubble which formed around them as the cloud squeezed against it, trying to break the bubble which protected its prey.

"It works! Ha! It actually works!" Kendrith celebrated in disbelief.

"Kendrith, it's not leaving!" George stated.

The malicious entity was not a cloud as Kendrith seemed to have first believed, but rather black grains of sand which clumped together, scratching against the barrier with the occasional blue flare that came from a recoil. The creature wrapped them in a cocoon, blocking off their vision from the rest of the forest. It sounded like a swarm of locusts trying to devour them.

"It's okay, it can't get in. Let's just keep going," Kendrith said.

Suddenly a large centipede scuttled over the surface of the barrier, a woman's face on the very front, and then it vanished.

"Kendrith?" George said with fright.

"We're safe."

A young girl slid across the surface, body splattered over the bubble.

"George," gasped the girl. She was no older than a young child, with freckled cheeks and dirty blond hair.

She clung to the bubble for only a moment, torn away by the turbulent storm. Pleading desperation was visible in her eyes as she called for the young bard.

"Lily?" George shouted in disbelief. Fear showed in his eyes as he stepped back.

"No!" Kendrith called out, but it was too late. Kendrith watched as the scared bard vanished behind the consuming storm. There was recognition in the boy's eyes. He knew the girl.

"Lily!" Kendrith could hear George call from within the ravenous storm.

"George!" Kendrith called out himself, but it was in vain—he couldn't see anything past the swarm.

The centipede returned, the face of the woman screeching at the bubble, furious that it couldn't get through. The woman's cheeks tore apart to reveal the webbing of flesh; the sound of jawbones dislocating as pincers uncurled from within the monstrous maw which stretched thick saliva; a tongue several inches in length licked against Kendrith's protective bubble, blue sparks grinding against the tongue like a blade against steel.

The bones flared violently in Kendrith's hand as he strained against the storm. His entire body weighed heavy, his limbs were ready to give in to fatigue and collapse, but pure will kept him on his feet. As he steadied the hand which held the rattling bones, he called out once more, "George!"

Kendrith could no longer hear the sound of George calling for the girl over the sound of the storm, but he was soon visited by his own past. "Weak," Kendrith's grandfather said, disappointment in his eyes. No sooner did he come before he departed again.

"This isn't real," Kendrith whispered to himself. The roiling storm of grains turning more fevered.

"You are no son of mine. Just a disappointment." Next it was the projection of his father, fitted in an opulent suit with a tailored vest and the draped chain of his pocket watch. He sported a groomed salt-and-pepper beard and unbidden contempt in his eyes.

"This isn't real," Kendrith whispered again. His composure was all but gone, its walls beaten down by the battering ram of his past.

"Save me, Kendrith!" The third figure to visit him was a beautiful woman with scarlet hair and strength to her. Kendrith remembered her as the embodiment of hope and strength, two things that he tried so desperately to inherit. But the only thing that Kendrith's mother wanted at that moment was to be saved—great rending stone teeth chopped down on her, tearing her back into the storm as just her screams remained.

"This isn't real!" Kendrith collapsed to his knees, roaring the words as if the realisation would steel his heart.

The grains swarmed around, breaking Kendrith down piece by piece. The blue light of Simantiar's bones began to wane.

Kendrith panted—he was so tired. His arms ached, the wound in his shoulder burned, and the feeling in his legs faded. He had lost a lot of blood.

"George," he whispered, struggling back to his feet and continuing his advance through the relentless swarm. "I need to find George."

George was all alone now—just the glow of Simantiar's bones bleeding through white knuckles and the rapturous entity that circled him. But the glow gave him hope, it protected him and shone a piercing light that kept the darkness at bay.

"Lily?" he called out again. That was where his mind had gone. It wasn't possible, was it? No, he was certain. The freckled cheeks. The dirty blond hair. Her eyes. It was definitely his sister.

"Lily!" he called out again, struggling to hear his own voice over the sound of the swarm. Holding Simantiar's bones high, he waved them left and right, finding the bubble of grains shift to the sway of the barrier.

He kept calling. There was a second voice in the storm. Faint, but still there. Kendrith was calling for him too, but George only held out an ear for any sign of his dead sister.

Once again his sister clashed against the barrier, fear in her eyes. "George! Save me, George! Don't let me die again!"

The voice tore through George's heart and the words pierced even deeper. Tears streaked his cheeks—he never wanted to fail her; he never wanted her to die.

"George. Save me."

"How? Tell me how!"

"Drop the bones, George. Let me in." The eyes were Lily's, George didn't deny this. The same unwavering trust that she always had for her older brother was there.

George lowered his hand, the grip on the bones loosening. He missed his sister dearly. He wanted nothing more than to see her again. And there she was, gripping the edge of the bubble, wishing only to be in her brother's arms again.

The storm squeezed against the barrier.

George imagined a world where Lily was still alive, thinking of her laughter, of the two of them joining arms and travelling the distant lands, completing the quest and standing in front of the golden vaults together. They could find Simantiar and travel past the dipping mountains and follow the fish in the sky, have Kendrith become a part of their family, and laugh all the way there with Simantiar's jokes.

Lily smiled tenderly, lovingly, at her brother; a single tear as she was about to reunite with George.

"You are not Lily," George finally said. The words were a stark and cold realisation. Simply admitting it made him want to reach into his chest and tear the pain from his heart. He wanted nothing more than to believe that the girl before him was his sister, even just pretend. But he had made a promise to his real sister before she died. He would find the golden gates. Another tear ran down his cheek. "You are not my sister," he said, lip quivering.

The girl suddenly turned her desperate expression of compassion and love into one of furious and inexplicable wrath that made her seem anything but human. Her complexion turned a sickly grey. Her hair aged into broken strands. Her cheeks turned hollow And her eyes became as black as the swirling grains.

The shrill shriek the demon gave from her was a thing of nightmares.

George raised the bones back into the air and walked on. "Kendrith!" He now knew who he truly had to look for; he never should have left his side. But it was too late. By the time that George had pulled himself together, he knew his path had already diverged from Kendrith's.

Chapter 9

When George awoke, it was with a start. The stench of the place immediately invaded his nostrils with a gagging rancidity. His cheek was wet with something thick and sticky. He groaned at the feeling.

Where am I? the boy wondered, rising to his feet.

"K—" George was about to raise his voice, but then thought better of it. He had enough of making naive mistakes. He wasn't a child anymore and knew that shouting out names like that was simply an invitation for unwanted guests.

Instead, he looked around and noticed the wet and sagged appearance of where he found himself. His heart sank. It was a swamp.

George could suddenly hear voices. Gurgles and snarls and unnerving high-pitched snickering. The bard hid behind a willow tree and leaned past his cover.

"Hobbers," he whispered with fearful realisation. Kendrith wasn't exaggerating how unsightly the creatures were. In fact, George wondered if Kendrith had downplayed their repugnance.

There were three Hobbers on the other side of a small bog, ostensibly having some form of argument. Though George wasn't sure, with how disgustingly primitive their language sounded—mixing grunts and gurgles with the occasional rolling of phlegm forced to their mouth—it could have been possible that they were asking about each other's day and their mother's health, and George thought that it still sounded like they were talking about the size of their morning shit.

They were truly quite small, hunched, and not even reaching George's waist in size. Their legs were thin and very long compared to their round upper body.

George noted how they seemed to bend their knees to have their springlike posture support their disproportionate body frame as their legs were comically disproportionate to their torso. Their heads were round and slightly pointed. Their lips were thin and angled close to their chins while their noses were just as tiny—most probably to make space for the massive eyes which took up the most space on their large, confused faces.

Each eyeball flitted around independently from the other. One of them observing the scene of a Hobber who was pranked on for a laugh, while the other eye was peeled for nothing in particular. It wasn't just how they looked, it was also the unnatural and slimy way they moved; always finding something to toy with for their amusement.

George returned to the cover of his tree, deciding to hide until the Hobbers had moved on, and then come up with a plan.

But his breath in his throat as he looked up at the Hobber that stood less than a foot away from him. He could smell the noisome and putrid stench which they gave off—something comparable to sickly mould and rolling in their own filth. Yet the creature simply eyed George with curiosity. Its eyes blinked independently from each other, first the left, then the right. It cocked its head and leaned in closer.

Thoughts raced through George's mind, as fear settled in. He remained remarkably still, finding it impossible to contain his breath. The bard gagged as the Hobber came face-to-face with George. He recoiled, turning away and pinching his nose shut as the Hobber was just an inch away. Rotting teeth lined its deteriorated gums. Black strands of hair dangled like weeds.

Slowly, George reached to the small of his back as the Hobber reached out a four-fingered hand to George's cheek. Its skin was equally wet and sticky as it was rough to the touch. George felt a little bit of bile jump into his throat.

The Hobber suddenly smiled, as if realising what it had just found.

Just as the creature was going to raise its voice and call for its comrades with glee, George seized the moment, drawing out Kendrith's dagger in a flash and bringing the blade up to the creature's chin, sheathing it in its flesh.

The Hobber was suddenly paralysed with shock. It looked to George with confusion, as if it were betrayed, as if it wondered why George would hurt it if it only wanted to play with and torture him. One eye blinked, and the other one slumped with a slight twitch.

Thick disgusting blood that even matched the Hobber in its sickly look oozed from the wound. It never managed to call for its comrades, twitching and letting off the occasional grunt as it choked on its own blood.

George held its gaze—a cold look as he watched the life leave the Hobber's eyes.

A slight memory flashed into George's mind—the look of a man the first time he took their life. "I'm sorry," George kept saying. But no, he felt nothing as the Hobber went limp.

George felt himself lose control—the "Other" was taking the reins, another side of George he would see through the fractured mirror inside his soul. He recalled the whispers, the promises it made to protect him, to keep him company, to make sure he wasn't alone. It was like the stagnant water at the bottom of a well, unmoving, unperturbed—numb to pain and fear.

George had felt the Other less and less over the past couple of months, first as he had found Simantiar, the first true companionship he had had in the years since Lily had died and then with Kendrith, the dark implications of his other half seemed to be no more than a shadow.

But if George's smile, cunning, and luck all failed, the killer within him certainly would not.

"Fuck!" Gaven kicked the dirt at his feet. "Fuck, fuck, fuck!" The hollower had already fled, one of its legs severed in the process. It didn't matter, it would soon build itself a new leg with sinew and bone and flesh.

Salo didn't say anything, his sword limp in his hand, several notches marking both of their blades.

Hank finally returned from his pursuit as Gaven dropped his sword and paced towards his comrade, grabbing him by the collar. "Tell me you got them," Gaven demanded, spittle flying in Hank's face.

Hank didn't say anything, looking away instead.

"Fuck!" Gaven pushed Hank away, having him stumble backwards. "Useless, the both of you! If you just stuck that first arrow in that fucking merc's head right from the start we could have that child by now." Gaven turned away in frustration.

"I told you to let me get closer! That the fog was obscuring my view and I didn't have a clear shot, but you insisted I take it!" Hank challenged, finger pointing and cheeks turning red.

Gaven spun on his heel, his distaste plain for all to see. "Are you talking back to me?" Gaven paced towards Hank again, a look in his eyes that promised something far worse than just shoving.

"Boss, stop." Salo jumped between them, concern in his eyes. He didn't like it when Gaven and Hank fought.

Gaven shrugged the gentle giant away and went to sit on a stone boulder, facing away from the other two as he removed his hat and scratched at the scar that marked his face.

"Where did they go?" Gaven asked.

Hank remained silent until Gaven turned around and looked him straight in the eye. "Where did they go?"

"That's just it—they went through the centre," Hank finally said.

Gaven's eyes widened. "What? Are you sure about that?"

Hank nodded.

Gaven turned away again, mumbling to himself.

"So, they are goners?" Salo asked with his lisp.

"No. That merc isn't dumb; I have seen him before." Gaven considered this. It was true that Kendrith was rash and brazen, but his reputation was downplayed. In a matter of seconds he processed not just their attack, but how to deal with them and deduced the ladder of power. What was even more impressive was how he immediately saw the hollower not as an enemy, but as an opportunity.

Gaven bit his nails, starting with his thumb, a habit he always had when deep in thought. He knew that Kendrith wasn't stupid—there must have been a plan.

"Hey, but it wasn't all in vain," Hank said.

Gaven turned around to Hank who now had a big grin on his face, pulling out a couple of bones from his bag; Gaven's eyes widened. "How did you get those?"

"The boy fell while he was running and a couple of the bones fell from his bag."

Gaven now walked over to him and took one in his hands.

"We can go home now. We'd make a selling out of these! Besides, the boy and mercenary are as good as dead—no one survives the centre."

"No."

"What do you mean no?"

"I mean, no. This"—Gaven held the bones in his hand—"is our ticket through the centre." Gaven smiled.

"Boss, are you sure?" Salo asked.

"Trust me." Gaven saw the uncertainty in their eyes, he looked down at the bones and didn't blame them. *Am I crazy?* he pondered. It was a big risk to take on a hunch. In fact, now that he thought about it, the boy and Kendrith certainly must have acted on a hunch as well.

He looked back up at Salo and Hank who regarded him with pleading eyes. They trusted him. It was a fact that Gaven often forgot and not often enough appreciated.

"Salo, what were you most gifted at as a child?"

Salo pondered for a moment, he seemed to hesitate as if it were a trick question. "Playing the flute, boss."

"Right, right. You were so good, in fact, that people would come from all around to hear the wonderboy and his flute!" Gaven pronounced.

Salo just looked down to his stubby fingers clenching open and shut as if something was missing in his grasp.

"And then you had your growth spurt—it seemed like all was going well for good ol' Salo! Turning into a strong, handsome man. But then, as if fuelled by all that praise, your growing never stopped, did it?" Salo's eyes teared up as he was forced to relive it all. They were still among the spirits of the dead, their wailing sounds calling out as if they deigned to be the choir of Salo's tragedy.

"Your fingers became too stubby, too clumsy to play. What did your parents do when your fat fingers couldn't play anymore? They abused you, shunned you."

"Gaven, not now, we better leave," Hank said, putting one arm on Gaven's shoulder. The mists drifted along like an ephemeral blanket to their messed-up bedtime story.

"You fought back, couldn't take their beating anymore."

"It was an accident," Salo defended.

"But no one else thought that, did they?"

Salo remained quiet.

One down. Gaven turned to Hank. "And what about you?"

Hank stepped back as Gaven took one step forward. "A wife who cheated on you? The love of your life? A happy family? You think you have it all and then some handsome—"

"Stop, Gaven. I get it." Hank let out a defeated sigh.

"We are victims! Not of your wife"—he pointed to Hank. "Or of your parents"—he pointed at Salo—"but to the universe!" He pointed to the grey skies.

"And me? How did the world betray me, you may ask? Well, I am stuck with you two bozos, aren't I?" Salo and Hank laughed at the joke, Gaven's arms wide open and his smile true.

"What do we always say?" Gaven asked.

"If the world wants to make us villains," Salo started.

"Then let's kill and plunder like villains," Hank finished.

The three nodded silently, no more words needed to be spoken. Except for the fact that Salo allowed himself a slight tear.

As Gaven led the way with bones in hands, he started to look back at their pasts. Their hopes and dreams. How they were all brought together.

The three neared the heart of the forest, wading through the running river and onto the other side.

"I will go ahead—stay behind me; hold the bones in your hands."

Hank and Salo nodded.

And that was that. Gaven offered the two an out. He offered them hope, and it was just on the other end of a murderous malevolent centre within the Forest of the Dead.

The bones within their hands flared blue and a body of black mass suddenly came into view. "Stay close," Gaven said.

Simantiar rolled onto the riverbed, the tail of a fish flapping restlessly in his mouth until the skull spat it out. "I should have just stayed in the tomb," he said.

Simantiar stayed on the shore for a while, the water of the stream clashing into him relentlessly. He played back the events before he landed in the water. The sudden panic in George's eyes, the fear. He felt sad to be separated from the boy and in spite of all his teasing, George had truly grown on him. There was an innocence to the bard that reminded Simantiar of a past, of a familiar sensation though the memory that was supposed to accompany it was still marred.

George was genuinely scared for Simantiar, and that touched the old wizard. "I hope that kid is okay." Though he convinced himself that as long as Kendrith was with him the boy would be safe.

Simantiar looked around and noticed that the scenery wasn't terrifying. Quite the contrary—it looked like something out of a fairy-tale. Birds chirping, trees growing vibrantly with the promise of life and luscious green weeds covering the land like young sprites still in the springtime of their life.

"Hmm, not so 'dead-ish' as usual," the wizard mused. He had no clue where George and Kendrith had gone and no idea about how he was going to go about finding them. He noticed that the light which pierced the canopy brightened and assumed that the sun was coming up. A whole day had passed since their pursuit and Simantiar's water tour.

"'It will be fun,' they said. 'Let's go on an adventure and find an imaginary vault,' they said. Now here I am in a forest that is trying to kill me as a skull on a body of water." He sighed. "How did I fall so low?"

Suddenly, as if feeling the wizard's lonely ramblings, a woodpecker flew down and landed on a small throwing stone right beside the skull. It cocked its head back and forth with idle curiosity.

"Well. Aren't you a cutie—ow!" The bird suddenly began to peck the wizard.

"Stop that!" Simantiar demanded, hopping around. "Great. A thousand-year-old wizard is now the plaything of a little bird—things can't get any worse."

The wizard turned to the bird and realised it had stopped pecking him. It jumped onto Simantiar's head, leaning over so that its upside down head peered into Simantiar's empty sockets. "You're right, birdie! I can't continue to stay in a state of self-loathing! I need to find George and Kendrith."

"I think I will call you Pecky. Ow!" Pecky pecked one of Simantiar's empty sockets and the wizard laughed.

The wizard's spirits were lifted, and with newfound energy he decided he needed to find George and Kendrith as quickly as he could. But how? He was just a skull without feet. He didn't even know where to start.

His figurative heart stood still as Simantiar realised he needed to reach deep into his memories to recall the ancient incantations that he long since had no use for.

With hesitance, the wizard allowed a small opening to the chaotic realm of his old life and tried hard to meander past the memories of battle and pain.

"I need a body," the wizard realised, looking all around him and stopping at a clump of discarded tree branches. "Hmm."

The wizard hobbled over to a short stick and tried desperately to get one end in his mouth, but failed. Without lips the task proved impossible. Of course, limbs would have also helped.

Pecky seemed to realise what the odd skull was trying to do, for it jumped down and lifted the stick up for Simantiar, putting it between his teeth.

"Thank you," said Simantiar.

And so, Simantiar tried painstakingly to draw magical circles. When he still had a body to move in, the mage didn't have need for such circles— they were things taught to children when still learning the basics of magic. But now, without a body and with the world's magical reserves drained, this was the best he could do.

He tried his best to keep the circle straight, but found that no matter how he tried, with his lack of dexterity and an unfortunate angle he could not form a proper circle.

"It looks like a monkey was electrocuted while trying to draw a circle..." Simantiar commented.

His eyes veered off to stare at Pecky. "Maybe..."

Deciding it was worth a shot, Simantiar continued to eye the bird, focusing with every ounce of his being and drawing upon the feeling within himself.

There. He could feel the path. A thread escaped his essence and came to worm itself onto Pecky. Broken off from the binding of his skeletal form and binding itself to Pecky in hopes of being understood.

"Help me find the other two idiots, and I will show you a world unlike any other," Simantiar said. It seemed to have worked, for Pecky flew over to the branch in Simantiar's mouth and took it into its grasp.

It took some getting used to and using splinters no bigger than the size of a thumb, but the bird eventually was able to recreate the images which it found in Simantiar's consciousness to satisfactory proportions.

"This will be the start of a great friendship," Simantiar said approvingly, as he watched the bird's masterwork. Pecky flew over and perched itself on the skull, giving a happy peck of its own and a chirp.

Simantiar waddled to the centre of the three triangulating circles and spoke the incantations. The words came to his lips like ghosts spoken from the past.

The earth rose to his demands as Pecky flew from Simantiar and up to the branch of a tree to watch the magic unfold from a safe distance.

Soil coiled. Twigs rose. And, in no time at all, the pieces all came together to form a small body of branches and leaves. Three flexing fingers made of twigs and pine needles formed each wooden hand and two-toed feet held up a spindly body. Simantiar's new form was no bigger than a toddler, perhaps even smaller. But the wizard felt more alive than he had in years. It was nothing more than a little touch of mobility, but that was enough to remind him of what it was like to have flexing fingers and straddling toes.

Days passed by and Simantiar tried hard to remember the rest of his sealed memories. He wandered the woods trying to get a scale of the land, but his new form could travel only so far before falling apart. The distance he could cover proved rather disappointing.

"You wouldn't happen to know the way out?" Simantiar asked Pecky. The bird just pecked his skull and rose to a branch up above where an opening provided itself, as if to imply the way out was with wings. "Great use you are," Simantiar grumbled.

It was when the skull reached a clearing that he found something, or rather someone, that made him understand where he was.

A creature turned to the small curious skull. Its entire body was fashioned by coiling and intertwining oak with the lower body of an elk and the upper torso of a large man. Its eyes glowed an emerald green with leaves sprouting from its body. Wayward branches sprang from its head like antlers of wood sprouting spring leaves of their own. Further greenery from a weeping willow draped its scalp like a mane of flowing hair.

"Well, aren't you a curious one," it said with a low tender voice formed by the flowing contortion of wood.

Simantiar stepped back as he regarded the being. Everything about the creature was majestic and humbling.

"Stand back," Simantiar said as the creature stepped towards the old wizard.

"I mean you no harm, little one." It spoke with a deep and old voice that carried pain born from experience. Weathered and old like the body he bore. But still the voice he spoke with carried undulated compassion and worry.

"Little one? Look here, you giant forest nymph—if you come too close you could die."

The sage-like being laughed a throaty thing. It was bemused by Simantiar's claims as it reached down and picked him up into his palms made of thin branches. Simantiar and the being were now face-to-face, and the wizard could see the features of the mystical creature in full detail. How the branches twisted and writhed to form new facial expressions like a tandem choreography of vines.

Pecky flew over and perched itself on the being's propped finger. The bird leaned in as so too did the creature as if going for a kiss.

"Whoa, whoa, whoa, this is not appropriate! Think of the children!" Simantiar chastened.

The wooden being's mouth opened so that Simantiar could see its tongue emerge—or not a tongue, but rather a worm. Pecky ripped it out from inside and devoured it.

"I think I'm going to hurl," Simantiar said.

"It is good to see you again, old friend," said the being.

"Old friend? Do I know you, tree-person? And would people please stop manhandling me? I'm not a toy."

The being didn't respond right away, grunting instead like an old man who had to rise from his seat as he put Simantiar back down.

"My name is Cernunnos. I am the great guardian of these woods. And you, my old friend, are Simantiar the Great, the Pride of Yumia, the Legend of Eindeheid."

Simantiar stumbled over his words. Syllable after syllable fought for dominance over which of his plethora of questions to ask first. All in all, it just resulted in incoherent and nonsensical gibberish.

Simantiar finally stopped, composed himself, and asked the one question that took precedence out of all: "How do you know me?"

"Know you?" Cernunnos asked. "We are old friends, you and I."

"But how?"

"You know how, little one."

"My past life?"

Cernunnos did not reply, but he had no need to. Simantiar knew it to be true.

"Why did you not collapse when you came near me?"

"Why would I?" The being frowned.

"Because everything magical I touch falls apart."

The old thing chuckled. "You think me to be powered by magic? I am far beyond such fancies."

"What do you mean?"

Cernunnos lifted his wooden hands and regarded the world around him. "Nature is my creator—I am given form and life by the nature that encompasses me. I am not the simple fancy musings of sorcery—I am the world's gift to itself. There are more powerful things, more fundamental laws in life than the ability to temporarily distort reality. Even after all your lifetimes lived, you still have so much to learn.

"Though that is a peculiar quality of yours to negate magic, I don't recall you having that in your past life."

Cernunnos turned away from Simantiar.

"Wait!" the skull called out, having to run after the reverent being which paced away slowly while Pecky found a seat on Cernunnos's shoulder.

"Wait, you don't just bloody drop a declaration like that on somebody and leave, it's rude." Simantiar struggled to keep pace, so Cernunnos picked the little thing up with a groan and a roll of its emerald eyes, and placed the tiny wizard on his other shoulder.

"I am beginning to remember how annoying you are," the being spoke slowly as the branches of its body groaned to voice the being's annoyance.

"Excuse me?"

"'Don't pick me up.' 'Don't walk so fast.' Always complaints with you!" Though Cernunnos spoke as if he were irritated, his mood seemed quite affable to Simantiar.

Simantiar remained silent for a few moments, his feet dangling over the shoulder. "You are no George, but your shoulder ain't half bad." Pecky all the while flew back and forth from the being's head, then perched on its antlers, and burrowed into Cernunnos's chest for what Simantiar could only imagine was food.

"I know you seem to know me and all, but I feel like I am at a disadvantage here. Who are you to me?"

"What do you remember of your old life?" Cernunnos asked.

"Bits and pieces. My mother. A boy called Usellyes. A war. Conflict. Blood and screams." The more Simantiar recalled, the less he was in control of the words that slipped from his tongue. A floodgate opened that he struggled to close as much as his memories struggled to form.

Cernunnos nodded with a deep and contemplative groan. "Yes, it is no wonder that your memories are so distraught. And what do you remember of your time within the tomb?"

Simantiar suddenly went dead silent. He couldn't talk about that time. Even if he wanted to, the whole thing was just a hazy darkness that knotted his tongue and prevented him from speaking. "Nothing." That was all he could muster. It wasn't entirely a lie, but it wasn't entirely the truth either. More so than war and conflict, blood and death, it was that hell that he spent over a millennium in that haunted the ancient wizard. No life, no beings, no death or connections. He was alone for an eternity in that chasm. As days drew into years, the wizard had grown numb and his mind went quiet. Time stood still within those caverns and the skull drew on cold dead eyes.

He couldn't remember how long he spent in there—all he could muster was the feeling of his mind growing cold and going into a deep and hollow slumber—and then a light, the sight of a boy groaning as he broke through the final door.

Life returned into the dead skull's eyes and he was awoken by the sudden unsure and dainty look of a young boy—his saviour.

He recalled how the first words he ever spoke to someone after being entombed for over a thousand years was about scratching an itch on a nonexistent nose.

"And what is our relationship?" Simantiar asked, changing the subject.

"We are friends. At least, that is how you put it. I insisted that I didn't need a human friend, that all you do is destroy the nature I swore to protect as guardian of these woods. But you came when you could and brought me gifts. Adamant that you could learn much from nature." The being laughed at the memory. "You were so angry about how the other mages insisted that magic was all they needed to know. Called them ignorant."

"And that is how we became friends?"

The old guardian grunted and the moving bark of its body groaned. "Let's go with tolerate." Simantiar went quiet, and though he did not remember the being, he couldn't help but feel safe in its presence—it was familiar to say the least.

"So, tell me all you know about the past. Who was I really? What do my memories mean? What happened all those years ago? And why was I in a tomb?"

"But you already know."

"I do?"

The old being groaned again as it reached over, touching a finger made of vines against the skull's forehead.

"In here; your memories never left you, but you chose to keep them locked away."

"How do I release them?"

Cernunnos did not reply with words, but rather by entering a clearing within the woods. Simantiar noticed a circular depression and steps protruding from all around the perimeter. All manner of overgrowth from grass to moss to vines claimed the circle, enveloping it, yet the primordial power which emanated was unmistakable to Simantiar.

"Here." The guardian lowered Simantiar to the floor as Pecky joined him, perching on the skull's head with a brand new worm it gulped down—Simantiar did not want to know where that one was from.

The old wizard walked slowly, using the several levels as steps to lean over and hold the ledge before falling to the next step.

"What is this?" Simantiar asked, looking back up at the foreboding guardian as he walked to the epicentre. The being emanated mystic reverence, the way its centaur-like body of forestry tapped a hoof against the floor and its broad chest with mystical spiral patterns hidden under a mane of shrubbery poked out.

"A way to find your memories, and with them, return to some of your former strength as when you were alive. You wanted to learn from nature? Then let it guide you. Become one with the ground below you and remember—magic can be controlled, it can be harnessed, for without control destruction is its recompense.

"But nature is not to be harnessed, it is not to be controlled, it is to be let free and twist like coiling vines left to grow. Like water that form rivers. Let nature guide you and let go of the reins." Cernunnos then raised his three-fingered palm made of coiled vines.

"Become one with nature instead of controlling it—only then can there be unity." Cernunnos's final words echoed as if coming from the forest itself; it carried wisdom, but also timeless power. Not the kind of power which creates flames to destroy, but rather the type of power which would take its time patiently for time is of no consequence. The type of power which will have waves clash against boulders and chip away for years or have vines that grow upon the makings of man and claim it in time."

And as if to prove his point, the vines that formed Cernunnos's arm coiled and twisted, a green light escaping from within, and the forest obeyed—no—the forest *listened,* it obliged. The vines slithered away as if reversing through time, the grass returned to Tiria, and the moss faded as if to return to its creator.

"Amazing," Simantiar gasped.

The skull turned to the being once more, seeking guidance. "But how?"

Cernunnos stepped into the circle and looked down at the skull. "Once you go in there, there is no turning back. There are memories that you locked away for a reason. Are you sure you wish to do this?"

Simantiar hesitated but only for a moment. He could not run away from his past forever. "And what about my friends? I need to find them."

"As long as they are part of this world, nature's reach cannot be eluded."

"How do I start? Do I like—sit down and cross my legs? Some monk chanting? Maybe a spiritual dance? But I don't know if I can cross my legs."

"Just shut up," said Cernunnos uncharacteristically with rolling eyes. It reached down, the bark of its body creaking as the guardian's fingers grew longer and reached in through the skull's sockets. Pecky flew away as more and more of the vines circled around and wrapped Simantiar. A sudden soft emerald glow escaped from the skull until the soft blue light of its own sockets vanished and Simantiar became as still as would be expected of a skull.

"Good luck, old friend," Cernunnos said.

Chapter 10

"Simantiar..."

Nothing.

"Simantiar!"

The young boy suddenly awoke with a start as the entire class exploded into laughter. He wiped the dreams from his eyes and yawned as if it were his bed that he awoke in and not a classroom full of hysterical children and a very annoyed teacher.

"Sorry, Miss Clarisse, what was the question again?" he asked, and the class dissolved into a second round of laughter.

Miss Clarisse was built similarly to the lean switch she wielded to frighten her students when they weren't listening.

She wasn't particularly old nor was she particularly young. Yet, she was old enough for the wrinkles on her face to make her seem more weathered than not. But if there was nothing else to go by, her unrivalled temper and boundless reserves of energy made her the cause of a lot of uneasy nights for Simantiar.

Miss Clarisse put on her infamous smile, one that was annoyingly deceptive. It seemed loving and understanding, but it was simply a sign that her patience was wearing thin. Simantiar noticed it often looked like a branch that was bending, and the moment it snapped was the moment Simantiar knew he had it coming.

"Where does magic come from?" Her smile held, on the verge of breaking.

Simantiar hesitated. "Ugh—well, I kind of just think of what I want to do and—*poof*, it kind of happens."

There was no snapping of the branch, no sudden enraged outburst, only a defeated sigh from Miss Clarisse as she pushed her spectacles down her nose so she could pinch the bridge in frustration.

"Your natural talent with magic may just prove to be your undoing, Mr. Trufin."

"Yes, Usellyes, please save me." Simantiar knew that Miss Clarisse wasn't all gloom and doom. She did have a loving side to her, but it was reserved for Usellyes alone. He was her model student, sharing an intrigue and love for magic that rivalled her own.

Simantiar looked over to Usellyes and noticed his best friend lower his hand.

It had been six years since they had met on that fateful day in the garden, and the boy had grown well into his new life. Simantiar himself was handsome even at the age of twelve. His curly golden hair gave him a regal aura. Full-bodied cheeks made his smile even more warming, while his energy and confidence drew people to him.

Unparalleled magical talent, looks, naturally sociable: the boy seemed to have it all. And for quite some time, he was the one that girls would chatter about as one does in school.

Yet in time, Usellyes caught up to him. If Simantiar was the sun, Usellyes was the moon.

The black-haired boy was not rowdy like Simantiar, not the life of the party, and his attractiveness came from a soft and tender tranquility that soothed in contrast to his gregarious friend. His lips were thinner, his face longer and angled with hollowed cheeks. There was a cold sharpness to his stare that made him seem entirely stoic as he walked around with his placid expression.

Though he always seemed timid and sorrowful, that wasn't the case. Simantiar's popularity brought attention to Usellyes. It was when people talked to the dark-haired and quiet boy, and saw him smile tenderly, that they recognised the good inside his heart was like the still waters of a lake in moonlight.

"Umm…" Usellyes hesitated, before finally summoning the courage to speak, "it depends on the source we are talking about. There are different theories and claims, with all of them having their own theories.

Archaeological findings suggest that ancient civilisations saw magic as a gift from gods, bottomless wells of power to give man the ability to stand for itself, while others believe it is an interconnected part of all that is. Scholars such Betemies Nafurn believe that—"

Miss Clarisse laughed delightedly and raised her hand. "Wait, wait, Usellyes. This isn't advanced magical theory. You have several years before discussing such complicated concepts. For now, just tell me about the basic and most accepted idea behind magic."

Usellyes went silent and Simantiar noticed his friend fold his hands together—it was something he did when he felt like he said something stupid. "Of course." Doubt was heard in the boy's voice, but still he pressed on.

"The most popular theory at the moment comes from the Vranian Calendar sixth century after the ordinance of advancement. A theorist ahead of his time theorised that the world—or rather reality—is built through a weave of fabric that can't be seen with the naked eye and that it holds everything together, 'the constant' he called it. At the time, the theory was archaic and not quite fleshed out, but further research showed that he set the groundwork for finding that this interconnected reality binds us all, and by tapping into that weave we can temporarily distort reality."

Miss Clarisse smiled as one would to their own child when they had reason to be proud. She was beyond pleased. Simantiar knew that Usellyes still managed to overexplain the theory, but no one dared complain.

"Let's call it there." And as if it were a sudden race, most of the students packed their things up in a hurry, excited at the prospect of doing something other than studying. Books slammed together, writing equipment clattered, and in no time at all, everyone packed their things and left as the sound of their chatter turned softer and softer outside of the classroom. The last was Usellyes who always took his time, and thus, the rest stayed with.

"Hey, Usellyes, let's do something," Simantiar said as they were the only two left in the classroom.

"I wanted to go to the library."

Simantiar rolled his eyes. "You always go to the library, one day of lying around won't harm you."

"And one day of studying wouldn't harm you either."

Simantiar punched his friend in the arm with a playful smile and Usellyes returned it. The golden-haired boy was the one person that Usellyes never worried about saying the wrong thing with, not once.

"Let's go to our spot."

The dark-haired boy looked up at his friend as he packed the last of his things and pondered with a blank expression. "Fine," he finally said, smiling.

They walked out of the golden gates of their school, but instead of walking back towards Simantiar's home or Usellyes's dorms, they headed to a secluded area behind an alleyway.

The boys looked left and then right, and when they were certain that no one was there to catch them, Simantiar lifted his hand up into the air and pinched it—drawing back something invisible as if he were peeling it. The resistance was there, a slight shine and glimmer in the air like bending glass.

"There." Simantiar wrapped himself in the invisible fabric.

"Oooooooooooouuuuuuuu—I'm a ghoooooooooost," Simantiar mimicked the drawn-out drawl of a ghost as he was now nothing more than a floating head. "You study too hard Usellyes and are making your best friend look bad!" Simantiar continued as Usellyes laughed.

"Which one?" Usellyes teased.

"Dick." Simantiar gave the laughing boy another invisible punch.

Simantiar wrapped Usellyes up in the cloak. They could still see all that was around them, but knew that none could peer inside.

"Ready?" Simantiar asked.

Usellyes nodded.

With a soft incantation, the bending of knees, and a blue wispy glow that came from Simantiar's eyes, drifting along coloured lips, their feet left the ground and they rose into the air.

Usellyes's grip tightened around Simantiar's neck as the two rose higher and higher. Simantiar knew that his friend, as always, looked down despite being afraid of heights. He asked Usellyes once why he does it, *Just because I am afraid doesn't mean that I shouldn't experience it,* the boy would say.

They reached their destination in a matter of minutes: a ledge pressed into the side of a mountain and facing Eindeiheid, the great magical school made for those seen as the best of the best in wizardry.

Though their flight was impossibly fast, their landing was gracious, slow, and controlled.

Simantiar pulled the cloak from his hands and a slight shimmer in the air suggested that it vanished. Suddenly, the elements and the thin air became abundantly clear.

The two boys sat on the ledge and it was Usellyes who murmured a few words and created a bubble of warmth to ward off the gripping cold winds that inhabited those heights.

"I wish I could use magic like you." Usellyes smiled, seemingly upset that his ball of warmth was nothing compared to Simantiar's abilities. They weren't very different when they had first met, and though Usellyes could perform magic that was far beyond anyone else in their grade, he still paled in comparison to Simantiar. Simantiar knew this, but tried his best to never let Usellyes feel that way.

The ability to create an invisibility cloak and the magic of flight were abilities approved only for graduated mages, yet the two of them weren't even apprentices.

"Well, I wish I could be as studious as you," Simantiar said.

"What's the point of knowing the theory if you can't do the actual magic?"

Simantiar laughed. "You've got me there. I don't know, I just kind of think of it in my fantasies and figure a way to do the magic I want. It kind of...connects."

"That makes zero sense."

Another laugh. "I know."

They sat in silence for a while, watching how the sun caused the framework and gorgeous architecture of Eindeiheid to glisten radiantly. A steeple of boundless knowledge. Simantiar as well as Usellyes dreamed of entering that academy. One for the knowledge, and the other for the prestige.

"But you know what?"

The black-haired boy suddenly turned to his friend.

"With my magic and your knowledge, we will be unstoppable," Simantiar said.

Usellyes smiled. "Yes, that we will be."

Usellyes placed his hand on top of Simantiar's, and neither of them said a word as they looked up towards the academy. This was their spot. Two fish circling each other within their small world just like back at the garden. And together, they stared at not just the academy, but at what the future may hold.

School was the same as always the following day.

Courses on magical theory, and breathing techniques on how to control one's magic if one were to lose control. Including relaxation techniques and focus training.

Other inklings of courses included a focus on potential future career choices from healing roles to court councils to warrior knights to arcane fighters to general practitioners—the school propagated the importance of having a clear goal early on.

It was noon as Simantiar, Usellyes, and several others spent their daily hour-long respite from classes in the schoolyard. The yard had a sense of verticality to it, risen platforms that floated in stationary positions, stairways of stone connecting them all to form almost an ascending series of platforms shaped into a laurel wreath. The first two platforms began at the very bottom and moved upwards to the following levels.

All around them were the drifting blocks of stone that students could bounce off from platform to platform—it was supposed to promote motor sensibility and mental acuity. Though at the very bottom was a field that on the chance that a child would lose control and plummet, the feather fall magic would soften their descent.

When first they were permitted access to the area, Simantiar and the others would intentionally climb and jump from the ends to feel the rush of going from a roaring plummet into a soft, drifting descent.

Simantiar, Usellyes, and a few of their friends sat upon a block on the third level. There they had the comforts of a long tabled bench where they could sit and joke.

"By my pigtails, I think the sun is planning on roasting us alive." It was Emilie that spoke, and indeed she did have pigtails. If her freckled cheeks were anything to go by, one would assume she quite regularly enjoyed the sun, but Simantiar knew that she also enjoyed complaining even more.

"Better than having to sit in Miss Clarisse's class," Noima complained.

"Oh, don't you worry. As long as Simantiar continues to be the pain in the ass that he is and Usellyes keeps saving him, we have nothing to worry about," said Zaros as he sat on the edge of the long table, one leg dangling and the other drawn to his chest as if he were a languid and confident adventurer.

"Oh, come now, why do I even have to be here? I can already perform magic at a far higher level than most graduates!" Simantiar complained.

The others seemed to take some offence to that, except for Usellyes who sat at the end of one of the benches and read the class book to himself while the others bickered among themselves.

"You may be gifted at improvising magic, but there is no way you will ever enter a king's court when you can't even comment on simple magical theory." Now it was Usellyes talking and the others fell quiet at such an event. Usellyes having something to say on his own accord was always a rare occurrence, but whenever it did happen, it was because what he had to say was worth listening to.

The others started laughing as Simantiar went over and grabbed him in a headlock.

"Ah, now you finally have something to say when it has to do with my own shortcomings. Never is it: 'Oh, Simantiar, you are so great, can you teach me how to do magic?'" Simantiar put on a very high-pitched and mockingly posh voice for Usellyes.

"What's the point? You wouldn't even be able to show me anyway." The laughter grew even louder as Usellyes gave Simantiar a bemused smirk. It didn't bother Simantiar—he enjoyed that he could be the cause for everyone's laughter.

"Hey, Sim, come check this out." Ciro motioned from the back as she leaned over the platform's edge, peering below.

Simantiar was always the curious type as he abandoned one source of laughter for the other. He jumped forward onto his belly and said a quick spell to remove any force of impact, followed by a quick spell which made him slide across the surface like a seal on ice.

When finally he stopped, he did not do so on the precipice of the platform, but rather continued sliding through air as if there was a layer of unseen glass.

He pretended not to notice as his entire body remained in midair and he lay on his side, his head propped up by a planted elbow and tucked hand.

"What am I looking at?" Simantiar didn't turn to see if the others were amazed by the fluidity he had just cast all those spells. It was cooler that way.

"There is that girl again," Ciro said.

"What was her name again?" Simantiar asked.

"Joselyn," Emilie recalled as she joined Ciro at the lip.

"Ah yeah." Simantiar looked down to her. Joselyn just sat there with her back to a stone column as she read a book all by herself.

"Should we talk to her?" Noima asked.

"Doesn't really seem like she is interested though. She never really hung out with us no matter how often we asked," Zaros replied.

"She isn't that adept at magic, is she?" Ciro asked.

"Not really. She has been struggling in the practical lessons with the spells," commented Emilie.

"I mean, you're only good at fighting. Maybe she has some other talent?"

Ciro went red at Noima's remark as she rose to her feet and balled a fist. "Yeah? I can show you how good at fighting I am."

Simantiar laughed at the theatrics as Ciro rose and Emilie jumped in front of her.

Ciro stood slightly taller than Emilie, but Emilie was fearless and was always the one who held Ciro's short temper in check. "There are arcane fighters, Ciro, and Miss Clarisse already said that you show promise in that field."

"Yeah, she meant it in a bad way," Zaros absently commented.

"Zaros!" Emilie admonished.

Ciro went even redder, her boyish demeanour shining through again as her body tensed, ready for a fight.

"Yeah? Well, at least my only talent with magic isn't sculpting useless things!" Ciro challenged.

Zaros seemed to ready a retort of his own before a stagnant and placating tenor stilled their conflict.

"Joselyn is diligent, if nothing else." All heads veered to the rarest voice which was once again Usellyes. There seemed to be some form of unspoken kinship between Joselyn and him. Of course he would understand the amount of effort that went into studying and the fulfilment it granted. Indeed, Joselyn also quite often did well in Miss Clarisse's sessions though her practical abilities fell short.

"Let's help her a bit." Simantiar, without so much as a second to consider it, waved a nonchalant finger about. At first, one struggled to notice what he had done. But then, Joselyn's legs seemed to stretch. Then a panicked scream from her. Her shadow started to grow in size.

"Simantiar! What are you doing?" Emilie demanded.

Next thing anyone could see was Joselyn beginning to float up slowly as her book fell from her lap to the ground. The girl faced down, screaming. Her hand reached and stretched out for the book as if it could save her.

"Simantiar, I don't think she's enjoying that," Ciro said, poking her head over the lip of the platform.

"It's fine." Simantiar curled his finger up as the girl screamed all the air out of her lungs, shooting up in a matter of seconds till she was face-to-face with Simantiar and the others.

Joselyn was desperately trying to clutch her skirt and hold it down. Her cheeks flushed and murmurs began to form from below.

"Sorry about that." Another wave of Simantiar's finger and the skirt seemed to unmake itself and change as if by the hands of an invisible tailor. When they reformed, they did so as loose-fitting trousers that reached Joselyn's heels.

"So, I believe we've met before. I am Simantiar and this is Emilie, Ciro, Zaros, Noima, and Usellyes."

Her eyes momentarily settled on Usellyes before she averted her gaze and fierce burning red filled her cheeks.

"Uh, Simantiar…" Noima tried to intersede.

"Put me down!" Joselyn screamed.

"But we saw that you are alone, and we'd like to get to know you a bit."

In an effort to make her laugh, or even just entertain Joselyn, Simantiar made her fly up to the sky. His gaze and that of all the others followed her flitting screams up and then left and right and coursing through the air in a figure eight as she bobbed back and forth before landing her at the platform.

"Ta-da!" Simantiar declared, positive that it must have entertained her.

Joselyn's hair was a rowdy mess, her knees buckled, and her teeth clattered. Her eyes were wild and frenzied from the ride.

It started to dawn on Simantiar that perhaps Joselyn didn't enjoy it as much as he thought she would.

"Pl-please take me down," she said through trembling lips.

Simantiar was the one who was frozen still, now. He didn't get it. He loved to fly through the sky the way she did.

"It's okay." Usellyes was the one who stepped forward, his docile and tempered aura helping to still some of the fear instilled into the girl as he guided her slowly down the steps. She clung on to him with every step.

"Nicely done," spoke a sardonic Zaros from behind Simantiar.

"Ow." Someone must have nudged him in the ribs.

Simantiar suddenly felt sour all of a sudden.

"I'm home." Simantiar wasn't his usual self for the rest of the day.

He wondered. Did he do something wrong? He tried to apologise to Joselyn. But she just bowed her head and paced in the opposite direction.

When all else failed he hesitantly resorted once more to another magic trick, and another one after that, and another one after that. Till he was called into the principal's office.

With his head bowed and a wave of regret and doubt wafting over him, Simantiar dragged himself through the pristine halls of his mother's mansion.

"Simantiar." It came from his right, his mother's voice. It was still one of love, but also one of regret.

Simantiar stepped back and turned to see the dimly lit room where his mother waited. It was already dark. Usellyes had also seemed more distant than usual that day. The only reason Simantiar was late was because he didn't want to go home.

His mother stood there, cane in her hand as she leaned on it, her legs hidden behind a long blouse with thorned roses patterned on the fabric that reached her feet.

"Come, sit. We need to talk," she said. There was hurt in Giselle's eyes. A profound, but loving sadness for the talk that was to come.

She let Simantiar know of the message she had received of the events that took place and asked him what happened.

Simantiar began to tell her. The more he retold the events the more he realised that he did do something wrong, and a great heavy pit formed in his heart that ached.

They sat on two opposite, cushioned armchairs, a small round table between them and the city of Yumia in its stark night beauty as it glowed with latent magic though the full-length window. Timmy, the family dog was curled up beside Simantiar's feet getting petted by his curled toes.

"I was just trying to show her a good time," Simantiar insisted.

"I know, Simantiar. I know. But it's not that easy. You scared the little girl. Multiple times."

"I know!" Simantiar lashed out, burying his head between drawn-in knees.

Giselle put down the tea that Sebastian had poured her before he was relieved for the night.

"Perhaps it is partially my fault."

Simantiar looked up at that, failing to understand.

"Any child gifted with such talents will eventually hit a wall. Believe they are entitled to the rest of the world simply because they were born with gifts. But that's not true. They will progress only so far as their talents permit. Or they will try to solve everything with their talents when even magic cannot do everything."

Simantiar frowned, confused. "But I can create things out of thin air. I can perform incredible things that make others smile."

Giselle rose from her seat, taking her cane and limping to a dark corner of the room. She returned with a potted flower, a scion sprouting through the dirt.

"I want you to tend to this flower and make it grow," Giselle said, though it seemed as if she wasn't entirely finished.

Simantiar looked to the pot and snapped his fingers and the flower grew instantly.

He was confused already, but even more so when he saw his mother's dissatisfaction and defeated sigh.

"Simantiar. Does magic make you friends?"

"Well, there is Zoras, Ciro, Usellyes: they became my friends."

"Because of your laugh." Giselle pulled on his cheeks, earning herself a chuckle through the gloom of Simantiar's heart. "Because of your smile." She poked his dimples for another buttoned laugh. "They enjoy your jokes." She now tickled him as they laughed together. "But not because of your magic. I watched the one thing you offered Usellyes that made the boy cherish you since the first day. Safety. Familiarity. Understanding. You helped him make friends."

Giselle glanced over to the beautifully grown and healthy potted basil leaves that Simantiar invoked.

"There is no love in this." Giselle touched the leaves with such pity and saddened remorse.

"The things in life that truly matter take time, care, patience. A friend is like this pot. You tend to it, take care of it, be patient with it. And when it sprouts, the result will be all the more beautiful because of it. That was what your father taught me."

Simantiar pondered for a second, the memory of an unknown father battling that of a lesson that planted its own seed. And Simantiar knew that this time, he had no choice but to let the plant grow by itself.

"If you could bring Father back with magic so I could see him, would you?"

Giselle seemed shocked. "No. There are just some things in life that stay the way they should. As much as he would have loved you." Giselle tickled the boy, and despite the laughter, Simantiar felt a sudden profound sadness for a person he never got to meet.

"Simantiar, I wish to share with you a story."

"What kind of story?" asked Simantiar suddenly excited.

"The tale of Hubys."

"Is that another legendary mage of old?"

Giselle chuckled. "He is the most powerful of wizards to have ever lived."

Simantiar suddenly felt threatened at the thought. "We'll see about that," he pouted.

Giselle laughed again before settling down, clearing her throat, and beginning her story.

"Once there was a man named Hubys. His skill and talent far outmatched any other mage."

"Like me!" Simantiar proclaimed proudly.

Giselle didn't allow it to break her stride. "He formed temples out of forest trees, formed cities from thin air that float in the sky. Lifted mountains and cut winding rivers. The world was his playground. But soon, magic became his very being. His feet never touched the floor, for why should a man so powerful resort to walking like a commoner? His very body merged with forest trees for he was beyond having a mortal form. He would become the fish that trailed through rivers, the eagle that soared up above the clouds, the stone that sat and watched everything in reserved stillness. One day, Hubys turned into the wind itself, but never turned back. For he forgot what it was like to be human, and magic was all that defined him."

Simantiar was still, and then a deep primal fear he never knew was there evoked itself and he began to cry—small tears at first that turned into a cascade.

He clung to his mother. "Mom," he spoke through a pained throat and in between sobs. "Will that happen to me? I don't want to turn into wind and vanish."

Giselle chuckled, seemingly pleased at the reaction as she held her son lovingly and tight.

"Don't worry, Simantiar. As long as you don't forget that you are human. That the true magic is the friends you make, and the bonds you forge outside of magic will never let you forget who you really are. Only he who lets himself be lured by the temptation will fade to dust one day and never return."

Simantiar had a sudden existential dread emerge. "Am I human too?" he asked.

"One day you may be known as Simantiar the Great. Seen as the greatest wizard who ever lived. But to me you will always be Simantiar the human." This suddenly comforted the young boy as he spent the rest of the night clinging desperately to his mother, never realising when it was that he cried himself to sleep in her arms.

Chapter 11

"It's warm, Mother."

"Shush, my child." Mona Brosnorth put a damp cloth against her son's forehead. She was tender and caring just as any mother would be, but she looked nothing like a normal mother. Her arms were corded with muscle, and her scars were visible in the soft candlelight. Her entire body forged as if for war.

Yet still, her tender touch and care soothed the fevered boy.

"Sing me something," the boy said with a hoarse throat.

The mother chuckled. "Like what?"

"Anything."

The mother happily obliged, humming the tune to the Vranian tale, a tale of a hero that rose within the darkness and brought with him light, a story of a god that opposed fiends. How he loved that tale, how he longed to hold that sword and match the feats performed by the winged Vrania. How he longed to be like his mother and grandfather.

The boy could still hear the hum as it turned distant. His mother's voice became an echo that drifted into silence.

Kendrith opened his eyes and realised it was all a dream. A dream from a distant past he longed to revisit, yet they were nothing more than ghosts of a time long lost.

His mother's touch, the bed he laid on, the candle's glow, the lullaby, and his childhood: all of it was gone. The one thing that wasn't was the flaring warmth which he realised was a screaming shoulder and the fever that accompanied it. Yet this time, he had no mother to coddle him—he had no one.

"George." Kendrith suddenly remembered the boy. He looked around and saw no sign of him.

"George," he said again, trying to rise to his feet, but even his very limbs had deserted him—buckling knees gave way under the strain, as he collapsed to the floor and clasped his wounded shoulder. The merc could only gasp for air.

"I must find George." Kendrith was growing delirious, driven by duty in the face of his predicament.

"What's the most important rule when you are being a guide?" The words suddenly came to him from a long-ago past, words that must have found their way to the surface when Kendrith visited the memory of his mother.

"To protect our charge!" Kendrith remembered with what confidence he answered the question, that it was absolutely obvious and the first lesson at the guild.

"No!" Instead, Kendrith was rewarded with a stick over the head.

"Ow!"

"The first rule of being a guide is to take care of yourself." Kendrith's grandfather knelt down to him, a giant face-to-face with a young boy.

"How do you expect to save anyone if you are injured and on the verge of death? All you would be doing is getting each other killed."

"But the guild said—"

"To hell with the darn guild! They are just trying to fill up their own coffers."

"So, they don't care about their members?"

Kendrith's grandfather chuckled. "I never said that. Idiots like us willing to risk our lives are hard to come by and are an asset. Just that the reputation they hold as a guild would be on the line if every customer of theirs ended up dead in a ditch."

Kendrith didn't quite understand, which was it? Did they care more for their members or customers?

"Look, just remember this: no matter what happens, you can't save anyone if you are about to die yourself. You want to save your employer? Make sure you can move yourself. And pray to the gods that they aren't stupid enough to die in the meantime."

Kendrith nodded.

Drifting in and out of his delirium, Kendrith returned to the moment, touching his shoulder tenderly at the memory of the old man. "Thank you," he said. Even after all those years, his grandfather was still lecturing him. Kendrith couldn't help but smile.

He knew that his grandfather spoke the truth. But what of George? Could the boy protect himself? Kendrith thought back to the young boy and smiled.

George was nothing like Kendrith when he was his age. Kendrith was always reckless and foolhardy, running into danger with reckless abandon.

George, on the other hand, was smart. Yet still, Kendrith saw himself in the young boy, perhaps fancying the idea of a younger brother. He knew that George showed little skill with sword and blade, but he more than made up for it with cunning. Their first meeting and the way the boy had saved them from the pursuing husks was more than evident of that. The hunter wasn't sure if it was just hopeful thinking, but he decided that George would survive on his own for a little while.

He forced himself to rise again, not driven by the need to find and save a young boy, but by the need to survive.

"Where am I?" Kendrith wondered; the woods looked tranquil and a lot more like a normal forest.

It wasn't covered in fog so he knew he had left the spectral lands. He could tell it looked nothing like a swamp. That left the dryads, the domain of the husks or the one that drew paranormal beings of all sorts.

Honestly, he wasn't sure which would be worse at the moment, for him and for George.

Kendrith stumbled to a clearing where a tree had been severed from its roots and had collapsed, creating a natural refuge from the elements.

"Shoulder first," he told himself, as his stomach growled. "Okay, food first."

Kendrith reached into his satchel and tried to bury the worry that came from noticing how light his bag had become.

Reaching in, he pulled out a few emergency brisket rations and began to chew on them, including rummaged dark berries from a nearby bramble that he yanked. The man could tell that he was running on fumes, as a fog clouded his mind as his most primal instincts managed to tell him that food was to be eaten.

"Water," he said, as he struggled to squeeze every last sorrowful drop from his waterskin.

Kendrith struggled to his feet; it didn't take long for his ears to catch the subtle sounds of a running river. Just the sound itself sated his shrivelled will.

With newfound energy, he hastened his pace, his gait changing from a drunken and slow man into that of a drunken and hastened man.

When he finally reached the source of the sound, welcoming the rushing stream, he turned around a tree and was about to lay his drought-afflicted lips to the running water. It was only his instincts that saved the man, years of experience that took over even in his delirious state.

He saw the large hulking beast before hearing its soft roar. Kendrith retreated behind the tree, more out of reflex than conscious decision, panting heavily.

He dared to look around the corner to see the bear grunting, several fish hauled from the water with a swipe of its paw.

"Can't catch a break," he murmured to himself. The hunter retreated back into the cover of trees and walked down the path to where he would be able to drink without having to worry about an inconvenience that could decapitate him with just a swing.

Kendrith returned to his clearing, his bag and blades were still in the precarious hideout covered with leaves and branches underneath the fallen tree.

Being partially nourished with food and water, Kendrith felt part of his mind begin to awaken, but with the awareness, the agony in his shoulder became all the more apparent as it flared and screamed at the man.

Fever was taking its hold, and Kendrith's thoughts kept going back to his mother and the sweet lullaby she sang.

The man sat underneath the fallen tree and leaned against a boulder planted conveniently behind him. He removed his red-stained cloak slowly, grunting and freezing every time his shoulder screamed at him as he grimaced with the pain. Next he proceeded to remove the brown shirt to reveal the tunic underneath.

The whole area around his shoulder was red with blood, pooling around the wound like the imprint of a continent. "Fuck." He chuckled to himself, it was certainly a lot of blood, more than he thought to have lost. "Grandpa would be furious with me."

The arrow had certainly done a number on his shoulder.

He didn't bother removing the tunic. Instead, he tore off the sleeve with his good arm, though the fatigue which nestled into his bones made it a gruelling task.

"By Mordan's phallus." He let loose several more curses of obscure gods.

Next, he reached into his vial belt and took a reddish swirl, removing the stopper and gulping it down. The sharp taste made his neck tense. It was a potion to kill the pain and accelerate healing. Next, he took out a small leather-wrapped bag, opening it to reveal a few surgical implements.

Taking one of the pliers in his good hand, he reached for the remaining arrow shaft. His muscles tensed, his breathing accelerated, and his cheeks inflated with every hyperventilated breath as he prepared himself. His vision blurred as the man tensed and tugged at what remained of the arrow embedded in his shoulder.

Birds broke free from the canopy as Kendrith's groan turned into a bestial roar. He hoped that the sound of wounded prey wouldn't attract predators, but at the time, the arrow was his primary concern.

It didn't come out like a loose tooth from a child—the thing was stubborn, embedded deep into a shoulder that continued to fight and contract for over an hour, driving the tip ever deeper like a parasite.

The progress was slow, like a nail being pulled out of wood, but finally, the arrow came loose with a spurt of blood and a sudden wave of exhaustion.

Sleep came to claim the exhausted hunter till the nascent feeling of dread forced him awake again. He couldn't fall asleep, not yet.Kendrith gathered his sewing kit as shivering fingers tried to thread the needle. His digits struggled to obey him, going cold and numb.

He felt his delirium worsen with every passing moment, his vision failing. The implements slipped from loose fingers and clattered to the floor. He was running out time.

Kendrith began to pant, his eyes becoming heavy as he hunched forward with deep and tired breaths. He just wanted to sleep. To dream of his mother singing him a lullaby and feeling her touch. But he knew that if he allowed himself to go to sleep now, he would never wake up.

With what little will he still had, Kendrith reached into his vials again, but his blurred vision and shaking hands made it hard to take hold of the vial he wanted. He hoped the one he grabbed was lavender, as he put the stopper to his teeth and unplugged it, dripping the contents onto his shoulder instead of drinking it. He was gratified by the sizzling sound and the agonising burn—the scent of burnt hair and skin suddenly wafted in the air and mixed with spilt blood.

Heavy arms took the sleeve and bandaged the shoulder to the best of his ability until numb fingers fell to the ground and his body betrayed him.

His body could take no more. It begged for rest. The hunter collapsed under the refuge of a fallen tree that tried desperately to protect the unconscious man within a forest of predators.

"George," whispered Kendrith as he fell into a deep slumber.

"Kendrith."

Kendrith turned to his friend John. Another striking example of untouchable prestige within the academy. His short brown hair was kept impeccably groomed, and his smile already showed promise for the game of politics. He wore the school's uniform: a high-class tailored waistcoat of deep blue over a brown shirt. "The boys and I will be going by the lake, to see who can skip rocks the farthest. You coming?"

Kendrith simply stared out the window and down at the departing students. He always made sure to get a seat by a window, not to look down below, but to have a view at the promise of a vast world filled with adventure just beyond the hem of trees. "Sorry, I have plans," he said, keeping his eyes on the horizon of trees and faraway mountains.

John sighed. "The guild?"

Kendrith didn't answer his question, picked up his few books, and rose to leave. "I have to go."

"If your dad finds out, he's going to kill you again."

"Then I won't let him find out," Kendrith called back with a smirk.

Despite his cold shoulder to John, Kendrith liked his company. He liked the company of many of his classmates. But as the years drew by, a deep longing for what the world had to offer made him grow distant, not with his friends, but with his life as a whole. He couldn't help but feel like a caged bird, born to a life where he felt as if he didn't belong.

With head bowed, Kendrith departed from the building surrounded by the excited chatter of children frantically trying to take advantage of the fleeting day.

Kendrith walked over to a fountain in the school's yard; swimming fish caused the surface to ripple. As the water settled, he regarded his own reflection. He was still just a child, more than halfway through his eleventh year and sighing with defeat at the prospect that he had to wait several more until he could leave home.

He was fully aware that some would give up an arm and leg for the chance to live his life. Opulence beyond comprehension, only the best of food and a bed that felt like one slept upon the clouds. Simply being born into his father's wealth meant he had his entire future set. Yet, he would give it all up in a heartbeat if it meant he could travel to the white-lands far to the north over treacherous oceans or travel east to where there is only sand as far as the eye can see. "A sea of sand" the stories called it. The only taste Kendrith had ever gotten of the stories were the tales that he would hear from travellers or from textbooks in class. His heart ached to be like one of those adventurers.

Kendrith gave one final look at his young expression in the fountain. He had already allowed his black hair to grow out and frame his face with part of it pulled back into a half ponytail and what remained draped over his nape.

With lost frustration at his helplessness, Kendrith slapped against the water.

He knew what would cheer him up—it always did: the guild.

It resembled his own academy in many ways. Perhaps it wasn't as exquisite in its golden frames or intricate carvings, but it held an aura of modest confidence. It didn't need the academy's glamour, for it had reputation.

There was a wall that surrounded the building and reached four times Kendrith's own height.

Kendrith threw his bag over his shoulder and placed his foot on the side of a tree, taking hold of a branch and grunting as he hauled himself up.

Almost daily he repeated this routine, perching himself in the depression of the tree as if it had been specifically grown in such a way to provide Kendrith with a view of the guild's courtyard.

Kendrith eagerly stared out at the ensuing clashing of swords and training that took place. Lines formed for the chance to throw nets and spears at targets. Grappling men created grooves in a sand pit as they rolled through it. Kendrith reached into his bag and rummaged for the apple he had saved, his eyes never leaving the field, as if worried that just a single moment of not watching the men practise would be a waste. He would move his arms back and forth, trying to match the movements that were being drilled into the men.

The boy bit into his apple and watched as commands were barked, his feet swaying over the edge.

"Up! Always keep your blade between you and your enemy!"

"What kind of stance is that?"

"Werewolves? A bloody leprechaun would tear you apart!"

Kendrith smiled; he was right, his spirits were already lifted.

He wasn't sure what it was, but the sound of commands being called, of people gasping for air with arms to their knees, or the sight of a whole group having to do laps because of one person's failure just brought a thrill to Kendrith that could only be trumped if he were to actually be part of it all.

Maybe he didn't feel like he belonged at the school, but even if it was just beyond the wall of the guild where he heard the newest trainees being brutally beaten or the veterans exchanging blades, he thought he could get a glimpse of the life he was supposed to be born into.

Kendrith averted his gaze, crunching down on the final bite and tossing the apple away. He saw the man he was looking for—mountainous and foreboding with every step taken. The man wasn't always there, but when he was, Kendrith dropped everything in a frantic hurry to meet him at the gate.

Kendrith continued to chew on his last bite as he took his bags and hurriedly climbed down the tree, slipping in the process and crashing onto the floor.

"Ow." It wasn't the first time his hurried descent caused him to have an even quicker landing.

Kendrith rubbed the back of his head with a pained expression as he clambered to his feet and ran.

"Grandpa!" Kendrith approached the hulking bear-sized man that happened to come in his direction.

"For the love of Balan, won't you leave me in peace?" the bearded man said.

The boy ran up to him, and what felt like the hundredth time, repeated the same words every time he saw his grandfather. "Veteran-Hunter Haggen Brosnorth, train me!"

"Nope." Despite the cordial and titled greeting, Kendrith's grandfather simply ignored the boy and kept walking. "Now get out of here before your father finds you and gives you a beating."

"Dad doesn't know I am here."

"Then I will tell him—maybe then he will keep you away."

Kendrith clenched his fists as a fury rose in his little stomach. He was a child about to stand his ground against a bear. He ran in front of his grandfather and blocked his path, and though he had no fists the size of boulders nor was he built like an ox, the young boy had a fire in his eyes that didn't seem like it would die out anytime soon.

"He could beat me to an inch of my life and I would still come. He could rob me of my legs and I would crawl my way here. Even if he takes my arms I would fight with a sword between my teeth."

Haggen stopped in his tracks and stared with the eyes of an owl at the whelp before him. The old man was definitely entertained. He crossed his arms and gave the boy a bemused smile. "You wouldn't be much of a threat like that." Haggen joked, but there was no humour in the boy's eyes.

The old man finally sighed and dropped his arms, his affable expression suddenly replaced by a rueful one. "Kid, you know why I can't train you."

"Because my father won't allow it."

"I don't give a bleeding damn what that man allows or doesn't allow." A slight moment of fury was heard in Haggen's voice. Even when his words overflowed with anger, they were controlled and bridled flames.

The rage in him died out as soon as it had risen, and he sighed once more. "I can't send another one of my flesh and blood to their death." Haggen was a monstrous man, and tales sometimes compared him to the legend of Balan: the man made of mountains. That was until Haggen became a legend of his own.

Kendrith felt his own flame die out, as he lowered his gaze. Still, the boy frowned, feelings of sadness fighting against his unquenchable desire.

"I'm sorry, boy," Haggen said with a pained voice.

Kendrith wanted to scream obscenities, swear upon his life that he would be a hunter, promise that no cage made of stone or steel or love would keep him from his dream.

Yet, he didn't say a word, all of the things raging within him like a tempestuous storm struggled to get out.

Kendrith was happy with the prospect of visiting the guild daily, perhaps running into his grandfather and replaying the whole act of him asking to be his apprentice only to be turned down. He didn't mind the act, because he was sure that one day, he would be taken in.

But now, he wasn't so sure anymore.

"I have to go. There is something urgent." Haggen walked past Kendrith with urgent strides.

Kendrith turned on his own heel, the wind suddenly taken from his sails as he dragged himself home.

He opened the door to his family's estate, where a vast foyer that reached three storeys greeted him. One could say that the foyer was pointlessly large and a waste of space, but Jaylen, Kendrith's father, made good use of the space regardless.

A exquisite large rug covered the floor, and small polished tables were tucked between the supporting columns to the left and right of the foyer which held the balustrade above with a grand stairway before him which divided left and right.

"Good day, Master Kendrith. I hope school was pleasant," Fletcher said at the door.

"Yeah, sure," the boy said half-heartedly, not even trying to seem in high spirits. He wondered if Fletcher was a sign of more ill tidings.

"Master Jaylen has requested your presence in his study."

Kendrith sighed, he was right: there was more cause for suffering.

Every step Kendrith took proved heavier than the last. The carpeted hallway seemingly closed in on him as dimly lit wall lamps meshed the bronze light with the dark wood of the hall.

From each side Kendrith was surrounded by portraits of ancestors or nobility. When not the portrait of a person, it would instead show painted renditions of more recent conflicts such as warships firing cannons on piers and smoking debris. Kendrith recognised the image from his history books: it was the battle of Celemy.

A war between the Gullian Empire that ruled on its own continent and his own country of Bedal.

"Who is that?" Kendrith had asked his mother a long time ago, pointing to the back of a hooded figure who stood atop a slanted and tiled dome while holding on to a bird spike. Kendrith recalled that she stared at the painting often.

"The hero of Celemy," Mona had said, holding Kendrith tight in her arms. "Nobody knows who she is…or even if she existed. But when the Gullian Empire invaded, she was the one who stepped in and fought tooth and nail to protect the port town."

Kendrith looked out at the rendition, the rising waves of water, the horizon spotted with the telling bowed curves of ships as parts of buildings lay in ruin and smoke.

"The Gullian Empire has been trying to invade Lenaren for a very long time."

"Why?" Kendrith had asked.

She had shrugged. "Because people want more. The reason may not always be the same, but the want is always there."

"How do you know it is a woman?" Kendrith had asked, looking to his mother. The classes always seemed to have portrayed the figure as a man and stating that he never existed. But was a myth spread by the officials to spur morale.

Mona had just smiled and looked down to Kendrith. "Just a feeling," she had said with a wink.

Kendrith realised he grasped for his mother's locket. It was something he always did when he wished for her courage and strength.

There were other paintings of older wars still, vague renditions of artists that had tried to capture a long since dubitable war between mages and dark entities of unknown origin. The mages were clear to make out—long robes with haggard faces emitting radiant magic from their bodies—while the fiends were less distinguishable. The painters portrayed dark misty outlines of horned and scrawny bodies of black masses with burning red eyes and sharp teeth—surely embellished by their own interpretations.

There was one painting in particular that Kendrith always stopped at, for it gave him strength just before he would visit his father. It was another fanciful rendition of a tale where the artist took liberties, but it didn't matter to Kendrith, even if the tale was just a story, he appreciated what it represented.

It was the story of a god—Vrania. The guild named itself after the hero: The Wings of Vrania. Kendrith saw the black swirling mass of demonic bodies create a dark deluge, and at the foreground of the painting was a being of strength and light that challenged the darkness—an island unto himself. Vrania bore glorious white wings that spread open, a magnificent relic of blue energy radiated in his hand, and scores of fiends were depicted blinded or hurdling back in Vrania's presence.

And just like that Kendrith was ready for his father.

"Father?" Kendrith asked as he pressed open the door to his father's study just enough to squeeze through.

The study itself was even darker than the hallway, a fireplace crackling to the left and a soft candle allowing Kendrith's father to sign away at the piled papers on his desk.

"You called?" Kendrith added in case his father hadn't noticed his entry.

Jaylen ignored his son, and continued to scribble on another piece of paper, before putting it on another growing pile. "Yes, Kendrith. Come here." Jaylen permitted himself the effort to speak during the transition from one paper to the next without his eyes leaving the table, as if just a moment's distraction could result in his workload doubling.

Kendrith shrank back. People were scared of him at his school; he had gotten into plenty of fights and his sharp wolflike gaze made him more than intimidating. Even the mountainous figure of his own grandfather did not scare Kendrith, but his father was another story.

The boy suddenly became very small, with hands cupped before him and a bowed head as he stepped slowly to the desk as if on trial.

Kendrith waited patiently, his head bowed for quite some time. The only thing that could be heard was the crackling fireplace and the quiet, but frantic scribbling of a man at work.

"I know where you went today," Jaylen finally said, his attention still on the stacks of paper before him.

Kendrith looked up with shock and stuttered, unsure of what to say. There was nothing *to* say. He looked back down, not denying the claim.

"How?" Kendrith finally asked.

"I have known for quite some time—it isn't relevant how I know."

Kendrith squeezed his fists tight. Did his grandfather actually snitch?

Jaylen sighed. "I gave it time, Kendrith. Hoped this whole nonsense was a phase. That you would grow up and let go of this childish fantasy."

The young boy couldn't take it anymore, and he snapped. Jaylen wasn't just insulting his dream, he was insulting his mother.

"That's not what Mom thought!"

Jaylen pounded his fist against the table and faced the boy who almost jumped out of his skin. Where before his voice was a cold and bureaucratic thing, it now at least carried emotion.

"And look at where that got her! Mona is buried beneath the ground! How noble a prize indeed!"

Jaylen looked at his son through rimmed spectacles. Age had not yet robbed him of his appeal, but his lack of sleep had made the bags under his eyes apparent and wrinkles slowly crept onto his skin. Yet the curled and groomed moustache as well as his combed hairline still informed of Jaylen's unrelenting need for order.

Kendrith rarely saw his father exhibit such emotion. There was a frenzy to Jaylen's eyes that made the young boy hesitate.

The man sighed; it was a long thing that told of his exhaustion. He just wanted to lie down. Instead, Jaylen reverted to the composed bureaucratic persona he had as if it was professionalism that was called for when dealing with his son.

"You will cease such nonsense immediately and grow up. I have plans to leave behind all that I have earned so that you may carry it on. As from now on, you will return home directly after your schooling and partake in extra lessons designed to have you take over when the time is right."

"But—"

"You may leave," Jaylen interrupted, returning to his work.

Kendrith didn't leave—he tightened his fists until his knuckles turned a ghostly white and his body trembled.

"No."

Even Jaylen was startled by the boy's defiance. "I beg your pardon?"

"I said no," Kendrith spoke the words even louder. Did his voice tremble out of passion or fear? Perhaps both, thought the boy.

"You wish for me to sit around here with ball and chain in a small room of useless items and scribble away like a prisoner? You call this living? You think Mother would approve?"

"Your mother is dead! And I won't allow my only son to die as she did!"

"Oh? So I'm your son now? You sure don't act like my father."

Jaylen rose with murder in his eyes. His cheeks were flushed and lips quivered. Kendrith thought he had done it now, pushed his father over the edge.

Yet just as quickly his father let out a deep sigh and composed himself again. He pushed his spectacles back up the bridge of his nose and sat back down. If it were even possible, it sounded like Jaylen's voice had become even more indifferent and callous as he returned to his stack of papers.

"Sleep well," was all Jayden said.

The dreaded confrontation ended the way it always did, with Kendrith leaving furiously and wondering why he ever feared such a coward.

Kendrith collapsed onto his bed, the sheets a welcome comfort as the first of his tears broke free and ran down his cheek. He tried hard to hold them back, telling himself that he was a man. But no, he was still just a child and entirely helpless.

Kendrith reached into his shirt and pulled free a locket with a sapphire gem cut smoothly round and fitted inside. Kendrith pressed it and the lock opened with a click. "When you're ready," it said. Kendrith squeezed the locket in his hands as if willing the time to come. On the other side of the locket Kendrith saw the miniature likeness of his mother, sitting regally with an opulent dress and hanging locks. From that painting alone, nobody would have figured her to have been a worthy huntress.

The boy recalled the day when the hunters returned to Kendrith's household and informed him of his mother's fate. The body they carried was truly his mother's despite the fact that the entire left side of her torso and body had been bitten clean off. Though even in death, there was a strong beauty to her that was undeniable, how peaceful she seemed, almost as if she would be woken from her slumber at any moment and travel to the next impending danger.

Kendrith would dream of the events even though he was never there. She didn't die in the Forest of the Dead, but rather on the northern outskirts during a scouting mission in the uncharted lands. Her body was the only one recovered after a scouting team was sent, led by Haggen to find her and her team. Rumor had it that grandfather broke down over the body of her only daughter.

Her team had been halted at the border by what they called the Great Beast, a gigantic four-legged beast that prowled between the upper reaches and the eastern mountains, reports spoke of a monster of stone. It had the face of a man as if carved from stone, and a mane of forestry. The rest of its body was cramped and stout, with the limbs of a lion. Its size, apparently, was enough so that when it walked through the forest, its large stout body caused the canopy of trees to ripple, like a shark parting water just below the depths.

Kendrith knew without a shadow of a doubt that if he were to fall asleep, those memories would come back to haunt him. To see his mother's helpless struggle. How calm she seemed in death. And the pendant which she left for her son.

"When you are ready," he whispered the words. He knew that his mother would have supported his dreams regardless of her own death. He was the son of Mona Brosnorth—daughter of Haggen Brosnorth. The need for adventure compelled them and nothing would stand in their way.

Kendrith rose from his bed, and decided not to dream again of his mother's fate, but instead to start his own journey, to stand atop the shoulders of giants as they had and become a giant himself.

He opened the window to his room and looked down from the second floor at the assortment of bushes.

He then looked out towards the huddled houses of the town and beyond even that towards the dark outline of the forest.

His grandfather didn't live among the people. "Too noisy," he complained. He preferred the quiet life living in a hut outside.

Kendrith squeezed the locket once more for strength, before looking down at the drop before him. He could only hope that the bush he was aiming for would cushion his fall as he stepped onto the rim and leaned out.

Kendrith wasn't sure if it was the unruly and dubious nature of night or the way his feet carried him farther and farther from home, but he had never truly felt as free as he did in that one moment. There was an uneasy beating in his heart that made it thrum rapidly, a coldness to the space as if his heart had suddenly shrunk and chilled air filled it.

Cold sweat drenched his skin, frantic thoughts bounced around his skull, and fear tried to cloak him. And even though the boy was frightened, he embraced that fear. It was true that he had no idea what he was doing; it was true that he was running towards the Forest of the Dead's borders when night robbed him of sight. Yet as hard as fear may have tried, Kendrith simply ran faster and faster; the rush he felt was intoxicating. He laughed—the boy laughed because he didn't understand the way his heart beat against his chest, because he didn't know what to do with the fear that touched him in the form of cold sweat. He didn't understand any of it and yet he loved it—the feeling of danger. It was as if his heart truly beat for the very first time.

Kendrith laughed because he had no other way to express the turmoil of roiling emotions that raged within him. Raging not like the clash of battle, but rather like tempestuous seas.

The rush he felt could carry him only so far, holding just the right amount of motivation to bring him beyond the town walls and onto the roads.

The town might as well have been called a city due to its size. It was seen as a protective refuge for all those who travelled that far and encountered the supernatural remnants of a time when the world was still overflowing with magic.

Kendrith gave another look towards the cage he had called home, soft lights meekly offering a challenge towards the night. The wind blew and grass blades swayed. The chill touched Kendrith as a final warning before the foreboding shadow of trees.

He took deep breaths and his heart failed to still itself. This was it. He knew that whatever he played at in the past was just fanciful musings. With the rush during his escape fading, he now began to understand the fear that gripped him. The doubt that tried to make its claim. He knew that there was no turning back, even if he found his grandfather and didn't get killed by whatever the night had to offer, there was no guarantee that he would be taken in.

And neither would Father. The thought made him clench his fists, and he welcomed the anger for it gave him resolve, yet it wasn't that anger that gave him strength.

Instead, he recalled his mother's message, "When you're ready."

Anger faded, fear died, and the boy's mind became silent. He stepped past into the shadow of trees.

Chapter 12

He wasn't at the Forest of the Dead, and his grandfather's hut wasn't that deep, yet the night made its demons brave; a lone werewolf that drifted towards the outskirts, or an Arachna—spiders the size of bears—or even a pack of wolves could find the presence of a lost and defenceless boy wandering where he shouldn't.

The night didn't just make monsters brave, it also stoked the fear that bubbled within, giving it the power of imagination. Like a shadow, fear wrapped itself around Kendrith's young heart and began to squeeze, *Is that a spectre?* it whispered to him as the slightest shade moved within the corner of the boy's eye.

Kendrith kept his hands before him in a meagre attempt to fend off whatever may lurk in the woods; another cold breeze rustled the canopy and lifted leaves from soil.

"Come on, Kendrith, be brave." His voice was breaking, and he was scared. Kendrith spoke the words not to somehow conjure strength, but rather to fend off the uneasy silence which made the fearful whispers deafening.

As he wandered through the forest, the boy realised he had no idea where he was. The few times he did travel to his grandfather's lodging, he used the beaten path and remembered the spread of trees. Yet, having his attention directed towards the shifting shadows born of fear had led him in unknown directions. As the night thickened and his surroundings darkened, the boy found that he could only make out the apparent outline of silhouettes.

He couldn't tell up from down, left from right, or back from front. The boy truly didn't know how to retrace his steps or if he should walk forward or back.

He grasped at his chest and squeezed his mother's locket to lend him strength.

Kendrith tried to think, looking for any sign of terrain that looked even remotely familiar. Yet, fear brought with it doubt, and clouded his mind.

Kendrith finally came to a tree and slid down its bark. He had not given up, not yet, but he had no idea of where to go next.

"Come on, someone give me a sign," the boy whispered, not to his mother, but to anyone who would lend an ear. He was desperate and lost, a child that always had others to rely on. He realised then how it was the first time that he tried to do something for himself, and it may have been the last.

"Was it worth it?" he wondered silently, sure that his father would ask the same thing when they buried him.

Crunching leaves. Kendrith stood up; was it a sign? "Grandfather?" He called out hopefully. Kendrith saw a dark figure emerge from behind a tree, it certainly was large enough to be Haggen, but the hope for that died almost as soon as it came. He took note of the bristling hairs that outlined the towering beast.

"Please don't be a bear, please don't be a bear, please don't be a bear," Kendrith kept whispering to himself.

It wasn't a bear. The beast sniffed at the air and turned to the young boy leaning against a tree. It rose up to its full height to reveal razor-sharp canines through a snarling snout. Its fur seemed to be woven from the night sky, and its talons could tear through steel like butter—it was indeed a werewolf.

"Bear! I will take the bear!" Kendrith cried out as he stumbled to his feet not a moment too soon as the beast lunged forward and buried its fangs into the tree.

Kendrith didn't stop to look back—he just ran as fast as his legs would carry him. The sound of splintered wood followed by the gallop of heavy limbs against the soil closed in.

Kendrith turned a corner just barely avoiding the snapping jaws of the werewolf that snarled at its missed meal. Kendrith dodged and weaved his way through trees which caused the beast to break through the gap or stop and rear its weight which proved difficult with its powerful body building momentum. The beast drifted uncontrollably at another failed bite, taking with him only a piece of Kendrith's torn vest. Its body crashed into a boulder, a yelp escaping it.

Another small gap. Another hard turn. Suddenly, Kendrith saw a tree hollow and, with an agile skip and hop, leapt through it. The boy rolled and came to a stop as the tree suddenly shook from its very foundations with a loud thud, leaves drifting down from the swaying treetop. The werewolf clambered at Kendrith, managing to get only an arm and its head through the hole; saliva splattering everywhere like a rabid dog.

The beast clawed at the air, snarling with frustration as if it could magically extend its reach and grab the boy.

The tree creaked as the werewolf pushed forward, but it held strong and bought Kendrith time as more leaves showered down from the rattling branches.

Before Kendrith picked himself up, he realised that the tree looked very familiar. *The path!*

Kendrith knew exactly where he was. "This isn't what I meant when I asked for a sign..." he complained to the universe and kept on running.

He ran without pursuit only for several seconds before the boy heard the sound of exploding bark followed by a hungry howl.

The hut came into view and Kendrith found himself beyond relieved.

"Grandfather!" Kendrith said, knocking hard against the hut door. "Open up!"

No response came. Kendrith looked behind him and barely noticed the silhouette getting closer.

"Grandfather Haggen!" A final plea of desperation as the beast leapt.

Yet, the werewolf never reached its destination.

The hulking arm of Haggen Brosnorth had grabbed the monster by its throat as it flew through the air. The werewolf now lay suspended several feet from the floor, snarling and reaching for the bearded titan.

With a mighty roar, Haggen cratered the beast to the floor as a cloud of dust formed around the impact.

The creature yelped like a wounded pup and before it could pick itself up, Haggen hafted his axe and brought it down in one clean swing that splattered him with fresh werewolf blood.

The beast was still, as Haggen rose slowly to his full form. Muscles bulged and veins writhed. He pulled out the axe blade with a wet splurt and turned slowly to Kendrith as if he was his next prey. "Inside. Now." Cold were the worlds which Haggen Brosnorth spoke; Kendrith had never heard his grandfather so furious.

"Of all the stupid, irresponsible things you could have done." Haggen Brosnorth paced back and forth within his hut, just a few candles to meagrely oppose total darkness. His hut was built large, with a tall roof, but with little that furnished his home. It was better so, otherwise he would have been dragging his entire home back and forth with all his pacing.

Kendrith didn't say anything. He didn't regret coming to his grandfather, in fact, he was quite proud of himself. It was the first bit of proof that he wouldn't just make false promises, but back them up as well. It was proof that he braved the night and had the will to become a hunter. Even if all he did was run away from a hungry werewolf, it dawned on the boy that he outsmarted the beast and was able to outrun it even with his childish physique. But one thing he did feel apologetic of: he didn't wish to make his grandfather worry.

So, the boy simply looked down to his hands and accepted any condescending insults that came his way.

Finally, Haggen stopped his tirade and must have come to realise that he already said every bit of adult platitude one could, and twice over. The old man rubbed the nape of his neck with a sigh. Just moments ago he took down a monstrous werewolf as if swatting a fly, yet when it came to disciplining kids, he seemed at a loss.

"Look, just get some sleep, I will take you back home tomorrow."

"No," Kendrith spoke the words with his head still lowered, and though his voice had still not broken, not even a drop of doubt stained his conviction.

"Excuse me?"

"I'm not going back." The boy looked up to his grandfather. Whenever their paths crossed, Kendrith was stubborn, insistent that he become Haggen's apprentice. Yet, there was no passionate flame that reflected in the boy's eyes this time. If anything, it was just the soft glow of candlelight that showed a boy who accepted the fact that he would never become his grandfather's apprentice, but still he would always return. The stare was cold and stoic, devoid of passion, and yet Haggen saw the boy's resolve.

"Look, I already told you—there is no way I can train you. Your mother's death still stains my hand. I enabled her and it cost her her life. A father should never outlive their own child, let alone their grandchild."

Kendrith fell silent for a moment, not because he admitted defeat, but because he considered his words carefully. The boy found that with flames of passion stilled and his mind gone tranquil, it was far easier to sort his thoughts. "Do you remember when the circus came?"

Haggen crossed his arms and chuckled. "Of course."

"Do you remember the acrobats? How they swung with such freedom through the air? Or the abnormal freaks that exposed themselves?"

Haggen must have thought the boy was about to make some speech about the claim for freedom, to do what one wants.

Kendrith paused for a moment, and then looked deep into his grandfather's eyes. "Do you remember the caged tiger?" Kendrith's eyes were pleading, and Haggen's softening eyes betrayed his understanding.

"Did that tiger look happy to you? How it was caged inside, the dead look it had in its eyes. Its heart beat and its jaws expanded into yawns. But did it truly live? Its eyes blinked, but all I saw were vapid things that simply waited for true death."

Kendrith trusted that Haggen knew exactly what he was talking about, the feeling of being confined behind the safety of walls was torturous to the boy. Kendrith thought quite often of that tiger, going through the motions day in and day out but never living. It was a hollow look that wanted to be filled with adventure.

Kendrith finally reached into his shirt and pulled out a locket. "Mother certainly understood." The boy looked at the pendant with longing, his finger caressing the azure surface that had a shine from the candle glow.

The boy tossed the pendant to his grandfather who snatched it out of the air.

"Open it," Kendrith said.

Haggen Brosnorth complied and opened it to find a scribbled message from his mother.

"When you're ready," the titan read aloud.

"I am sure that my mother felt more alive in those years than she would have behind closed doors; if she were here now, she wouldn't curse you for sending her down that path, she would love you for it. If she has given me her blessing, why can't you?"

The titan looked to Kendrith with watery eyes. This was a man who was synonymous with the simple idea of strength. He was the mountain of Haven. He was a paragon of The Wings of Vrania. When new initiates joined the guild, he was seen as the goal to strive for. And yet, a small chisel cracked against his steeled heart and it gave way to the first of tears.

"I am going to go out there with or without your blessing. I certainly will not go back home. If you truly wish to ensure that I live a long life, then train me so I don't die a foolish death."

Kendrith wasn't sure what had come over him—it was rare for him to be so serious and talkative. Perhaps the spirit of his mother graced him with the words he needed to speak in that moment.

It sufficed. Behind the privacy of walls and far away from the town of Haven, a large titan fell to his knees and wailed in tears.

Kendrith simply watched and he did not speak. He just allowed for the most feared and respected man in all those parts to let it out. One of Mona's earliest lessons for Kendrith was that people needed to cry, and that those tears became the foundation upon where one's sorrows lamented so the brave could venture on.

The lesson hadn't eluded Kendrith, as he sat there listening to the pained sobs of his grandfather and the tears that puddled upon the wooden floor. Surely Haggen carried a lot of guilt for what happened to Mona. And perhaps the thought of robbing his grandson of a mother didn't help.

So, the titan wailed to his heart's content and clutched the small pendant in his giant hands, holding it against his chest.

Kendrith had never seen such a vulnerable moment from his grandfather, but he understood it. In fact, it comforted him. His grandfather must have been in pain for so long, and the catharsis of his cries brought with it freedom.

The following days proved awkward. After years of denying Kendrith as his apprentice, Haggen needed to adjust to how he would raise the child. Not to mention that his moment of vulnerability left a strange air between the two.

But with a few days of adjustment, the two simply accepted that this was how their new life would begin and they eased into the training.

"I don't understand why I need to still study all this," Kendrith complained. "I left the academy."

"Knowledge is the greatest weapon you will have. No axe or sword would ever be able to replace your mind. In fact, all other tools are simply there to complement your knowledge."

"Yeah, yeah, you already said that," Kendrith said as he turned to the next page and sighed, his bored expression leaning against a propped arm.

"I was just expecting more sword fighting," the boy said.

"In time." Haggen paused. "You remind me of myself, you know?"

"I do?" Kendrith asked.

Haggen nodded. "When I was young. Passion and excitement towards adventure, yet no interest in books. Mona on the other hand"—Haggen made a bewildered face—"was the complete opposite. She was disciplined, never complained, and always put in 100 percent of her effort in whatever it was that was asked of her. She was prodigious in every way." As Haggen reminisced, there seemed to be a sadness to his voice.

"Well, okay then," Kendrith started. "In that case, I will put in even more effort." Kendrith suddenly buried his head in the books with newfound zeal.

Haggen chuckled.

"Did you send the letter?" Haggen asked, drawing Kendrith out of his stride no sooner than he had found it.

"What letter?" Kendrith pretended not to know what his grandfather was talking about.

"Don't play dumb with me, boy. I see you at the table writing under candlelight every night. Did you send the letter to your father?"

Kendrith hesitated, before finally admitting that he had. "I went home at daybreak and dropped it before the gates."

"Good." Haggen pressed the topic no further.

Kendrith continued to read from the book, and though he had finally done what he wanted to despite his father's wishes, he could not bring himself to loathe that man. He was his father, after all.

He recalled the letter he had written, one that had taken many alterations and rewrites, frustrating and tiring with every new draft.

Dear Father, it read.

I have run away. I know you do not approve of my dream, but I cannot do as you wish. I have gone to live with Grandpa Haggen as an apprentice, and he will train me to become a hunter.

I don't expect you to understand.

I am sorry I couldn't be the son you had hoped for. I am sure you are disappointed in me. But despite everything, I have to do this.

Just know that I will always love you.

Your loving son, Kendrith.

Chapter 13

"No. Again." The practise sword parted from Kendrith's grip as the boy fell to his rear.

Three years had passed since Kendrith had moved in with his grandfather; Haggen Brosnorth had fallen into his role as master completely in that time and showed little mercy when training Kendrith.

On more than one occasion did a man visit who was sent by Jaylen or the town guards, but there was nothing they could do as Haggen chased them away and insisted that Kendrith was under his care. And one does not oppose Haggen Brosnorth.

Kendrith groaned, rose to his feet, and looked at his hands. They were covered in blisters and calluses, hands that never knew the taste of labour now shook under the toil. His hair was no longer well groomed—instead it was stuffed into a ponytail to ensure that it would never get in his way. His body also bore several bruises and light scars. Corded muscle started to show over what used to be smooth skin.

"How am I supposed to match you when your weight dwarfs mine several times over?" the boy asked, closing his reddened fists to quell his shaking.

Haggen grunted. "Are you going to ask a bear to take it easy on you? Perhaps when hunted by another werewolf you will invite it for a cup of tea?"

Kendrith didn't say anything, his grandfather spoke truth. The creatures of the forest would never take it easy on him, so he shouldn't expect his grandfather to do so either.

Most of Kendrith's daily routine had been studying the bestiary and what worked against which creatures, though Haggen still forced the boy to study the more scholarly subjects that Kendrith had hoped to leave behind at the academy such as mapping or arithmetic.

During the first several months, Haggen had taught the boy how to hunt for animals, to blend in with his surroundings, and to move across the land like soft wind passing through trees. To string arrow to bow, and to fire at prey like a knife through air.

The titan of a man taught Kendrith how to skin animals and create a fire to cook with. How to concoct alchemical brews, and which plants were poisonous and which weren't, which healed, and which sated. How using the frog strait along with devil's nail could easily give a boost of energy, but add a willow tuft and it suddenly turned into bubbling acid.

It was good that Kendrith used that time to learn diligently, for he spent the first month of his second year living by himself within the vicinity of the hut. Tasked with hunting and foraging for his own food. A nearby stream was used for fish and water. Haggen did not help, did not intervene, even when Kendrith became sick from eating the wrong type of berries Haggen would ignore his wailing cries.

Up until that point, the boy had never needed to do anything for himself.

His first attempt at cooking was less than satisfactory, as Haggen ended up heaving the contents of the pot.

"I bet the fever from that potion was just revenge for my cooking," Kendrith would joke, remembering how sick he had gotten the first time he concocted a brew.

Yet after a gruelling three years, the boy's progress was stalwart.

On top of sword play, hunting, cooking, and studying, there was another challenge that Kendrith had to face. Not by his grandfather's order, but his own.

His entire life was lived for by others. Others cooking for him, clothing him, grooming him. He had no need to lift a single finger.

The first few months were imperative to showing how seriously he took his dream. The past three years were imperative to show that he would succeed at it. More than once the boy doubted if he truly had the mettle to be a hunter. More than once he found the task too much and just wanted to collapse. Perhaps submit to his old life. Yet something inside him never allowed him to. Even when his arms felt like they would fall from their shoulders, he still moved forward.

Perhaps it would have been the truth he would have to carry with himself wherever he went, that he failed, gave up. Perhaps it would be the feeling that he failed his mother. Perhaps it would have been the ridicule. Or perhaps it was the smugness with which his father would regard him as if to say "I told you so."

In all likelihood, it was a mix of all and more that kept Kendrith moving.

With silent lips and screaming eyes he stared on.

Kendrith looked at his grandfather and noticed another form that his doubt had taken. How could he ever live up to the man known as the epitome of strength? How many more months would it take before he could be considered more than just fodder for the forest of death or the uncharted lands to the north?

"Do you remember how you survived the stray werewolf?"

"How could I forget when you keep reminding me?"

Haggen chuckled. "How did you escape it?" the titan asked.

Kendrith considered a moment. "Well, I used the terrain."

Haggen nodded approvingly. "There will be beasts far larger than you out there. Faster, stronger. Creatures born to kill—don't try to outmatch them with strength, but rather with cunning. If you fight such a beast head-on you will die."

Kendrith said nothing.

"Let's stop there for today; I have an errand for you to run."

Kendrith raised his eyebrows curiously.

"I made an order at the blacksmith for a sword. It will be yours to use."

Kendrith caught the coin pouch midflight and looked at the bag hesitantly.

Even if Kendrith could put his reluctance into words, his grandfather had already turned away to walk into his hut.

The boy stood there for a while, looking at the pouch. *Three years*, he mused. It had been three years since he last was in the city of Haven. Three years since he had left school and ran away from home. Three years since he had sent his father the letter and heard nothing in return.

He looked nothing like the son of a rich man, with grimy hair and dirt-stained hands, grey-and-brown clothing dirtied by years rolling around the mud. The boy had grown taller, his usual slim demeanour now translated to a trained and tempered form with a focus on alacrity.

Would anyone even recognise him? How would they react?

Kendrith bounced the coin purse, tossing it up into the air and catching it with a swing of his hand; he chuckled. Kendrith hoped to brave the perils of the forest, yet found himself scared of returning to a life he had abandoned.

The closer he wandered to the city walls, the heavier his heart pounded.

Time spent in the forest had taught the boy confidence—he now knew how to cook, how to survive, how to hunt, and how to fight. Even so, as Haven drew into sight, he couldn't help but feel uneasy. What if someone he knew approached him? What would he say? What if it were John?

"Hey John," he said out loud with a forced smile and waving hand.

No, no. It felt too awkward.

"Hey John."

No, too cold.

At the third attempt to practise his greeting the boy sighed and gave up. Was it always so nerve-racking and difficult to talk to people? Kendrith hadn't really considered that his closest talking companion was his own grandfather, and the man wasn't exactly known for his tableside manners.

The forest had turned into his home and he felt at ease there. Now it was as if Haven had turned into a place that warranted caution—wolves prowling the streets dressed as humans.

With every step Kendrith felt as if he was going back in time to when he was nothing more than a dreaming boy, a feeling which made itself fully known the moment he passed the city walls. His heart quickened. The bustle of the market and loud chatter did little to ease him; he wondered if the town was always so crowded.

Pushing aside paranoid fears of watching eyes and heated discussions, Kendrith hurried his pace, walking straight for the blacksmith through trafficking shoppers, savvy vendors, and clustered crowds.

Kendrith caught one glance after another. Was it a passing gaze or did people look at him with recognition?

The blacksmith's shop stood just around a corner beside the bakery. A sudden pang of nostalgia came over the boy as he recognised the scent of rising dough—his mother always stopped by for a fresh loaf.

Lost in the memory he failed to notice the path before him and crashed straight into someone.

Suddenly, the burning heat of a furnace washed over him and he returned to the present as he found himself knocked down to the floor.

"I'm sorry," Kendrith immediately muttered, his broken nerves turning him into a child. He looked up expecting a familiar face. Perhaps John, or Fletcher running errands for his father, or perhaps even Jaylen himself.

He looked up to notice that the person was a girl, with piercing blue eyes covered partially by a cowl. How predatory, yet beautiful those blue eyes were like a panther along a treetop. Her features were slim and demure, a quaint look to her that only served to accentuate the sharpness of her gaze. The small glint of brunette hair framed her face. Everything about her seemed deceptively frail, but for the scar that marked her cheek and would have marred her beauty for most...not to Kendrith however.

Kendrith stammered, trying to find the right words to say, but the sudden rush of thoughts ended up getting clogged in his throat.

The girl never did say anything nor acknowledged the dazed boy except for a moment of eye contact. A stare that Kendrith found familiar. One of cold alertness and focus, caution and warning—yet under it all, a glimmer of fear. Kendrith became fully aware that this girl was not his mother, yet everything about her reminded him of Mona.

What felt like a lifetime was just a moment as the girl absconded between the shifting crowds.

Kendrith continued to glance at the dangerously beautiful girl draped in a cowl till the moment he couldn't. In that one moment, Kendrith forgot all about the town of Haven and its scrutinising eyes.

Chapter 14

The Hobbers continued their depraved laughter. They were mocking one of their brethren who happened to lame his foot. The creature dragged its crooked appendage across the floor with great effort while the others laughed, rolling on their backs as if it was the world's funniest joke.

Suddenly, one of the Hobbers walked over to his kin, not to help, but to add to the merriment. With a crude stone lifted in its dainty hands, the creature threw the rock onto the Hobber's other leg, the crushing sound of bone was only barely audible over the rekindled raucous laughter.

The creature cried out in pain as friends and family laughed at his suffering.

The creature lay there, crying out with agony as another boulder toppled right onto the Hobber's skull, putting him out of his misery. But the Hobbers would not cease their laughter for quite some time.

One of the younger children laughed with ecstatic glee as he waddled back and forth. Suddenly, one of the older Hobbers grabbed the young child by the shoulder and scolded him, pointing up towards a soft incline and scowling at the young creature for getting too close.

Just like that, the laughter died down, as the Hobbers were reminded of their new unwelcome neighbour.

Even from there, with just a couple of yards distance they could see the first signs of danger. Their brothers and sisters were dismembered, pieces of their body parts hanging from trees. Limbs scattered the heads placed to watch their brothers. Or at least in essence, for their eyes had been removed and placed all over the trees, lending bark and wood the ability to peer at new unfortunate souls that might venture too close.

Hobbers relished pain and suffering, they thought it to be the most comical display in the world. Yet when they saw not misery, but only the dismembered remains of their kin, it was hard to laugh.

Within that circle was a young boy that became known as a demon to the Hobbers.

Soft winds that blew through swamp trees and sunk steel into the flesh of unsuspecting victims.

That was all that George was within the swamp—a wind that carried one away and displayed them for all to see. That was how he imagined that the creatures down below saw him as he observed their vile exchanges.

The bard had captured and skewered a string of frogs which burnt over a fire. The thing cackled as the critters roasted; he stepped back from the spectacle to his meal.

The boy was safe within, no Hobber had dared venture into his camp, just as there was a centre to the Forest of the Dead—he was the centre to the swamp. Feeling safe within his barrier of fear, George reached into his bag and pulled out his most treasured possession—a book that was all he had to remind himself of a sister he had long lost.

The black mass within the centre had torn open wounds that had healed long ago, and the thing festered. He mourned Lily, with a hate growing within him for how powerless he had been to save her.

George turned the book to another page, one that told the story of a praying mantis who loved and wished to be loved—but no matter who it tried to hug would end up cut into pieces with its sickled appendages, whoever it tried to kiss would end up devoured by its mandibles. It was one of the darker tales within, but it made the boy wonder. Was he like that? A being wanting to love and be happy as he once had, but whose arms now shed blood because it was all he could do?

George once watched a praying mantis as a child, how still it was upon that leaf, never moving, until a hapless bee drew too close and the mantis struck, its sickle arms like a harvester's scythe. George was bewildered, amazed at how the unfortunate never saw death come.

George opened his book and turned to the picture of the golden gates instead, running his fingers along it. The boy read it aloud to the sound of crackling flames for what felt like the thousandth time. And even though his lips read of the book, his mind wandered to the memories of when his sister was still alive.

"Thief! Thief!" called a man, pointing towards a crowd that quickly swallowed a young girl into the shifting tides of the market.

"Catch her! She stole my coins!"

The girl seemed to be safe from her pursuers, daring a look to see the growing distance till she crashed into another guard.

"Not so fast." Lily looked up and saw a guard grabbing her by the shoulder; she repressed the need to gulp.

George waited and watched from the alleyway. Should he jump in? No. Best he waited.

"Did you steal from that man?"

Lily looked down to her feet. "No, sir," she said unconvincingly as the well-dressed man caught up to them, rasping for air with hands to his knees.

"Don't lie!" demanded the red-faced man, struggling to be taken seriously with each breath he took.

The guard looked down to the innocent girl who suddenly reached into a woven pocket and pulled out several coins. "I was hungry, and I thought this sir was showing how kind of heart he is by giving several coins. I didn't mean to steal it; if he wants his coins, I would happily give them back."

Lily had an innocence to her voice that would make anyone doubt her ability to do evil.

Even the man who made the claim suddenly seemed doubtful. "No, not that. My coin purse," he said, sounding almost guilty for even daring to interrogate the girl.

Lily simply shook her head. "I took no coin purse from you, sir, but if you have been robbed, here," Lily said with compassionate eyes as she held out the coins. Her look was one of guilt and of love.

"No, no. It's all right, you need it more than I do," the man said, noticeably uncomfortable as the crowds grew all around.

"Behave," the guard said, and Lily nodded complacently.

The girl dropped the coins into her pocket and walked away with her head bowed.

"Nothing to see!" called out the guard and dispersed prying eyes.

"Lily!" George called out with a hushed voice, motioning to her from the shadows as the girl skipped with a bright freckled grin.

George smiled at her victoriously and tossed the clinking bag of coins with a wide smirk. "Too easy," he said.

Suddenly, Lily didn't seem like an innocent and unsure little girl, but rather a deviously plotting urchin that better suited her talents.

Her lip tugged into a smirk. "Well, how can anybody suspect me with these eyes?" As if putting on a mask, her face suddenly transformed back into that of a clueless child with rheumy eyes that blinked innocently.

George laughed. "Yeah, yeah; let's go."

Lily smiled and nodded as George took her hand and they slithered through the city into their small den.

Their home was part of a run-down complex with a torn roof. They had fixed it using cloth and parchment to keep most of the elements away, but the winds proved more tenacious as the two would huddle up under covers to ward off the cold.

Yet on that day, the weather was pleasant as the two sat together shoulder to shoulder, bread in hand and turning the pages of their favourite book. Just to be safe, they had stowed it away under the floorboards.

They didn't know how to read, but always made up their own stories about the golden vault.

"Maybe it's the doorway into a glorious kingdom! With a kind king and queen and a beautiful princess!" Lily mused.

"Or maybe it holds a sea of gold as far as the eye can see! That way we don't have to live in torn down homes like this or steal."

"Maybe...if you had that much gold, what would you buy?"

George pondered the question for a second. Suddenly, his eyes widened and his lips turned into a knowing smile. "I would buy us a trained monkey!" he said proudly and Lily laughed at the absurd claim.

"You are rich, and you would buy a monkey?"

The boy nodded. "Or better yet, an army of monkeys!"

Lily was in tears. "But why?"

"So, that we could command them to smite our foes!"

"But how about a *normal* army, then?"

"Okay yeah, but what if I want the monkey to do tricks every now and then?"

Lily wiped away her tears as she forced the laughter from her throat. "If we ever become that rich, there is no way I am giving you power over it."

George simply smiled. He knew the claim was absurd, but it was the most absurd of claims he said with a serious expression that Lily found funniest, and he never grew tired of fuelling that laughter.

"What would you do with that kind of money?" George asked as Lily rested her head on his shoulder.

"I would buy us a proper house, maybe a really comfy bed. Perhaps adopt the homeless children so they never have to live as we did. A dog, perhaps, for us to play with."

George nodded. "That would be nice."

Their serene moment was suddenly broken by Lily's cough. A haggard and nascent thing that wouldn't quell down until her face was red and her eyes watered.

"Are you okay?"

"Yeah, I'm fine," she said. "Just a little cough." One more into her fist for good measure.

Gaven let loose no curse words, spat no insults, just a primal cry of frustration given life as he pounded against a tree.

"Gaven." Hank's voice was soft in a way that suggested his concern for Gaven went beyond just the relationship of leader and accomplice.

Gaven dropped to the floor, fists going from hammering trees to the soil as tears ran freely.

"Gaven," Hank said, still with a consoling tone, but louder this time. But no matter what he did, Gaven cried out louder and louder.

"Fuck!" the scarred man finally shouted in overwhelming frustration. His hands shook, tears flowed without constraint.

"Fuck!" he roared a second time. His neck muscles strained and his cheeks red, his eyes watery and filled with desperation. The word was mixed and fuelled by the guilt and sorrow he felt.

Hank stumbled over to where Gaven knelt and fell to his knees as well, the two of them dropped the games, they weren't power-hungry men who tried to make the world kneel to their whims—they were just desperate and pitiful scroungers playing pretend.

Hank embraced the large man and perhaps if it were for any other reason Gaven would have shoved him aside. But the brutish and scary man simply allowed himself the moment of weakness, clutching at Hank's shoulder for support, clambering and tugging at him as if letting go would have him plummet into the endless depths of his own despair.

"It's all my fault," Gaven finally managed in between sobs and reddened cheeks.

"Stop it," Hank said. The man looked over to where Salo was, or at least what remained of the man, and let loose tears of his own.

The thing that troubled Gaven most about the pain he felt was not the suffering that tugged at him, but the promise of realisation. It took time to process a death, especially one as sudden as Salo's; death's touch never simply came and went—its presence lingered always like an infection. It was the realisation that dawned on the mourner—the realisation that something was missing; a hollowness, a gap left in the conversation where once there was cause for laughter. It was this piece that death tore away from Hank and Gaven. The two were far more concerned about how they would feel when the realisation was given time to rot and fester in their minds.

The events played over and over in their minds as they saw the still and statuesque remains of their friend.

The mass of black grains had come for them as a cloud of malevolence—the way it ground against the bubble that protected them, the blue layer that flared to its touch.

Even though their sight was blocked, Gaven recalled how he had looked ahead and could see the promise of riches.

The thrill didn't last long; Gaven had lurched back with a cry reminiscent of a childhood he thought he had left behind. His father's image pierced through the swirling black grains and pressing against the bubble. It wasn't a face of compassion or joy from seeing his son, it was one of undulated rage. Thick brows frowning with pudgy cheeks. *You are a disappointment! Always getting into trouble! What have you got to offer, other than an unsightly face and making problems for everyone?*

Gaven gathered his composure quickly, but the doubt he thought was left in his past suddenly returned to him, accompanying the image of a man who still haunted his dreams.

"It's not real, don't be fooled," Gaven had said. He was glad that Hank and Salo stood behind him, for he wasn't sure that his expression had expressed confidence.

The image of Gaven's father suddenly changed, his mouth splitting down the middle through the jaw, as the entire lower half of the face parted like a monstrous flower, turning into terrifying mandibles before disappearing back into the raging storm of black grains.

The next image that plastered the bubble showed a group of voluptuous women with hungry eyes, several of them carrying golden coins within their cleavage with pieces dropping to the floor as the women squished their breasts against the bubble.

"Let us in, oh, Gaven. What stories we have told of your legend. We will fulfil *all* of your dreams." Though Gaven seemed like a cold-hearted opportunist, he still found that women, especially attractive ones, made him weak at the knees and at a loss for words. Even more so when the suggestive scantily clad women snickered the way they did. Although he knew the projections before him were nothing more than demons, he felt a sudden primal lust inch within him as it did most men.

The storm spoke his language, and though it didn't take much to drive away the feelings that stirred within him as his dreams dangled before his very eyes, Gaven still felt disappointment at not jumping at the opportunity.

No transformations this time, just coins turning into black grains as they plopped to the floor followed by the women that returned to the swirling storm. But it was the sudden claws that scratched at the bubble which drew the trio's attention. The magic of the bones glowed bright as the blue bubble bent to the force.

"Hank! My sweet darling!" Hank turned to the voice. The curly blond locks and innocent expression of his wife seemed even more beautiful than the real thing, strengthened by Hank's quiet longing as he recalled only the most cherished moments spent with his wife, the long nights of contemplation, leaving her image infallible compared to the real thing. An image recreated right before him with longing in her eyes reserved for one man.

"Elisabeth?" Hank said in disbelief.

"It's not real!" Gaven turned to him, the sudden possibility of hope proving to be too much for Hank.

"Hank!" Gaven called out again. The burly Hank turned to Gaven, to the man who Hank trusted with all his being. "It's not real!" Gaven cried.

Hank knew that; his chest heaved, his eyes moved back and forth as all his hopes were thrown back at him and the fishing line swayed before him with his wife on the hook.

The problem with a broken heart was not love itself, but rather the promise of love. Hank didn't mind the idea that the image was a lie, it was comforting even so. Even if he were to walk into his death, at least for just a moment, he could pretend things had never changed.

"Hank!" Gaven gripped his friend, shaking him. Friend looked upon friend, and Hank could see the desperation in Gaven's eyes.

"This isn't real," he whispered, a whisper of submission. Hank knew that Gaven would never stop him if he wished to walk over to his wife, but it was that plea of desperation that woke Hank from his trance.

It took all his will and reopened wounds which had long ago left ugly scars, but even so, Hank stepped back, his soul tearing apart as the image faded into grains. "I'm sorry," Hank whispered softly.

Yet, within their moment of newly solidified friendship, Salo's nerves proved far more wanting.

"Salo! Get over here!" The man and women which plastered the bubble were diminutive and seemed ready to collapse—there was no way they could match Salo's strength or size—but it didn't matter. Their weapon was their title as mother and father.

"Mommy! Please, no!" Salo begged, stepping back.

"Salo! It's not real!"

The man turned child suddenly squatted down into a fetal position. "I'm sorry, Mom! I will try harder!"

"Are you talking back to your mother?" The man suddenly unbuckled his belt—no, not a belt, the scuttling centipede legs revealing its true nature as the phantom pulled it taut and the centipede head chittered against the bubble.

"No please, Daddy! I will try harder! I will play music!"

"You ungrateful child! After all we have given you!" The father raised the belt over his head and Salo retreated just like that. He was no longer the fearsome Salo, brother to Gaven and Hank—he was now just a boy who had become too big to play the flute.

There was no place for magical bones within this past, so Salo dropped the bones and ran into the embrace of the storm.

When Hank and Gaven awoke unscathed on the other side, they found their memories cloudy, their minds trying to piece together the events which had unfolded.

The notion of a magical black cloud of grain which threw monsters at them seemed to be the musings of a bad dream, but then the reality dawned on them as they searched for their brother.

It didn't take long for them to find Salo, and though his eyes were wide open and he seemed alive, if only for a moment, it didn't take Hank or

Gaven long to realise the truth of what they saw. Once again they had played the events over and over in their minds.

Salo seemed surprisingly peaceful at that moment, his lower half nowhere to be seen, but the remains of his flesh had been put together to form a hauntingly large flute of sinew and flesh and bone and skin to match his own burly size. And though the gentle giant did not move, nor did any sound come from the perversion of an instrument, he still seemed surprisingly at peace.

Chapter 15

The night clouded the streets as silence nestled in narrow gaps and crevices. This part of the city bustled with merchants and the hopeful during the day. Desperate men would wear hopeful smiles as they each tried to raise their voices over the others, promising wares unlike any other. Yet, at night, the city would sleep and its nightmares would come forward.

Though not in great abundance, for if the day merchants were like birds that took their pick of worms, the night harboured critters that crawled within the shadows. Both held desperation, though those that roamed the night featured a desperation of another, darker kind. Curved blades were tucked under coats and sashes hid faces. The occasional lost soul wandered the streets with hollow eyes, scratching at irritated limbs.

The way their feet dragged against the ground, their scratching was audible in the silence. Those that waited to pounce from the shadows left them alone in peace, for there would be nothing worthwhile to gain.

Within the coldness of this slumbering night, a boy crept his way through a window as if he were a shadow.

George had never before tried to steal from those that sat higher up on the pecking order, for if caught, it could cause him far more trouble. He never needed to. Lily and George always did enough to get by and they played smart. They constantly reminded each other to not be blinded by greed or take unnecessary risks.

Yet George had no choice in the matter, Lily was sick, and he needed the medicine.

Though it was the first time he entered the home of a healer, his heart proved still. He could feel it beat against his chest, a hammer that pressed against his ribs, the pulse thrummed in his ear, but the beat was steady, rhythmic like the beating wings of a sparrow.

As the curtains swayed from his intrusion, George took in a single deep breath.

It was George's upbringing that taught him wit. How object A moves into object B and how one can meander through it all and be a part of the coursing sands; it was much like a conversation.

So, he became one with the house, finding one object to hide behind followed by the next, the shadows aiding him in his approach.

Like wind blowing through the halls, the doors opened slightly, and just like the wind George slithered unnoticed from room to room: through guest rooms and workstations and lounges filled with such scrupulous attention that it deigned the impression that everything was placed with purpose. From rolled-out carpets to hung paintings to organised and measured seating arrangements. Even the night dust in the air felt of a higher calibre compared to the ruin he and his sister called home.

He could understand there was a sort of humble reservation to which the room apartment was planned out that suggested careful presentation of one's wealth without trying to be ostentatious. But all George saw was the brandishing of wealth.

Finally, George stumbled into the room he had been looking for—the one filled with vials and bottles and containers of labelled contents. Some seemed to be dark viscous materials within small glass bottles, while others contained shelved herbs growing from pots, or cabinets stocked with tinctures. For all the order, the room stank something noisome.

His fingers grazed anything that seemed to have healing properties: vials with mixtures within, bigger mixtures with letters George didn't even try to read.

Due to his illiteracy, all books were ignored, and the contents of liquids and herbs were smelt instead. George tried to drown away the thought that he had no idea what he was doing; he could not afford to fall into that line of thinking. The best he could hope to do was believe that something within the healer's wares would save Lily's life.

George removed his hood, taking a whiff of one vial followed by the next. Some made him pull away and retch from the pungent stench, as if they were dung roiled in swamp water, others left a sweet, yet acidic scent which made his nose hair tickle and scrunch up.

Something caught his eyes. Not a vial. Not some herbs. Nothing that was for healing.

It was a slanted and standing work desk with an unfurled scroll and instruments strewn about it. Beside the table stood crates where more rolled-up scrolls jutted from.

Perhaps it was the contents of the book he and Lily would read that fascinated George and drew him towards the table or just plain curiosity, but for a moment he let himself wander from the medicinal bottles to the contents of the work desk.

His fingers trailed the coarse and rough texture of the page—an old etching that depicted what seemed like lands and pyramids or tombs being drawn. George smiled, unable to express the strange familiarity that came with the etching. No doubt Lily would love the drawings. The top of the page showed a robed man who seemed to perform great magical feats. The boy was glad that there was little writing, and even the glyphs that were present were in no language George had seen before.

The last pictogram depicted not the wizard, but a skull with crossbones.

A sound. The doorknob rattled. George had only moments to react.

As quickly as he could manage, George shuffled between the crates of scrolls as the bleeding lantern light chased the shadows away, and muffled footsteps entered the room.

Silence. Quiet. George tried his best to blend into what little shadows were left as the footsteps neared. No words were said. Carefully. He tried to nestle deeper into his hiding spot.

The lantern light dashed back and forth. George cupped his mouth to stifle even his breath before it dared betray him. His mind raced. What if he was caught? Who would care for Lily? Would they put him in the gallows? Or would he be tried and put to death? He was too young for that, wasn't he? He didn't want to be thrown behind bars. He couldn't leave Lily alone.

The footsteps neared the workstation. The lantern forced all things into the light.

George was going to be found, he knew it. The light would reveal him. Should he fight? George curled his fingers into a fist.

The footsteps faded, the lantern light retreating. George shuddered. The bleeding light finally vanished behind a shutting door. It was only then that George noticed he was holding his breath.

And just like the wind that came and went, George returned to his run-down excuse of a home with little to ever suggest he was there in the first place. In his hands he held several ointments and tinctures, whatever smelled as if it carried some healing properties. And along with that he carried the scroll he had seen before—the man had so many. Surely he wouldn't miss a single one?

He hesitated at the door, sitting at the footsteps and taking a sip from some form of brandy that he had stolen.

He knew Lily was on the other side of that door, waiting for him, and he knew that if he walked inside, that the reality of her situation would wash over him all over again. But when he sat outside, he could pretend that he would be greeted by a wide smile, and a book turned to a page with golden gates on her lap. George smiled at the thought of being able to add another page to their collection.

George finally braved the courage to enter. "Lily, I'm back," he said.

She never replied.

"Gotcha!" Perhaps if it were any other reason minus the Hobbers, George would have been grateful for being pulled out of that memory. But the man who grabbed at George and pulled him from his seat was not a welcome sight.

George squirmed and thrashed, but it made little difference. Though he was nimble and quick like the wind, nothing he did would allow him to escape once caught. George stopped trying to pry the monstrous hands that cupped his mouth and circled his stomach; he looked up into the eyes of his aggressor and found a raven's stare looking back with a wicked smile.

George did not hesitate for a moment. In one swift flash, his hand grasped for his knife and slashed upwards into the face of his aggressor.

The man released his grip and cried out in pain as both hands clasped a ruined eye. "Fuck!" he bellowed.

And so George ran, the wind was free once more, yet he failed to notice the second man who grabbed George and pried the knife from his hands.

"You okay, Gaven?" the man asked with concern.

"No, I am not fucking okay, *Hank*. I just lost an eye to that bleeding kid. Shit, it hurts."

George thrashed the same way a squirrel might in the hands of a predator, yet without a weapon, his chances proved fleeting.

Gaven cursed again, turning around and tearing a sleeve from his shoulders which he used to bandage his mangled eye.

"Hank, tie up the kid while I fix this fucking mess."

George had his arms bound together as he hung from a tree, grunting as the rope rubbed against his wrists and his feet dangled in the air.

"You okay?" Hank asked.

"Stop asking me that, of course I'm not."

Blood streaked the wounded man's cheeks, and whatever it was that kept him going George knew it would not end well for him.

"Now," Gaven said, turning to the boy with a snarl as the makeshift bandage ran diagonally from scalp to socket, the rags stained red to mark the spot where once was an eye. The man was suddenly leagues more unpleasant.

George tensed, his arms clumping up, his muscles tightening, and his lips pursed. He readied himself for whatever Gaven's blade would find to pierce.

"Aren't you going to tell me to go easy on the kid?" Gaven asked Hank.

"After what we went through today? Fuck 'im. Fuck the kid up."

Gaven smiled gleefully at that.

Yet, George's eyes widened, for the man that was fuelled with unwavering rage held his blade against the one thing that George had not considered, and it was the one place that made George lose all composure.

"Please no! Don't!" George pleaded, his pursed lips loosening instantly at the sight of his book held against the tip of the knife.

"Please! Harm me instead if you have to!"

"Oh, don't worry, I will be coming to you next, boy. I will take my sweet time carving my will onto every single inch of your body. But first, I will tear this book to shreds and enjoy every moment of it."

"No, stop! Please, I'm sorry!" It didn't matter, George's eyes widened in disbelief with every given second, and tears brimmed his eyes as he realised how helpless he was.

And just like that, the blade pierced through the cover and George felt as if it was his heart that was run through. How cold and hollow his chest felt at that moment and how his tears ran free.

"No!" Time and time again the blade ripped through the pages. Time and time again George felt as if Lily was dying all over again.

Fugue misted within the boy's mind as the world lost its order and things failed to make sense. He caught glimpses of his past from when Lily looked at him with fading eyes; how her laugh echoed when she still was alive.

Every last piece of memory defiled and torn apart just like the pages of the book.

It rained pieces of paper as the pages and binding came apart. The wretched man tore more and more.

"No!" It was a loud and desperate roar that reverberated with George's sorrow. The boy pulled on his arms, the pain of his wrists turning numb at the sight of what was his only reminder of a sister he had made a promise to. Skin rubbed against the rope as blood began to escape from open wounds.

Two things gave way at that moment—one was the sound of George's mind as it snapped, for the darkness within him that had turned into a slithering blade took over.

The second thing was the rope, as chafed and bleeding wrists pulled themselves free and the boy fell to the floor.

It all happened in a blur. The boy said no words as he leapt far and wide in front of the man. There was no way that George could match Gaven in a bout of strength, but he could help guide the blade.

As the knife came down for another stab, George pushed it away and towards Gaven's stomach. The blade struck home as the raven-eyed man stumbled back in shock.

George did not hesitate to grip the knife and, with a resounding roar, drive the blade up the man's stomach. Tearing it loose and following the man's example, he stabbed over and over until the man stumbled back with shocked eyes and pale lips.

It soon became impossible to tell where the blade had struck, for the blood pooled and covered Gaven's entire torso, only for the man to fall back wide-eyed and staring at the canopy as the first of Gaven's insides escaped, guts bursting out into a pool of blood.

The sound of steel unsheathing itself was heard behind him; George turned swiftly on his heel and ducked under the sweeping blade as his own knife slashed deeply above Hank's knee, gratified by the pained cries of the man falling to his knees. George gave him no time to repose, driving the bloodstained steel deep through Hank's chin.

Suddenly silence.

A cloud roiled over George's mind. His eyes were in a constant state of frenzy as he struggled to retain his grasp on reality.

Still the world lay shattered before his feet as he struggled to piece them together, and soon that world took the form of torn pages from a book.

So, as his limbs trembled, George did the one thing his broken mind knew how—he mounted the still living Gaven who choked on his own blood with blade in hand.

George's eyes were that of a crazed animal, frantic and without composure, while the last eye of Gaven stared at George with desperation, pleading for mercy like a hapless child.

And so George continued, his blade striking home over and over until his hands turned numb.

Birds broke from their perches and trailed into the sky, ejected by the sudden roar of a young boy who gave from him a cry so wild till it turned into frail sobs brimming with unmatched sorrow.

Chapter 16

"George," muttered Kendrith as he unsheathed the blade with a wet splurt; the beast he had just slain was a cockatrice, a creature with a serpentine body that carried itself on two legs and bore webbed wings, its head that of a rooster.

It had already been days since Kendrith had recovered from his fever and got to laying the plot of land. But his right arm would be of little use propped in the makeshift sling that used to be his shirt. What remained was the dirtied white tunic underneath, his coat still draped his shoulders, and a bandolier which held daggers and vials.

The infection which threatened his life had been battled and won, but still the gash had become grisly from all the fighting and running. Even though the fever had gone, replaced by a soreness which permeated his body, pain still shot through his shoulder with the slightest movement. On top of that, the days spent in a fevered sweat with rationed food made it a task by itself to eat and hydrate once he had duly recovered, even with the fugue that clouded his mind. But at that moment, he didn't have the luxury to worry.

He was glad that he heard the wailing of the young boy and could follow the general direction, even if it was to the swamp and away from the city of Haven; on the other hand, dread filled the mercenary as he could tell that whatever situation George had found himself in, it could not have been good.

"Please, stay alive till I get there," Kendrith whispered to himself as his feet blurred at every stride, even when sore and brought to its bitter limit, Kendrith's nimble alacrity proved astonishing.

It didn't take long for the surroundings to shift towards wetlands; pudgy soil and haggard trees announced the change of environment. It took even less time for Kendrith's breath to heave and his lungs to burn. His feet lost their rhythm as one foot slowed or dragged; the merc almost tripped on several occasions. And yet even as the man's vision blurred and every breath turned into fire, he struggled forward on heavy limbs.

When finally Kendrith entered the swamp, he worried that he would struggle to find George, but that was soon put to rest as he found the first of the displayed Hobber corpses. All of them in a perimeter that formed a circle—it was a warning. Kendrith no longer ran forward, his breath deep and ragged, his thighs burning. *Is this George's doing?* he pondered. The thought that George was capable of such cruelty seemed impossible.

The more Kendrith walked into the closed-off circle, the more grisly the warnings became. Giant Hobber eyes were forced to observe his passing, vile dangling heads seemed confused rather than fearful, and limbs were strewn all over to pave the way to promised death.

Yet there was another thing, a sound. Kendrith could not tell what it was at first, yet every step made it more audible, until Kendrith recognised the familiar sound of steel piercing flesh over and over again.

Kendrith walked into the clearing to find a decrepit and smoking fireplace, the body of a man with wide eyes and a tear that strolled down his cold cheek, and the familiar back of a young boy mounted atop a limp cadaver. With both of George's blood-soaked hands gripped around the hilt, Kendrith watched the blade be brought down time and time again.

The soil around the boy was stained red from the dead bandit's corpse.

"George," Kendrith whispered.

Nothing.

The boy continued to lift his quivering hands and stab continuously with numb rhythm.

"George," Kendrith called louder this time, hoping that the bloodstained boy would turn and reveal anyone other than George. Perhaps a Hobber in human clothing, or any other boy for that matter. *But please don't let it be George,* Kendrith thought, though he knew without a shadow of doubt the familiar back of the innocent child.

George was naive and didn't seem to be very good at much, but he was hopeful and caring, qualities Kendrith silently praised. He tried hard to see

George as nothing more than another job, but as he looked at that diminutive back and the burden it seemed to carry on those lithe shoulders, Kendrith found it more and more difficult.

"George!" Kendrith finally called out louder, but still no response.

He moved closer, stopping as his step didn't give off the wet splurt of mud, but rather the crumple of paper and noticed the tattered pages of a book which haloed the boy and gutted thief.

Pain struck Kendrith; he was beginning to understand. He understood how much that book had meant to George. How tearing it apart must have had the boy snap as his heart was torn to pieces just like the pages—Kendrith knew what pain and anguish the boy must have felt.

"George, stop it!"

Kendrith strode over and placed a hand on George's shoulder.

A sudden blur as only instinct saved Kendrith from the passing blade.

Kendrith ducked under the blade's path.

"George, it's me—" Kendrith never finished the sentence as George's blade searched for fresh meat to pierce. He saw the dead look in George's eyes framed by blood, a look driven by the most primal instincts that made him an instrument of death; there was no recognition in the boy's gaze.

"George!" Still nothing as the blade advanced.

The boy lacked form and grace, his swings wide open and his feet off balance, yet there was a reckless, swift edge to the alacrity with which George swung as the sound of swishing air accompanied his movements.

"George!" Kendrith stopped retreating. In a swift motion to match George's own he redirected the blade with his good hand, forcing George off balance. Kendrith did not relinquish the hold, twisting the arm over and extending George's wrist gratified by a loud, pained cry as the blade fell to bury itself in the mud.

"Stop, George! It's me!" Kendrith said as he spun George around and embraced him, hindering his movements as George struggled against the man.

"It's me," Kendrith whispered into George's ear as Kendrith did his best to chasten his arms. The sound of clothes and blood rubbing against each other was heard, and muddy feet splashing on wet ground as Kendrith kept whispering words of comfort.

Finally, he could feel George ease his struggle, each twist turning weaker than the last until the boy just stopped.

"It's me," Kendrith whispered even quieter as George sounded the softest of whines. It started as a hollow-stomached struggle that Kendrith sensed through George's quivering lips against his chest, until it burst forth as a harrowing cry, one that screamed of pain and anguish. Curled fingers clambered and pulled on Kendrith's garments as such lamented cries of true pain rang out, unlike any Kendrith had ever heard.

"It's okay. I'm here now. It's okay," reassured Kendrith, but all George could do was sound his despair.

Within the crying and the tears and the death, Kendrith noticed only too late the Hobbers that surrounded them.

Chapter 17

At those heights, the winds proved relentless. Far away from the exchange of common folk, the temple of Eindeiheid, the esteemed and proud academy of mages, stood erect against the face of the mountain.

The reason for why the school was so high up had nothing to do with practicality. In fact, it sacrificed practicality to become a symbol—those atop the mountain were no longer human, but rather gods.

Far away from the musings of those below, everything among the clouds proved to be completely alien from the daily workings of life.

Howling gusts of wind faced against the bracing mountain. While the winds below offered a comforting breeze which caressed one's skin, the winds of Eindeiheid were like wild stallions.

The harsh living conditions and the cold embrace of the academy didn't just offer the idea of an unattainable form of being, but was there to condition a mage if one wished to become a god.

The cold rush of wind made bones rattle, and the thin air robbed one's breath as deprived muscles burned and ached. Yet a mage still needed to build, to weave the world to their design and that required concentration.

There was no law among the clouds, no rules to keep the elements in check; chaos reigned and it was from that chaos that mages learnt.

With cold winds that made teeth clatter, thin air that made lungs heave, mages would find their calm within the barren skies as they learnt to master their minds even when exposed to the harshest of environments.

All of that which was Eindeiheid, all of that which it symbolised, and all of which it tried to teach was hammered into Simantiar, Usellyes, Noima, Ciro, Zaros, and Emilie over the course of seven years.

Mylor Hershaw, the head of the academy and the man who discovered Usellyes as a child, led the class personally. His robes were a deep blue like the depths of the ocean and his full white-and-black beard compensated for the shine on his naked scalp.

Simantiar and the others stood in their own magenta robes, though they had worked their way from the white of acolytes to the yellow of apprentices and now the deepest shade of red for senior mages, the trek towards their blue robes seemed still so far as they waded through the thickening muck and mud.

They were in the academy's own contained garden. Through the use of magic it spliced several different ecological biomes and divided them into sections like a cut of cake.

Simantiar began to drool at the thought of cake. How long had it been since he indulged such cravings? Too long in his opinion.

"Mr. Trufin. Are you listening?"

Soft snickering arose to Mylor's queries.

"Yes, sir."

"Well great, would you like to repeat what I said? For my sake. My memory isn't what it used to be and I seem to have lost my train of thought."

Simantiar sighed, playing along. "You wish for us to wander the garden and find animals that speak towards the type of companion we wish to find. Because of the simplistic nature of many animals untainted by the curse of sentience and still bearing their natural bond with the weave of creation. Thus, you want us to find the animal which best represents the path we wish to forge based on the studies we made regarding animal types and their symbolic bonds."

Mylor nodded his head, a move which could have been interpreted as a slight bow. "Very good, Simantiar. But perhaps having my students listen to what I have to share is just the bare minimum of the requirement to be attending this academy."

Simantiar smiled, feeling as if he had outsmarted Mylor. But no sooner did the fancy form before Simantiar shook the thought away. Mylor was clever. Beyond clever. His raw magical prowess may not have been able to contend with Simantiar's or several other mages for that note. But what he lacked in force he more than made up for in tact. Mylor. Known to have refined his magic to an art form, his spells were as sharply forged as his own mind.

The headmaster turned to the garden.

Up above, the biome itself was sealed and domed by slices of dimensional magic. Each sky for each biome as different as if stepping upon each border, teleporting the mage instead of the biomes being transported to the academy. And that was precisely the case.

"There are a total of fifty different biomes to be found, from winter lands of crested snow all the way to the arid sand dunes of the east. And among these locations you will find a myriad of different animals." Mylor extended his wrist as from the end of his loose embroidered sleeve several golden snakes slithered through the air and towards each and every gathered student.

Several yelps and ouches escaped the crowd as the serpents bit down on the arms of the students and coiled their lengths about the biceps before suddenly losing that shine and seeming no different from an ordinary golden arm ring fashioned after a wrapped serpent.

"These arm rings will ensure that you are bound to this academy. I apologise for the precaution, but there have been several occasions where students decided to remove the armband." Mylor's gaze wandered over to Simantiar expectantly. "Despite our advice."

He returned his attention to the body of students. "You do not need to take or collect any as a familiar if you do not wish to. What I simply ask is that you find a bond which fits your intuition and keep it planted firmly in mind. You have the rest of the day to find your animal."

Simantiar yelped as the serpent finally coiled up his arm with such tender and demure patience till bared fangs shot out and pierced into Simantiar's flesh. He winced at the sudden shot of pain and watched as the snake became a glistening bronze-gold ornament.

The arched wooden doors creaked on their hinges as they opened. Murmurs arose and heads turned to see who had entered the garden.

"Excuse me, please make way, passing through," spoke a lazulite-robed mage who waded through the crowd of students. As he finally made his way to the front, his head shrouded by the mage robe he wore, the mage shuffled skittishly towards Mylor before leaning in and whispering into his ear.

The headmaster nodded. Once. Twice. "Understood," he said.

The mage shuffled back towards the doors and the students now openly made way.

Simantiar's gaze shifted from the man to Mylor to catch the headmaster's deep dark eyes staring at him intensely. It lasted only a moment, as his gaze returned to the body of students.

"What are you waiting for? Go!" He waved his arms and smiled at the statement as everyone ran into the woods.

As Simantiar walked forward, Mylor intercepted him and grabbed him by the biceps.

"Where is it?" Mylor asked. Whatever the mage from before had whispered into his ear now transferred as venom into the headmaster's query. Simantiar never heard such urgency or anger in the jovial voice of the headmaster.

"Where is what?" Simantiar asked.

Mylor's grip tightened, his piercing brown eyes looking directly at Simantiar's with great scrutiny. The eyes narrowed, the lips tightened into a line.

The grip loosened.

Mylor's smile returned, his usual affable and welcoming self at the front.

The headmaster straightened Simantiar's robes and dusted his shoulders.

"My mistake. Go on. Enjoy yourself," he encouraged.

Simantiar strode on, looking back constantly as the other students already looked into brushes or simply strode deeper into the forest. Mylor's gaze continued to follow Simantiar, his hands at his back, his smile reassuring. But something about that gaze told Simantiar that something had perturbed the archmage greatly.

The first biome past the gated hall was a simple forest. Certainly holding packs of wolves, bears, deer, foxes, and critters like squirrels or rabbits. All of it incredibly unappealing to Simantiar.

Each biome itself stretched far enough that one could explore it for a couple of hours till all of it was properly mapped.

"I really wish to take a look at the arctic biome, but perhaps will end up going towards the jungle," Ciro had said. "I would love a tiger! I heard their ferociousness is something to be admired! But the supposed timber wargs of the north could also be something interesting."

When they were younger, the others had joked that Ciro was more of a boy than the others put together. She had a certain proclivity for getting into fights, and something which seemed brazen and rash soon enough began to show itself as a rough talent for combat.

She had already received an invitation to train among arcane fighters after her graduation, and the training she committed herself to prepared her body for just such an endeavour.

Her wavy black hair was certainly always short and her rather fair skin always finding a darker shade as she trained under the sun's glare. It did not surprise Simantiar at all that Ciro came from Sorofa—she certainly matched their competitive and determined zeal.

Simantiar had faced her a couple of times in sparring sessions—he would win a great deal of times when all rules were permitted, but never stood a chance when the type of magic was restricted to contact spells. He truly believed that Ciro's limbs were faster than he could even think.

Emilie wanted something cute, a rabbit was her first choice as she stayed at the first biome.

Simantiar wandered through as some strolled through the forest while others were carried by forest vines or by the wind. Others buried their heads in hollowed tree trunks or stalked hoofprints.

Noima was never quite certain of what he wanted. He even knocked on Simantiar's door and spent several hours discussing potential choices before Simantiar evicted him.

Zaros on the other hand couldn't stop talking about his attraction towards an arachnid familiar—something to help him further diversify his art was the goal.

Simantiar's arm itched as he absent-mindedly went to scratch it only to feel the squeeze of the tightening serpent as it sprang to life again.

"Okay, no petting, got it," he noted to himself.

"Ah, Simantiar. Any idea what you are looking for?"

Simantiar turned to find the wide-mouthed grin of Moran. He had a rather exotic accent when he spoke, apparently having travelled from Okoria where they had schools of magic of their own, but their reputation as a school of magic was quite wanting and Simantiar regretted to admit that it sounded quite squalid.

Moran was tall and hefty in stature. His father seemed to be a man of connections and pulled strings to send Moran to Eindeheid. Despite Moran's tendency to be rather talkative, his topics of choice were things which he somehow managed to stretch over several minutes when they could have been cut down to just three words.

Though all things considered, Moran was a good person, and Simantiar most definitely harboured no dislike towards him.

"Not yet, Moran," Simantiar replied. "I am just looking. I don't think I will pick out a familiar."

"Yes, yes. I am also quite confused. You see, my father used to always say…"

Simantiar learnt to trail off and stare towards the serene branches of leaning trees and watch the leaves shift while Moran rumbled on.

"…so, I was thinking of maybe like an owl or something. I heard owls are very smart. And did you know their feathers make it so that they are incredibly quiet in flight?"

Looking around, Simantiar noticed the familiar form just ahead that he was looking for. Usellyes strode alone through the forest grounds, but something felt…off.

A thought came to Simantiar as he turned to Moran. "Well, Noima was just telling me he discovered an owl nest earlier. Maybe you should go ask him?"

Moran brightened at the notion. "I will at once! Thank you, my friend!" Moran paced away hastily, thrilled at the prospect.

Simantiar turned back towards where he had seen Usellyes earlier to find him turning another corner, and silently he followed.

Usellyes seemed as if he tried to be inconspicuous, checking his surroundings for unwanted attention. Everything about his behaviour intrigued Simantiar, a friend who was usually so well behaved, so fastidious, so cautious, suddenly seemed to be hiding something. Simantiar smiled at the notion—this was far more intriguing than finding a spirit animal; he repressed the urge to roll his eyes.

Usellyes trudged farther on, and Simantiar peeled away the air and wrapped himself in a blanket that granted him invisibility.

The two moved forward together, an additional spell making it so that a bubble around Simantiar blocked out any sound from escaping him and another to make him as light as a feather so he left no prints in the soil.

The original sense of curiosity which originally humoured Simantiar had grown sour with every step of Usellyes he shadowed. What could Usellyes possibly be hiding with such fastidious caution? Did it have something to do with why Mylor seemed suddenly so frazzled?

Soon, the forest faded away, the orange glow of a setting sun bleeding through summer trees till suddenly another border revealed itself. Smoky blue vapor formed into what seemed like ropes stretched across the forest floor. The other side of it revealed the thick and dense jungle trees of kapok and rubber.

Darkness reigned supreme as Simantiar stepped over the magical border and into a new ecosystem, a distant bird call swept over like a chilling breeze, echoing what Simantiar assumed would be the first of many warnings.

More and more that promise of adventure faded away as dark thoughts played at Simantiar—what could Usellyes possibly be searching for?

The night swept through the lands and the tightly packed trees overhead simply loomed menacingly. Thick blankets of moss covered the floor and trees, vines, and exposed roots stretched across the path and suffocated Simantiar beneath his tarp. The sudden shift from potentially pleasant summer day towards arid and humid made the experience all the more inebriating. Simantiar could feel his heart beat almost as deafeningly as the steps that Usellyes took with supposed purpose.

The man was looking for something.

He rummaged through hollowed-out trees trunks, pieces of bark, anything that would hide insects underneath.

"What are you looking for?" Simantiar softly whispered beneath his breath.

Suddenly, a shadow shifted on the ground and scuttled away. Usellyes leapt, following it along.

Simantiar tried hard to keep pace, suddenly running through the forest grounds.

The vines and roots which covered the floor conspired to make him trip.

Suddenly, Simantiar cast his fourth spell midjump, his mind a tranquil sea though underneath it was a tumultuous current. Simantiar's feet phased through the littered objects, nothing able to grasp him as his limbs turned into wispy-coloured vapor only to then reassemble flesh and bone again.

He sprinted, keeping pace as best he could.

The scuttling thing on the floor was now clear to be a centipede.

A thought crept up, remembering the studies of lost and forgotten lore and stories regarding ancient creatures. Simantiar knew the jungle they were in was situated somewhere along the eastern lands.

Simantiar never had a chance to finish his thoughts, as the clearing of trees gave way to a desolate and unforgiving desert of shifting snow and an awe-inspiring visage of rising mountain peaks encrusted in ice.

The centipede vanished upon reaching the border as it never traversed to the arctic plane.

Just the chirping of cicadas nestled in their crevices and what sounded like a far-off abysmally deep groan that emerged from inside the heart of the biome could be heard.

"Damn it!" Usellyes voiced his irritation as his hands clambered for the insect at the last second only to miss.

He rose to his knees, panting.

Simantiar tried hard to remember what was so important about the centipede, why Usellyes tried so hard to reach it.

Suddenly, the kneeling mage reached into his pouch and pulled from it something that glistened. It was a key. It shimmered a deeper bronze than the arm rings they were forced to wear, with a dragon imprint coiled around the teeth of the key.

Admiring it for just a second, Usellyes then took to his arm and stabbed the key into the serpent.

Simantiar saw it hiss before seeing the shadowy image of the serpent writhe and then fall to the floor, slithering away.

"No, no, no." Usellyes clambered forward trying desperately to grasp it, but it eluded his grip and vanished into the thick, hanging vines of a tree.

Simantiar heard something, and looking down he saw the slithering bronze serpent and reached to grab it.

The thing went rigid and stiff in his hand as Simantiar watched it bite its own tail. Simantiar proceeded to pocket it.

Usellyes looked past the border and then back towards the path he came from.

With apparent determination he rose to his feet, wiped at his dirtied robe, and vanished past the border.

Simantiar waved away his invisible tarp and stood among the thick, encrusted jungle trees that creased him with sweat.

Looking down, he unfurled the serpent in his hand that had coiled into an inanimate ring.

The key unlocked the arm ring—Mylor would certainly be mad. Simantiar wondered if he should go back and let Mylor know what happened.

No. Usellyes would be alone across the entire world on a foreign continent.

Simantiar looked to his own arm ring and reached for it, the serpent's scales shifted and rattled as it tightened its grip.

He tried to phase his arm through it, remove the beast, reason with it, but nothing seemed to work.

Finally, Simantiar thought back to the key and a stray thought occurred to him.

"Maybe?" he pondered.

It was like an abstract realisation, the kind where a sudden simple solution presented itself for a problem that persisted for days. Would it even work?

Simantiar waved his hand, imagining the key that Usellyes had waved around, returning to the image and entrusting the familiar tinge of essence it emitted and copying it into the key. His eyes closed. And when they opened, he firmly held a key with a small dragon coiled around the teeth of it.

He moved it to the serpent and unfastened it from his arm, and having taken note of Usellyes's own blunder, he snatched it up the moment it fell to the floor.

As the serpent went to bite him one more time, Simantiar whipped its head against a tree as the serpent went limp, curling into a circle as it too bit its own tail and went incredibly still.

As Simantiar looked up, the arctic dunes of endless snow were gone and the way to where Usellyes vanished was now revealing itself.

"I should have taken a step into the snow," Simantiar said, his hair matted with sweat and his skin sticky, cicadas chirping in full choir as Simantiar tried to loosen the robes and shirt that clung to his pits.

"This better be worth it," he groused, trudging on the path and finding the first footprint of Usellyes.

Simantiar contemplated calling out for his friend. Obviously whatever it was that Usellyes was doing, he wanted to keep it secret.

Following the telling trail of sunken footprints, disturbed soil, and broken twigs, Simantiar decided to shadow Usellyes for the moment.

It didn't take long till the first footsteps were audible, followed by the familiar form of Usellyes himself.

"Where is it?" Usellyes muttered to himself, high knees stepping over protruding roots and moss-covered stones as he seemed to scan the forest floor.

Eventually, a cavernous cave revealed itself—its opening a wide yawning maw of endless darkness, the soft echo of water dripping inside. Simantiar begged that Usellyes wouldn't go inside—it was the second time Usellyes walked on and vanished from his sight.

It was also the second time Simantiar gave off a long sigh and followed along.

The *drip drop* was deafening. Simantiar called upon his fifth spell to grant him feline eyes, but even that did little for the stark barren darkness that filled the cavern. Why did Usellyes not summon any light? Where was he going? That and many more questions accompanied him.

The anxiety crept inside like weeds scaling a building, slow but deliberate and suffocating. The shadows crept inside and tendrils worked their way into Simantiar's very being as Usellyes's name became more and more present in his trembling throat.

"Usellyes," it came as a frightened whisper.

Drip.

"Usellyes!" Simantiar's mind broke and the word was screamed and echoed through the darkness.

"Simantiar?" a familiar voice called back from the dark—it was scared.

"Where are you?" Simantiar called out, summoning a ball of light to chase away the shadows.

Sudden steps strode towards Simantiar the moment they lit and a waving hand absconded the flash of light the moment it appeared.

"No!" the whisper from Usellyes was harsh.

"No light," the command sounded almost pleading. Usellyes was scared.

"Did you just cast Void on my light?" Simantiar queried.

"Shh!"

"Where are we?" Simantiar asked, lowering his voice and following Usellyes's example, acting on the side of caution, though Simantiar felt that if there was something out there, the whispering would make no difference.

"Why are you here?" Usellyes countered with his own question, his whispered query harsh and direct.

"Where are we, Usellyes?" Simantiar asked again, the nausea and trepidation that came from being in the unknown dark shook his resolve.

"You shouldn't be here."

The sound of skittering feet echoed. The dripping was now like the sound of a drum.

From the corners of what little light Simantiar was offered he saw the outline of whatever skittering abomination pounced upon them, its vile screech the thing of nightmares.

Simantiar grabbed Usellyes's robes and pulled him to the ground as the monstrous outline of a centipede leapt over them—its pincers just barely missing them.

"We need to get out," Simantiar stated with clear desperation. He extended his palm, trying to summon a ball of light to little avail. His mind was too chaotic, as fear robbed him of clarity and all he could hear was his consciousness telling him to escape.

The second time it was Usellyes that pulled Simantiar out of harm's way, the sound of skittering legs proved deafening as it surrounded them. The lack of light made it seem like a sea of skittering beasts with venomous bites filled the endless caverns.

"Come on," Simantiar said to himself.

His breaths frantic, the practised tranquility of his mind was now frenzied clashing waves as dark clouds roiled over.

"Simantiar! Hurry!" Usellyes urged.

Finally, Simantiar closed his eyes, although it made little difference to what he was able to see before him anyway. But yet still it was a different type of darkness, it was his. A darkness he chose, one he could control. The skittering legs became distant. The looming threat of pouncing centipedes was a hollow thing in the back of his mind. He couldn't still his mind and pay attention to the creatures at the same time. So, he didn't. Either he calmed himself and gave them a chance at survival or they would die.

A ball of radiant light the size of a cartwheel bloomed in his palm. The darkness fell away to reveal the source of the skittering as thousands upon thousands of small centipedes scuttled over each other like a sea of moving legs.

There was little to see of the larger ones as they absconded into the shadows and only the last set of vestigial legs the length and size of human legs remained before also vanishing.

"Run," Simantiar advised as the two ran across the sea of centipedes, the sound of their skittering still echoing against the cavern walls. Simantiar felt an itch that stretched across his entire body, a cold shiver that ran down his spine at the thought of even one centipede having found an opening to crawl inside.

The ball dimmed.

He shook the thought from his head. He needed to concentrate.

The two kicked away mounds of piling centipedes and rushed through.

Simantiar turned to make sure Usellyes was keeping up, as his friend lowered himself to the ground for a moment and held an opened container. He scooped up several of the tiny little creatures and closed the lid. A shrill cry escaped the annals of the cavern.

"What are you doing?" Simantiar demanded.

"This is what I came for!" Usellyes objected as he pocketed the container.

They continued to run, the winding paths giving no sign of exit until a soft shine of light revealed itself reflecting its silver glow against a rocky wall.

"There!" Simantiar cheered, hope arising in him once more.

"I lost my arm ring!" Usellyes stated as if he suddenly remembered.

"No, you didn't." Simantiar reached into his bag and removed one of the serpents coiled into a circle and biting its tail.

Thousands of heavy legs thudded against the cavern floor before Simantiar felt the heavy body clash against him and send him and Usellyes hurtling to the floor. The sound of bronze shattering momentarily outrang the skittering of insect feet.

The sea of centipedes had divided, allowing the two to land on solid ground. Contemplative chitters and skitters observed them as they groaned. Simantiar looked up to see the serpent arm ring shattered in half with bronze pieces strewn all about as his ball of light flickered and then darkened.

"Get up…" Simantiar stated.

Simantiar could hear Usellyes try to rise and gather his bearings, but seemed to fare as little as Simantiar did.

"Simantiar…" Usellyes sounded as if he were weeping.

"Please, do your thing," the man sounded desperate.

It dawned on Simantiar that Usellyes was probably too shaken, too scared to conjure any spells.

"Please, you're Simantiar, capable of casting spells that even the most elite struggle with. Please, you have to save me."

The pleading desperation in his friend's voice wounded Simantiar.

A change in the air, and Simantiar pounced to his feet and stretched his arms out at exactly the moment when one of the monstrous centipedes pounced upon them only to be recoiled by the barrier that sparked blue with the collision.

A second centipede.

Then a third.

They pounced and lunged with their large insidious mandibles as venom dripped from their pincers.

The momentary sparks of light were like lightning strikes, illuminating the terrified and pallid expression of Usellyes, frozen still on his rear.

Simantiar couldn't move—his concentration frayed, his mind frenzied and straining with the fear that fuelled him.

With a sudden act of desperation, Simantiar stretched out a hand with the second arm ring and whispered a command in between his lips as the serpent sprang to life and shot out at Usellyes, coiling his arm and biting him before suddenly being torn from where he lay. He screamed, a sudden shocked cry as Usellyes was yanked through the air, traveling farther and farther towards the cavern entrance and out into the forest.

The creatures did not relent, having eyes only for Simantiar as they pounced and lunged with unbridled fury.

They tested the barrier, moving along its fringes and knocking their weight again and again to find where best they might find an opening. The creatures were intelligent.

A centipede to Simantiar's rear knocked against the barrier, and it gave way slightly before repelling them. It froze for a moment, chittering as it swayed upright like a serpent waiting to strike. Its pincers chattered and its legs rippled.

The others seemed to understand the motion as they too rose and mimicked the behaviour.

Are they communicating? Simantiar wondered. His thought absconded the moment another beast clashed into the barrier.

A second one worked its way to Simantiar's rear and the two doubled the force of their impact on the barrier. Simantiar winced, sweat dripping from his brow and forming puddles at his feet.

Another pound and it sounded like the cracking of stone.

I hope Usellyes got away in time.

The barrier gave way, the sound like breaking thunder, and the two centipedes flew straight for Simantiar as a gust of wind lifted him off his feet and sent him reeling into a backflip. A simple lift of his fingers coalesced the puddle of sweat into an icicle that shot straight through the beast's head and it let loose an inhuman shrill cry of pain.

The first of the monsters writhed in pain as Simantiar landed on the back of the second. He took a moment to whisper words into his hands before spreading them wide open and clapping his cupped palms onto the centipede's head.

The sound thundered through the cavern halls and caused loose rubble to rain from above, the resulting force sending the sea of centipedes back like rising waves as the mounted centipede's exoskeleton shattered and its head turned to mush from the vacumous force of the clap.

Stalactites shook free from the ceiling and upon their descent, Simantiar redirected their paths so that they embedded themselves on the floor in front of him and created a traversable path free of centipedes.

He leapt from one to the next as the feverous and enraged sounds of the last remaining centipede sent shivers down to Simantiar's bones.

The beast slithered after him, chasing Simantiar down as a final gust of wind absconded him the same way it tore Usellyes out earlier.

The way was open, the first of the moss-encrusted trees draped with manes of vine revealed themselves as Simantiar shot out like a spear striking true.

Centipedes arose with terrifying coordination, forming into a wall that blocked out the exit.

Simantiar braced his arms before him and with a desperate cry rammed through the centipede wall and into freedom. With frantic fear he scampered to his feet and tore off whatever centipedes crawled on him. Reaching around to his back to see what remained.

His mind was shattered, his concentration gone.

The last giant centipede came like a vile obsidian tongue unfurling from within the abyssal maw as it reeled up till it was a meter tall, then two. It loomed over Simantiar until its very legs rippled and its pincers chittered in anticipation.

Simantiar clambered back, his hand reaching to grab the tree for support as his eyes closed for what he believed was the final time.

The strike never came, but rather he heard the sound of a pained cry and the taut stretching of vines and ruffling of foliage.

Simantiar opened his eyes to find the tree he leaned against had reached down and constrained the centipede, lifting it from the floor and entangling it with ropes of vine. The beast screeched, an equal mix of desperation and anger. Soon enough, the sounds turned into a muffled struggle underneath the tightened vines, and then after, there was no sound or movement at all, just a massive coiled and bundled cocoon of jungle greens.

A minute had passed, then two. The wraps unfurled and a limp and unmoving body fell to the forest floor. The creature was truly massive.

It was over. He lived. And hopefully Usellyes lived too. Suddenly the mage vomited out whatever it was that he ate that morning to the floor. He gasped, frantic. He felt cold despite the humid air that clung to his skin. The sound of the chittering could still be heard from within the caverns.

He needed to get out of there as quickly as possible.

Simantiar struggled to his feet and roamed the jungle trees, trying to get anywhere as long as it was away from what will be filling his nightmares for the weeks to come.

Simantiar dropped behind a tree and rested. His legs ached, his mouth was dry, and he could still taste the acidic contents of his vomit. His arms lay splayed before him as he breathed haggard breaths.

Suddenly, he looked up to the tree that he rested on. How did it save him? Did he use magic in a moment of desperation? That isn't how it ever worked…

He stared up and though the trees stayed unmoving, Simantiar couldn't help but feel that they observed him.

"How am I going to get back home?" Simantiar wondered.

He looked down to his palms. There was teleportation magic…but he had never used it before. At least, not long distances. Only within certain limits. The farther away it was, the harder the travel seemed to be.

"What do I have to lose?" Simantiar wondered.

With his mind frayed and still in shock, Simantiar crossed his legs and concentrated.

He remembered the walls of the academy. The garden. The library with its floating books and endless dimensional stairways. The practise ranges filled with animated dummies and the alchemy lab that was a chemist's wet dream, or the botany hall with its selection of herbs.

Simantiar focused. The slight scent of polished walls undercut whenever he passed by the alchemist lab. That one spot where the sun would shine through a window set upon a stairway for thirty minutes before moving on every morning.

The corner he always knew to find Usellyes.

The cute new lunchboxes that Emilie would pack. The way Zaros and Moran joked to one another and played portal goals, or the questions that Noima had and would ask Simantiar about rather than Usellyes, or that knock on Simantiar's door which came as sure as the rising sun.

He felt it. It was there. In his mind's eye. He suddenly felt a warmth. He was so far away from the humid jungle.

Actually, it really did smell like a freshly baked loaf of bread. Was that Ciro's perfume? She only ever wore it when she was in the mood. The moss-covered floor felt surprisingly hard.

Simantiar opened his eyes. He was back at the academy meditating in the middle of the hall as students wandered to and fro, all of them staring with beguiled and curious eyes, murmuring about what a horrid stench suddenly filled the hall.

Simantiar rose to his feet and brushed what dirt he could off himself before sprinting down the halls. He stuck out sorely, as the others walked with properly untarnished robes, books being carried in folded arms.

Simantiar ran across the open air arch bridge made of stone to his dorm. Surely the others were still at the garden finding their animal of choice while Simantiar blurred past the veined white marble halls and into his room.

The door shut behind him and Simantiar found his heavy laboured breaths blurring his vision—he was hyperventilating. His heart pounded in his ears, and his fingers trembled uncontrollably, fear granting fervor to wide eyes that looked to every corner which cast shadows.

"You're okay," Simantiar reassured himself over and over. The cluttered mess that was his room was reminiscent of the jungle he had left behind. Scattered clumps of branched oak as an arcane conductor, dull crystals held a three-day-old mug, bedsheets were strewn over an unmade bed, two stacks of dirty plates, and unorganized class notes left in some semblance of something Simantiar tried to call a filing system.

Chapter 18

A scream, a roar. Something filled with the purest of emotions broke into Simantiar's memories, like a faraway echo of a time in the future, as he returned to the present.

"What is it?" the guardian of the forest, Cernunnos, asked.

"George," Simantiar spoke the word as if remembering a long-forgotten friend. It wasn't that Simantiar had forgotten about Kendrith and George and the situation they were in, but having been taken deep into the past and the most hidden reserves of his memories caused him to be lost in forgotten times.

"I must go," Simantiar said.

"But your memories aren't fully restored yet, and nor are your powers."

"Doesn't matter, George needs me."

The guardian of the forest let out a contemplative hum before finally nodding. "Very well, you should have found that a great portion of your powers have returned with your memory, but use them sparingly. It is at this point as much your power, as it is your life force."

Simantiar nodded before standing on his branched feet—it was true. He could feel how his touch upon the universe had strengthened, the same feeling of bending reality coming back to him.

Though before, erecting his body of wood and branches and soil proved a challenge, he now found it as simple as slipping on a glove. Even without a magical circle, branches and leaves and twigs all gathered to him, piece by piece, erecting an even taller body of wood until Simantiar's skull was placed on the shoulders of wood and twigs. He felt the distant touch of a tree that had saved his life, and then he felt the interconnected touch of nature altogether as his lips cast the incantations, but primarily he sought the forest for help as Cernunnos had shown him.

"Thank you," Simantiar said, "for everything."

Cernunnos nodded to his old friend as Simantiar turned to a run.

It didn't take long for Simantiar to stop and come running back to the ancient being.

"How do I find them?"

Cernunnos was stunned for a moment, but only chuckled with a shake of his head. "You never change, old friend." The being placed a wooden thumb to Simantiar's bony forehead as the world faded away from the mage for a second, before coming back as everything. The trees, the birds, the worms within the soil. The coursing wind and the running streams—all of it bound by a single endless and thin thread.

And there it was, through the eyes of the forest Simantiar could feel the touch of Kendrith and George, and most alarmingly, the touch of hundreds of little creatures which began to swarm in from all sides.

Cernunnos released his touch, and Simantiar felt the world go distant again, his sight barred and his reach shortened.

"Go, old friend. And remember, nature has bestowed its touch upon you. You are as one with the world as I am. Its tether may be weak, but it is there. Find it. Let it be your eyes."

Simantiar was grateful to his friend, one he had not remembered in a long time and still did not remember. But in spite all of that, he was happy to have met him again.

"Keep moving!" Kendrith barked, but George moved towards the slowly creeping Hobbers, their tongues writhing in the air as their vile gullets opened wide to cry their sickening sounds.

"George!"

The boy bent over, picking up as many of the torn pages as he could and trying to put them together.

"For crying out loud!" Kendrith knew that he could never convince George to abandon the book, nor would he ask him to. If he wanted to the boy to hurry up, he needed to help.

Kendrith leapt in front of George, separating the shoulder of one Hobber that dared venture too close.

The spell that George had wafted over the Hobbers was broken, fear born out of their own imagination, and as the fog lifted, it showed that the mirage of a lion was nothing more than the shadow of a small kitten mourning over a torn book.

"Hurry up!" Kendrith pushed as he felled another Hobber. He couldn't keep going on for much longer, and it wouldn't take long till the swarm overwhelmed them like a tide.

George frantically salvaged as much as he could, stuffing torn pages back into a halved cover.

"George!"

Finally George turned with the pages pressed tight against his chest, as Kendrith followed suit and fled with him.

"Keep moving," Kendrith panted through gasping lungs and aching legs.

A Hobber leapt from the trees and fell limp to the ground at Kendrith's swing.

"Where do we go?" George asked, back to his old self save the splatters of blood like some crude and macabre art display with poor taste.

"Just keep going," Kendrith said, yet none of his words were spoken with much of a plan or confidence.

As the two ran, panicked and exhausted, trial after trial having worn them down till only the need to live kept pushing them. Yet as the swarm of Hobbers grew in number, creeping out of their holes, the idea of surviving seemed to become more and more unrealistic.

As George turned around to observe the growing numbers, his foot broke through the wet soil, careening him over the side of an incline.

"George!" Kendrith barked, and George could only scream as he rolled down the side.

The mercenary leapt after him and watched as George's roll was broken by a large standing stone which impeded his retreat.

Kendrith surfed down the decline and turned his back to George defensively. "Whatever happens, stay behind me," Kendrith said, lifting the blade as the horde of Hobbers swarmed together, a deluge of vile swamp creatures with spears at the ready with tongues hanging hungrily.

The first of the Hobbers raced towards Kendrith and so the first of their blood was spilled. With the floodgates opened, Hobber after Hobber raced for Kendrith with momentum and numbers as they spilled down the wet slope. Kendrith's usual grace now forsaken, each move was harsh and rustic, it was only desperation and the promise of death that lent him strength.

"What the—" Kendrith began.

Hobber after Hobber were flung to the sides, screaming with comical surprise as they soared in numbers through the air. A sudden heaping mass of branches, foliage, and other forestry rose like a mound of compost till it just kept rising and rising into a giant, limbed heap.

Kendrith stopped his killing, the Hobbers ceased their assault, and all of them turned to stare at the being that entered the fray.

"Kendrith, what is that?"

"I...I don't know; I've never seen a creature like that before."

All they could see was a headless giant made of forestry. Wood upon wood stacked upon itself to create towering trunk-legs, long and bending arms made of twisting vines and roots and trees that swatted the Hobbers like nuisance pests. Great mound pauldrons of moss and earth panzered the being's shoulders, coiling vines criss-crossed the inner skeleton of the titan, a great, broadly fashioned chest and a stout body gave it a wide berth as it got to work sweeping the Hobbers as dirt crumbled from it like sand in an hourglass.

It was only when the towering giant stepped forward to give a clear view of its visage that Kendrith saw the familiar thing sitting atop its torso of roots and foliage.

"Is that..." Kendrith began.

George simply laughed, in spite of all that just transpired, in spite of his book being torn to shreds, the bard let loose an ecstatic cheer.

"It's Simantiar!" he called out.

"Well, I'll be damned," Kendrith said, watching the howling giant controlled by a small skull cleave through the Hobbers like wheat.

"I am Simantiar! Destroyer of worlds!" Simantiar boomed, ostensibly lost in the rush of it all as he rolled on through the disgusting little beings.

"Fear me!" he demanded with a low, villainous laugh as what remained of the Hobbers fell back and retreated with phlegmed, disgusting gurgles voicing their reluctance.

When Simantiar neared Kendrith and George, he knelt down on creaking wooden knees that stretched the ligaments of vines and great hands of four-fingered wood rested on his knees. Simantiar easily stood at four times Kendrith's own height and five times as wide.

"I never thought I would say this, but damn it is good to see you again," Kendrith mused.

"Right back at ya," Simantiar returned, seemingly happy to have found the two unharmed.

A bird suddenly flew from the canopy of trees with a streak of red at its skull, black wings tucked into their fold, and a lightly splotched brown underbelly.

"Oh, may I introduce you to Pecky, my new companion during my time in the woods."

Kendrith and George waved gingerly.

"Right, let's get to it," Simantiar declared as his body suddenly started to fall apart, twigs and leaves sliding from his giant body as an oversize chunk of wood that was his leg toppled to the floor with a sudden quake. Kendrith and George fell back a short distance as more and more parts fell to the floor.

Soon, the rest finally toppled and collapsed all at once except for Simantiar himself who landed in Kendrith's hands.

"O', fair knight! How noble of thou to catch me during mine own plummet. I believeth it be now owed a kiss upon my pale thin lips," Simantiar professed, his voice like a parodied damsel in distress— incredibly high-pitched and theatrical as his skeletal teeth chomped and smooching noises came from him.

Kendrith didn't hesitate for a second as he playfully took Simantiar and kissed him on cold rough lips. When human and skeletal lips parted, they both spat out into the dirt.

"I was kidding! I didn't expect you to actually—"

Kendrith cut him off with a big grin. "So, you can grow an entire giant body, but insist on using me as your personal steed?" Kendrith joked.

"Hey, I just saved you from an army of those disgusting things and I'm all tuckered out!"

Kendrith chuckled. "As you wish, majesty." Pecky also found a spot on Kendrith's shoulder, gratified by a defeated sigh of submission.

"Majesty, aye? I could get used to that. Just no more kissing. You are wayyyy too young for me. I don't know how things are done in this era, but where I come from, that kind of thing is frowned upon."

Simantiar leaned towards George. "Be careful of this one." The hushed whisper was anything but quiet.

They laughed, a sound that Kendrith only then realised was something he had missed.

Simantiar turned to George, and before he could say anything his eyes went to the state of the book within the boy's arms. George must have noticed, for he squeezed the torn thing even tighter.

They were silent for a moment until Simantiar finally spoke. "I might be able to fix it."

George's eyes widened and his lips parted in surprise.

"I mean it when I say 'try'—can't promise that I will succeed."

George simply nodded with a smile, that little bit of hope that Simantiar offered was more than enough it seemed as George smiled.

"It's good to see you again, kid."

"You too."

And so, after scavenging the rest of the torn pages, now darkened and damp with mud, the rest of their journey continued without interruptions.

A trip through the forest that should have taken up to a week ended up taking far longer.

Simantiar shared the story of the ancient guardian of the forest he had met, and the fact that he had remembered much of his past from when he still walked as a human.

Kendrith simply shared the fact that he relived his own past, but spoke nothing more of it.

George shared nothing of his experiences, and nobody dared ask. There were some things better left forgotten within the Forest of the Dead and Kendrith thought better than to ask.

Pecky on the other hand chirped some foolish nonsense to all four corners of Kendrith's shoulder that no one understood.

Still, Simantiar humoured him. "Really, Pecky? What happened next?" he would ask.

Within the next few days as the rest of their journey progressed without circumstance, the trio finally broke through the last of the trees to glimpse the city of Haven—a glorious town with elaborate homes peeking out from the surrounding walls that closed them in; a single opened portcullis welcomed them in the early light of morning.

"Finally," Kendrith said, "we're home."

Chapter 19

The town of Haven was unlike anything that George had ever seen. Though he could tell it was not the biggest of cities, it certainly wasn't small either, and it certainly bustled with riches.

The buildings themselves were clustered with stone walkways, and steam rose from wafting kilns. The lingering scent of earthy bread with the sweetness of raisins made him salivate and his mouth watered. Having eaten cooked frog for the past week he understood the displeased growl of his stomach.

In the distance the sound of chickens could faintly be heard beneath the hubbub of conversations clashing into a mesh of indecipherable clucks, the sound of working hammers cutting through laughter and greetings, and merchants selling produce.

All the houses were built with the finest craftsmanship. There didn't seem to be many people, but those who were present had the luxury of a comfortable life. Homes were plated with crafted designs that bracketed glass-paned windows and hung from rooftops with a gleam of silver. George wondered if the filigree markings of silver were not just a fashion statement, but also a way to protect them from darker apparitions.

George hugged his book even more tightly, but more out of sheer awe than reservations. He had seen great structures and pyramids and wandered cities before, but the level of concentrated craftsmanship and identity that struck him was new. A chirp from his shoulder seemed to share his opinion as Pecky chirped and bounced all over with fluttering wings, taking in the view.

In a bittersweet moment of sorrow and nostalgia, he wished his sister, Lily, could have been there to see it with him—she would have loved it.

George took note of the clustered homes. The closer they ventured into the centre of the city the more apparent the divide of comfort became, from languorous to downright absurd.

Mainly four establishments were worthy of note in George's eyes towards the centre which he had already noticed as the tallest structures peaking from outside the walls.

"What is that house over there at the end?" George asked in regard to the most luxurious and sizable building; it was built like a palace. Two roads met just before that final building and merged into a circular spot with a beautiful fountain taking up most of the space. The circular stone base told the tale of a winged hero battling hordes of monsters. Right behind the fountain was a gate, and behind that a massive garden filled with topiary animals.

"The home of the duke. He is in charge of the town."

"That one?" George pointed to another building.

Kendrith smiled. "That used to be my school—it is an academy."

George looked up to Kendrith for a second, and found it hard to imagine that such a haggard and rough individual could have ever been in a classroom, let alone a school environment.

George then turned to the third establishment, and from the sound of steel clashing against steel and raucous orders, he deduced what it must be. "Is that the hunter's guild?"

Kendrith nodded. "The Wings of Vrania."

"And that one?" George pointed.

Kendrith seemed to hesitate for a moment. George turned and saw the moment of doubt in Kendrith's eyes betray him, a reluctance to speak.

"The house of a merchant. He deals in the exchange of rare magical artifacts, purchases new ones, and gives old ones for a price to neighbouring kingdoms as a dignitary. You can consider him a messenger of notable affairs for treaty arrangements."

"Magical artifacts?" George's eyes widened.

"Calm down," Kendrith said. "Most magical artifacts are useless unless in the hands of someone who can cast magic, and even those that aren't end up being extremely rare and never used. They are a status symbol of notability. Anyone who wishes to form a treaty or rises to a position of worth is bestowed such an item."

George left it at that, not wishing to pry further. "And where is your home?"

"We passed it."

"So, where are we going?"

"I first have business at the guild."

George placed a hand to his bag to feel the familiar shape of a skull. Unlike before, Simantiar now sat perfectly still inside.

George and Kendrith waltzed through the front gate of the guild into the courtyard. All around them, people were exchanging blows with practise swords, yet none of their voracity seemed to have dulled due to the constant shouting of their trainers. The harsh and short demands were only outdone by the clash of steel and strained roars.

At the centre of the courtyard was an statue of an erect mountainous man, just the image alone expelled an aura of brute strength and fortitude. It depicted a bearded figure with hulking muscles, an axe held strong before him as if to challenge those who wished to rise against him, be they beast or man.

"Who is that?" George asked.

"Haggen Brosnorth: the strongest hunter this guild has ever had...and my grandfather."

George was stunned, the figure truly seemed like a force to be reckoned with.

"Can I meet him?"

"Sure. At his grave," Kendrith said as he continued their advance.

George stuttered, wondering if he should apologise. Instead, he thought it wiser to keep walking.

As the two continued into the building, George was blown away. The ceiling of the foyer reached three storeys high, and each side of the entrance had wooden carved mannequins outfitted with glistening armour and weapons which presumably belonged to notable figures.

From each side of the foyer, doors opened and people went about their tasks, from cooks to smartly dressed figures and all the way to cleaners.

"Incredible," George said. Pecky, however, seemed more overwhelmed by the sudden cacophony.

"You haven't seen the half of it."

The two climbed the stairs at the end of the foyer which split into the left and right balustraded walkways.

George suddenly felt very small as people passed by, trying to make himself a little smaller in the hope that he wouldn't draw any unwanted attention.

"We're here," said Kendrith, knocking.

"Come in," said a voice on the other side.

As Kendrith went to open the door, he paused. "Wait here."

"But why?"

"Just trust me," Kendrith said, moving into the room before George had a chance to argue.

George waited for close to an hour, the occasional elated sentence audible through the crafted wood of the door. It was hard to tell if the exchange was agreeable at times or telling of a heated debate, yet George waited patiently until the toll of their travels and his empty stomach finally washed over him and his eyes fell heavy.

"Hey, George, wake up."

George awoke in a daze, forgetting for a moment where he was.

"It's okay, it's just me," Kendrith said with his head lowered to the seated boy, a hand on George's shoulder.

"Let's go."

George and Kendrith finally left, walking under the glow of a setting sun to Kendrith's home.

"That's your home?" George asked. It wasn't a particularly amazing home when compared to the dozens of others George had admired, but it wasn't small either. It showed modest yet true craftsmanship and if nothing else, it had a homey and quaint appearance to it which George came to appreciate.

When they entered, the place seemed almost abandoned. It wasn't remarkably tidy, but still seemed somewhat organised.

"Though this is where I live, we don't usually stay here for long before the next quest."

"We?" George prodded.

"I don't own this place alone. Perhaps you will meet her—she should have returned now as well."

George didn't inquire further, He was sure to find out in time.

Kendrith lit a few candles to chase away the darkness; although the place was dusty, it seemed welcoming all the same to George.

"Could someone *please* get me out of here?" George suddenly remembered Simantiar stowed away in his bag, and reached inside to take the old wizard out.

"Sorry," George said.

"You turn into a giant tree to save the life of friends and this is how they repay you," said a bitter Simantiar, but George just smiled, it was as if things had returned to normal.

Kendrith seemed to hesitate for a moment. "George, I would like to rediscuss the payment that I have been owed."

George nodded in understanding. He understood how much of a burden the escort mission ended up being. It was right to compensate Kendrith for the efforts.

As George reached into his pouch Kendrith raised a hand. "I don't want coinage."

Kendrith pulled out a seat and motioned for George to join him. George frowned, not understanding what was going on as he took his seat and placed Simantiar on the table, Pecky now jumping onto Simantiar and giving him a curious peck.

"Instead of gold, I would like to ask for five of Simantiar's bones."

George looked to Simantiar. It was clear that they were, in the end, his bones, and to make such a trade without asking first seemed wrong.

"You already tossed some away as if they were dog food to those husks so please, by all means, go for it."

George hesitated.

"Really, it's okay," Simantiar said, more sincere this time. "Not like I will be needing them."

George reached into his bag and handed over five bones as Kendrith pocketed four and gave one back.

When George seemed puzzled Kendrith just smiled. "I usually expect to have to haggle with the customer and wanted to negotiate for only three. Since you willingly gave me five, I will return one back to you." Kendrith winked.

"Gee, what a gentleman," Simantiar mocked.

"What did you talk about at the guild?" George finally asked.

Kendrith had his back turned to the boy as he cleared the tables and folded articles.

"I had to report on the trip, and also the fact that I have been injured and won't be able to go out on a mission until I have healed."

George's eyes widened. "What about my quest?" he asked.

"That's the other thing I asked about. I already found another person to take you up the route you need to go. It won't be cheap, but from what I can tell, money won't be an issue for you."

George bit his lip. Did the dangers they braved really mean so little to Kendrith? Yet he could not argue—the deal was that Kendrith only carry him through the forest, nothing more.

As if sensing George's frustration, Kendrith's shoulders sagged, and he turned to the boy.

"You will be far safer in the hands of a licenced veteran. Plus, with me injured, I am no good up there."

George lowered his gaze and nodded reluctantly.

"It will be in a week's time so you have time to gain your strength back as well. You may stay with me until then."

"Thank you," George said. He felt as if it had just become too formal, as if they had become strangers again and hadn't just survived an entire ordeal that fashioned a bond. George suddenly felt very, very foolish. He guessed with the payment made and the contract sealed everything was already done and handled.

"And so our deal is done," Kendrith said. It was silent for a long time until the door to the home opened once more and a hooded figure stepped in.

The woman had piercing blue eyes with a slim face, brunette hair, and a scar that ran down the side of her cheek.

"Ah." Kendrith walked over to the woman and wrapped an arm around her. "This is my beloved, Kristen." Kristen removed the hood to reveal a warming and sharp-featured face with long and thin features.

Despite her scar, there was a modest beauty to the woman as she smiled with perfect, yet charmingly small teeth.

"I'm gone for a month and you are already bringing home strays?" she mused with a chuckle and kissed Kendrith with some difficulty through curled and laughing lips.

Kendrith seemed to have been infected by the energy for he laughed too; it was a warm thing that George had not seen before.

"Kristen, this is George. He was my charge through the forest, and he will be staying with us for a couple of days."

"Perfect!" Kristen announced as she conjured a loaf of steaming bread and cuts of smoked ham and butter. "Food is always better when shared."

Kendrith gasped in playful surprise. "Did I tell you that I love you?" he joked.

Kristen pretended to ponder the thought. "Once or twice." Another kiss.

George's stomach growled at the sight.

"My god, is he cute!" George looked up to find Kristen leaning over and ruffling his hair.

With an empty stomach and little reason for merriment George could do little to keep away his annoyance as he brushed aside Kristen's hand and rose to his feet. "I am not a damn child, and I don't need you to pity me." George stormed out of the house and slammed the door behind him.

Kendrith could only watch as George left. Part of him wanted to follow and see what suddenly irked him so. Yet the other part made him plant his feet and give George some distance.

"Was it something I said?" Kristen asked.

"I doubt it," said an equally confused Simantiar. Pecky gave a chirp as if in agreement.

"What in the name of Vrania?" Kristen leapt backwards against the wall. "The...the skull. It talked."

"I have a name—are all people these days so rude?" Simantiar jested.

"Kristen, honey. I can explain."

"This ought to be good." Kristen managed to barely collect herself.

Chapter 20

George wandered through the town, eventually coming to an inn. Perhaps it was the cheering or echo of occasional laughter that drew him in or the familiar scent of lingering ale. Regardless, he now stood under the hanging wooden sign creaking on rusted hinges that read Lost Dreams with a fading trail of dust above the name.

George chuckled, *What a sappy name for an inn.* Though it did the trick, George stepped inside, for the temptation of something was better than the promise of nothing.

There weren't many in the bar—few well-dressed men who seemed to retire after a long day's work, other burly men with dirtied sleeves pulled to their elbows and foam adding to already filled beards, with the occasional woman who though may have lacked in size, still matched the energy of their colleagues. They were all nestled into their own clusters, creating little islands of conversation and laughter.

George avoided them, thinking that even if he could find a way into their circle that all he would do was bring rain to their islands. So, he sat at the bar, hoping that their laughter would infect him instead.

"What will it be?" asked the barkeep leaning against the table and his affable smile challenged George's sour mood.

"Ale would be great."

The man nodded and set to work. George liked the bartender—he wasn't particularly friendly to the point where one would doubt his intentions nor was he particularly aggressive as if George had insulted his mother in a distant past. To which George always preferred the latter.

Too often did fake smiles hide vile intentions for him that he preferred at least to know who to keep away from.

"You must be new to town." The voice belonged to a colossal man who took a seat of his own; George couldn't help but feel sorry for the groaning stool that strained to hold his neighbour.

Eying the man up and down, George tensed—the last time he was in a bar and approached someone he ended up being chased across the Forest of the Dead, and this giant seemed like the last three built into one.

It took all he could muster to not recoil; the domineering figure was like a rather gregarious and well-spoken bull. George nodded gingerly at the previous statement.

"Knew it!" The man bellowed a bemused chuckle as he slapped George across the back, causing him to shoot out the contents of his drink and choke, his tankard spilling all over the bar.

"Oh, I'm so sorry," the large man's apology was meek in contrast to his boisterous demeanour, but also sincere as he pat George down with ginormous fingers while the taste of bitter ale burnt the back of George's throat and dripped from his nostrils.

George waved him away in between coughs and brushed himself down. "It's all right," George wheezed.

"Brokk, I'd like to replace this young man's drink and also pay his share."

The barkeep nodded, not even trying to hide his bemused smile at the comical display.

"And what will you hav—"

"Soran's the name." The giant introduced himself with a smile as jovial as his own stature and an outstretched hand that George took hesitantly— the man's palm was surprisingly soft and moisturized.

Soran turned to Brokk. "Ah yes, sorry for cutting you off. I would love some of that whisky of yours."

Brokk nodded and turned to the counter.

"What may I call you, newcomer?" A toothy grin revealed pearl-white teeth underneath a well-cared-for moustache.

"George." The handshake was firm; the man could probably break every bone in George's hand with a tight squeeze, but Soran displayed confident restraint.

"I knew you weren't from around here," Soran said with a wide grin as if relishing victory in a game that George wasn't even playing.

"It isn't a small town, but there isn't much traffic. And the traffic that does take place is for business practises or diplomatic missions. And you don't seem to be the type."

"Why?" George challenged as a fresh tankard was placed in front of him.

Soran seemed taken aback for a moment. "Partially because you seem too young," he admitted. "But you also don't seem to be dressed the part."

George didn't respond, simply draining down the bitter ale as the foam moustached his upper lip.

"Got some despair to drown out?" It was Brokk that placed the query, his smile reassuring and tempered in comparison to that of Soran's.

"Brokk, a man's business is his own. It is rude to pry."

George took a moment to more clearly take in the giant. Just like with Brokk, George couldn't quite manage to dislike Soran and felt his own tension ease.

Soran was boisterous, but also genuine. Large brown eyes stared out as if to catch as much wonder and joy they could possibly witness, His groomed and slicked-back golden hair smelt of berries, or perhaps the scent was coming from an incredibly well-fashioned and curled moustache including unpocked and flawless skin. His arms and chest stretched out the white shirt he wore and the pantaloons were so brown they were akin to darkened wood straining at the sheer size of Soran's thighs. The man seemed simultaneously overwhelming and regal all at once.

"Are you going to tell me that I am too young to be gloomy?" George challenged.

"Not at all. My pops always told me that men need to process their feelings. That is the only way that wounds heal. So please, by all means, drain the ale; cry, rage, do something you will regret. If that will make you wake up tomorrow with regret instead of lament then all the better," Brokk stated.

George suddenly looked to Brokk, glad that he wasn't being belittled…it was refreshing. "You really think so?"

"I would listen to Brokk. My mentor would come here all the time when needing to vent, many do—much wisdom to be found with Brokk." Soran turned to Brokk with a shared smile. "And don't forget Kendrith."

Brokk chuckled. "Oh, don't remind me."

George's ears stood up at the mention of Kendrith. Trying his best to remain inconspicuous, George cupped his tankard and gave his best attempt at pretending he had never heard of him before.

"I have this regular at my bar," Brokk began, explaining to George, "Kendrith is his name. Knew him from when he was wee little." The barkeep raised a horizontal palm as he lowered it to the ground, earning a smile from George. George was grateful Brokk didn't gloat the way others did when they cheered him up.

"He would visit with his grandfather, Haggen Brosnorth. Little did Kendrith know that his father would inquire about his health. If he is still in one piece. Too much pride in stubborn men, I tell you." A knowing glance was shared with Soran. "Anyway. That boy lost much in his life. A loving and strong mother—my, what a striking beauty she was. Not because she was born with rosy cheeks or plump lips, but because that woman would *own* the room she entered. Mona Brosnorth she was called. And then years after his grandfather. Two legends gone." The barkeep shook his head regretfully with pursed lips that said "It's a damn shame."

Soran joined in at the remark. "Their time came far too soon."

George found that he was leaning in listening intently. He felt a strange sense of comfort towards Soran and Brokk as they recounted Kendrith's youth.

"And Kendrith—" George caught himself, noticing that the keep was pretty sharp of mind. "I mean, this man. He was also young and foolish?"

"Foolish? He was brazen. Stubborn. Wouldn't stop asking his grandfather to teach him, and then Haggen would come to me and complain all the time. It was infuriating!" There was a surge in the man's inflections, more so than before—a natural storyteller and it seemed as if Brokk stepped his act up a notch when George showed to know Kendrith. George didn't mind however. It helped learning about Kendrith's past.

"He would be the centre of town gossip whenever something went wrong because the kid was acting out." Brokk paused for a moment contemplatively.

"Kendrith knew what it was like to lose someone, so every relationship since has been hard to make." George wondered if the words were meant for him…or if the barkeep just talked in reminiscence, peering through the bottom of a glass he was polishing as if it were a looking glass to a distant past.

George turned to the room and saw a lute leaning against a chair in the corner. "Would you mind if I…" he trailed off.

"Please. Help yourself. A free round of ale if it is something worthwhile too."

George strode over to the seat and grabbed the lute, fingers drifting familiarly over strings as they began to pluck by themselves, remembering the motions.

The melody was one of healing, a soft and hurt tune, but familiar in its universality. The men and women around the bar slowly faded out of their conversations as their heads turned and they found themselves part of George's new land.

George tried to ignore Soran who stuck out like a sore thumb at the bar, a private conversation between him and Brokk taking place. Was he just imagining it? Or was Soran's look one of curious appraisal that lingered on George.

"Ow," Kendrith winced at the sudden tug.

"Stop being such a baby. And to think you are related to Haggen Brosnorth," said Kristen as she tightened the bandage around Kendrith's healing shoulder.

"Not just related, he is my grandfather."

"A fact you still insist on making public knowledge." Kristen's remark sounded almost slightly annoyed.

"We talked about this—if people will come to know me, it will be for what I have accomplished, not who I am related to. But even so, I am proud of the one who trained me, and have no reason to hide that." Though even Kendrith couldn't deny the air of pretentiousness to his words.

Kendrith and Kristen sat silently within their room, just the soft glow of candles allowing Kristen to stitch his wound, apply ointments, and change the bandages.

"You really did a number on your shoulder."

"Well, it was a shame that the three bandits and the hollower never really gave me the time to treat it when I could."

"Maybe ask them nicely next time?" Kristen's head popped over Kendrith's shoulder, illuminated by the candles as she teased her love. They both laughed.

"I will keep that in mind."

"So, what's with the boy?" Kristen finally asked. It was the third time that she tried to bring up the subject, but it was the first time that Kendrith didn't avoid it.

He just sighed, wincing slightly at the movement. "I don't know. One second everything is going well and the next minute he just runs out of the house."

Kendrith and Simantiar had already explained what had taken place, all the way from the start. Kristen seemed to be in shock and found it hard to believe the absurdity of the tale. It was only after Simantiar performed his magical feats of lifting objects up or forming bodies out of discarded goods that Kristen started to believe it all.

"There are just some things you won't know till you talk to the boy," Kristen said.

"Talk to him? I just had the job of bringing him here safely, and I did that."

"Done."

"Yeah, done," Kendrith replied, thinking it was a question.

"No, I mean I am done with the stitches. You are definitely not done with George." Kristen began wrapping the wound. "You both went through so much and it sounds like luck was a factor in it all. That kind of event bonds you. Maybe he is upset that none of that mattered to you."

Kendrith wondered for a while. "But I can't do anything about that. George has to keep going and I don't have the training or licence to travel north."

"I am not telling you what to do, just what is the case. I know this is going to eat away at you. So, if you want to fix it fast, at least talk to him."

Kendrith transitioned from a sigh into a wince. "Perhaps you're right."

"How much did you tell the guild?" Kristen asked after a moment's silence. Kendrith knew she was trying to distract him from the pain.

"Just what they needed to know."

"So, nothing."

Kendrith didn't deny it.

"Do you think Beynard knows you were keeping stuff from him?"

"That man has wits sharper than any knife—of course he knows. But he also knows that if I am hiding something, it is for good reason. Just looks at me with these eyes that say 'just don't bring it to the guild.'"

"Did he ask about the boy?"

"He did. I made up some story that his parents had passed and left behind a fortune. That he wanted to pass into the mountains."

"Did he buy it?"

"A kid with that much wealth to his name? Of course he didn't. I don't even think that is all the gold he is carrying around."

"Done," Kristen said again as she cut off the rest of the gauze. His arm was now wrapped in a sling. "Don't move too much or your stitches will open."

"Thank you."

Kristen never replied, only cleaned up the rest of her medical appliances.

"So, who did you find to take the boy?"

"Logan."

Kristen eyed Kendrith with disbelief.

"Can he even afford someone like Logan?"

"I told you, the child is stupidly rich."

"Where does the gold even come from?"

"Never asked. None of my business."

Kristen fell into Kendrith's arms as both allowed themselves to fall into the comfort of their bedding. Neither of the two blew out the candles quite yet.

They both fell silent for a while, as Kristen's fingers trailed along the scars on Kendrith's torso absent-mindedly, like feeling the rough edges of a map. "Tell me more about the skull."

"Simantiar? Apparently, he is an ancient wizard from forgotten times. Mother used to sing about him when I was a child. Of course there were different variations, folktales, but fabled legends as well." Kendrith paused. "I never would have thought him to be real."

Kendrith suddenly unfurled his fist to reveal the four bones tucked within, Kristen eyed the bones with equal measure concern as well as fascination.

"It's almost as if it were fate that brought you together, wasn't it? If what you say about his bones is true, you can finally retrieve that which your mother left you."

"You know I don't believe in that nonsense." Kendrith seemed almost insulted, and Kristen chuckled. She enjoyed teasing him.

"Then what about our meeting? Was it not fate?" she teased, pulling his gaze to her as she rest her head upon his bare chest, dangerously playfully biting on her lower lip.

"If I remember correctly, we tried to kill each other."

"Isn't that how love starts?"

Kendrith didn't reply as just as they were about to embrace in a passionate kiss, there was a knock at the front door.

Chapter 21

Between the rests he took from fixing George's book and everything else, Simantiar was given little time to sort through his fractured memories. That night he returned to the past life he no longer remembered, to the memory of a frightened and frayed mind.

The sound of crickets returned like a distant phantom of a sound.

Then a knock that made Simantiar leap from his place in his dorm room.

"Simantiar? Is that you?" said a voice from the other side. It was Mylor. "Simantiar, let me in."

Simantiar shuddered. No. He needed time.

"Simantiar." The doorknob rattled as someone tried to enter.

"Ahh!" Simantiar cried out, as his terrified fearful hands waved forward in a momentary clasp of lucidity as an air of magic blanketed the door and locked it tight with arcane magic.

"Simantiar! Open this door! What happened out there?"

"Please, leave me alone." Simantiar was shocked at the sound of his breaking voice. Had he ever been so chillingly terrified?

"Simantiar!" Mylor shouted, the evoking of the name: a command. But Simantiar couldn't move. His breathing was laden and heavy.

The rattling stopped. The voice vanished. Only the very alive echo of crickets filled Simantiar's insanity. The chitter of centipede legs skittering in his eardrum.

Time passed by. Simantiar had no way to tell how long.

Footsteps on the other side. A presence? The rattling of a key. The faint sound of broken magic like a deflated shimmer. The doorknob turned and the door opened to reveal the faces of onlookers staring down with anger and judgment towards Simantiar, a gaze that soon turned to concern at whatever it was that they saw.

"Simantiar." Mylor's voice turned incredibly caring as he rushed forward and draped his robes across Simantiar's body protectively. Usellyes had stood on the other end, a key in his hand, and something in his eyes that Simantiar couldn't quite place…was it disappointment? Anger? Disgust?

A simple wave of Mylor's hand and the door closed on its own to the sound of dissenting voices barred from seeing the usually affable and cherubic Simantiar at his greatest low, bereft of all his usual merriment.

Another moment later and a brief flash of darkness before Simantiar found himself in the comfort of Mylor's study.

He had never been there, usually only at his office, but his study was something else.

The momentary repose granted him a chance to appreciate the many wonders of the study.

A colour palate composed mostly of brown and some deep red presented itself, a circular panelled window behind his desk gave way to a clouded view below and a blue sky above that blended into the black starry space above.

Artifacts lay strewn about although Simantiar's study was brazen and without order, Mylor's study had a certain charm to the odds and ends like a toymaker's workshop.

Shining golden tools lay about unfurled maps, books of leather binding filled shelves that rose all along curved walls. The scent of earth cologne, polished wood, and dried leather hung in the air.

As Mylor walked through the maze of stacked books and dishevelled instruments, a glowing blue squirrel leapt from its burrow of makeshift clutter and onto the shoulder of Mylor.

Mylor returned with several tools cradled in his arms and got to work immediately.

He tugged, pulled, spread, and inserted a myriad of tools into every one of Simantiar's facial orifices. Even if Simantiar was able to object he doubted Mylor would comply.

A sudden light shone into Simantiar's eye from an instrument used and abandoned too quickly for Simantiar to place.

"You were in the jungle, weren't you?" Mylor queried, his hands working quickly with his tools and a grave urgency in his voice.

Simantiar nodded feebly.

A few more tests and objects were pressed against him.

A few more moments as if to confirm his suspicion. "Centipede?"

Simantiar started with wide eyes at Mylor.

Mylor nodded. "I thought so." His lips were a thin line.

The man rose to his full form and chanted a spell of old. Blue streaks of flowing ribbon went from one clawed hand to the other as Mylor brushed his tarp of magic over Simantiar and let it settle.

It glided slowly down, drifting over the confused student.

"This will hurt," Mylor's warning was barely given before the magic absorbed itself around Simantiar's arm. Pain shot through it.

"We're not done," Mylor informed him.

Suddenly the pain centred around his stomach and the blue aura travelled there. A sudden wriggling sensation spread through him that left Simantiar cold and malaise.

"Almost," Mylor said through gritted teeth.

The wriggling became clearer, the feeling of something just underneath his flesh. Simantiar cried out in agony.

Simantiar could hear the centipede chittering once more and realised it wasn't the cicada that he could hear.

The pain worked its way upon his chest and then his throat, finally into his eye as Simantiar screamed unlike ever before.

"Hold still!" Mylor ordered as he grunted and pulled.

The pain felt like a hot knife being inserted into Simantiar's eye and the last fringes of his mind seemed close to unravelling. But it was nothing compared to the sense of relief that Simantiar experienced once the vile creature was out like the expelling of contained pressure.

The thing writhed like a contorting whip, its many reddish legs striding back and forth, its pincers biting to seize any flesh which presented itself.

Simantiar grasped at his eye, breathing a sigh of relief to feel it still present.

His mind returned to its usual self, he felt...calm. Or as calm as one could be given the circumstances.

Mylor squeezed his fists as the meter-long centipede turned to ash.

The glowing blue squirrel lifted its double-tailed rear as if to pounce and sucked in the remains of the centipede, absorbing it into the rattling blue fluff of its tail.

A moment later when it all vanished, the cute creature sneezed a bit of the dust away and rattled its head.

"Good Stinky." Mylor gave the magical squirrel a treat that it nibbled in both of its tiny hands.

Simantiar panted, and the horror passed as his mind no longer felt as if it was on the verge of breaking. But he relaxed too soon. Mylor's gaze shifted to him and now that the cause for concern had fled, only murderous judgment awaited.

"You will tell me everything that happened." His tenor was now that of a disciplinarian.

Simantiar and Usellyes sat in front of the work desk in Mylor's office.

The headmaster hadn't said anything yet. He simply paced back and forth, occasionally granting the two mages contemplative glances as if considering his verdict.

He finally stopped and splayed his palms out on the table and stared at the two without a trace of humour or warmth.

As Usellyes was about to open his mouth, Simantiar cut him off. "It was all my fault—I wandered off and had stolen the key. I was irresponsible and overestimated my abilities, thinking I could find more curious beasts deeper in the biomes. Usellyes just happened to find the key when I dropped it and followed me in. He tried to save me."

Usellyes looked to Simantiar with restless eyes, though what worked itself behind that placid expression Simantiar could only guess.

Simantiar looked at his friend with stoic and confident resolve— Usellyes were to take the offer. Whatever it was that Usellyes needed the centipede for, it must have been important. He also had no doubt it would be confiscated if Mylor were to find out.

"Is this true?" Mylor queried pointedly.

"Yes. It's true." The words seemed forced from Usellyes's stiff lips. There was reluctance and malice in that statement.

Mylor sighed. Simantiar wasn't sure if he bought it, but there was nothing really he could do when both parties agreed to the same story.

"The good thing is that no one was hurt, and it is best if this is kept away from the board. For both your sakes, and mine."

Mylor considered for a moment longer.

"Simantiar, a whole month in locked meditation."

Simantiar's eyes widened. He wasn't surprised by the severity of the punishment, but rather the type and extent. The chamber was supposed to be a time for self-reflection and tending to one's own maturity, but never had he heard of a meditative punishment lasting an entire month. That was without sleep, without food, without water, without toilet breaks.

He would remain animated and time dilation would result in the locking of bodily functions so that he would be bereft of all those things he needed to survive, but his mind would be able to meditate endlessly.

"But that's—"

"Fair," Simantiar cut Usellyes off. He could hear his friend clench his fist defiantly as the leather cushioning of his chair grew taut.

"And you, Usellyes, a week."

Usellyes rose from the seat and charged off.

Simantiar sat there and tapped his knees to drown out the awkward silence.

"I don't know what you are hiding, but it better have been worth it," Mylor said.

Simantiar gave no response that would either deny or confirm Mylor's suspicions. The man was too clever to insult him like that.

"You are dismissed," Mylor said, veering his attention to some paperwork.

"Before the meditation, would it be okay if I take a shower first?" Simantiar asked.

"No."

Usellyes was waiting outside as Simantiar emerged, and all that bottled fury bubbled to the surface as the man charged forward and shoved Simantiar away.

"You think you're better than me?" he challenged, another shove as Simantiar stumbled back for the second time.

"Why did you take the fall for me? Did you think I wouldn't be able to handle it? Do you think me too weak? To always stand in your shadow and have you protect me?" Usellyes's voice became ever louder and louder.

"You think I couldn't take the punishment? Is that it?" A final shove and Simantiar fell to the floor.

"I don't need your protection," Usellyes remarked with a finger pointing down at Simantiar.

"I never said you did." Simantiar's reply was soft and submissive. He didn't know what had Usellyes so riled up, but didn't want to fuel it.

"Whatever it was that possessed you to capture those centipedes, it must have been for good reason." Simantiar rose from the ground. "You use your time off to find urchins and feed them, heal the wounded during the semester breaks on your travels, and even on your break times you study new ways to improve lives. Whatever your reason, I trust it was justified."

Though it silenced and somewhat tempered Usellyes, his shoulders still shrugged up and down from the enraged breaths he was taking, his eyes that of a feverous beast. "I don't need you to protect me."

"No, you don't. But what can I do when you beg me to save you?" The moment Simantiar said those words he regretted it.

Usellyes cheeks flushed red, not out of anger, but out of sheer embarrassment.

Usellyes stepped up to Simantiar till the warmth from his breath could be felt on Simantiar's cheeks. "I challenge you to Magus Tha when you come out of meditation," Usellyes spat the words before reeling away towards the mediation chamber.

The guards that stood watch and served as security for the Eindeheid were arcane fighters, and their blades were infused with magical auras that took their teachings from the first arcane fighter, Vrania himself. Two outside and two at the door stood watch as Simantiar and Usellyes closed their eyes and drifted upon spiralling ribbons of arcane blue channels.

The first day proved the most gruelling, as Simantiar found his focus drifting in and out as he tried to anchor his consciousness to his breathing. After a time, the world beyond faded and time became irrelevant—he had found his centre.

He could hear the distant sound of people coming and going, but it felt so far away to his ears; Simantiar felt as if he floated upon a black abyss within his mind's eye.

The first week had passed and the most that Simantiar noticed was the end of Usellyes's meditation. He could hear the final exhale, sense the slow glide as feet touched the floor with such calm and radiating intensity like a wave of heat from a furnace. Simantiar sensed the daggers shot through piercing eyes even if he could not see it himself. It was the most disrupting moment in the meditation, but he didn't let it get to him.

In the past, the most Simantiar had spent within the chamber was six hours, and that was only because of a class that demanded it. He had never actually taken a chance to appreciate the tranquillity that came with the meditation.

His thoughts would travel often to trees, trees from the jungle, the one that saved him, reliving that event through the mind's eye and observing it with a calm stillness.

But then, he thought of all trees, trees from his childhood, then he thought to nature, a babbling brook or whistling wind or swaying grass.

A strange thought occurred to Simantiar, had he found his animal?

The month had passed and Simantiar ventured a rather rare visit towards the library.

He borrowed three books, all on magic types, animal companions, and spirit bonds and combed through the contents.

"What are you doing here?" Simantiar looked up to find it was Emilie accompanied by a bunny on her shoulder.

"We haven't seen you in a month and the first place we find you is in a library? Are you okay? Did you have a fever?" she joked.

Simantiar gratified her joke with a soft, numb chuckle before nodding. "Yeah, I'm fine. Congrats on the bunny."

Emilie looked over to her shoulder as if she forgot it was there and smiled at the reminder.

"Ah yes, I named him Captain Peanut, 'cause of his fur." She tussled the bunny's head. Already a salmon pink began to lightly coat Peanut's fur and Simantiar spared a fleeting thought about how long it would remain a fitting name.

Emilie returned to Simantiar. "I heard what happened. You got in trouble for something, huh? Meditation for a month? That's rather excessive."

"Well, it was well deserved." Simantiar turned a page to see diagrams and depictions of greatly vined trees and their history.

"What are you doing?" Emilie leant in with her usual inability to read the room and then, deciding it wasn't enough, she worked her way around the table to really invade on Simantiar's reading.

"Ah, Tiria magic."

"What?" Simantiar asked.

"Well. You know how the weave is just everything—you can interact with all of life and call upon its shape using the weave, right?"

Simantiar seemed confused.

"Well, I guess you are an exception. You just kind of imagine the end result, and you don't need an image," she amended.

Simantiar must have still looked lost as Emilie gave an exaggerated sigh. "Look, this is Tiria magic. But it is not really used."

"Why is it called Tiria magic?"

"Well, because it is bound to nature. It calls upon forest trees and all else to grant you its power."

"And why is it not used? That sounds quite useful."

Emilie nodded in agreement. "Not only useful, but incredibly powerful too."

"So, what's the issue?"

Emilie pondered for a second. "Most magic is…about control, seizing an object in your mind and bending it to your will. But Tiria magic…it's just unreliable. It's not about taking control. It's about asking nature for help. Sometimes nature complies, but one day it may stop. It is not very reliable since you can't force nature to obey you. It *chooses* to help."

Simantiar began to understand with a brimming sense of fascination. For as long as he could remember, magic simply obeyed his every whim and command as if it were an extension of his limbs. He never had to really think about it in the same way no one really thinks about using their legs. But a thought that never really occurred to him was the use of Tiria magic wasn't seized, it was earned. This was something that wasn't just handed to him without a challenge.

Another thought occurred to Simantiar. "Where is Usellyes?"

"In the lab." She leaned in to whisper, "You helped him smuggle in those centipedes, didn't you?"

Simantiar nodded, suddenly feeling as if he had done something he shouldn't have.

"What are they?" Simantiar asked.

"Omukade, centipedes from the eastern forests and jungles. They represent usurpation. They can channel magic and fill themselves as a vessel to contain any source of power, but they can also contain or concentrate such power to force control."

"Why does he need that?" Simantiar asked.

"Usellyes said it can be used to channel magic for those who cannot cast it. Perhaps provide a reserve for magic to help the less fortunate. But he is just experimenting with it for now. It is true that the Omukade are known for being a type of container of information."

They went quiet for a moment.

"You know, your Magus Tha is tomorrow. What happened between you two?"

"I don't know," replied Simantiar.

"Well, whatever it is, work it out. It will be awkward for the rest of us if the two of you are having a lover's quarrel."

Simantiar smiled at the quip more sincerely this time as Emilie left him with his thoughts.

Atop the mountain that held Eindeheid there was a courtyard that looked outwards to passing clouds below and an unforgiving sun above, a sun that come night would dip past the peaks of mountains and poke through clouds before vanishing.

The courtyard was by no means lavish, all the magic and wonder that took place, took place inside the academy itself.

What one found outside on the courtyard was a cliff peering down to the cities below and a raised plateau of stone on which all Magus Tha were held.

The plateau was an arena meant for all disputes to be handled where pain was meant to be felt, but no injury was permanent and no death was possible.

The plateau's radius proved large enough for the players to move unabated and not have to worry about being cornered—at least to begin with. The entire crowd of a hundred curious onlookers themselves could have easily crammed into the provided space.

Simantiar's feet shifted restlessly, and he looked down to the bareness, how cold the cracked stone marble felt to his skin and the trafficking rush of wind made his toes curl from numbing cold. The etched filigree patterns had long since faded and eroded from countless battles and exposure to the elements.

Simantiar looked back up to Usellyes who burnt with stoic conviction like a hot blue flame—concentrated, yet seething with power. His long black hair was gone, and he instead sported a short trim. Simantiar had made no such change; his blond curls were bunched into a ponytail that stretched his hair taut over his scalp. His usual cherubic and vibrant cheeks deflated, only the purpose at hand in his mind.

The two had eschewed their magenta mage robes and instead replaced them with loose-fitting white shirts and baggy black trousers, both of which had their ends wrapped as to keep them from fluttering endlessly.

"Kick his ass, Usellyes!" Simantiar heard Zaros call from somewhere in the crowd, followed by a curt shushing from Ciro.

Simantiar chuckled to himself, but looking up at Usellyes, his friend seemed to share no such humour…just a need for vindication in those piercing dagger eyes.

"Welcome," began Mylor as he stood at the outer rim of the arena. "This Magus Tha has been sanctioned by the board of Eindeheid and as such, this battle will follow the rules of a Magus Tha. All magic is allowed…" *Except for the forbidden ones,* thought Simantiar privately to himself, but that was a given. "Any attempt to kill or maim will not be permanent and your safety will be ensured as is my responsibility." A low, bemused chuckle came from the crowd.

Mylor continued to read aloud the rest of the rules as Usellyes stared with blazing intensity at Simantiar.

"Do you plan on winning?" Usellyes asked.

It seemed like a strange question. "Why wouldn't I?"

"Because you never care."

"Come on, Usellyes. We are brothers—you are the closest friend I have had. I know you have some issues, but at the end of the day I just hope we can settle our differences."

Usellyes nodded regretfully. "I see. So, you haven't come here with the intent to win?"

"I guess not," Simantiar admitted.

"If you value our friendship, you won't hold back." The gravity of Usellyes's tone fell upon Simantiar like the weight of the mountain they stood on. Was it a threat? He didn't want to gravely hurt Usellyes, even if no injury was permanent.

Mylor reached the end of the statements. "No spells will be able to enter the arena and none can leave, magical elements can be called in from outside as a catalyst, but no conjured spells will be able to enter. Finally, the match will be decided by mock death, loss of consciousness, inability to continue, surrender, or by being knocked out of bounds: this includes disappearing completely underground. It is within my right for any reason I see fit to step in and stop the Magus Tha prematurely."

Mylor turned towards Simantiar. "Understood?"

Simantiar nodded. "Yes," he said, warming up his calves by bouncing on his toes. *What spells should I use first?* he wondered.

"Do you understand?" Mylor asked, turning towards Usellyes.

"Yes." What a chillingly cold reply Usellyes gave, colder than even the wind that blew past and tugged at your warmth, colder than the winter lands of perpetual storms far to the north, a coldness not born of snow or wind, but of emptiness; short, emotionless, as if he barely even heard the question, all his attention was reserved for Simantiar alone.

Mylor hesitated.

Usellyes turned to Mylor. "I said yes."

Mylor didn't seem to like Usellyes's glare or tone one bit, and a passing gust of wind howled atop the precipice as all breaths were held. The passing seconds seemed agonizingly slow.

Finally Mylor relented.

"Begin." The word accompanied by a straightened palm through the air marked the commencement.

Whispers deluged in a frantic blur of speed-casting from Simantiar and Usellyes. A rather new talent popular among the younger mages that was not favoured by more senior casters for it was very easy to twist your tongue and slip up, and what then? What would one do when suddenly you had to start from the beginning or even worse—cast a spell that backfires?

The fact that Simantiar and Usellyes casted spells at the speed which they did only spoke towards their confidence…or arrogance.

The last syllable on Simantiar's lip fell away like a whisper spoken by a whisper; a moment later Simantiar inhaled deep into his lungs and made the breath of Balan take form.

From his expanded lungs came loose a torrent of wind, his body leaning forward, a leg stretched out behind him to brace against the evicted air.

The wind clashed against the risen wall that Usellyes sprouted in front of him. Sudden surprised screams erupted from the crowd as the wind pressure raised their robes and brushed against them, plotting to send students plummeting over the end.

"Take this seriously!" called Usellyes from behind his wall.

Unseen, Usellyes invoked sudden twirling stalactites that shot out with the sound of cutting wind from his conjured defense.

Simantiar reeled back, heightened sense and instinct having him dodge one, two—he suddenly summoned an invisible barrier of force that denied the other stakes of stone—but the final one found itself embedded in his leg. Simantiar gave a cry as a wave of hot pain shot up from his punctured thigh. He turned to see the sly portal barely the size of a ball fitted into a palm which opened and flanked Simantiar from the side.

He looked down to the gaping, protruding stake of stone and shattered it with a spell, the punctured hole running free with blood.

Using his barrier, Simantiar turned its rigid form into a free-flowing blanket, spreading it over his wound to stop the bleeding. A few more silent words and the spell took the form of mock muscle fibres and ligaments to keep him moving.

Usellyes was not done. No sooner did Simantiar cover the bleeding mess did the wall fall into mush and slurp its way towards him like sludging ooze.

Simantiar spoke a few more words, raising a hand up to the sky and slapping it to the ground.

Nothing happened at first till Simantiar continued to evoke his magic and raise his palms as the sound of a roaring furnace erupted and a wave of immense heat washed across all present.

A thin pillar of a flaming rod emerged from the floor, growing taller the more his palm distanced itself from the ground as flames licked the air around its blazing shaft like millions of demonic tongues stuck to its burning red body.

When Simantiar finally lifted what came to be a glowing hot spear aloft and the sweat at his palms sizzled to the touch, he brought it over his shoulder and prepared to throw.

"Ignis Ra Gungnar!" The spear of flame shot forward like lightning, his grip and hands only lent it direction, but the force of ejection was wholly its own.

Flames burst from the shaft of the spear and turned into great wings of fire as the rush of passing air made all shield their faces.

Simantiar never had a chance to see what happened except for the fact that the sludge of stone had turned into crumbling clay and then there was a loud explosive collision that left his ears ringing and the mountain trembling.

Simantiar fell to his knees, the ache in his leg pulsing and distant. Blurry eyes looked up to find the cracked outlines of a shattered barrier fixing itself.

What Simantiar failed to see was the sudden knee that knocked him under the chin.

The mage went flying, his world turned upside down. The clouds rolled beneath him.

Never was a chance given to collect himself as the weight of fists bore down on him faster than any syllables or spells could leave his tongue.

The world doubled over. *Where am I? Are these Usellyes's fists?* The punches did not relent. He heard the distant sounds of worried murmurs.

This was no magic. It was a simple street fight.

"Fight me!" demanded a voice somewhere far off in the distance.

Simantiar tried to mutter something else, but a knock upside the head and a hand clasped to his mouth permitted no such thing. There was the smell of blood in the air. *Is someone bleeding?* he wondered.

"Fight me!" It was a command.

One knock sent him reeling deeper into the depths, another one and his skull knocked against the concrete floor and sent a shock of lucidity through him.

Something touched Simantiar, a feeling, a sensation like a thread grasped in umbral darkness. A sensation of perplexed understanding.

A gust of wind pushed Usellyes off his body and flipped Usellyes backwards on his feet. Simantiar's vision coloured red with his own blood. The surrounding murmurs were clearer.

"Usellyes, you are going too far!" Zaros called out. He had run up to the barrier and pressed his hands on it.

"Headmaster, please stop the fight," Emilie pleaded.

Simantiar turned towards Mylor who seemed to seriously be considering it, his eyes staring out with affectionate concern. Simantiar could tell by the clenched fists that he was trying to stay rational.

"What are you doing, Usellyes?" asked a concerned Moran.

"Usellyes! Stop hurting him!" Desperation was in Noima's tone.

"I will kick your ass!" threatened Ciro. Simantiar chuckled inwardly a little, thinking how Ciro always tried to be a hard-ass.

Simantiar wondered if his vision was playing tricks on him. Wondered if he truly watched Joselyn standing among the crowds, the only one who seemed cold and unfazed with what transpired. Simantiar chuckled at the sickening humour. Still she didn't forgive him. Still she resented him.

He rose to his feet.

"No need to stop the fight," Simantiar said with a chuckle that portrayed unwarranted confidence, spitting a cracked and bloody tooth that rattled to the floor.

"It will be over in a second." He winked towards Emilie, his smile weak. He wondered if he actually had winked as trembling knees struggled to remain standing.

"Thanks for waiting," Simantiar said to Usellyes.

Usellyes took his stance again, blood dripping to the floor from his fists. "Today is the day that I outgrow you." Finally an explanation. Finally an answer. The realisation struck Simantiar as heavy as Usellyes's own fists.

Was that how Usellyes truly felt? Simantiar wondered. He tried to come up with excuses to himself. Usellyes misunderstood, he was having issues of his own, Simantiar didn't try to overshadow him…but was it true? A part of Simantiar, a guilty seed he never knew was there took root and sprouted as a sapling through the dirt.

A sudden wave of shame washed over him. He had been lazy, disingenuous, insincere. Usellyes was fighting for something, something he believed in. Again. Like every other time. Yet, it was all just a light breeze to Simantiar, another thing to do for fun, another thing to not take seriously as he lay there getting pummelled and just accepted that was how it would go.

Did he really conjure that barrier because it was the best choice…or because he was too lazy to do something else? Simantiar wondered…did he actually care if he won? Would he just laugh it off when everything came to an end while everyone knew he hadn't given it his best? If he had really thrown that spear with the intent to win rather than show off, or even really gone all out with his breath of Balan…would the fight already be over?

Was that how Usellyes always felt? Perhaps. Maybe it was the knock to Simantiar's head that finally shook him to his senses, but if Usellyes fought for something so important to him, then Simantiar deserved to meet him halfway.

"I will be getting serious now," Simantiar noted.

"That's a first," Usellyes remarked.

Was that a joke? Simantiar could tell the light signs of a smirk on Usellyes's lips.

Simantiar could still feel the thread, a light fringe of a touch at the tips of his finger. He tugged on it.

The puddle of blood by Usellyes obeyed without a single incantation, piercing right out and puncturing the unsuspecting Usellyes as an icicle of blood.

"When did he do the incantation?" rose one murmur from the crowd.

"Was it when he was being punched?" asked another. The murmurs meshed into incoherent sounds among the crowds.

"Good one," Usellyes chuckled, holding his sides as he watched Simantiar for what he would do next.

A quick word from Usellyes's lips sent the stench of burning flesh up into the air, his sides burnt, and then the wind took the scent away with another passing gust.

However, Simantiar never let the wind pass by completely; he rotated on his heels and spun his hand around as the wind veered in its path, flowing back towards Simantiar as he tossed it forward and blew the air into Usellyes.

Without a second to react, Usellyes chanted as the air tried to pry him off his feet. The ground opened and swallowed his legs up to the knee while a second chant formed on his lips.

More and more gusts of air escaped Simantiar's hand, not grabbed by the wind, but evoked at his swings. It wasn't a chant, it wasn't a spell—it was his thoughts given form. It all felt...so natural.

Clay men erupted from below to seize Simantiar, clinging and clambering, the ground beneath his feet turned to pudding as he was slowly dragged under.

Usellyes was trying to win on a technicality.

Another thought, as Simantiar's imagination ran wild. He splayed his hands and pressed them down as the clay men crumbled and joined the quicksand of stone. The pull of the clay stopped, before suddenly reversing in direction and pushing Simantiar up. The clay at his feet and around him armoured Simantiar as he jumped out of the cratered ruin in the floor.

Each smooth step forward was taken as if the armour were part of him as he swung his arms and the hardened pieces of stones soared from him towards Usellyes.

Hampered and wounded, the dark-haired mage slashed across the air as extended streaks of lightning cut down the flying masonry.

The extended length of lightning coiled itself by Usellyes's anchored feet as he stepped out of his own restraints.

The crowds were silent, not a word spoken. The crackle of lightning was audible over the sound of a passing breeze.

The whip began to shorten before becoming taut, forming into a thick dagger of flayed energy. Usellyes thrust forward, the lightning dagger turning into a poled lance as they extended in a literal flash.

Yet it all seemed so...slow to Simantiar.

The tip of the lightning shattered and frayed like strands of static blue as it collided with the barrier. With a wave of Simantiar's hand the lightning started to collapse and form into wind through a transmutation spell working its way down the electrical shaft.

As the transformation worked its way down the spear, more and more of the sparks pulled into wind that gathered at Simantiar's call, cocooning him in a sphere of magical domed wind that harnessed the power of a storm.

Usellyes seemed to mutter something in his final moment of shock. Simantiar never heard what it was, but he could well imagine. The lightning vanished and the air that wrapped Simantiar with it.

The world suddenly became distant, as if taken away from Simantiar.

Perhaps it was a calculated plan in the moment, but most likely it was a spell cast in a moment of sheer panic. A moment that made Usellyes realise that he was providing Simantiar with his next attack, so Usellyes must have cast the spell of void to dissipate the lightning, and with it, the wind that was still bound to it.

So, there Simantiar toppled to his knee, in pained gasps, the air that was created, the air that he breathed in, all removed in an instant.

An agonizing breath that gave no sound within the vacuum that he was stranded in as the surrounding air began to fill the empty space.

Usellyes seemed to have noticed what had happened before Simantiar, for before a fresh set of air could fill the void left behind, Usellyes summoned a barrier that encased Simantiar and forced him to crouch even lower.

Painful, forced gasps silently pressured his lungs. It felt like his chest was going to explode, the sound of his heart drummed in his ears with panic. His vision was blurry.

"Stop it," the lips moved, but the words never sounded in the bubble as black spots filled Simantiar's vision.

Everything vanished. The barrier blocking him. The pain in his lungs faded without even an ache as if it was never there.

Looking around, no one spoke, no breeze howled past, and no clouds roiled over. Usellyes stood frozen with a grimace as the worried and shocked faces of students filled the background.

Simantiar looked around him with clear eyes, clearer than they had ever been. He could see things he'd never noticed. He sensed the bead of sweat frozen upon a cheek, the breath in the middle of an inhale, the most miniscule of tendered moles or protruding veins, the softest of heartbeats coming from a small, insignificant worm buried in the bark of a hollowed tree trunk at the base of the mountain.

He looked to the sky with the first breath of air he could feel.

Clouds no longer moved. He saw the frozen form of birds passing by. Even the sun seemed to have come to a stop.

The command he uttered earlier gave form to his will, and his will was obeyed.

But that wasn't all—as time froze still, Simantiar felt as if he could touch the world.

He reached out to the sky knowing full well, as he felt the very being of all that was, of what he was capable of—he feared it. The warnings of his mother quelled the rising euphoria that tickled every drop of blood in his veins and reminded him he was human.

But the voice seemed so…distant.

With a flick of his wrist, the sun flew by and the starry night came instead. With another flick of his wrist, the universe passed him by again. Simantiar stood there wondering what it was like to have found the little flicker that allowed him to tug at the world's strings as if it were a puppet, and he its marionettist. He motioned for the universe to come closer and watched as the stars of the night blazed past him, scanning through the solar system and then the galaxy as if going on a stroll.

Another wave of his hand and he watched the faces of Mylor, his friends, and his teachers vanish, as the school of Eindeiheid suddenly was deconstructed and snow, plants, trees, animals, all things passed him by in a blur of Tiria's history and endless seasons.

Simantiar realised that he could no longer just bend reality, but he could change it to his will, and that reality terrified him.

With another wave he returned to his fight, still frozen in time. Simantiar walked around the place, watching his friend, with what zeal he seized that opportunity to suffocate Simantiar, as if all the passion and desire he had built was clearly visible upon Usellyes's expression.

Simantiar looked to his friend and envied him.

Simantiar was lazy, carefree, and without any ambitions. Yet, Usellyes was a man of discipline with a good heart that wanted to help the world with a frightening amount of dedication to match.

A realisation struck Simantiar harder and more true than any attack, a feeling more pronounced and hollow than the absence of air that suffocated him. He vowed to face Usellyes with everything he had, and he did. But what point was there to it now? He felt as if he could erase Usellyes from existence with a simple flick of the wrist and that made him go cold like never before. His fingers trembled as he beheld them. What utter horror for any man or woman to have such power.

He was just a kid. A truth that he brazenly mocked or ignored in the past…but now, he knew he was just a kid with the power of a god and the sheer immensity of that contrast frayed his mind in a way that centipede never could.

He felt so hollow at that moment—what point was there to winning if it wasn't earned? Usellyes was strong because he worked to be strong, yet Simantiar was strong because he was born that way. And yet, he wondered, what point was there to power when there was nothing to strive for?

All in that one moment, the mage felt large and yet small; he felt scared; he felt important and yet so insignificant.

And so he sighed.

The loop of time began to move once more, yet it moved in reverse, gaining speed.

The streaks of fire in the form of lightning gone, the conjured gusts of wind taken away, the raised blocks of stone returned to their original points.

In a blinding flash, the whole duel was undone.

There they were again, Usellyes standing against Simantiar.

Simantiar raised his hands and Usellyes tensed as if to ready himself, yet he could never have predicted Simantiar's first and final move.

"I forfeit," Simantiar said.

Usellyes licked his lips as he approached the podium, the gathered students all silent as they waited patiently for the words of the honoured graduate.

The boy who was scraped up off the streets, glazed with dirt and rusted like chipped steel, had forged himself anew from the dark metals which he was. He never saw his upbringing before the academy as a weakness, but as a strength. It humbled him and helped him become cold steel which waded through the river. He was calm, precise, and fluid.

It had been years since Simantiar and Usellyes's duel and though their relationship had changed, and a new bond of trust and understanding had formed since then, the innocence they nurtured since their meeting was irrevocably gone forever. Simantiar was sure that Usellyes had never entirely forgiven him for forfeiting the match before it had begun.

And so began Usellyes's speech: "Magic," he paused, "it allows us to bend reality, to turn dreams and wishes, fanciful musings, into reality. I stand here before you today, because despite my circumstance of birth, my diligent studying and magical prowess was taken note of by our teachers. Yet, I wish to address all of you under another pretext." Usellyes eyed his friend who sat upon the front row with his sharp and calm stare. Simantiar simply watched Usellyes with respect.

Usellyes's eyes returned to the crowd. "I wish to address you as opportunity. If magic is capable of bending reality to how we see fit, to chisel the world into a sculpture of our own making, then let us do that to make a perfect world. A world where children must not go through what I have, where love can be found and cherished, while death and strife is abolished. Mylor, our headmaster, taught that to me when he saw my potential and took me in. And I want to follow that example.

"Let us put our efforts into using our magic and creating sustainable food for the less fortunate, to make hunger a thing of the past. To heal and mend rather than break and burn. We graduate here today, going from acolyte to full-fledged mages, and now set out to recreate the world in our image. Although I wouldn't mind if our graduate robes had come in a different colour." Usellyes looked down to his robes with mock indifference which earned him a laugh from the crowd.

"If I can escape my circumstance of birth, then who is to say that anything is impossible? This isn't the end of our journey, fellow mages. No—this is only just the beginning."

The entire crowd rose in an uproar, all of them draped in their blue robes of varying designs, while their applause was like thunder among the clouds with no roof to hold the resounding cheers.

Yet, it was only Simantiar who did not clap, nor did he rise from his seat, but what he did offer instead was a single tear and sombre smile, for his friend had truly outgrown him in every way possible. He regretted not being as diligent as his friend and envied Usellyes's resolve. And knew that if he could do it all over again, that he still wouldn't be able to.

As the ceremonies wrapped up, and many of the students took flight upon soaring winds or tamed hawks and griffins or whatever was their spell of choice, Simantiar took a seat by the tipped ledge at the end of the cliff which permitted a look towards the sifting clouds below and the Magus Tha plateau just behind.

His feet dangled over the end as familiar footsteps approached from behind. Simantiar did not need to look to know it was Usellyes who took a seat beside him.

"So, I guess this is it," Simantiar said.

"I guess it is," Usellyes replied, neither of them turning to the other as a strong gust blew into them. When they first arrived at the academy, the grip of the winds would steal their warmth and cause them to shiver uncontrollably, but as they sat there it was nothing more than a small breeze—capable of fazing them as much as the wind fazed the mountain which they sat upon.

"Are you sure you don't wish to stay here at the academy?" Usellyes asked.

Simantiar only smiled and then shook his head. "This is your dream, not mine. I need to find my own purpose."

Simantiar looked to his friend and saw with what admiration Usellyes regarded him and this saddened Simantiar. For in truth, Simantiar felt as if he were the one who fell into his adversary's shadow; he admired Usellyes, looking up to his friend with such enduring admiration and respect.

Simantiar didn't speak of this, however, for how could Usellyes ever understand. His own aimless path was not something he could speak about, not even with Usellyes.

"Stay well, Usellyes."

The friend nodded and rose to leave. That would be the last time they would see each other for many years, but whatever may be said between them was done so unspoken. They would meet again one day.

Though the prospect of graduation saddened Simantiar, it was the idea of parting with his friend that truly left a bottomless pit in his heart. Already he had said goodbye to the others, even Joselyn for one final attempt to mend past mistakes, but some things were unchangeable.

And as Simantiar watched his friend leave, sorrow gripping at his heart, the manifested body which Simantiar had created began to disintegrate into dust. He was never there—Simantiar hadn't been there in years. He had departed and left an image of himself to finish and graduate from the academy.

It wouldn't be right to call it a clone, nor would it be right to call it Simantiar. For the man had ascended into incomprehensible measures, the image he had left was as real as he, the only difference being that Simantiar had understood form, space, and omnipresence: for Simantiar had broken through the keyhole of reality and found the mechanism of the universe.

Chapter 22

"A knife," Kristen began, "is as much a part of your body as you are of it. It is not just the arm you wave around or the leg that carries you, it is the air you breathe. An essential part of keeping you alive that you can remove from a person's view in an instant."

Kristen demonstrated as she explained, brandishing a short dagger with a slight curve and making it vanish before George's very eyes. George couldn't help but blink in astonishment, trying to process how the sharp glint of steel disappeared into nothingness.

"I will be teaching you as much as I can with what little time we have together, but in essence, here is what you need to know: win at all costs. Honour is a luxury that can only be afforded to those who have been born into the top of the food chain. They are the sparrow that lands to take worms for feasting, and we are the worm that needs to fight dirty to level the playing field."

George only nodded. He understood the words on the surface, but still knew that to truly comprehend what Kristen had said to him, he would have to learn with his soul.

"So, instead of a short dagger, wouldn't it make sense to use one of Kendrith's swords?" George nodded over to the hunter who sat upon a tree stump with his arm still in a sling, and right beside him sat a propped Simantiar. The three had gone into the woods for a little quiet.

"Kendrith, would you be so kind?" Kristen asked. The merc bit down on a peach, its juices staining his shirt as he pulled out his steel sword from its sheath and tossed it at George's feet.

The boy reached down for the blade, grasping its hilt in both hands and lifting it off the ground.

"Good, now strike me," Kristen said.

George looked over at Kendrith, who took another bite from his peach and watched without a word.

With a few breaths in and out, George held the sword before him. Kristen stood straight without a stance, waiting for George to make the first move.

George had no wasted movements. Focusing entirely on his body, the way he leaned forward, how gravity pulled him towards his target, and when he finally swung the blade through the air in a wide arc, he didn't just use his arms, he twisted his entire body.

Yet, Kristen simply hopped back out of the blade's reach and kicked at the dirt on the ground which flew into George's eyes.

George cried in sudden surprise and spat out whatever contents had found themselves in his mouth as panicked hands rubbed at his eyes. It was all the time Kristen needed to grab George's wrist and unhinge the blade from his grip.

"We are the worms that fight against the sparrow," Kristen repeated, pressing her vanishing blade into George's neck. "Just as I lack the strength of a man, I cannot afford to fight like one. Same as you, you do not have the muscle tone required to swing a sword properly, and when you miss, the blade carries you even farther, leaving you wide open."

"So, how do we fight?" George asked, rubbing his neck as Kristen removed the blade.

"We fight with what has been given to us." Kristen cupped her breasts. "Sexuality." Then she pressed a tear from her eyes. "Vulnerability." Then she pinched George's cheek with a smile. "Innocence."

George laughed and failed to repress the reddening of his cheeks.

Kristen chuckled. "Exactly like that."

"And remember, if fighting a man bigger than you, their pride will also be strong. Fighting with what is between their legs instead of using their mind. Exploit that, make them emotional, then you will have your opening."

Kristen distanced herself. "Besides, teaching someone to play dirty in a few days is far easier than teaching someone how to wield a sword. The world is your playground, use it."

George smiled. "I think I understand now."

"Oh? Do you?"

"Yes." George's smile widened, as he lifted a dagger before him. Kristen's eyes widened, reaching to her belt to notice the absence of another hidden dagger. Yet, she wasn't upset—instead, she smiled. She seemed excited in every way.

"Good, very good," she said smiling.

"Again," Kristen said as she nodded approvingly.

George took note that Kristen used praise sparingly, offering just enough to keep George motivated, but not so much as to allow it to get to his head. He didn't mind. He actually preferred it.

Yet to the boy, the role which Kristen filled in his life comforted him. He had never had a mother to dote on him, and he was too busy worrying about his own sister to ever be wistful of such luxuries, yet at that moment, as his dagger cut through the air and pierced the tree's bark, he wondered if this was what it was like to have a mother. He relished her approval.

"That's enough for today." George collapsed, only just realising how tired he was, but still he couldn't help but smile as his chest heaved hampered breaths, too tired even to wipe the sweat from his brow.

The sun had begun its descent, as bright blue skies dulled into shades of a warm orange.

"Shall we check on Simantiar?" Kristen had asked the boy.

George looked over to the skull perched atop shoulders made from wood. The body that Simantiar bore seemed more and more pragmatic, with padded leaves serving as shoulders, twined vines corded to form a strengthened chest with the rest of the vines pulled taut to create an abdomen. His lithe and long arms extended from his torso, strong and spiralled wood copying the flexing of leg muscles to ensure maximum efficiency. He would meditate, taking mock breaths in and out not for the purpose of living, but rather as an anchor to the world as Pecky chirped from the treetop along with a few other singing birds before coming down to Simantiar and singing to him instead.

George heard the expanding and groaning sound of stretched bark and wood at every inhale, noted by the expanding chest of forestry, only to then have the sound of wood and vine relax from the bending motions.

Over the past days, Simantiar seemed far from his lively self, quieter and distant as if something bothered him.

He would sit among a clearing of trees most of the time to recollect the fractured memories of his past; his wooden legs crossed, vines extending that burrowed into the soil below like roots or dangled from nearby trees like plugs. He seemed almost like an obscure part of the surrounding forest and the way the breeze passed and drifting leaves covered him, the forest seemed to agree.

"He will come when he is ready," George said. Over the course of a week, Simantiar had taken a far more serious demeanour as more and more of his past returned to him. Less and less was he the jovial, mirthful skull that George had come to know him as. It surely was reassuring, especially since Simantiar had said that he may be able to repair the book. George tried hard to remember that Simantiar made no guarantees, but he couldn't help but hope.

The last of the sun's light had almost faded as within the humble, but cosy home of Kendrith and Kristen supper was had.

"Slow down, you're going to suffocate before you even finish your quest at this rate." Kendrith joked as George tore into his portion of puckered beef. It must have been expensive and George had no intention of letting the opportunity pass him by. Though George had much coin upon him, he never quite found the opportunity nor the city to enjoy life's more extravagant pleasures.

"Just let him enjoy it," Kristen said with a smile.

Dinner continued with Simantiar regaling those gathered around the table with the newly reacquired memories of his past. He told them of his childhood, what the world was like when rich with magic.

Suddenly, the air before them shimmered like fairy dust, an image forming that showed Simantiar's past. How thick the fabric of creation used to be, the creatures that lived within the world, recreated stills of Simantiar's memories; the whole room filled with gasps and astonished remarks. Pecky took flight and chirped while flying back and forth through the images.

"So, this Usellyes was stronger than you? I mean, you messed up. But he ended up winning because you couldn't breathe anymore, right?" George asked as Simantiar retold the story of their duel, though certain parts were left vague.

"That he was."

"And handsome too," Kristen said with doe eyes.

"I'm right here," Kendrith complained.

"I wish *he* was right here," Kristen joked and the table laughed as Kendrith flicked a piece of beef from his fork at Kristen.

"What happened to Usellyes?" asked George.

"I honestly don't know, haven't gotten that far yet in my memories."

"So, where are you now?"

"I am travelling the world, learning of all types of magic and creatures that are hidden from the rest of mankind. One of them was the guardian from the Forest of the Dead. I also recently travelled north in my memories to the home of frost giants. Mighty trolls with fur as white as the snow that surrounds them. Then the home of dragon-kind tucked beneath caverns within volcanoes."

"Are they all dragons?"

"Some. Dragon-kind aren't necessarily dragons. It was mostly filled with humanoid reptilian beings that looked like lizards more than dragons. They served the few dragons who still remained like a beehive protecting its queen."

"Amazing."

"It truly was," Simantiar sounded wistful to the memories.

"And…" George hesitated, as the others looked to him expectantly. "Do you think you can fix my book?" Not only did George want the book back for what it represented, but for the clues it held to finding the golden gates.

"You said when you uncover more of your past then you might have a clue to fixing it. Did you?"

Simantiar hesitated for a moment. He hadn't donned a body, but rather rested as a normal talking skull. "I'll try," he said, though there wasn't much confidence in the statement. That didn't bother George as his excitement became apparent.

Dinner drew to a close and George played some tunes on his own lute after an uproar of clapping chants from the crowd. The lute had seen better days, but the surrounding company made the lute seem more pristine than it ever was before. George had watched silently for a moment, imagining that at the end of the smiling and expecting faces sat Lily, as young and unmarred as he remembered her. George didn't recall ever having so many people gathered around, people who knew his name. Knew of his dream. Heard his laughter day after day.

He let the lute show how his heart felt before they called it a night.

Kendrith and Kristen retreated to their quarters as George slept in the dining room with Simantiar and Pecky.

As always, Simantiar remained on the table with the torn pieces of the book before him. The wizard tried to reassemble it piece by piece, to scour his memories for any clues that could help. And as always he struggled, yet he felt as if day by day he was closer to the answers. He felt as if the torn pieces could be fitted together in time. But his true concern were the pieces of paper that George wasn't able to retrieve when attacked by the Hobbers.

Simantiar assumed that in theory, he could still put the book back together, but how he would achieve such a thing was a completely different question. Simantiar noticed how his past self grasped at that thread in the darkness…that comprehension that felt like enlightenment as it was harped about in thousands of elusive texts. But as he was then, he couldn't grasp the feeling. It felt more like a tug at the heart each time he tried to relive that sensation rather one of the mind, a fleeting idea long lost to him. Maybe he had to collect more memories for that feeling to return? Regardless, as he was, he was calling upon a pool of power not as that he used in his past…he was lost.

"How is your shoulder?" asked Kristen as she closed the door behind her.

"Better. I can move it," said Kendrith, rotating his stiff shoulders to test it.

"So, are you going to keep wearing the sling?"

Kendrith nodded. "I need people to think I am still unable to move."

"When are you going to do it?"

"Tonight."

Kristen suddenly seemed concerned, a fact that did not escape Kendrith. "Don't worry, I will make it back," he reassured her.

"Are you sure you don't want my help?"

Kendrith sighed, considering the offer and even wanting to say yes. "This is something I have to do alone; plus, I need you to be my alibi."

Kristen said no more, nodding reluctantly.

Kendrith pulled out a drawer, taking a small bundle of wrapped cloth and opening it to reveal Simantiar's four bones.

"You think it will work?"

"It has to—this is the only option we have." Kendrith tucked them away. He looked to Kristen with hopeful and worried eyes. "This is it."

"No coming back."

Kendrith nodded, as they lost themselves in each other's embrace for what could be the final time.

Chapter 23

Kendrith had followed the path countless times before, the only difference being that back then, it was during the light of day rather than the cover of night.

The hours before had passed without incident, Kristen continuing her tutelage as George continued to be a promising and tentative student. Kendrith observed more of George's training than any day before, watching his progress with great interest and confirming his suspicions of George's natural proclivity for combat—he was fast on his feet, both literally and figuratively. But perhaps the true reason for why Kendrith had observed him for that much longer was because they had only two more days before George would continue towards the uncharted lands. Kendrith didn't know how it made him feel.

Shaking the ruminations, he decided to focus on the task at hand— there would be enough time for that later.

Looking up to his former home, Kendrith took note of its sleek walls dripping with silver-rimmed windows and largely crafted filigree silver nailed to the sides like wisps of shining leaves; they were perfect for showing off your wealth and keeping certain supernatural beasts at bay, but also perfect for scaling the wall and breaking in.

Kendrith had abandoned someone behind those ornate walls long ago, a boy caged within the confines of birthrights and grooming while beyond those bars was a world the boy's wings would never soar towards. Kendrith abandoned the boy there the day he ran, but he could still feel the presence, the nagging anxiety which roiled just beneath the depths whenever he looked upon it. He then considered not just the cries of a boy left behind, but the father he hadn't seen since, a relationship that if there ever was any chance of mending, was ruined the moment Kendrith fell in love with Kristen.

That was the second thought that Kendrith shook from him, with a calming breath that joined a passing wind he centred himself and stilled his wayward heart. He was ready.

Pulling the sagging hood over his head to aid the shadows in their task of obscuring his approach, he stepped forward.

Jaylen Feller was a man of opportunity, gathering and selling artifacts of lost ages and providing them as symbols of power to rising dignitaries. Thus a man with so much wealth and so many connections was sure to be a threat to many. There had been a couple of attempts on his life over the ages, thus it was no surprise that the security which patrolled the grounds had also gone up; lanterns peeled away the darkness as they made their rounds.

Kendrith withdrew a vial which usually would reveal a golden hue as ferocious as a tiger's pelt, yet with the poor illumination of the night sky, it seemed like a dull and dark orange. Kendrith downed its contents, pulling a cloth over his nose to conceal his face even further.

A few more moments passed as the man tensed his neck muscles, clenched and flexed his fingers, his feet shuffling against the wooden branch of the tree he perched on. The world was asleep but for the soft chirping of grasshoppers that rung their rhythmic chorus, the lonely hoot of an owl distant within the fringes of uncharted lands, and the shuffling of patrolling feet.

Kendrith leapt, his feet taking off from the branch quietly, only a slight rustle and a few falling leaves to ever hint at his being as if he were just passing wind. He glided through the air with little noise, a shadowy stain in one's peripheral vision as he soared above the unsuspecting guard below and his fingers found purchase upon a windowsill, dangling like rags left to dry.

Kendrith waited, his arms still, his legs unmoving.

Now, figured the shadow of night, as he gently tapped the window.

Kendrith's fingers hung from the few inches of stone offered to him and gagged any complaint about his aching shoulder.

As expected, the window opened outwards, without missing a beat, yet with no sign of impatience, Kendrith pulled himself up and through the window in one swift movement.

"What in—" was all that the guard could voice as Kendrith moved like the shadow he embodied. He curled around the guard as a phantom, a hand clasped against the mouth and Kendrith's arms locked under the guard's arms to prevent him from struggling.

Kendrith procured another vial of a swirling, lavender-purple, liquid into his gloved palm, removing the stopper and placing the sudden aroma which the vial expelled right under the guard's flaring nostrils.

The man eased his struggle, his writhing legs losing strength, his eyelids turning heavy, and soon the man turned limp and fell to the ground.

Kendrith sat the man down with his head against the wall. He had no time to hide the unconscious body. Kendrith could only hope that by the time the guard was found, that he would already be gone.

Though Kendrith entered the building from the window on the third floor, his target was below. The hunter skulked the darkness with careful steps, striding over to the walkway that looked down to the ground floor in search of any more patrolling guards.

Uncurling his gloved hands, Kendrith counted the four bones. He could no longer still his heart. He was so close to his family's legacy, to his mother's final gift to him, to that which belonged to Haggar Brosnorth. And all of it would be found the deeper he delved into the belly of an abandoned home.

Excitement merged with the fear of his youth to knock upon Kendrith's nerves—he was close.

A shadow could hide behind any object it desired, but a shadow that was brought up in a house since the day it was born became the home itself. Hiding behind objects that Kendrith knew intimately, blending it with the walls and ornaments to avoid observant eyes.

Kendrith passed by only a few guards on his way to the resting quarters and work rooms of the servants, going past the kitchen and stopping at a plain and intentionally unremarkable wooden door. Kendrith knew the lie that it was, what truth it plotted to hide.

With two procured prongs Kendrith picked the lock and was gratified by a satisfying click.

And so, Kendrith stepped into the darkness with an old and creaking set of stairs to guide him down.

The man gulped, his family's legacy awaited him, yet somehow, Kendrith felt as if the darkness would swallow him whole if given the chance.

The path down the spiralling stairs seemed to go on endlessly, each step bringing Kendrith closer and closer to complete darkness until everything was pitch-black. Kendrith knew that even his potions wouldn't be able to pierce the complete darkness below.

Heavy boots creaked against the wooden steps, a heartpoundingly loud echo with each creak as if years of silence made the steps relish the chance at being heard. Each step was slow and patient, and Kendrith noticed the sound of his breath and wondered if it was always that loud.

A step, but no creaking wood, instead Kendrith heard the muffled surface of hard marble—and there was something else in the air, a sound that drowned out his own breathing, a hum like from one of those energy coils that his grandfather once showed him.

I'm getting close, Kendrith thought.

The lower Kendrith continued to climb, the clearer the humming became and then the slightest hue of light was seen—so soft that Kendrith at first wondered if the darkness had seeped into his mind and was causing him to imagine things, but no, there it was again. A soft blue hue pulsing like a snoozing heart.

As Kendrith descended the final step, a gasp escaped his agape lips—he had found the source of the pulsing light. The blue hue bathed him with its soft shine, and lines of power ran across the floor and walls with straight and angled turns to form some sort of network. Some lines continued on till Kendrith's feet while others ended with round circles as if to denote the end of a circuit. Each one of the power lines seemed to change course and direction without real patterns, but Kendrith could tell that each change and shift was done with purpose; calculated geometrically to perform at its utmost efficiency.

Kendrith stepped forward, careful and in awe of what ancient technology he now approached, with what power it radiated, and how insignificant it made him. It felt as if he was travelling back in time to a world he had only heard of in stories and, until that moment, felt so far away that it might as well just have been stories and myths.

The power lines continued to pulse, the blue light radiating and basking the small room in its ancient glow. Kendrith approached a door from which a large circular centre had several lines meet. Was it the source? Or did the line power it? Kendrith wasn't sure.

Reaching into his pocket, Kendrith removed the bones as they radiated a glow of their own in tandem with the pulsing rhythm of the ley lines.

Hesitantly, Kendrith stepped forward, avoiding the blue streams of power as if fearing to awaken the slumbering world of old.

The closer he got, the louder the hum of the magic became, pulsing to the rhythm of the light until only the constant hum of the bright epicentre was audible.

Lifting Simantiar's bones, he noticed the light within his palms brightening as if in response to the concentrated magic. He took one in his hands and lifted it to the epicentre with caution as the core also flared in response, flaring ever brighter before dwindling out.

Kendrith could see how the magic from the bone depleted as it neutralised the core, the blue shine now evaporating like vapour to the touch.

Kendrith gritted his teeth, the light though dulled still persisted and the door unfazed. "I have not come this far to be held back by a door."

With renewed resolve, Kendrith took the second bone into his hand and pressed it against the light, magic brightening to the touch of the bones as they rattled with the sheer force of the power. The warmth of the ancient magic flared brightly and heat washed over him.

With a final roar, the light brightened in a final act of defiance, blinding Kendrith and causing him to cover his eyes, as the whole chamber began to rattle and the sound of cracking bone was heard over the quaking.

Silence, and the lights dimmed. Kendrith looked up to see the final moment before darkness returned, though the etched pattern of ley lines were still burnt into his vision.

And as if on cue, the circular panel rumbled before him, splitting down the middle with debris falling from the shifting stone of old magic. The split panel divided, opening up a path before him into the vast chamber hidden below his father's manor as fresh rays of pulsing blue light filled the cavern once more.

Kendrith looked to the bones in his hands and noticed how they had blackened to charcoal before crumbling apart as if burnt in a fire.

He curled his fingers over the final two determinedly, whatever trials still awaited him, he would not be denied.

Kendrith stepped forward to witness the long expanding hall as wide as the mansion that stood just above the surface as mirroring thick pillars coursing with lines of power held up a ceiling that was just as tall.

No walls or clutter divided the vast chamber as Kendrith heard his echoing steps resound within the chamber as if to serenade the first sign of life in millennia.

Kendrith looked closer at the power lines which coursed endlessly like guided ravines of magic in far more intrinsically complicated patterns. Though the air outside this hall was stuffy and thick, the chamber within was bright and clear like a breath of fresh air during a sunny day.

At the very end of the vast hall Kendrith could see his long-awaited prize. His hand grabbed at his mother's locket as if grasping at his faith, and limp murmurs escaped his lips. "It's true," he said.

He was so close to reaching his birthright, that which brought him to those halls and something that none of his ancestors had ever managed.

Kendrith removed the sapphire locket and opened it with a comforting click to read the note. "When you're ready," Kendrith read the words aloud. All the times before it sounded like a distant echo, a haze of a phrase that Mona never actually spoke, but Kendrith attributed to her nonetheless.

"If only you were here to see this," he whispered with a longing smile. He knew how proud she would have been.

As Kendrith stepped forward, taking in the sheer nature of the pillars which surrounded him and the pulsing lights as if the very floor pulsed with life, he couldn't help but feel the touch of the old world and the awe it instilled.

Kendrith now stood before the impressive sculpture which held the beautiful blade with both its chiselled hands as the end of the sword pointed down.

Kendrith recognised the winged figure immediately as Vrania, and the upside down blade that was held in both hands, Kendrith recognised as well. "The blade of Vrania," he said as if not doing so would reduce it all to a fleeting dream.

The statue had the features of a long-haired man with a stoic expression of duty despite the colourless stone eyes staring out. Muscular, corded arms grabbed the hilt and lean broad shoulders had folded feathered wings on the back; it had a sense of gravitas to the depiction of Vrania that made Kendrith wonder what the myth was like in person.

The sword was etched with glowing blue runes running down its steel while the rest of the aura that surrounded it gleamed bright with power like a ghostly sheath encasing it. A crescent pommel with ancient leather wrapped the hilt itself, and the sword was a double-edged long sword with a slight wider berth than what Kendrith usually dealt with.

On either side of the winged statue sat kneeling golems with fists to the ground as if in servitude.

Behind the statue, Kendrith saw the mural likeness of a shrouded priest gifting the blade to a kneeling Vrania. Just behind the priest one could see the stout dwarven appearance of Ivaldi hammering away at an anvil. Other heroic depictions formed like the towering mountain of Balan and deities which Kendrith had never seen before. For a brief moment Kendrith fancied the image of Balan to be that of his late grandfather, Haggen. The thought brought a wistful smile to his lips.

Kendrith neared the blade and watched the runes glow at his approach.

A weapon as old as the creation of the world itself was at the tip of his fingers.

And just like that, Kendrith's moment was disrupted as he heard the sound of shifting stone.

Kendrith stepped back, first wondering if it were the figure of Vrania having come to life, but then he turned, now noticing the flanking bodies of stone chiselled to be upon one knee and their fists pressed to the floor.

Power lines came to life all around the two golems and life sparked into their vacant eyes as pits of blue light.

The figures groaned and strained as they rose, rubble falling from their long-dormant bodies as the same criss-cross of power lines which marked the chamber became filled with the familiar pattern of coursing ethereal blue.

They turned their hulking forms of stone and peered down at Kendrith as if he were a bug to crush.

Chapter 24

The two giants came rushing for Kendrith, their eyes ablaze with singular purpose—to protect the last remnant of Vrania.

In a flourish, two daggers from the small of Kendrith's back spun in his palms with a satisfying whir, but he doubted their usefulness against the titans before him.

He had brought them out of security rather than necessity, his two larger swords made for man and beast were left at home for they would have only made it harder to hide. But Kendrith knew the weight of his blade made no difference to the giants of stone as they might as well have been toothpicks.

Kendrith ran, creating distance between himself and the golems, already weighing the options that presented themselves to him.

One step forward, two back, Kendrith measured their intelligence. Playing it safe, he watched with great care at how the monsters stumbled forward on heavy limbs, the way they swayed, the way their eyes wandered without forethought—whatever magic powered the beasts didn't grant them intelligence; their purpose seemed singular, their goal without vision.

Kendrith could have easily outrun them, but it would have defeated the purpose of breaking into his father's house. He stepped back just out of reach as a golem bent over with stubby digits. Kendrith remembered his grandfather's teachings, a memory flashing in his mind of chasing chickens. "Remember, even if you are faster, you will lose speed every time you bend over." Haggen's voice rang in his mind, laughing every time Kendrith tried to catch one of the fluttering winged birds—Kendrith still wasn't so sure if his grandfather was training him, or making a fool out of him.

Kendrith stifled a grin, pulling himself back to the present, yet always grateful for even the oddest of Haggen's teaching.

Each time one of the golems stepped closer, Kendrith took a few more steps back, watching as the two towering structures stepped closer and closer, one foot after the other with dumb eyes.

The giants stumbled gingerly on stone legs as they tried to reach Kendrith. Finally their grinding shoulders and rubbing bodies tripping over one another sent them crashing to the floor in a pile that raised a cloud of damaged stone with it.

Running through the risen dust and hopping with grace onto a ginormous finger, Kendrith ran up the arm and leapt upon a stone face, as he buried the blade of his dagger into the glowing socket of the splayed golem and felt the blade pierce…nothing; just the vibrating buzz of magic coursed through the hollow socket.

The machinations stumbled to their feet as the one Kendrith battled proceeded to backhand him into the air with such force that his dagger snapped with the audible echo of steel ringing through the halls.

Kendrith crashed into a pillar and gasped, all the air evicted from his lungs as he came crashing down with a pained cough and rasp for air.

His lungs tried desperately for air in great choked heaves as the golems loomed. In a desperate attempt to escape them, Kendrith rolled moments before the weight of a golem's foot came cratering down.

Forcing himself to his feet as the first inkling of air returned to a smarting chest, Kendrith stared down in shock at the destruction caused by the weight of the stomp.

He noticed then in his moment of panic that the power line was destroyed and the entire connection suddenly was cut of power.

"Of course," Kendrith said to himself, an idea coming to mind.

Kendrith ran, not looking back, but hearing and feeling the earth quake beneath him as the giant golems pursued him.

Retreating behind a pillar, Kendrith threw away his broken dagger and reached into his pocket to pull out a yellow vial. He downed the contents, feeling the ache in his chest dull and his senses heighten; it was an all too familiar rush which took him now.

The golems came from either side, one already reaching out with its large fingers. Yet, wise to the move and all too fast—in one quick blur Kendrith hopped off his feet, one hand pressing down upon the giant's thumb and using it to gain ever greater height. He ran up the beast's arm for a second time, swift as a cat, as the other arm came to snatch him with slow, clumsy movements while Kendrith might as well have been the wind as he leapt upon its face.

The structure stumbled backwards as Kendrith shouted to the opposite golem with curt insults. The creature watched as empty eyes loomed on Kendrith. It raised its fist and swung just as Kendrith jumped out of the way.

The sound of stone shattering crumbled stone filled the hall as the now headless golem fell to the floor in a shallow grave made by its own descent.

"One down, one more to go," Kendrith said, pulling out the last of Simantiar's bones. His mind raced almost as quickly as his body and his heart seemed to beat doubly fast. He was riding the rush like a wave and let it guide him. He smiled at the thrill and speed as the wind whipped his hair and coursing calves braced him to a leaning halt.

With a dashing sprint, Kendrith slid under the golem's feet, as the giant's hands reached to grasp at nothing.

Swerving on the ball of his foot, Kendrith sprinted back and towards the final golem.

With a soaring jump, Kendrith stabbed into the cracks of one of the golem's power lines and used the momentum to swing even higher into the air and abandon his remaining dagger. Landing on its knee, he scaled up its body and around, onto the arm, and still climbing with unparalleled alacrity.

"Let's see if I can't do it a second time." Kendrith leapt upon the structure's eyes and away as the golem's own fist struck.

The structure fell with a long, heavy groan from a mouthless face. But it wasn't over, the animated structure began to rise.

"A few more of those and—" Kendrith never got to finish his thought, stunned as large stone-like fingers closed around him.

Kendrith gasped, turning helplessly to see the rubble which rolled down a headless golem.

"Should have known," Kendrith admitted as the life was squeezed from his lungs, his ribs bending at the strain.

Kendrith looked at the ruin of the golem's head and noticed a small hole in the centre where the blue magic seemed to gather, smoking from the surface like vapour.

Kendrith struggled, his hands still free from the golem's grasp as he revealed a single of Simantiar's bones to toss into what remained of the golem's head.

At first nothing happened, but then Kendrith watched as the golem went rigid, struggling to move, the light of its body flickering until the creature convulsed and its light was extinguished before it collapsed into a pile of rubble as its threads of magic came undone.

Kendrith squeezed himself through the dead golem's grasp, coming free at last and breathing in the sweetest breath of air he had in a long time if it weren't for the sudden pain at his side.

"Goblin shit," he cursed, feeling the effects of his potion wear off and the aching of torn muscles pushed to their limit.

Kendrith turned back to the remaining golem standing on its feet.

Without the potion running in his veins, Kendrith was running out of options as the soreness of bruised ribs and aching bones made themselves be felt.

"The sword," Kendrith realised.

Kendrith limped towards the statue as quickly as his feet would carry him, finally returning to the blade as the statue of Vrania seemed to look down upon Kendrith with stoic judgment.

His fingers shook as they wrapped themselves around the imposing hilt of the blade.

The blue pulse of the blade became brighter, runes which ran down its steel quickening.

Kendrith could hear the quaking feet behind draw near; Kendrith tugged, pulling back and forth with all his weight, teeth gritted and groaning as the booming strides matched his frenzied heartbeat—the blade wouldn't relent.

The sword seemed to pulse more and more.

The feet which quaked were now deafening to Kendrith's ears. He couldn't tell how close it had come.

How ironic, Kendrith thought, *to have come so close to the sword of Vrania only to die at its feet.*

Yet, the giant froze, and a new blue glow shone upon the golem like a soft rippling pulse of a sleeping heart. However, the glow came not from the sword, but from Kendrith himself.

He looked down to see his mother's pendant glowing, the sapphire gem radiating an energizing warmth. He wasn't sure when it had come loose from his garments.

Kendrith knew it was different to the pulse of the room: softer, more loving; it seemed to almost have a mind of its own, almost as if it were…communicating.

The golem came to a stop, dropping down to a knee and fists to the floor in submission.

Kendrith didn't understand. He looked down again at the pulsing gem, like an ebb and flow of shore waves, its glow a lighter blue than that of the room. "Mother?" Kendrith wondered hesitantly.

Turning to the statue, the blue glow now shone in Vrania's image.

Though confused Kendrith did not question it. He removed the pendant from his neck and raised it to the sword, watching as it glowed even brighter in response.

"Perhaps…" Kendrith looked closer and noticed the little indentation at the hilt of the blade where something was to be fitted. Kendrith looked closer at the sapphire gem and removed it from its gilded frame before fitting it into the slot.

The statue brightened with a blue hue that was not like that of the hall, but that of the gem.

Kendrith watched in wonder as it came to life.

Kendrith tensed for a moment, thinking there was now a second trial to be had.

Yet it never came, instead, the statue held the sword in both hands and extended it out to Kendrith in an act of bestowal.

Kendrith was overcome by the sheer gravity of the act that left his hands trembling and doubt filling his bones. What felt like the shadow of Vrania that peered at Kendrith and deemed him unworthy now held out arguably the most fabled sword in existence.

Trembling hands grabbed for it as if expecting to be smitten for his folly. What pristine aura the sword expelled could have only been described as divine, a fact that filled Kendrith with great reverence.

The large chamber faded in the blue light, the coursing power lines dimmed to a soft hue before finally all the power lines began to retreat from the entrance and return to the statue of Vrania and disappear behind the mural.

That is when Kendrith understood, the chamber wasn't powering the blade, but rather the blade was powering the chamber.

Chapter 25

Feelings roiled within the young hunter—he had finally achieved what countless before him could not. He had passed through the vaulted walls of his home and retrieved that which was believed to be a simple legend.

Part of Kendrith felt invincible, an inexplicable rush and sense of awe filling him at the glistening sword in his hands that put him out of time and made him acutely aware of his existence, but also his insignificance.

A faint glow came from the runes etched into the sword. The glyphs were none that Kendrith had ever seen before, and the curves and elegance with which the runes were chiselled told of the meticulous care and attention that was involved. The aura pulsed like a timid heartbeat that brightened, then dimmed over and over.

It was a chance to shape an epic in his name, brandishing the blade and matching legends of old. But for all intents and purposes the hilt felt...awkward and ill-fitting in his grasp, his mother's gem pressing into his palm and the usual comforting weight which weighed against his chest now gone.

"What now?" Kendrith wondered.

As if sensing his hesitance the sword's glow flickered, dimmed, and then vanished all at once, leaving Kendrith to his ruminations. Something about that eased his breathing, made him unclench tense muscles he didn't even know were being tensed...he hated that. Was he really so unprepared?

Lost in his thoughts he continued to exit the chamber of the lost world, a ruin hidden by the grandiose home of his childhood. Kendrith felt for the walls as he slowly found his way to the door. Careful and heavy steps led him up towards the surface, but a piece of him was left behind.

The victory he felt, the rush at holding history in his hands felt so...fleeting, so vague. This was what he had always wanted, wasn't it? He recalled the tales of how bright the sword gleamed for those it championed, yet for Kendrith, it was nothing more than a relic.

Hiding within the shadow of the doorway, his new blade was tucked behind his cloak as footsteps marched by. The mansion had livened up—perhaps the sound of the stomping golems had reverberated throughout the foundations or they had found the guard which Kendrith had put to sleep.

Yet somehow, it didn't seem to trouble him, for his turmoil of indelible doubt left him fugue-minded. He felt...drained.

Kendrith walked out into the dark shadows of the kitchen without incident, silver moonlight shining through to colour the tiles grey.

Like a ghost, Kendrith simply glided through the halls of his home, gone like a whisper the moment cautioned eyes turned a corner.

Perhaps it was the blade in his hand? What did his fear of his childhood home matter anymore? The fear of getting caught by guards. The fear he had for his father. It all suddenly seemed so inconsequential in the presence of the sword; Kendrith's world suddenly seemed far larger, feeling as if he were stranded on a boat within the dark waters of the sea, as if the truth of how wide the surface was paled in comparison with the darkness of the depths.

He wanted to become a hero. Like his grandfather. Like his mother. Suddenly it didn't matter what blessing his father wanted to give or didn't. But doubt still whirled inside the man. What if he failed? What if he gave his father another reason to be right? It did not topple his conviction, but it sure threatened his foundations.

But one thing became unmistakably clear for Kendrith as he veered away from the exit and headed up the stairs. It was time to pay his father a visit.

Jaylen Feller entered his study, opening one of the double doors just enough to allow himself entry. Kendrith watched him through flowing white curtains which gave his father a ghostly impression.

The years weighed heavily on the man. More and more books piled up in the study, sheets of paper carpeted the floor, and the familiar scent of bourbon which had always smelt of maturity meshed with the scent of oak now smelt of stress and exhaustion as the toils of age showed themselves.

A sudden pang of guilt hit Kendrith, one that was always present and he tried hard to suppress. Everyone talked about the stress that parents have over leaving something behind for their children to secure their future, but no one ever discussed the guilt carried by children who chose to reject that gift. All that toil, all that hard work, driven by a singular cause only to then be so timidly rejected by a child who never asked for any of it.

There it was—the chains of Jaylen's own making—a legacy with no one to inherit it, left to toil on with what he had built because giving it away now would leave him hollow.

Jaylen's grey hairs came in streaks, slicked back to cover as much of the thinning as they could, fault lines marked the corners of his eyes as the slumped man pinched the bridge of his nose and let out at an exaggerated sigh. It would seem as if the only thing that would interest him was sleep, a notion that became ever more apparent as he stumbled, bracing himself against the wooden headrest of an armchair.

The only comfort was the cracking of burning firewood that Kendrith had tended and lit.

"Did I light the fireplace?" the man murmured to himself, unaware of Kendrith's presence.

The man rose to his full stature, straightening his austere dull grey jacket and fixing the rounded spectacles. Yet, all of that effort crumbled quicker than the time it took to fix as he stared out towards the three arched windows of his study. The two left and right were empty, but a moaning breeze rushed through the one in the middle to reveal the broad-shouldered man who stood leaning on the windowsill.

Kendrith swirled the polished brown contents of his glass before taking a sip. He was already on his second and found each sip instilling more and more foolish courage.

Jaylen turned around for a moment as if to call for the guards, but something made him hesitate.

The man slowly spun back towards Kendrith with cautious eyes.

"If you are here to kill me you better get it over with—I have a ton of work still waiting on me. Otherwise, piss off before I call the guards." The words were spoken without any humour, more a threat than anything else.

Kendrith couldn't help but chuckle. "It's good to see you too, Father," Kendrith said, realising the shadow of his father was what Kendrith had truly feared, not the haggard and exhausted man before him who was riddled with age.

Kendrith eyed the man before him—now that he was standing closer he could more clearly see the ravages of time that aged his father. Creases and wrinkles formed valleys below and under sunken eyes. A liver spot showed on his left cheek and heavy eyes struggled to stay open. There was a sudden profound sadness that washed over Kendrith—he was surprised to find guilt at the fact that he hadn't been there to watch his father grow old. Kendrith always had respect for his father, but seeing him so frail felt like an injustice.

The only emotion expressed by the man was disbelief. It had certainly been a decade since last they saw each other. His glance fell on the blade which rested on Kendrith's lap, confusion knitting his brows, but then, stark realisation.

"Is that?"

Kendrith only nodded, a sombre smile on his face as he turned away to look at the moon, mere days away from shining fully.

"And is that?" He pointed at the gem upon the hilt as if seeing his late wife's face looking back at him.

"Yeah, that's Mom's. Turned out it was the key to retrieving the sword."

Jaylen let out a soft chuckle. "So, you are the reason for all this commotion."

Kendrith stayed quiet as he heard the shuffling of feet and grunts.

"What are you doing here, Kendrith?" Jaylen's query was direct, but there was a hint of caution to his words, as if fearing he might scare his only son away after not seeing him for ten years.

Kendrith looked down to his newly won prize.

"Other than that," Jaylen amended.

Kendrith smiled.

"Want to join me?" Kendrith asked with a wayward smile as he lifted his glass implicatively.

Jaylen hesitated, but the man knew an olive branch when he saw one and nodded with deep consideration.

The two of them climbed out the window with a second glass and the remaining whisky in hand. They sat side by side on the slanted tile roof which gave a view of swaying tree branches and a sea of quiet homes, the outline of the uncharted land trees just beyond that like a dark mound of earth.

"Do you remember we used to come here when you were really young? Your mother too. We would look at the stars and talk for hours on end." The words Jaylen spoke were supposed to be comforting nostalgia, reminiscing about better times. But all it served to do was make Kendrith wonder how everything went so wrong. Another thought he drowned with another sip of his drink.

Several moments passed by in silence, Kendrith not minding it in the least, but his father seemed to be searching for the right words to say.

Jaylen finally settled. "So, you finally did it."

"Did what?" Kendrith asked, knowing the answer, but he still wanted to hear it.

Jaylen simply nodded over to the blade.

"I guess I did."

"Even after all my efforts to stop you from going down this path."

"Yep."

"You never answered my question. Why are you here?" The query was equal measures restraint and contention.

Kendrith allowed himself time to find the right words, a patience grown from the absence of urgency, surely instilled by the liquid courage that swirled in his hand. He took his time, looking at how the contortion of the glass reflected what little light shone on it from the moon above.

"It's been ten years. Do I need a reason to see my father?"

Jaylen nodded. "It has been ten years, ten years too long. So, why now?"

Kendrith shrugged. "You didn't reach out to me either."

"I sure tried more than you did! Your grandfather didn't exactly make it an easy endeavour."

"You weren't trying to reconnect, you were trying to drag me back to a future I never wanted!"

"Is it so wrong to want to keep my son safe?"

"You know what? It was a mistake coming here." Kendrith rose to stand and noticed the subtle wave of alcohol working its influence.

"Wait…" What a feeble request it was that came from Jaylen as a rogue hand grasped desperately upon Kendrith's sleeve. Jaylen simply looked straight ahead, eyes blinking manically as Kendrith took note of the slight tremble to his father's grip.

"Please stay, I'm sorry."

Kendrith sighed. He came here to reconcile, not to make things worse.

There was something else now in Jaylen's expression…sorrow. Perhaps even doubt?

Kendrith realised then that his father was trying to find words he never used before. Perhaps wondering what words a father would use rather than a businessman. And now, when the time finally came, he didn't know what to say to his son after so long and neither did Kendrith. It felt as if he were walking on a rickety bridge on the verge of collapsing.

"Are you still angry that I left?" Kendrith asked, the only question which came to mind.

Jaylen's words were spoken with audible exhaustion. "Angry? I was furious. After all the effort I put into securing your future, making sure you didn't humour your foolish whims, chasing some sort of fantasy, and still you did everything in your power to defy me."

Kendrith began to wonder if his coming was a bad idea, but then his father said something which shocked him to his very core—words that only bore fruit by the contents of his own glass.

"And yet you did it anyway. Do I agree with your decision? No…but I would be lying if I said I wasn't proud of you. Even if I could stop you now I would, but I know when I should cut my losses. I know you think that I failed as a father, and perhaps in many ways I have. But I tried my best. And surely you liberating me from the sword of Vrania will only stoke your flame."

Kendrith looked over to his father and watched as the man stared up at the moon with deep-rooted sorrow. Rheumy eyes began to water, but the tears never came—even the moustache and beard seemed to be nothing more than a burden on sunken skin.

"I'm sorry I ran out on you." Now it was Jaylen's turn to look shocked, an apology was the last thing he expected.

"I don't agree with what you've done. I still look back to my childhood with regret and what could have been, but I also understand, and wish to mend as much as can be. I know you did what you thought was best. And coming here now, I know I was wrong to not visit you." Kendrith shrugged as a distant owl's hoot sounded like encouragement. Taking in a deep breath he continued, "I was wrong." The words came loud and quick like ripping off a bandage, but when it was done, a sense of relief washed over him.

"I was wrong to leave without telling you. I was wrong to not visit for the past ten years and avoid you when we lived in the same town. I used to think it was because I was still angry at you. But the truth is I was scared.

My hands still shook when I broke into the study…it's just as I remembered it. The scent and everything." Kendrith turned to his father. "I was scared of coming back, seeing the hurt and disappointment in your eyes for not being as you wanted me to be."

Jaylen nodded, his lips pursed and his reply solemn. "I am also sorry. I realised far too late that my attempts at leaving you a settled and worthy life just drove you further away…even if you are partnered with the very person who tried to kill me." Only the final part held some trace of Jaylen's previous malice.

"Dad, you know her story. It's different now." Kendrith was surprised to find how he let the claim pass. He saw his father more clearly than ever before and realised he was not a monster, he was just another human trying his best.

Jaylen gave a defeated sigh. "I guess you're right." He didn't sound entirely convinced.

The two looked out to the moon once more, allowing a more comfortable silence to fill the space between them now, the aching tension of Kendrith's heart now softened.

"If you are still here for a time, I'd like to invite you over, and you can share all your adventures with me," Jaylen offered.

"You want to hear about them?"

"Not one bit." They both laughed at that.

Kendrith felt the tense air between the two unwind and loosen. Was it genuine or was it because of the alcohol? It didn't matter—what mattered was that they both made the effort, and talked like father and son just like they had when Mona was still with them and smiled lovingly.

"Do you remember that one time when you dressed up as a dragon and ran around the house?" Jaylen asked, a great big goofy smile as he recalled the memory.

"No?" Kendrith chuckled and felt a light warmth at seeing his father express such joy as he retold the stories.

"You would dress up as a dragon and your mother would pretend to be a great knight looking for the big bad dragon that terrorised the lands of Fellania. She would actually go and question each cook and servant if they had heard rumours of the dragon and they would play along and tell your mother to travel to Kitchenia where you were last seen, or consider crossing the perilous valley of Hallwayton."

"Who came up with those dreadful names?!" Kendrith asked as his chest heaved from laughing so hard, the commotion of the restless guards still audible as they called each other for news.

"Your mother, of course!" Jaylen joined in on the laughter.

"Eventually, she would come across your lair where you stacked pillows into a fort, and you pretended loose items to be your treasure." His laughing turned sombre as he neared the end of the story, as if he was rueful to return to a world where his love no longer was present.

"Every single time it would end with the dragon beating the knight…because she loved you, and loved playing along just to hear your laughter at the very end."

How does one contend with such an ending? Kendrith did not know what to say that would continue the train of happy memories.

Eventually, everyone had to return to the present.

"…And you can also invite Kristen when you visit. I guess it is time to meet my daughter-in-law."

Kendrith gave a heartfelt chuckle, happily accepting the change of topic. "We aren't married."

"You aren't?" A look of disbelief.

"Not really interested. We are happy as is. But I would happily bring her along."

Kendrith fell quiet for a time, staring at the blade with understanding. "But I can't right now, I have a job waiting for me."

Jaylen didn't seem to approve, but knew better than to speak out. It was something that meant the world to Kendrith. Understanding that even though they did not see eye to eye, Kendrith did what he had to do.

"Where will you be going?" Jaylen asked.

"Not too sure, but I will be heading towards the northern lands, heading east. Something about a vault."

Jaylen's eyes widened. "To the uncharted lands?"

Kendrith nodded and expected a rebuttal, and even though he could see how his father pursed tight lips waiting to explode, he kept quiet instead.

"Be careful," was the closest Jaylen came to voicing his disapproval.

"What was it like, getting the blade after so long?" Jaylen asked after a moment of quiet, sounding genuinely curious.

Despite your insistence that it couldn't be done? Kendrith thought.

"Rather…anticlimactic," Kendrith confessed.

"Anticlimactic?"

"I just…I don't know. It was supposed to feel right. Like justification that I am going on the right path. That the world does have something in store for me."

"And you didn't feel that way?"

"Not really. More like I am out of my depth. Sure, I got the sword, but so far my tasks have been escort missions through the Forest of the Dead. I haven't really achieved anything. No broader escorts to other cities or exploring the uncharted lands."

Jaylen nodded. "You know, as a child, you never really dreamt of getting the sword. You dreamt of becoming a legend. Like your grandfather." Jaylen shuddered at the mention of Haggen, almost as if remembering something he'd rather forget. "The same way I wanted to uphold the family legacy and maintain my reputation, not garner wealth and power—that was just a side product.

"Perhaps in the same way the sword was never supposed to be the end of it all, just an accessory towards that goal. "

Kendrith looked down to the blade. "Everyone tells me of my talents, my natural acuity for combat. My skills. I am supposed to be good at this. Yet, the blade does not shine for me. Perhaps this is it, this is my limit."

Jaylen seemed to consider his next words. "Talent is the greatest bane of all. It convinces you that you are different, prodigious, a natural. Yet, when you hit a wall—and trust me, we all do—you suddenly have to put in the effort and are convinced that is your limit. It's not, that is where the real work begins."

"So, if I put in the effort, do you think I can end up like Mom and Granddad?"

"If I say no, will you stop this?"

"Definitely not."

Jaylen gave out a chuckle and gingerly wrapped an arm around his boy, tugging slightly—then perhaps thinking better of it, he let go and cleared his throat to hide his awkwardness. "There you have your answer," he said to take away from the embrassment. "I don't know if you will make it. But does it matter? You are going to try anyway. Just promise you will come back to me." His eyes were almost pleading and desperate. What emotions must have roiled beneath them.

"But what about the sword?"

Jaylen blinked. "How can the sword shine for you if you don't even believe in yourself? The sword doesn't make you a hero, the sword just happens to belong to one."

Kendrith nodded. If the words were supposed to provide comfort they did, but it came at the cost of dread—dread at the tasks that were yet to come.

A knock suddenly came from the study.

"You have the guards in quite an uproar looking for you."

Kendrith simply smiled as Jaylen stood up to get back into his study.

"Your mother would have been proud," he said before reentering his study.

"Thanks, Dad."

As Kendrith was about to leave, Jaylen spoke his final words. "And Kendrith?" Kendrith turned back to see his father, the old man hesitate, like a clump stuck in his throat that had to be forced out. "I love you."

It didn't sound like a declaration…more like a promise. Kendrith and Jaylen weren't foolish to think that all their problems were solved, but the groundwork was laid for a better tomorrow. Though awkward and strange, Kendrith was glad he buried his pride and came to reconcile.

The words meant the world to Kendrith and he didn't even realise it. His voice gave the slightest sign of breaking before he replied, "I love you too, Dad. I will be visiting you when I return, so be prepared."

The only thing which chased away the shadows within Kendrith's room was the lamp which burnt with fish oil, perched upon the nightstand, a humble glow offering respite from the darkness and illuminating the mauve bruise atop his ribs.

"You are lucky they didn't break," Kristen said as she tended to him.

Kendrith couldn't help but notice how Kristen's eyes kept flickering over to the new relic which leaned against the wall of their room.

He smiled, knowing exactly how she must have felt, thinking how out of place the blade must have seemed as if a noble king was to sit at their dinner table.

"I'm not your nurse, you know. Perhaps try to not get injured every time you leave the house," Kristen teased as she always did, but the mirth which usually coloured her tone was absent.

Kendrith tried to change the subject. "How is George's training coming along?"

Kristen looked up at him and each time he looked into those deep sea-blue eyes illuminated by the orange glow of the light, he couldn't help but realise all over again how deep his love for her went. It was that rare moment of lucidity where one acknowledged the sheer absurd luck that brought Kristen into his life, a brief realisation of her own will, her own identity, what made Kristen her own person, and what made her choose to fall in love with him.

"You were right—he is talented, and he takes to the training the same way a fish takes to water." Kendrith was avulsed from his rumination.

"But even so, with only two days left to train him, I don't know if he will be ready."

Kendrith looked down at that and was foolish to think Kristen wouldn't notice his hesitance.

"What's the matter?" she asked.

"I've decided to go with George."

Kristen's eyes widened. "Are you sure? The path is perilous, and you are not trained to guide anyone up there. The guild isn't going to accept this, and Logan is far better trained."

"Never said I would guide him, but go along with them. Logan will still be in charge. I can sign up as a volunteer. It also helps to prepare me for when I do want my licence."

Kristen sat up, looking deep into his eyes in search for answers. "Why the sudden change of heart?"

Kendrith licked his lips and braced his elbows under him as he lay on the bed. "After I found the sword…I didn't really feel it."

"What does that mean?"

"When I held it…it wasn't the way I imagined it. If this is a chance to get a step closer and realise my goals, then I have to take it. Perhaps along the way, I will be worthy.

"Am I going to be content with claiming that which I dreamt of since my mother told me the stories of old? Will lousy escort missions and cutting down husks do it? And then what? Retire and hang the sword on the wall? Plus, if it weren't for George and Simantiar, I wouldn't be having this discussion. I owe it to them to finish what was started."

Kendrith's eyes drifted to the reverently still blade. Though it was he who found it, who beat the golems and took the blade from underneath his home and carried it around, Kendrith couldn't help but feel as if he was not in control, as if the blade was still appraising his worth. "I wasn't seeing the big picture; this is just the beginning, a piece of the old world that was simply found in stories and books, something that seemed so far away as if entirely from another world."

He looked to Kristen. "But it isn't from another world. It's right below our feet, right at our doorstep, and one need just venture out and find the rest. Now that I have the blade, I can't just sit back in the comfort of our own house, but rather I need to go out into the world and put our family's birthright to use."

Kristen matched Kendrith's stare of determination and then nodded. "Then I will be joining you."

"Wait just a min—"

"There is no way you will get me to stay home. You know the promise we made each other, the promise I made to myself ever since what happened with Verron. There is a whole world waiting for us out there to be discovered, and I'll be damned before I let the love of my life discover all its wonders without me."

Kendrith knew three things, the first being how stubborn Kristen got once she set her mind to something, the second being how she would use their love for one another to get what she wanted, and the third being how Kendrith would always give in at the end.

"Plus, while Logan is watching George, who will be watching over you?" she mocked, returning to her old self with a teasing smile and leaned in for a tender kiss that made everything fade and yet fall in place all at once.

Suddenly, it felt right, and Kendrith wanted nothing more than to travel the world with Kristen at his side. Even the weight of the relic leaning against the wall seemed to fall away and become featherlight—he knew that with Kristen nothing was insurmountable.

Chapter 26

Nothingness.

The ground below one's feet, the cold marble at the touch of curling toes, the grainy soil of the forest or the feeling of wind through one's hair or the sun's warmth on skin: all of it had fallen away.

The world had lost its shape, gone from the material into absence without any form or shape, all of it turning into nothingness, into a single exhale which expanded and formed with every breath that Simantiar took.

Over the past couple of days, more and more of Simantiar's old power began to return, yet still it was but a drop in the emptied sea stricken by drought.

Bits and pieces like shadows of his old self coalesced, parchments coming together to take form and fill in the chasm which was once Simantiar so very long ago.

Within this dreamscape created of Simantiar's old mind the ancient wizard retreated, immaterial and at the mercy of the roiling abyss, one with all of it.

And just as his old self began to slowly but surely rebuild itself like parchment returning to plaster walls, the pages of George's book floated within the mindscape Simantiar had built.

His material shell still remained in the real world, lost in meditation as his spirit vaulted itself behind closed doors and continued to toil over the pages.

Pages imprinted as projections in his mind's eye, taking form within the abyss the same way a thought takes shape, like shifting ink on fleeting paper.

Simantiar sensed how the pages were tethered to George—his very essence was tied like an invisible thread as time and time again George had coveted the book with such love that the lingering warmth was like a soft spring heat after melting snow. And there was another thread, faint, barely noticeable, but undeniably present, intertwined with that of George into a braided spiral. Simantiar had no doubt that this one belonged to Lily, and true to her name Simantiar imagined a lily blossoming upon a grass hill overlooking a great swaying field over grass.

Simantiar remembered the classes of the institute, how symbolic relationships with objects in the world left behind wispy threads of their beings that bound them. The stronger the ties, the stronger the link; the more passionate the emotion, the darker the corresponding hue.

"Simantiar." The abyss fell apart, and the world took shape once more. Simantiar looked down from his perch to see George, Kristen, and Kendrith below him.

Simantiar had preferred to do his work among wildlife due to the teachings of an old friend he still did not remember.

Nestled within his crane of vines and away from the presence of humanity, he found his powers worked even stronger and his connection was even more pronounced where life flourished unrestrained.

The vines and branches from neighbouring trees coiled around Simantiar to create an intertwined hammock which held him aloft and tangled his enamel vessel ever further until moss blanketed him; the vines continued on, reaching down into the soil like roots.

Birds of all sorts, squirrels, deer, and all other wildlife gravitated to him, some that could reach that high resting upon his body, while those who couldn't napped below around the vines as if they knew Simantiar would protect them. Though Pecky seemed ostensibly protective and coveting as he screamed and brigaded the other birds and squirrels who also sought refuge within the gaps of Simantiar's form.

Yet all fled at the approach of George and the others, and Pecky seemed satisfied at that.

But the magic did not relent, dexterous vines worked endlessly before Simantiar, trying to put together torn pages to an old book. Simantiar knew that at the height of his power, the task would have been no different than a hand wave or a breath. But as he was, it felt more like trying to fit a puzzle with missing pieces.

Finally, the vines unravelled and Simantiar was carried down to the floor by the aid of what felt like an entire living forest.

His makeshift body stood lithe and strong, engineered in such a way to ensure the most efficiency: from springlike calves to taut muscle fibres, he was made for speed and explosive power.

"I am almost there. I just need some more time," Simantiar promised, growing tired of the constant interruptions.

"That's not why we are here," George exclaimed, seemingly delighted.

"We are coming with you on the quest," Kristen said as if it were no important matter.

Kendrith simply smiled affirmably with crossed arms.

"Yet, I don't know how far we can get without the book." Kendrith looked up to the vines as they continued to work even without Simantiar to guide them.

Simantiar sighed. "Truth be told, I am almost there, but something is still missing. A catalyst, of some sort, a way to bridge the gap in the connection and have the pages find themselves." Simantiar spoke only half of the truth. He was honest in his promise that the pages could be made to find themselves, but there was no way to clean the muddied pictures or replace the pages that were damaged and lost to the swamp. For that, he would have to turn back time.

Kendrith eyed him closely. "We might have something for that."

Slowly, the hunter removed a wrapped object to reveal a sword. Simantiar gasped in the way a skull might, a sudden connection which transcended time and more, as if violently trying to pull him into the past.

"What power—what sort of sword is this?" Simantiar asked, his arm reaching out to touch the blade, and watched as the sword brightened, as if recognising the old wizard.

Kendrith immediately pulled it away. "I wouldn't do that if I were you, don't want you sucking it dry."

Immediately Simantiar realised his mistake. He could see how the very aura of the blade gravitated to him like whisps of smoke dragged through a draught. But more than that, Simantiar could also see his own essence being pulled towards the sword. Whatever the relic was, it was powerful.

"It is the sword of Vrania," Kendrith said.

"The fabled blade of myth? Are you sure?" Simantiar asked.

"Well, until recently we all thought you were a folktale," Kristen teased.

Simantiar nodded, it was true, but even he doubted the existence of the blade.

The vines then, as if by their own will, returned the pages to Simantiar stacked and gift-wrapped perfectly to prevent the loss of even one page.

"Perhaps it is something best discussed within the privacy of your home."

Pecky seemed to have noticed something, for he proceeded to lean over and peck against Simantiar's scalp.

Chapter 27

There was something surprisingly apt about the body Simantiar donned, a temporary vessel for a time long past his own, a reminder that he did not truly belong there—an uninvited visitor more than anything else.

A drab and baggy monk's robe hid him from prying eyes, along with his hood drawn over his ivory skull and a slight spell of concealment to make eyes drift over him.

Upon entering Kendrith's home, the hunter moved to the centre of the dining room and moved the furniture aside.

"Help me move this." Kendrith, George, and Kristen each grabbed a corner of the table and lifted. Simantiar removed his hood and could have easily extended vines from his fingers to do the work, or simply instilled kinetic magic to push the table out of the way, or any number of things, but his mother's words worked their influence; Simantiar knew that everything had a time and place and instead joined in to lift the table normally.

Kendrith rolled away the unremarkable rug to reveal the telling lines of a trap door. He pulled on the ringed handle to reveal a short set of steps leading down.

Kristen reached for the lantern hanging beside their entrance door, lighting it quickly with a match and handing it to Kendrith. "Let's go," he said.

Kendrith led the way into a small basement. Pecky fluttered his wings in unease, jumping into Simantiar's lowered hood to hide.

The chamber was only a couple of square meters in size, but seemed large enough to hold an armoury and a couple of tables with their own workstations of alchemy, weaponry, and leatherworking. A lone grinding stone wheel sat in a corner while polished blades from daggers to swords of all sizes hung from a wooden board on the wall. Beside it was a worktable with assorted daggers and an unfinished bandolier, including a crossbow unstringed.

The lingering scent of oil filled the room including acidic and sweet scents surely from what turbid remains filled the stained alchemy beakers.

"What is this place?" George asked.

"Nothing special, just our room of operations, weapons, alchemy, and all other things to help us on our missions," Kristen said.

"And is that a map?" George pointed to the far side wall.

Kristen nodded.

There were two maps side by side—one focused inward towards more of the lands surrounding Haven which was made for escort missions, while the other showed an entire continent. She pointed at the telling signs of the town at the centre of the map, she then dragged her pointer finger down. "This is the Forest of the Dead which you passed through." The map even showed the centre of the forest, a great warning dotted that one should not enter, but with no explanation.

Simantiar noticed George's sudden shudder and smiled internally.

"I miss the place you know." Simantiar threw his arm around George in mock fashion. "We should get another tour guide and take another walk, but perhaps this time someone who knows what they are doing."

Kendrith and George both turned, giving Simantiar a grueling look, and only Kristen laughed at the notion. Pecky peeked from the hood as if feeling the affable mood and chirped.

Kristen returned to the map, pointing up north of the town towards the uncharted lands.

"This is where we will be headed, most of it is still unmapped territory."

"Why unmapped?" George asked.

"Routes to and fro can be done with planning, but the place is too dangerous for long-term settlements. Expeditions can gather only one bit at a time and single elites dying on the job hadn't been unheard of." Simantiar couldn't quite place it, but took note of the fleeting glance that Kristen and Kendrith shared.

George seemed to have noticed too. "What is it?" he asked.

After a brief moment of hesitance, it was Kendrith who spoke. "My mother and grandfather. My mother died when she came across the great beast of stone in the forest. My grandfather never returned. He is presumed dead." The words sank like heavy stone as Kendrith spoke them.

"That's reassuring," Simantiar commented.

"What is the 'beast of stone?'" George asked.

"A ferocious creature that lurks beneath the canopy of trees. It follows a mapped path across the forest, but sometimes trails off without warning. It is the main reason no permanent settlement could be made too far into the land because of its prowling," Kristen explained.

Kendrith shrugged. "We will manage." The man smiled and let his stern expression drop for one of reassurance. "Plus, we will have Logan coming with us."

Both Simantiar and George cocked their heads questionably. "Who is Logan?" Simantiar asked.

Kristen and Kendrith simply exchanged a knowing glance and smiled from ear to ear. "You'll see."

George turned his attention back to the map. "And what's that? Abandoned outpost?" George pointed to the western part of the uncharted lands.

"As it says, it's just an abandoned outpost, an emergency place of refuge stocked with emergency supplies in times of need. But the guild abandoned holding the spot for the amount of resources it required."

George turned to the other map. "And that is Lenaren?"

Kristen nodded. "The continent on which we are." She pointed at a small patch of land at the border of the continent. "And this is Bedal, the country which we are in." George stared at the map in awe.

"Right, enough dilly-dallying, let's get started," Simantiar said, thudding together his makeshift hands.

Kendrith and Kristen cleared a path, and a dented dummy fitted with armour was carried away from the centre of the room to make as much space as possible.

Kristen, Kendrith, George, and Pecky all stood against the wall beside the stairs, as if ready to escape should Simantiar's magic prove too much.

The ancient wizard sat on the stone floor, the robes he wore now removed to reveal the coiled veins that tensed into faux muscles like writhing worms with no ends, but that groaned like shifting bark.

His body began to unravel, veins extending outwards and taking apart the wrapped pages of George's book. Each tentacle worked meticulously and placed the pages in front of Simantiar in an order that formed out of trust for his instincts; he did not know the rhyme or reason for the system, he did not have to. The words of his old friend, Cernunnos, rang in his head, telling him nature was not to be controlled, how it was to be left to be free, and nature itself would tell him how it was to grow.

And so Simantiar allowed the veins freedom to sort the pages as they wished, like coursing water that continued to flow erratically.

Simantiar's ghostly sockets remained dim, the blue light now a soft thing within the darkness of his eyes as if at the very end of a vast cavern.

He could not feel the course of nature as strongly as he did within the forest, but it didn't matter. The veins which wrapped around him extended below, reaching through cracking stone and farther still, plugging the ancient wizard into all existence.

There was the sound of Kendrith's sword being unsheathed, the blade being placed delicately beside Simantiar.

Vines extended out from his ribs and lightly wrapped around the steel in careful reverence.

The reaction was instantaneous.

From a dull glow the sword brightened into a blinding flare, the runes upon it pulsing vehemently as tumultuous magic howled into soaring winds within the confined room, trying to break free. A beaker shattered. Books and scrolls rattled off tables into the wind as nail and wood creaked and groaned.

Simantiar's eyes suddenly exploded into life. A connection was made beyond anything that Simantiar had experienced—the power which coursed through him was unfathomable, almost unbearable. His eyes became a blaring beacon of blue light that exploded and filled the room, his mouth opening with even more blinding rays as if struggling to contain all that magic.

But the groundwork was laid, the soil ploughed to allow the waters to run free and form rivers.

The vines worked as they did, reassembling the pages, the stream now filling itself and the water taking its course from there, meandering the river and making it as nature intended.

Suddenly, it wasn't just the vines which led the way, but the winds too drove the pages this way and that, sorting them as they were made to be. A link formed. Not with George or Lily, but rather with itself as the book remembered what it once was.

And suddenly, even the pages that were missing came into existence, faint passages gleaming and turning corporeal.

"Simantiar!" Did someone call for him?

"Simantiar! Stop!" The winds continued their restless toil.

"Simantiar!" A hand now grasped his shoulder, and the wizard returned to the present, his eyes ebbing to their normal glow, the blade of Vrania returning to its tepid hue.

"What happened?" the wizard asked.

Kendrith was behind him, grasping at his shoulder, but looking straight ahead. Kendrith did not speak, he simply pointed to the pages before Simantiar.

The wizard turned, wondering what all the commotion was about, and then he understood.

"It can't be," the wizard murmured.

The pages floated before him, all assorted into one big page side by side, and the truth of it dawned on the wizard. "It's a map."

The pages formed into the surrounding parts, blue scribbles of the mountains forming as if ingrained into the very pages themselves followed by the forests and more. But it seemed different. Supposed cities lined the northern mountains and a path lead to the northeastern corner of the map.

"It's a map to the vault," George realised.

"The vault..." Kendrith started.

"Exists," Simantiar finished.

What was once a simple quest to fulfil a childish and dying promise to a little sister now became so much more.

The golden vault seemed to be real, hidden behind strong and intense magic.

But there was more to it, as the storm died down and the experience dawned on Simantiar, something else came to him. A memory, something long gone.

While he was lost within the endless world confined in that book, Simantiar felt the touch of his oldest and most dear friend—Usellyes.

The morning before the final trek, George had visited The Wings of Vrania and met Beynard. Countless times Beynard had warned him of the dangers of the quest at hand and to reconsider, but George rebutted every time. With just as many contracts and forms signed by George with a hastily scribbled signature and a hefty down payment delivered to the guild in the form of clattering gold coins tucked away in shoes and sewn into brown trouser seams, George was given the green light for his travel up north; a single moment was spared to consider what dangers may await him.

Chapter 28

At the break of dawn, George, Kendrith, Simantiar, and Kristen prepared to leave on the final stretch of George's quest.

Simantiar had abandoned his body and slipped away into George's satchel. It was only fitting that the last trek to the golden gates would continue just as it had begun. Pecky this time took a ride on George's shoulder. The boy seemed a little reserved and deep in thought ever since the book's repair.

"What is it?" Simantiar asked from within the shadows of the satchel as they walked through streets where vendors opened up shop.

"Nothing." George just smiled fleetingly.

Kendrith and Kristen had already gone ahead to the gate which faced out towards the northern territories.

George found that the two were not alone, but accompanied by a familiar hulking and handsome figure. A thick debonair moustache curled his regal lips, his white skin was moisturised, and the golden hair atop of his head was slicked back with glistening mousse. It was Soran.

Kendrith began to introduce him.

"George, this is Logan—he will be responsible for our travels henceforth."

"Logan? I thought your name was—"

George never got to finish what he was saying as Logan wrapped his bulging arm around him and gave a deafening laugh. "Oh, we've already met."

"You have?" Kristen asked.

"That's right," said the incredibly tall man. His voice booming with confidence that infected George—he was truly giant.

"Logan Van Dungen is the name." He reached out with beefy fingers. "I'm sorry for the alias I used with you earlier. I just thought it would be a good chance to meet the client without any names to get in the way."

George hesitated for a second time, but took it all the same.

The handshake was firm, cordial, Logan doing the shaking tug for the benefit of the two. George truly felt like a child in the presence of a goliath.

"When did you meet?" Kendrith asked.

"I went to a bar, Lost Dreams or something. There I came across Soran—I mean Logan. And the barkeep, Brokk."

Kendrith sighed. "I should have known this would happen. Logan likes to meet his charge before the actual escorting." Kendrith gave Logan a look of disapproval. "Did not think he would use an alias though."

"Oh, come now. No harm done." George wondered what Logan's secret was, but he wanted to trust and believe the large man.

Kendrith let it go and turned to George. "George, I need you to understand something: this is Logan's charge, not mine. Don't look to me or Kristen for guidance. We are just as much tourists as you are on this trek."

"Don't belittle him! He can see who is in charge."

George didn't know how to feel about Logan's deceit, but felt he would come to like him in time. Something about the well-groomed man made George feel as if he were taken straight out of a puppet show which sported the "manliest man in existence."

"Logan and I go way back. He is from a rare caste of hunters dating back generations who made a fortune out of their work. They are both hunters and nobility. He was also a good friend of my grandfather Haggen Brosnorth and his partner."

"Please, more like I was his student," Logan corrected.

Logan turned his gaze to George as if it were the first time, but his eyes looked past him and then his face broke into a wide playful grin. "And who might you be?" Logan asked, bending over with an extended finger.

George thought for a moment that Logan was going to stroke his cheek and lightly flinched. But instead, he reached out to George's shoulder upon where Pecky hopped onto the massive finger and chirped happily.

The bird approved of the new addition and hopped over to Logan's shoulder, looking up at the giant's face before poking its beak into the giant's moustache.

Logan seemed like a child filled with excitement. "Beak off the merchandise," Logan instructed, fixing the curled tip of his facial hair.

George only then realised how calculated the supposed visit of Logan was. He knew from the start of George's relationship to Kendrith. The man was cunning, smart, qualities that George usually shied away from…but he couldn't deny that Logan also seemed sincere. Plus, he trusted there was a reason Kendrith and Kristen vouched for him.

Logan's smile seemed to suddenly dwindle, now a sombre look in his eyes as he seemed to reminisce. "It is true, Haggen was a great man and a good friend, plus, he was the only man who could match me in strength."

"You mean beat you," Kristen teased.

The same overbearing humour returned to the man who straightened himself to his full height of almost seven feet and boomed another laugh. "I wish I could refute that claim but aye, no man was stronger than he."

George looked closer at his clothing. Logan's attire seemed to be a mix of regal colours supposed to signify nobility, yet also loose and thick enough to provide protection. Pauldrons made from heavy metal rested upon the right shoulder, and thick protective hide leather was fitted onto his vest with the banner of a lion set on the front. Golden colours meshed with brown upon his long-sleeved tunic while a rather dark blue coloured the breeches.

George simply confirmed what he already knew—the man wanted to be noticed.

"Well, let us get going while we are still ahead of the rising sun," Logan said, reaching up behind him and lifting up a hammer that stood with its head on the ground. As if the two-handed monstrous weapon weighed absolutely nothing, Logan swung the thing over his shoulder and gave a toothy smile with playful confidence.

As their travel commenced, George had already tried to provide payment to Logan, but the man seemed almost offended. "Why would I accept payment already? I still have to deliver you to your destination!" Logan had said. "And in one piece as well."

The early parts of the trek were slow, simple days back-to-back, camping under the canopy of trees which provided glimpses of a starry night.

The occasional husk patrolled the area, their tall statures and slumped silhouettes roaming the land.

Logan didn't seem to question it when both George and Kendrith asked to walk around the skulking monsters, and even if they were drawn to Simantiar's bones or the scent of Kendrith's new blade, the number of those present and their overwhelming new strength provided comfort to George.

Not to mention, he was fairly certain that Logan alone could reduce a whole pack of husks to ash in no time.

The first few days of trekking felt a lot like the first few days through the Forest of the Dead. Rummaging for berries or feeding on rations around a campfire, the occasional wildlife scampering along their peripheral vision only to then be skewered by swift blades.

Kendrith would spot movement from the corner of his eyes, spinning on the balls of his feet with blade in hand, ready to flick his wrist with a sudden exhale of his lungs, only to find the small creature already pierced to the bark of a tree.

Kendrith turned to Kristen, who was juggling another throwing knife in her hand and a teasing smile on her lips. "Maybe you will get the next one," she taunted, ahead of Kendrith by a lifetime, yet George felt comforted at the sight of his loving smile. He never had an interest in love. It was true. His affable and cherubic appearance had given him his fair share of fun in strangers' beds, but George wondered after the quest was over and his promise was kept…would he also settle down and find someone to love?

"Man, that boy really must have a small bladder," Logan complained.

George hid his blushing cheeks, a muffled laugh coming from his bag, as Kendrith laughed a deafening cry. It was a laugh unlike anything that the band had heard from him as he clutched his sides and wheezed gasping breaths, tears streaming his eyes.

"I don't think the joke was that funny," Kristen commented.

"Oh no, it's just that—déjà vu, I guess," Kendrith forced the words out over smiling lips. The last bit of laughter escaped him like fumes from a dying fire as he wiped the tears away.

"I can hear you!" George complained, disappearing behind a shrub.

"Less talking and more peeing," Logan called back, setting Kendrith on another laughing spree. "Is he really going to be okay? Must be the nerves."

As George opened his burlap sack to check on Simantiar, the skull was also cackling uncontrollably. "Oh, this brings back memories."

"I'm sure it does…" George commented wryly.

"Oh, come on, George, lighten up. This is it, we are going to find the golden vault." George smiled at that, putting a hand to the restored pages of the book. Feeling almost the touch of his own sister from when she was still alive. What an adventure it had been. The friend he had found in Simantiar against all odds, and the truth of his past and a world once forgotten.

The bond he had made with Kendrith and what little he had learnt from Kristen, and now Logan for the final stretch of his quest. George did not care if the vault was real or not, he simply wanted to keep his promise. He certainly did not expect to make such friends along the way, but he was happy for it.

"Now hurry up and pee so we can get on with it," Simantiar taunted. George blushed, not because he was being ridiculed, but rather because now that he thought about it, he really did have to go.

Logan was a man of professionalism, and he had asked a few times where the boy was headed or why Kendrith joined the adventure simply to make small talk and conversation, but when he could tell that none of them were too keen on telling too much, he kept to himself. Why they wanted to cross the northern plains was none of his concern, only that they did so in one piece.

"Where do we have to go?" Logan asked.

Kendrith showed him the map he had traced around in the basement, a line showed their travels northeast until they reached a large body of water centred about the mountain trail.

Kendrith recalled the second verse in the poem: Tucked under the dipping mountains and over the rising lakes.

He was unsure what was meant by dipping mountains or rising lakes, but there was indeed a lake situated atop of a mountain.

Logan's eyes suddenly narrowed, as he came to a halt.

"At this season the great beast is wandering through the centre."

Logan's eyes seemed to scan Kendrith for any reaction.

Kendrith understood the concern. He obviously had personal reasons to go and see the monster for himself.

He just nodded. "Then we will walk around." Kendrith couldn't help but remember the last image he saw of his mother, branded into his mind's eye as a half-discarded corpse.

Chapter 29

As the sun's light fadeed over the trees, the stars and moon took its place. Simantiar hid away in the refuge offered by George's bag, a campfire offering warmth and succour from the hostile night of the surrounding woods. Trees towered above, nature reclaimed and fed by whatever chaotic magic seeped into them that made them grow taller and wider.

"What are those sounds?" George asked.

"Animals," Logan answered.

"Doesn't sound like any animal I've ever heard of." Strange guttural calls like gurgling chickens or sudden deep shrieks that faded into a low growl filled the forest.

"That's because they aren't normal beasts. Their origins date back to the Great Cataclysm that fed their line with magic, changing them, transforming them. These woods are filled with creatures unlike any you would see elsewhere."

George swallowed his fear. "Should we be on the lookout?"

Logan reassured George, "Don't worry, the odd beast or two can be avoided if you know what to look for, and it's nothing that Kendrith and I can't handle."

"Speak for yourself, I am going to get my beauty sleep," Kendrith said snarkily, finding the right spot to sleep on.

George watched as Kristen sharpened one of her knives and inspected her equipment. George went over to her.

"Can I help?" he asked.

She smiled as she offered him her whetstone. "Well, there isn't much you can do, but here, you should learn to take care of your knives. Take care of them and they will take care of you."

George looked down to his sides, feeling the weight of the sheathed knives.

George gladly took the whetstone. "Like this?" George asked, grinding away at the edge.

Kristen gave a bemused chuckle. "You want to put the stone down on the ground, and then push away with the blade at an angle." Kristen showed George how it was done and George tried his best to follow the instructions.

George stared at Kristen for some time.

She laughed. "Out with it." Never looking to George, she continued her logistics.

"What?"

"You obviously have something on your mind, just say it."

George hesitated for a second. "How did you and Kendrith meet?"

Kristen turned to George with a curious and bemused frown. "Why the sudden question?"

George shrugged, sharpening his knives to a rhythm. "I don't know, I am curious, I guess."

She hesitating. "I tried to kill him."

The boy looked over in shock, earning a bemused laugh from her. "It's okay, really. It was a long time ago."

"What do you mean you tried to kill him?"

There was now a sombre look to the woman as she looked back on the past. She brought a hand up to her scar as she absently began to stroke it with a tender touch and stopped her inspection.

"When I was a child, I was taken in by a couple of hired mercenaries that raised me. Kendrith's father was my target—someone had hired us and wanted to get rid of the competition."

George hesitated for a moment. "Did you?"

Kristen laughed. "No! No, thankfully I never did end up doing it. The man is still alive."

"Kendrith never mentions him," George noted.

"They aren't exactly on the best of terms. Kendrith always wanted to follow in his mother's and grandfather's footsteps and become a fabled legend. But his father wanted him to take over the business."

George went quiet for a moment, his eyes straying to Kendrith's back as he lay on the forest floor, but George wasn't entirely convinced that he wasn't eavesdropping.

"So, what ended up happening?" George asked.

"Well, Kendrith stopped me. We fought and came very close to killing each other."

"And?"

"I was surrounded, and my cover was blown, as the guards and hunters from the guild came and captured me."

She looked to George with fondness at the memory. "Kendrith and his grandfather insisted that I be let free, on the grounds that I helped give up my associates." George couldn't quite place if the smile was one of fondness or sombre reminiscence. "I did it gladly." The final words spoken as if to herself.

"Were they captured?"

Kristen shrugged. "Some, not all, the main leader escaped."

"Aren't you worried that they will try to find you?"

"They tried initially. But after losing a couple of men in their foiled attempts they had given up. I have no idea what happened to them since."

George left it at that and let Kristen show how to perform his maintenance till, eventually, sleep came to claim them all.

One by one they dozed in the tender touch of sleep, and from there, with a trail of smoke rising from their extinguished campfire, Simantiar rose.

As all else was still, vines from trees and roots from Tiria slithered like serpents in the night, opening the flap of George's bag and rummaging inside, together dragging Simantiar out from within and dragging him into the shadow of trees.

Vines coiled into form, roots twisted and taut; tightening, stretching, taking form into a new body for Simantiar.

Simantiar looked up to the canopy of trees and beyond to the starry night, hearing the choir of crickets.

When Simantiar was content with the distance he made, vines came down from the trees to lift him into the air, and his feet left the ground, as vines of his own reached into the soil and connected him with Tiria.

And so, Simantiar faded into the realm of his mind once more, returning to a time long ago when he was still made of flesh and blood.

Simantiar had travelled the world, learning all that was to be learnt. Existing in a place beyond time, traveling like a phantom from place to place to learn whatever the world had to offer.

"Where will you be going?"

Simantiar turned around to see Cernunnos stride over to him, his tall form built from the leaves and vines of the forest, antlers of wood atop his head distinguishing him as the guardian of the forest.

"North—it has been a while since I have seen my friends and mother," Simantiar said.

"Oh, come now, Simantiar. Don't pretend as if you don't know about the goings-on in their lives."

Simantiar chuckled, throwing the bag over his shoulder. "No, seriously, I haven't been in touch with any of them, nor have I spied on them." Simantiar just smiled at his tall friend, one of the first he had made on his long travels to learn what the world had to offer. Cernunnos had taught Simantiar how to connect to the world around him, to become one with the trees and flow like nature itself.

Simantiar looked nothing like his groomed past, his wavy blond hair wild and down to his shoulders, a thick bushy beard covering his face.

"Even with all that power at your beck and call?" Cernunnos asked dubiously.

Something sombre fell over the all-powerful man. "Aye, perhaps there would have been a time when I wouldn't have thought twice about simply waving my hand and having the world be as I wished. Yet this boundless...potential of mine...it robs you of the world itself."

Simantiar meant every word he spoke, there was a wondrous contentedness at being powerless, a truth his mother had taught him; to appreciate arriving at one's destination with sore feet, how eating bland food becomes infinitely more delicious when ravaged by hunger, or the excitement of visiting loved ones after not seeing them for years on end.

"What is this? The foolhardy Simantiar showing restraint? Patience? Enjoying things as they come?" Cernunnos mocked.

"Ha!" Simantiar bellowed. "I will still blow up a mountain to sate my boredom—you give me too much credit."

Cernunnos chuckled. "Yes, perhaps I do, old friend."

"Well then, I will be off."

Cernnunous nodded. "Know that you are always welcome here."

Simantiar nodded back, leaving to head on home.

Beyond the forest heading north, Simantiar came across the town of Haven, a city powered by the very essence of magic. A long time ago, Simantiar's friendship with Cernunnos had created a peaceful pact between the humans and the beings of the forest. Using the centre of the forest which was a convergence point for all things magic, the town decided to leach parts of it to power their homes. In return, the humans respected the woods, only felling so many trees and hunting so many animals as to not harm the balance. Before, only strife compelled the battle of sylvan creatures and wizard humans.

The town was rather young, only showing the newest signs of infrastructure as people from all over ventured to start a new life. It featured tall structures with blue light bleeding through, the sound of construction as manors were being built. It was a humble and more honest venture towards a town with a purpose rather than the ostentatious marbling that Simantiar knew of in Yumia.

"Perhaps I should make a quick stop." Simantiar dropped by the big construction site, a drab cowl hugging his shoulders as he looked up to the building.

"Quite impressive, isn't it?" Simantiar turned to the voice, only to find his view obscured by a large torso. Craning his neck, Simantiar looked up at the gargantuan figure.

"You can say that again," Simantiar blurted, whistling, though he doubted the two of them were talking about the same thing.

"It belongs to my family, the Brosnorths."

Simantiar returned his gaze to the large construction.

"You must have quite a large family to need such a large place."

The large man chuckled. "I guess so…in a manner of speaking."

Simantiar turned to him with a puzzled look.

"It will be a guild house, responsible for training people to protect others from magical beasts."

"Right," Simantiar said, looking around. "What about that building over there?"

The man turned his gaze to where Simantiar was pointing. "That is an academy for magic."

"Really? Even though Eindeiheid is right next door?"

The man chuckled. "We can't all be as gifted as Usellyes."

The figure spoke of Usellyes's name just in passing, but Simantiar couldn't help smiling. "Yes, I suppose that is true."

"Plus, below its surface is apparently an item of great power which is being guarded by the mages."

"An item of great power?"

The man shrugged. "Just rumours as far as I can tell—none of us are privy to what it is they keep hidden."

"Right, I guess that would be the case."

"So, what can I do for the great Simantiar?"

Simantiar turned to the large figure.

"Do I know you?"

The man chuckled. "I wouldn't expect you to remember me, since we met when I was still a growing boy; you met with my father to develop a safe road system and escorts to provide a trading route. His name was Brandon Brosnorth. I am his son, Nigel Brosnorth." The man stuck out his hand, Simantiar went to shake it, feeling the iron grip of callused hands and laboured muscles.

"My father would be pleased to see you."

"I am sure he would."

Simantiar met with familiar faces in Haven. The years had not been kind to Brandon Brosnorth, age slowly eating away at his virility, the colour of his hair fading like oil from canvas, yet the full life he had lived was still apparent in his eyes. How much Simantiar longed for that simplicity. Then again, he sometimes wondered if he would ever appreciate it. He'd wonder if it was the plight of an introspective being to always contemplate that which could have been and to overlook that which was.

Whatever the case may have been, Simantiar simply smiled, taking a few cubes of sugar to stir into his tea. He looked into the steaming cup in his hand and relished in the smaller moment of simplicity—he simply enjoyed it as it was.

"Will you be staying?" Brandon asked. There was a rickety, yet disciplined quality to the way that Brandon spoke, like old wood still holding strong.

"Afraid not, I am just passing through."

The old man nodded, the few stubborn teeth in his mouth disappearing behind curled lips.

"Aye, I thought as much. Visiting that old academy of yours?"

Simantiar nodded. "Yes, I figured it was time to see old friends and family."

There was a knock on the door. "Speaking of old friends," Brandon said as the door opened to reveal a tall woman, age had only worked to add to her fine beauty and spring-infused smile.

"Emilie!" Simantiar rose from his seat and went over to embrace his childhood friend as she laughed joyously at being picked up like a flower from a field.

"Put me down!" she said through laughter.

"Simantiar!" A curt scream of joy was followed by more laughing.

"Hey! She's taken!" Simantiar turned to the doorway to find Zaros standing with a playful smile.

"Zaros!" Dropping Emilie like she was yesterday's goods to the sound of a scream, Simantiar ran over to Zaros and took him into a hard embrace that made them stumble back a few steps.

"It's been so long!" Simantiar stated.

"Yes, it has, since you've showered, apparently." Zaros pinched his nose in response.

"I didn't know you two were married!" Simantiar proclaimed.

"You are the most powerful wizard in creation and you can't conjure some soap?" Zaros said nasally as they both fell to the floor and the room resounded with laughter.

When the friends calmed down from the festivities of a welcome reunion, Simantiar, Emilie, and Zaros fell back to a room where they could talk and reminisce for old times' sake. Simantiar, out of courtesy, waved away his own scent like it was clothing to be discarded.

Zaros had grown into a lithe and strong-featured man. He wore a plain white shirt with a deep brown vest over it, and a soft bit of facial hair covered his chin, lower lip, and moustache. His face had continued to grow long with a sharp chin and hollow cheeks, a deep and rather stoic appearance to small and half-closed eyes as dark as the wavy black hair atop of his head.

But all of that didn't seem to clash with the warmth and approachability of his welcoming smile.

Emilie was much the same with her pigtails, more freckles added to smooth cheeks, and a deeper blue to her eyes, but there was a litheness to her figure like a swaying blade of grass.

"So married, huh?" Simantiar asked, taking an awkward sip of tea to fill the silence.

"Yes," said Zaros, taking Emilie's hand into his own as their simple wedding rings marked their fingers.

Zaros and Emilie shared of the time when Simantiar left. Emilie had been installed as the head of the academy within Haven, while Zaros ended up being a well-reputable artist mostly known for using transmutation magic to morph gems and stones or elements into differing shapes with curious patterns. Simantiar had even seen some of his work in far-off lands where he had overheard them speak of "Genuine Zaros work," though having been privy to the real thing, Simantiar knew that the item which was being peddled was most definitely not authentic.

The pieces of work lined the shelves mounted on walls. His personal favourite was a spiralling obsidian gem rising into a double helix which then suddenly shifted into a quicksilver-like appearance that continuously morphed and changed, but could never fully continue its rise. Other pieces included crystal-shelled toads that were frozen still or the volatile and extremely discomforting halves of a moon and sunstone gleaming silver and gold which trembled at the effort of repelling each other if it weren't for the shifting black bindings that glistened like umbral leeches and held the stones in bondage.

"So." Emilie placed her tea down, bringing Simantiar's attention back to them. "What stories have you from the past eleven years?"

Simantiar smiled. "Many; I have experienced magic unlike anything I have ever seen. Continents to the east which shift their theory onto positive and negative energy, lands which are inhabited by the strangest creatures I had ever seen hidden in lands of mist; I learnt the deepest secrets of water magic, and found creatures known as Djinn which are beings of magic gone sentient. I even found old runes of the beings before our time, the great Heralds themselves."

"Ridiculous, the Heralds are just a myth," Zaros scoffed.

"I just found signs of them—may very well have been designed by worshipers," Simantiar offered, though he wasn't entirely sure himself.

"How incredible," Emilie commented, giving off a sigh. "If only I was not bound to this post, I would have set off to experience it all myself."

"I am right here." Zaros gesticulated as if in disbelief. The comment earned a laugh from all present.

"What about you?" Simantiar asked. "How has it been in Haven? Everything looks like it is progressing well."

"Thanks to you. This town has really taken off. With the Brosnorths, we will be able to establish a guild for escorting individuals safely over unknown territory and with my academy, it can be a hub for new students or those who wish to widen their horizons."

"I saw the building—it's quite remarkable."

"That it is."

"How are the others?" Simantiar asked.

"Well, Ciro and Moran are working at the academy under Usellyes. Ciro truly embraced her combative side and became an arcane fighter."

"That's amazing! Already?" Simantiar declared, astonished.

Zaros nodded. "She was one of their youngest graduates and has already risen through the ranks to become one of their best. Moran, on the other hand, has shown a natural proclivity towards the study of machinations. He works under Usellyes and has recreated steam-powered recreations of animal followers."

"And what about Noima?" There was a tinge of worry in Simantiar's query, which faded away the moment he saw Emilie's and Zaros's smiles widen.

"He actually visited about a year ago. He went to live in Shorta and has taken a profession as a scholar—he travels the world and discovers new beings to write about in a bestiary for lesser-known creatures."

"Amazing, I should visit him as well! And Usellyes is doing well too, I suppose?"

Zaros and Emilie suddenly filled their expressions with worry. "Yes, yes he is," Emilie said as her smile faltered.

"Won't you stay the night?" Zaros asked.

Were they changing the subject? Simantiar wasn't sure.

Simantiar simply shook his head. "I must be on my way," he said, rising from his seat and throwing his sack over his shoulder.

Emilie rose and Simantiar extended a hand; she ignored it, going for the hug.

"I will make sure to visit," Simantiar said, letting go of Emilie only to be embraced even more firmly by Zaros.

"Make sure you do," Zaros replied.

As Simantiar was about to leave, Emilie spoke behind him. "Simantiar, there is something you should know. Usellyes has been…a little different."

"What do you mean?" Simantiar asked.

"I don't know the details, but he is taking part in a large project which has been getting some revolt. Mylor came out of retirement and took a seat once more on the council board to slow down Usellyes, but the details themselves are not clear. Whatever it is, there has been some controversy around it," Emilie explained with a pained look.

"Some say that Usellyes is trying to find a way to control the flow of Arcanum to more directly perform greater feats, perhaps even allow those without any magical ability to cast magic," Zaros added.

"That would be great, wouldn't it?" Simantiar asked, a little confused. "If he can find a way to bottle up a little bit, then it could have great results."

They went even quieter.

"It's not just a little bit. From what we heard, he could be planning to bottle all of it."

The blue of day faded into the yellow of dusk as the sun dipped over the horizon.

Simantiar continued to his home city of Yumia.

As he trudged on through the trees, he suddenly found the world—the moment—very familiar. But not from a past once experienced, but rather a future yet to come.

Simantiar turned to his side, and suddenly noticed a large moustached individual coming in with a mighty hammer.

"Who are you?!" the individual demanded.

Simantiar's eyes burst open, returning him to the present. He watched as the individual known as Logan came charging, hammer pulled back for a mighty swing.

Simantiar dodged the hammer by a hair's length as his vines pulled him to safety, the hammer barely missing him, as Logan used the momentum to turn once more, bringing the hammer down for an overhead swing.

Simantiar brought his knees to his chest, taking the impact from the hammer and tightening the vines in his feet into a spring, and using the charged momentum to propel away, landing clear and safe on his toes, his feet making barely a whisper at Tiria's touch.

"I don't know what you are, but one thing I do know—in all my days of hunting is that a creature with a skull for a head is never a friend."

"Hard to argue with that logic," Simantiar muttered under his figurative breath.

The wizard went into a fighting stance, bringing his right leg back and lowering his centre of gravity, open palms in front of him. The world he had left behind was returning, his spirit now falling into the motions of the northern monks who taught him the flow of energy so long ago atop snow-encrusted mountains.

Logan charged, his large stature and encumbering hammer did nothing to slow him down. His weapon was a blur, swinging into Simantiar's side. Yet, Simantiar had already become as light as a feather, using the sudden rush of wind to aid his sudden jump into the air. Simantiar's leg stepped against the swing, allowing the force to spin him like a corkscrew, using the sudden force to whip his own leg down onto Logan's shoulder.

The giant called out in surprise, knees buckling for just a moment, yet Logan stood. The man clenched his teeth, thighs as thick as surrounding trees tensed—he refused to fall.

Simantiar distanced himself—the giant was not to be taken lightly.

"Don't underestimate me, demon!" Logan gritted his teeth, reaching out to grab for Simantiar. Yet, his nimble body of vines proved too nimble, his flexible anatomy bending at an angle impossible for vertebrates to then kick off with his other leg and create even more distance.

Simantiar underestimated Logan's persistence and speed. The hulking man had already closed the gap, his large size in no way hampering his alacrity, and the veins on Logan's neck strained like thick ravines from a volcano.

Simantiar had no time to think of a counter, let alone to conjure a spell, as already the weight of the hammer swung at his side, slinging him to a tree which cracked its bark like a thunder's whip.

"Not bad," Simantiar said, thinking that he'd have certainly died if he were human.

Logan gave Simantiar no time to recover, already charging for his next attack.

Simantiar didn't move aside, instead spreading his legs into a squat and taking the charge head-on as the roots of his feet extended through the dirt and two more arms grew out of his back, waiting for the hammer's swing.

Simantiar brought his arms forward as they unravelled into cords of vines and roots and forestry before re-forming a split second later into a large spiralling spring the moment the hammer's impact reached him.

"I believe this belongs to you," Simantiar said; the spring pressed together, collecting the energy as the vines which anchored his feet strained at their task. Transforming the end of the spring into one giant flat surface, Simantiar released the coiled force.

All in a moment, as if by reflex, Logan grabbed on to Simantiar's neck before he was catapulted away.

The resounding impact sent Logan sliding back several feet, yet his muscles bulged and a guttural sound came from gritted teeth as he remained standing, yet Simantiar's own body broke away from his rooted feet.

"Got you," Logan said, panting triumphantly.

"Do you, now?" Simantiar teased as his entire body unravelled, the vines returning to their original shape as they coiled around Logan's body to bind his limbs, a single vine dangling Simantiar's head to the side as Logan strained against the bindings.

"This has been fun, but I think it's time for me to leave."

"You think you can hold me?" Logan asked as his cheeks reddened, straining against the vines that tore at the effort.

"Not at all, though know this—I am not your enemy." More vines reached down from the trees and picked up what remained of Simantiar's skull, absconding him off into the shadows.

One last strain and the vines binding Logan snapped, unravelling to the floor.

Footsteps approached, and it was Kendrith with steel sword at the ready.

"Logan! What is it?" Kendrith asked.

"Some weird creature, it was just a skull atop a body made up of vines."

Kendrith hesitated for a second. "Ye-yeah, that does sound weird."

"Sounds like a really lame enemy," Kendrith added, gratified by a sudden pebble which struck him in the back of the head. "Ow!"

Logan looked to the dark branches up above that swayed to the wind, shadows veiling whatever it was that crawled above.

"This one was different," Logan said.

"Different how?"

"It wasn't just some beast. It was intelligent—it was stalking us. Could even speak."

"Are you sure?" Kendrith asked, surely trying to protect Simantiar.

"I know what I saw," Logan said, raising his voice.

"Okay, I believe you."

Logan directed his gaze at Kendrith, questions seeming to fill him.

"Kendrith, is there something you are not telling me about this boy?"

"What do you mean?"

"Why follow us, why help me bring this boy even though this territory and route are not your field? What's so special about George that you would follow along?" Logan's question was accusatory, a boom which demanded truth, lest one face the consequences.

"Not to mention, I have noticed the higher numbers of husks that seem to be trailing behind us. When Beynard told me of a young bard wanting to travel the uncharted lands, I was curious. The only people who commission such a perilous travel are scholars, cartographers, or researchers, and even they don't do it unless commissioned to do so."

"Is that why you followed him? To find out a little bit more?" Kendrith queried.

Logan simply nodded. "To my surprise, he is an unremarkable young man with lots of gold to his name. Beynard said it was left to him by his family. I'm not buying it."

"You don't need to. And George is anything but unremarkable."

Logan calmed himself, taking a deep, mighty breath in and out. "You know that working in this field with only half the information can be fatal. And I know there is something you are hiding. I just hope that it won't get us killed."

Simantiar watched from the safety of the shadows, nothing but a skull with vines steadying him for a clear view, he watched as Kendrith seemed to consider his next words—was he about to tell the truth?

"The boy grew on me," Kendrith finally said. "Something about him, about his quest, about his honesty. I want to see it through with him. Plus, this is where my mother died, where my grandfather disappeared." Simantiar took note of Kendrith's sudden determined look. "If I wish to grow and step into their shoes, it is a place I also need to explore."

Logan sighed in defeat.

"Let's go back," he said.

A scream. "Kristen," Kendrith automatically concluded.

"Kendrith! Help!" called out the echoing voice of George.

Chapter 30

Kendrith and Logan raced back to the camp as quickly as they could.

There they found Kristen lying motionless in George's arms; a puncture wound apparent on her forearm, black vein-like lines spreading from the irritated red spot, viscous and clotting blood oozing from it as the black lines seemed to pulsate. Kristen struggled to breathe, her throat wheezing with every attempt, her eyes opening for mere moments before closing again like a butterfly's dying wing flutter; only the white of her eyes showed as the rest rolled back.

Pecky seemed equally alarmed as it chirped away and bounced across the scene.

"What happened?" Kendrith asked.

"Some strange multicoloured insect stung her."

Logan cursed under his breath, moving over to her, and waving Pecky aside.

"Where did it go?" Logan asked.

George pointed over to an area where his knife stabbed into the skull of the creature. It seemed scorpion-like, except for its shell with a multicoloured hue that seemed to keep pulsating rhythmically with the colours of the rainbow. Instead of just two pincers, the creature had four with two on each side. The ichor which trickled out of the stab wound was as black as tar, but it was still alive, twitching occasionally with its two-tailed stinger ready to strike.

"What is it?" Kendrith asked.

"It's called death's kiss," replied Logan.

"That doesn't sound good."

"No, no it's not." Logan slammed the knife down to its hilt, the arthropod giving off one last hissing squeal as Logan crushed the exoskeleton of the creature with an audible crunch. He tore out the knife with a twist, and the scorpion-like creature was split in two.

"It's venom is magical, but it is also potent. It is rare to come across them as they are scarce, but those who had been stung by it..." Logan trailed off, not bringing himself to finish the sentence.

"How do we treat it?" Kendrith asked.

"We can't from here, but there is a camp due west—we can reach it in half a day, faster if we hurry. The people there simply hunt for exotic creatures and sell them to the highest buyer, but there is a healer that can tend to her wounds."

"Camp west? Do you mean...?"

Logan nodded. "The abandoned outpost. I will explain later."

"Will she make it?" Kendrith's question went unanswered, the towering man already at work.

Kendrith grabbed Logan's arm, forcing the man to acknowledge him. "Will. She. Make. It?" The words were forced through gritted teeth, panic welling up inside him.

"I don't know," Logan admitted. "We need to hurry. Boy," Logan addressed George, "bring me my bag."

"And you, I need you to stay beside her at all times. Keep her awake as long as you can."

Kendrith nodded, relying on all he could muster to stay composed.

George returned with Logan's bag in hand. Kristen groaned in pain, the muscles under her puncture wound writhed, muscles contracting underneath to reveal the tense and tearing fibres of flesh. "What's happening to her?" George asked worriedly.

"The venom is a foreign body which she is rejecting. It is trying to change her."

"What do you mean 'change her?'" Kendrith asked with obvious panic, no matter how hard he tried to hide it.

"It is trying to turn her essence and body into something magical so it can accept the venom."

"And?" George asked, not grasping it.

"She's human, George. Her body won't be able to survive the process."

From his bag, Logan took a selection of dark herbs and leaves. A white-petaled flower Kendrith immediately recognised as feverhew, including bukwreath, collanroot, and grayweed which would be ground into a paste.

"This will keep her fever at bay and prevent infection, but we must hurry."

Logan looked around the base of the strange towering trees and found what he was looking for, a pointed three-pronged plant. "This is known as deep sucker."

The man pulled a couple from the base of the tree, the stems thick and hollow inside, much like a straw. Logan stabbed the stem into Kristen's wound, followed by a pained cry from her.

"What are you doing?" Kendrith demanded as Kristen faded in and out of consciousness.

That was when Kendrith noticed the plant was already at work, sucking up the magic within. The petals at the end began to grow, shift, and change colours from green to include cuts of red and blue and orange and pink and whatever else came to be. The leaves twisted and grew and spiralled into obtuse shapes as they made space to accommodate the strange magic.

"George, go and pluck some more. We will need it to contain the spread of the infection."

George didn't hesitate for a second, nodding and moving out. Kendrith noticed him pick up his bag on the way.

George plucked a couple of the plants and placed them gently into a herb pouch that hung from his belt, checking the stems to make sure they had the straw-like appearance.

When he felt confident he had enough, George went behind a tree and looked into his bag, Simantiar looking up at him.

"This is bad," George said.

"Yes, it is."

"Logan said it was magical. Do you think you could cure her with your magical negation abilities?"

"I don't know. It's risky."

"What do you mean?"

"What if the venom already infected her, would I be killing her too?"

"Is that how this works?"

"I don't know, George. I've never encountered such a creature before. Plus, Logan doesn't seem very fond of me."

"What do you mean?"

"He noticed me when I went to meditate, came running at me thinking I was a threat. For now, let's just see what his friends can do, if he thinks they can cure her, then maybe I won't need to reveal myself."

Kendrith carried Kristen on his back. "You'll be okay," he said, unsure if the words were to reassure her or himself.

With her legs saddled at Kendrith's hips and her hands tied around his neck, the band departed towards the not-so-abandoned outpost.

The trip took a couple of hours with a few short rests in between to change the bandaging and ointment for Kristen's wounds.

There was a light translucent shimmer to her skin, like an iridescent pool of water that rippled just underneath the surface. The black lines reached out farther like festering tree roots. At one point, the band heard a sudden crack and nothing else. Kristen breathed heavily, her arm suddenly twisted and broken.

"We must hurry," Logan said, unable to hide his worry.

Kendrith bit his lip, a single tear running down his cheek. Pecky, for all his energy, sat still and unmoving.

When the band reached the camp they were greeted with curious glances and prying eyes.

"Logan, what is this place? Not only is it not abandoned, it is a full-on settlement." Kendrith asked.

"Never said we would be welcome; just keep your wits about you and let me handle the talking."

The camp was small, but *camp* wasn't the right word. It had thatched homes and the nicer variants were with timber frames and wattle walls, but nothing made of stone. Temporary tents were placed with stained leather. Smoke which carried the scent of industrial coal or roasted meat rose from rooftops. The sounds of chickens could be heard over the back-and-forth of suspicious figures, as well as the clanking of hammer and steel which rang out like an echo.

A mountainous cliff wall closed the settlement inwards, the only thing that would permit further venture was a yawning cavernous cave veiled by shadows.

The biggest of the homes was a hut with a smoking chimney at the edge of the settlement towards the back.

Kendrith counted the potential threats, the weapons, the number of unaccounted places where a trap could spring. Kristen suddenly felt heavier, the weight of her life pressing down on him as he realised he could not retreat, only move forward.

He watched the alien cutthroat vagabonds that settled there, those who traded in the exchange of wild, unfamiliar chaos which resided that far into the teeming creatures that skulked the forest depths.

Kendrith watched the scene of a horse striding into camp, the bleeding remains of a quadrupedal creature being pulled along the floor, its neck fastened by a rope.

The creature was dark green, its head sported antlers the size of a man's arm, four closed eyes, and six deerlike legs; the dragged carcass painted the forest floor with its blood.

Kendrith turned to watch another behemoth, but this one was very much alive as it gave heavy, wheezing breaths from certainly crushed lungs through the encampment—how vapid its stare was with gaunt belly, taloned nubby fingers, and protruding tusks.

The creature stumbled behind a band of hunters, its hands chained, dragging a creature of its own behind it with the lower half missing. Just four lithe arms shown on the dismembered beast, three sets of eyes with each row closer and closer to the bridge of its long snout.

Kendrith began to realise the truth of the uncharted lands—how it was a governless and turbulent realm. If his trek through the Forest of the Dead was to survive a path past the amalgamations of known horrors, then the trek north was to survive that of the unknown. But there were people in the settlement who lived as renegades, profiting off a dangerous life.

"Don't trust anyone and avoid eye contact. We aren't home anymore."

Kendrith noticed George gulp at Logan's words, and kept his own wits sharp.

As Kendrith took in his surroundings, he noticed the vague absence of Pecky, who even then must have absconded to somewhere safe.

A man suddenly stood in their path. "Logan, it's been some time." The man was tall and broad, with a brown beard that was as well-kept as it could be in the environment he was in. He wore a leather vest with slotted daggers and many pockets for his own needs. A crossbow was slung over his shoulder with a whip and sword at his side.

"Yes, it has, Gerard." Logan approached the man with a sense of reserved familiarity, as they clasped arms knowingly.

The bearded man leaned past to see Kendrith and Kristen wrapped beside him. The man was broad, but still shorter than Logan. "Death's kiss?"

Logan nodded. "I need to see the healer, it is urgent."

Gerard scratched his beard. "You know the rules, you have to speak with Magnus."

Logan growled, Gerard stepped back apologetically. "My hands are tied here, Logan, either we fight about it while the girl's body is morphing, or you can go and talk with Magnus and get it over with."

Logan stepped forward, bumping into Gerard's shoulder and brushing him aside. "Some use you are."

"Nice to see you too."

"Give me Kristen," Logan said to Kendrith. The man's head was lowered, eyes trailing off into the distance.

Kendrith hesitated for a moment till Logan's eyes met his with sharp determination. Reluctantly, Kendrith unfastened Kristen and had Logan carry her in his arms.

"Wait here." Logan knocked on the door of the home Kendrith noticed earlier, the door opened as Logan ducked under the frame and entered.

A good thirty minutes had passed till Logan returned with Kristen in his arms. The black veins had now begun to climb up her throat—Kristen seemed in pain. Kendrith tenderly stroked her cheek.

"We can go," Logan said, his voice cold.

The healer's hut held many bedridden men, some just coughing and wheezing, already at death's door.

"So many people," George said.

"The men who hunt the beasts this far north live a dangerous life. Most are inexperienced novices who never live long," Logan said.

"So, why do they do it?"

"Because it's a living; desperation often throws caution to the wind."

The air within the hospice was nauseating, the stench of pus and blood and other fluids roiled into something noisome. A sweet stench that proved sickening, windows were left open to little avail, and the hanging incense only made the smell all the more pungent.

Walking through the beds, some empty, but marked with the blood and fluids of previous occupants, they finally reached a man tending the wounds of an injured fellow.

The person gasped horribly, bone-like spikes jutting out of his skin, one poking out of a stretched eye socket and cold sweat streaking sickly yellow skin.

"What horror," George muttered.

"Yes," said the man treating the patient. "Bone weevil got to him, doesn't have much longer left. All I can do is ease his pain." The man coughed, a tooth flying loose.

The healer turned to the band with a smile on his face and spectacles pushed up the bridge of his nose. "What can I help with?"

The man was short and thin, a round and academic look to him as the spectacles gave his size an eerie shine though more so than anything, someone who looked so short and friendly seemed oddly out of place.

Logan walked forward with Kristen in hand. "Death's kiss," he said.

"Hmm, yes, I can see that," the man replied, cupping his chin in thought.

"Can you help her?" Kendrith asked.

"I will certainly try."

"Gary." Logan spoke the name without a lilt of humour, it sunk down Gary's own smile and energy as he responded.

"I can't make any promises, but I will try."

"Thank you," Kendrith said.

The rest of Kendrith's day was spent with Logan learning about the forest. The situation had changed and Kendrith agreed that the more information he had the better. He understood that maps were useless, seeing as the forest changed naturally, shifting its foundation ever so slightly like waves constantly in motion. But the basic idea of the layout was always the same, dividing the town of Haven from the upper reaches.

Gerard joined Kendrith and Logan at the bar, catching up on old stories. Kendrith understood that Gerard wasn't like the others. A mean and calculating hunter, sure, but he was reliable. At the very least, Kendrith noticed that Logan had cause to trust him.

Logan was downing his third ale as Gerard shared another one of their adventures together. "This guy is crazy, I tell you! So, we were in the cave, and our torches suddenly blew out. What we originally thought to be a cockatrice turned out to be a dark stalker."

"You've gotta explain what a dark stalker is," Logan said half-heartedly, not really interested in the retelling of the story.

Gerard caught himself, already in a good mood based on the number of empty mugs at his side and foam stuck to his beard. "Right, well, a dark stalker lures you into dark areas using the sounds of creatures it has already eaten. It then extinguishes any light source you have and starts to tear at your flesh. With our torches extinguished and nothing to do, Logan lets himself get stabbed by the thing's claws so he could *grab* it, and go to town with his hammer."

"Sounds like a great hunt," Kendrith said, downing his ale and forcing a smile. He found himself too distracted by Kristen to think of anything else.

"Worrying won't help," Logan said.

Kendrith looked up in surprise. "I know."

"And visiting her every couple of minutes won't help either."

Kendrith looked defeated, irritation bubbling to the surface. "I know."

"She is recovering—just trust the doctor."

Kendrith nodded with a deflated sigh. "Sure, but can you explain what is this place? I thought the guild abandoned it. And why have you been uneasy ever since you entered that hut?"

"This place was abandoned officially a long time ago by the guild. But in time, freelance hunters and people out for money ended up filling the settlement. The guild has no control over the place but a sort of…quiet deal was made. We would provide food and resources to the settlement in return for their help whenever members of the guild would come by."

Kendrith shook his head in disbelief. He supposed it was naive of him to think that the guild was not running everything by the book, but the settlement seemed incredibly clandestine.

Logan looked over to Kendrith. "Kristen will need a couple of days to recover. The doctor said she has a good chance of making it, but it is yet to be seen. In the meantime, the payment for this is a rare creature born in the forest that Magnus wants me to hunt."

"You're leaving us?"

"I have no choice. Gerard will keep you company."

"What does he want you to hunt?"

"A new creature, apparently, its parts will be highly valued by some merchants."

"Logan, tell me one thing, are we safe here?"

Logan looked over to Kendrith, mulling over his answer. "No. But we had no other options but to come here. Whatever happens, keep the boy safe until I return."

Kendrith nodded.

"The people here aren't professionals like you or Logan over here," Gerard patted a hand on Logan's pauldron. "But for that, they have grit and can improvise, if they notice you have coin to your name you could be in danger. Magnus is seen as the overseer of this settlement, and there are very few people who actually live here. Most are those who travel in from their routes to go hunting for rare creatures and return. Spend all their coin on booze and a night in someone else's bed till empty pockets bring them back here."

"I know the kind," Kendrith said.

"No, no you don't, not like this." Gerard shook his head. "What you may have met before are those touched by the shadow of darkness. Those who come *here* are those driven mad by it. A touch of insanity that makes them as much a product of this place as the creatures it spews out."

"So, why are you here?"

Gerard smiles. "Because I am bloody well good at my job."

"So, join the guild?"

Gerard shook his head. "Tried that one in the past, not really my thing being told where and how to do my job. Prefer to have the will of passion guide me."

"And empty pockets?" Kendrith teased.

"So, you do have a sharp tongue too!" The two clunked their mugs and Kendrith found momentary comfort in the mirth.

"Kendrith, just be careful of Magnus," said Logan.

"What do you mean?"

"Magnus is a shrewd man. All he sees is profit. He seemed a little too eager to strike a deal for getting Kristen treated despite the material needed. I don't trust that man. I wonder how valuable the monster must be, and also how dangerous. There is a chance he is hiding the actual danger of the creature." Logan leaned over to whisper to Kendrith alone. "Be vigilant and get everyone back to Haven if I don't make it back in time."

At a shoddy and dull brown inn that lingered with the scent of oil, the band took their rest.

The next morning, Logan departed with a mixed bag of hunters. One such person came from the far east, his skin as dark and tanned as leather with a turban wrapped over his head, eagle-sharp eyes peering into your soul, and a cowl wrapped over his shoulders. The second was a woman and a seemingly eccentric hunter, with crafted traps of chain along with explosives and a crossbow of her own.

Logan promised to be back within a day or two at most.

Kendrith stalked the settlement where a wooden palisade was the first line of defence against creatures that came too close, though based on the unstained stakes of carved wood and Logan's own explanation, he knew that the settlement being attacked by such beasts was rare.

Kendrith took into account the numbers of potential enemies, making sure to keep detailed accounts of those who noticed his gaze. He didn't care about those who had the loudest bark and drowned themselves in booze immediately after getting their paychecks, but rather those whose stares spoke of cruel and pragmatic intelligence; for those who displayed caution warranted caution.

Next, Kendrith stalked the home of Magnus, but he never seemed to find the man leaving the hut. The people of the settlement also spoke very little of Magnus.

Kendrith contemplated what options he had left. Lastly, he looked over at the great cave at the end of the settlement. It was off-limits to anyone that wasn't Magnus or his own men. Gerard just said it was a depository for hunted animals, whereby they can be stored there, and Magnus himself pays a commission for any delivered animal.

Later in the day, when not enough things were there to distract Kendrith, he returned to Kristen's bedside. The doctor informed him that the spread of the venom was being contained, and the deep suckers were being used to drain the magical venom from her body. Her previously broken arm was fitted into a cast.

Though the news itself was a relief, Kristen still seemed as close to death's door as many others within the hospice. Kendrith spared a moment to notice that the man with spiked enamel growths of bone was missing, just a discoloured yellow bedsheet to ever tell of his suffering.

Suddenly, the door to the healer's office burst open, a great black leech wrestling with the gaunt Gary. The thing was only about half a meter in length, yet as thick as the healer's own torso. It writhed in the healer's arms, thin, long tentacles from its side slashed wildly with trails of slime from its shining umbral body, and its rounded mouth undulated to reveal rows of teeth. Kendrith grasped at the hilt of his sword beside him.

"Oh! It's quite all right!" the man said in an effort to sound reassuring despite gritted teeth and strained grunts. The creature suddenly gave a shrill scream.

"What is that?" Kendrith asked, as the doctor carried the beast over.

"A drain leech. Just like a normal leech, but for magic!" Gary sounded almost as if he brought it out for show-and-tell.

Kendrith's eyes widened. "You aren't planning to use that on Kristen?"

The doctor eyed Kendrith, almost forgetting about the creature. "Oh, not at all! I was planning on taking it out for a dance, maybe for dinner after, hoping it would suck me right off with that large maw of its—yes, of course it is for your damsel." Gary's head shook vehemently at the final statement, though his attempt at incredulity was more comical than chastising.

"Now help me move it if you want to save her."

Kendrith contained his worry and approached, holding the writhing beast along with the doctor to direct its mouth towards Kristen's arm. "Just don't let it latch on to your face! If it ain't magic, it will make do with your blood!"

The great thing latched on immediately, calming down instantly as the end of its body wagged and it suckled away at the magic.

Gary's breathing was hampered and heavy. "Like a crying babe suckling on a mother's teat. Finally, it is calm."

Kendrith looked over at him. "What a poor choice of words."

The doctor shrugged, returning to his room.

Kendrith sat there for a while, making sure that the creature meant Kristen no harm. Content with the process, and seeing the black lines thinning like water-starved roots, he sighed, and decided to call it a night.

The sun had begun to set when Kendrith left the hospice. He decided to return to the inn, first going to buy some grub brought in by a vendor that brought much needed food supplies from the town of Haven. If the food that came from the safe town of Adna struggled to arrive to Haven, it had an even worse time reaching this far out. The steep price pretty much spoke for itself.

As Kendrith was on his way back to his own lodging, carrying two loaves of bread in his hands with some jerky, sausage, cheese, and a particularly pricey bit of butter, he saw from the corner of his vision the familiar silhouette of Logan coming through the trees as the world began to turn grey for the night.

Kendrith rushed over to the man, noticing his empty hands. "Did you find the beast?" Kendrith asked.

Logan nodded. "Yes, but we will be needing your help to kill it."

"How is Kristen?" Logan asked, all of them back in their lodgings, beds made to sleep on hard floor, the actual bed left for George.

"She seems to be recovering, but I'm not sure about the specifics." Kendrith explained the receding symptoms, the thinning black lines, and the curious leech.

"Why do you need me?" Kendrith asked. "I don't know anything about the creatures you are hunting. Why not ask someone else?"

"You are more than qualified, you just lack the experience. Additionally, I need someone I trust. There is something about the other two I don't like."

"What do you mean?"

"I am just suspicious—something about all this seems off."

Kendrith weighed the different options brought to him. He was reluctant to leave Kristen in such a settlement ripe with those who were unbidden by the laws of society, where profit rather than virtue ruled as master.

Yet, Kendrith knew he would have been foolish not to put trust in Logan's gut instinct. If anything, he was the true successor of his own grandfather's teaching, nowhere near as tall or as formidable, but Logan truly proved to be the long shadow that was cast by Haggen Brosnorth.

"Why not Gerard?"

"I considered it, but I will be frank. The man is not the best at his craft. The truth is, the reason he never got into Vrania was because he wasn't good enough."

Kendrith nodded. "What about George and Kristen?"

"Well, Gerard will be here. He may be walking his way into an early grave, but as far as this lot goes, he can hold his own."

"Okay, I'll come with you. If there is something afoot, it would be best that we stick close in case anything were to happen."

Logan nodded. "At first light we meet to discuss battle plans and strategies. Now, get some sleep."

That night, Kendrith dozed off sitting at a wooden table beside the open window. The moon shone a bright silver grey above the canopy of the deadly forest. Strange enigmatic chirps and unsettling screeches, sounds which Kendrith couldn't quite place, reached the settlement like a whispering echo.

At night, the defences were put into place, the wooden gates closed, torches dulled using leather to soften the signs of tepid life, and the palisades pointed patiently towards the border of trees.

When sleep finally came to claim Kendrith, his last thoughts were about Kristen, and the time when they had first met.

Chapter 31

It had been a long time since Kendrith last dreamed of the past, of when he was still Haggen's student, and of how he had run away from home. All the events interrupted when he had to face the force of those Hobbers and find George.

But now, with his mind on Kristen, he sat there at the table and returned to that fateful first encounter when he came across the stunningly beautiful and lost visage of a scarred woman.

Even when Kendrith finally picked up the order and expected to feel the pride and excitement that came from the heft of his very own sword, he couldn't keep his mind off the short but stark encounter he had with a woman who commandeered his thoughts.

The boy blushed. "Everything okay, boy?" the blacksmith had asked, seeing Kendrith's cheeks redden.

"Is it the fumes getting to you?" The man was hefty, a loose tunic pulled over his blacksmith's body laden with sweat and coarse veins running down steaming muscles. A thick white moustache on the man's face moved as he spoke.

"N-no sir," Kendrith said.

The man squinted his eyes. "Ah, perhaps it is love?" Kendrith stood at attention, burning cheeks giving him away. The smith chuckled. "Ah, to be young again. Tell Haggen the sword is of prime material and that I am glad to work with him again. And for you, young boy, I provide a few words of wisdom. Love can be an elusive thing, a wisp of smoke or a burning candle.

Almost impossible to catch, but if you can, seize it. Even if it evades you, even if it burns you, at least for a moment, you grasped the impossible."

The large man nodded and his smile only shone through creased skin as his lips were hidden behind the white of his moustache. "The advice is for free." He winked.

Kendrith wasn't quite sure what the smith was yammering about. But he nodded. "I will take that under advisement." Kendrith paced back to Haggard, his stride fast and his mind even faster.

Kendrith returned to the cottage and sank into his bed that night thinking of the girl while his grandfather's snoring was as loud as ever even through the walls of his own room.

Kendrith had swung his sword earlier that day trying to distract himself, feeling the heft of his own sword and cutting through the haunting visage of what he already knew was instant affection.

When sleep didn't come, but wakeful dreams of romantic scenarios warmed his cheeks once more, the boy decided to venture out into the woods and distract himself.

Crickets of the night chirped their tune, an occasional owl hooted, and the ever-looming shadow of the forest of death transgressed upon their location.

The trees swayed ever so softly, and the smell of fertile soil wafted through the air. For the most part, the occasional soft rhythm of chirping crickets or hooting owls was like the snore of a forest that was mostly in a deep slumber.

Then Kendrith heard it before he saw it. Laughter. Like the kind one thought could be imagined.

Kendrith sharpened his senses, becoming fully awake as he followed the sound and didn't have to travel far till he saw the first signs of a camp giving itself away with the kindled fire that tore a hole into the sleeping night.

Kendrith moved closer. A patrol unit from the guild? Maybe an escorting caravan through the woods. But Kendrith knew there was no need for resupplying anytime soon.

Stalking the perimeter, Kendrith found a company of men drinking to their hearts content, instantly recognising that none of them came from the guild. The merry band numbered a dozen drunks. Kendrith deduced their rather brutish demeanor, thinking they might have been mercenaries. Perhaps venturing to travel up north towards the hunting grounds where mythical creatures were born. People who tried their hand at it rarely returned with anything to show for it, if they returned at all.

Wherever they came from with their stocky builds and their haggard looks, they didn't seem the mannered type. Kendrith considered retreating back to his home and informing his grandfather come morning. Until he caught a glimpse of an awfully familiar visage. The only figure among the rowdy bunch who stepped over piles of emptied wine pouches and inebriated bodies sprawled on the floor.

It was the same lithe and small girl Kendrith had seen earlier that day. She reached a man quite possibly in his thirties, but the limited campfire light and years of living on the road seemed to obscure the man's actual age, making him seem even older than he truly was; like a fine wine the man seemed to be handsome partly because of his age, but something underneath the surface suggested a bitter rotten taste to what would seem like a novelty. The man sat on a heavily laden backpack with a pan hanging down the side and a sleeping bag still strapped to the top. A knife in his hand shaved clean the surface of an apple, the firelight glistening off the steel edge.

A gruff voice spoke. "Did you find the target?"

The girl wore a cowl, removing the hood as she spoke.

"Yes," she said. A single word delivering every ounce of conceivable meaning behind it—meticulous, direct, no time for wasted effort.

"Good." The gruff man cut a piece off his apple, sliding the blade along with the slice into his mouth. "But we still need more information. Stalk the security detail and the house itself and get back to me."

Kendrith already turned to retreat, allowing the night to aid his repose as he fell away to hide from the camp's fire, realising that the band of raiders wasn't going to the hunting grounds up north, but rather pursued a target inside the town of Haven.

The next morning, Kendrith mulled over the events he had witnessed, contemplating if he should tell his grandfather or not.

He convinced himself that perhaps it would be best to find more definitive proof before pointing fingers, or that Haggen might report it all to the authorities and raise some flags.

But Kendrith knew the truth. He was hopelessly drawn in by the visage of the girl, seemingly young and innocent, but there surely was something about her that left an impression which Kendrith couldn't scrub away.

He wanted to know more about her, about her origin, about what she was doing with that pack of potent hyenas. Perhaps what Kendrith saw in her was an echo of a mother he lost long ago, and that echo turned into curiosity.

Kendrith awoke early the next day, tasked with running to town and aquiring equipment for alchemy, but instead returned to the camp to find any evidence of their numbers or anything else.

The only evidence of their presence was the faint smell of ash and smoke, depressed earth from the weight of their bodies, and the odd trail of urine marked against a tree.

Kendrith carried his sword with him this time, finding the weight of the pommel pressed against his palm to relax him.

A shift in the air, a slash of wind, primed reflexes—Kendrith's body moved before he knew why. A knife thrust itself into the bark of a tree, trembling with the force of the throw.

Kendrith turned around to see the girl who filled his thoughts.

"I don't appreciate being followed," she said. Brandishing more knives as she twisted her whole body back, her arm bent over her head and whipped it with such accuracy that it flew through the air steady and true.

Kendrith ducked, falling to his knees to avoid the first throw, rolling forward as the next knife flew right past and deep into the woods.

Kendrith fell back behind a tree. His heart beating, his hands shaking—Kendrith had trained for hunting beasts, but Haggen never told him how to fight a human.

Kendrith tried to move to the next cover, but the sudden thrust of another knife slashed him across the arm, causing him to reconsider.

"Who are you?" said the girl, her voice demanding an answer.

"Just someone passing by."

"Lies. You ran into me yesterday."

"That was a coincidence. I live close by with my grandfather."

"Is that why you stalked our camp in the middle of the night?"

Kendrith fell silent for a moment, realising that he couldn't weasel his way out of this one. He tried to understand what exactly it was that gave him away.

"How did you know I saw you?" Kendrith asked.

"I didn't." The girl's reply was daunting. "You just told me." Kendrith cursed his foolishness.

Then silence, as Kendrith waited. Seconds turned into a minute—he felt like it was a lifetime. Finally, when the sound of treading feet and the girl's voice could no longer be heard, Kendrith considered to dare a glance around the corner.

But he decided to not risk it. Drawing his blade, Kendrith held up the steel edge to see into the reflection—the girl was gone.

Another slash through the air, another instinctual reaction saving Kendrith's life as he tilted his blade and the cutting knife rebounded off its edge, cutting a bleeding gash above his brow.

Kendrith looked to see where the knife came from, following the supposed trajectory. Nothing. Another knife hissed through the air, finding its mark in Kendrith's shoulder.

He reeled back, the blood from his brow now blinding him in one eye. Kendrith worked his way around the tree again for more cover.

His breathing laboured, he reminded himself to stay calm, reminded himself of what his grandfather had taught him.

Kendrith checked his pouch, three vials inside. "Don't use more than one at once," his grandfather had told him. "Your body won't be able to handle it."

He looked at the contents, finding one meant for increasing the sensitivity of his skin and bristling hair, minute changes in airflow reacting against his skin to alert him of movement.

Haggen was training Kendrith to use it with blindfolds, to rely on his heightened sensitivity to dodge the pebbles that were being thrown at him. The many bruises that Kendrith would nurse spoke towards how inept he was at the task.

Another meant for increased blood flow into muscles to raise strength and explosive power for speed, and another that would give heightened reflexes.

Kendrith weighed his options at lightning speed. If he were to take a hit, he would know where the attacks were coming from, but by the time he got there, the girl might have changed location. She didn't need to kill him outright, just make him bleed out till he lost consciousness.

On the other hand, if he knew where the attacks were coming from, he might be able to close the distance, but still, by the time he would reach the cloaked girl he would bleed out to death.

But with the right reflexes, speed, and senses, he could just barely overcome the girl.

He hated to admit it, but his attacker far outclassed him. Kendrith eyed the bottles all at once, remembering how a single one would leave him feeling nauseous and in a fugue state for hours. His grandfather's warning returned, *Your metabolism and your body isn't adapted to take several changes all at once. Just a single extra mix of another bottle could kill you.*

Kendrith downed all three.

The roiling cocktail of dubious colours worked their way down Kendrith's throat as if through drainage, their toxic and enhancing properties working instantly. Kendrith clenched his fist and his teeth, as the veins on his neck strained at the excruciating pain that pulsed through him and the deafening heartbeat that drummed in his ears.

His eyes dilated with the force, and he arched his back, skull banging against the bark of the tree as foaming spittle dribbled from his lips. His heart raced with the force of a hundred stampeding horses. Skin stretched itself taut as muscle pushed to the surface, veins running across his skin like roads across a map. And as the pain began to reach its climax, peaking to new heights, the suffering and the world began to slow down to a dull hum and the undulating pain suddenly felt intoxicating.

He was aware of ant colonies marching through hollowed trees, a leaf falling from a distant tree, and a squirrel grinding its teeth down on nuts.

Kendrith tightened his already white fists, more foam on his lips. He could feel his bulging eyes pulse rhythmically with the beat of a burning heart.

He pushed himself to his feet as the bark of the tree broke to his steel-vise grip.

Another dagger aimed between his eyes whistled true, Kendrith caught the slender fine knife in a flashing bur, his mind pounding.

He lowered himself to the floor and pressed his heel against the tree, as the explosive power of his calves propelled him forward and the sound of breaking bark filled the air like thunder.

Kendrith could feel the numb, but present pain in his leg as he became slave to the ingested cocktail.

Another knife flew, coursing through the air deflected by his own steel.

A deluge of blades came like a breeze of air, the gap between each throw becoming shorter, the point of origin becoming less and less unpredictable.

Kendrith didn't think, he just did, as he could already feel the burn of torn ligaments and shredded muscle but still, he did not, could not stop.

Kendrith picked up a rock on his warpath, racing towards the girl.

He knew from the start that he could have attempted to fall back, return to Haggen, and warn him. But the exhilaration was too much to see reason.

His vision became blurry, as the heightened blood flow and gashing wounds made him bleed out faster than they could clot.

Within the ecstasy which he rode there was a moment of lucidity bubbling to the surface which told Kendrith he had to finish it quickly, and that he'd only have a single chance.

The knives came in bursts, no longer starting from unknown origins. The force and speed behind them seemed incredible.

Each throw became harder and harder to react to, but Kendrith no longer needed to sense the coming of the knives that bristled against his skin because he could now feel the throw itself.

He dodged each whiplike toss with such intensity that his mind was on the verge of cracking.

There. Kendrith curled back, tensing his arm, planting his feet, veins pulsating, as the stone cracked in his fierce grip. Finally, he reeled and tossed the stone with a force of his own. Still he could not see the girl, but he could sense where she was.

The stone pierced through a tree, the sound of bark snapping at the weight of the throw, burrowing, breaking through the other side.

An audible thud, and then silence.

"I-I did it." Kendrith's entire body heated up, boiling, a fever wafting over him as it felt like he was burning from within.

He collapsed. Multiple broken bones not used to the sudden explosive force, muscles and ligaments torn, blood pouring from him endlessly. But as the last vestige of his consciousness faded, the boy found himself to be smiling at his small victory.

Chapter 32

Kendrith's eyes fluttered open, a distant dream had made his night restless. His body felt tired and sore, distant and rigid as if he had been sleeping for a very, very long time. And even so the dream he had was already forgotten like a fleeting breath lost in a passing breeze.

A hefty hand collapsed on his shoulder.

"Come. We are about to discuss our plan," Logan said.

Kendrith stood up, sniffing under his armpits and wishing he had a chance to eat and take a shower. Perhaps even wash his clothes. But the thought of Kristen made all such luxuries wash away—he had to stay strong and help Logan finish his end of the bargain. Instead he just settled for a change of fresh clothes.

Kendrith stuffed his mouth with the previous night's procured jerky and sausage and moved on.

The meeting room had a couple of chairs and a long enough rectangular table for the sake of discussion. A couple of hunter weapons covered the walls, from barbed whips to simple swords to some more exotic instruments of death. But the whole display seemed tacky.

"The creature we encountered stands at about ten feet tall, and it has four hooved legs on each corner of its hips, moving about like a spider." As Logan described the monster, he roughly sketched the anatomy of the creature. Though rushed, it seemed that Logan still put emphasis on detail—making sure that the exact muscle composition were discernible as well as which body parts would pose a threat.

"The creature's torso stands like a totem pole, arms with no noticeable design growing out of the upper body. Additionally, two vertical mouths reach from head to hip where whole bodies can be thrown inside."

The thing that Logan seemed to draw was almost the stuff of nightmares. Kendrith recalled the creatures that he crossed in the Forest of the Dead, and though they were put together and marionetted by magic, these seemed to be chewed into a mess before being spat right back out.

From what Kendrith could see, there were easily dozens of arms growing out of the beast.

"The creature also has four faces, each covering one side of the head to provide no blind spot."

"Can the creature rotate its neck?" Kendrith asked.

"That is a good question." The dark-skinned man carried a thick accent. His skin tone and accent seemed to imply he was one of the Qalists: stemming from the sandy planes in the east, they were a tribe of warriors that learnt the art of sword-dance from the shifting sands. He had introduced himself earlier as Kasim.

"We didn't interact with it, from what I could tell—no. But we can never be too sure."

The fourth member, the crazed frantic-eyed woman smiled with pure excitement. "Doesn't matter, we can kill it with traps, lock it in one place, and hack it apart." Her voice was like that of a rusted metal grating against stone.

Kendrith began to understand Logan's concern—something about her didn't seem right, like her sanity was holding on by a thread, scaffolded by whatever madness kept her mind from breaking apart. Kendrith remembered the way she had introduced herself as Betty, with a wet handshake; he still wasn't sure why her hand was wet.

Kendrith looked back at his training, all the things that Haggen had taught him. To take advantage of a beast's one-track mind, of groups. However this time around, finding a blind spot would be difficult. Not just that, but he shared Logan's unease—could the other two really be trusted?

Kendrith left after the meeting to visit Kristen once more. She had improved a lot. Much of the magical venom had been sucked from her veins and what used to be thick suffocating roots of black that choked her body now were just thin withered strands like dry hay.

Her breathing had stabilised and she wasn't in peril anymore, but the fight was not yet over. The healer had said that the rest was up to her.

Kendrith pulled her brunette hair aside, tenderly pressed his lips to her forehead, and stroked her locks. A final loving brush against that scar which gave Kristen so much of her bright beauty.

Kendrith departed, setting out to complete the hunt, to bring back what remained of the monster and leave the place as soon as they were able to.

Chapter 33

George removed Simantiar from his bag, both of them resting in their room.

"How is Kristen?" Simantiar asked.

George shrugged. "Kendrith said she is recovering. The marks are receding and her breathing is stable."

"That's good. We should visit her," Simantiar said.

George nodded.

Early that morning he awoke to the sound of tapping against the bracketed window. Pecky was waiting on the other side and now found a temporary place on George's shoulder. The bird leaned forward and jumped down from George to land on Simantiar.

"Yes, I've missed you too," Simantiar commented dryly despite the pecks.

But despite George's words, he felt a pain, a nascent presence of lingering guilt.

He wasn't sure if he could face Kristen again when she awoke. Had he noticed the scuttling creature...George forced the thought dormant and returned Simantiar to his bag.

Gerard was waiting outside their room and trailed behind like a shadow.

George wasn't very young, but he wasn't imposing. Short and dainty, he had the body of an entertainer, not a killer. Thus he made it a point to avoid the cold stares of opportunistic men with hardened eyes; compassion running off them like rain through felled trees.

Trying his best to seem as small and insignificant as he could, George reached the hospice.

Several men coughed from their beds, and there were few women—few pursued that kind of life. Those women who fell upon times of desperation opted to earn coin selling their flesh instead of hunting it.

George took a seat, a simple wooden chair beside Kristen. She truly seemed better.

Rheumy eyes threatened runny tears. He took her hand in his eyes. "I'm sorry," he said. He had been there with her. He should have noticed.

He remembered her lying there, sound asleep. Only a ribbon of smoke rose from the snuffed fire, the stars shone bright above, and the forest was in disquieting slumber. The first show of a shimmering colour, scuttling feet as sheens shifted.

A sting. Shrill scream. George jumped instinctively, running over to whatever it was that attacked Kristen.

George remembered it all happening so fast, his body reacting on its own. Grabbing the thing and yanking it off by its tail. Twisting, the momentum carrying the creature away so it couldn't attack him too.

He slammed it with the entire force of his turn, a dagger skewering it to the floor.

George pressed his eyes shut as to will the memory away, tears running freely. His hand was placed on Kristen's and a tender thumb stroked her slender fingers.

Kristen's skin was rough, the hands of no brute, but of a crafter, of an artisan.

A shadow loomed behind as a sudden chill filled him.

He didn't duck, he didn't dodge out of the way, instead he jumped backwards knocking the chair into the attacker, and hearing a groan as it connected. Pecky fled through an open window.

Now standing, George noticed the dagger which had tried to strike him now stretched before him. With a firm grip on the arm George pulled it down with all his might onto his shoulder and heard the snap of bending joints before the cry of pain.

The dagger dropped. He sent an elbow into the attacker's stomach and was rewarded with a winded cough.

Every last move was taught to him by the same woman who lay there motionless.

George reached down for the fallen dagger and turned to see Gerard.

"I thought you were supposed to be on our side," George noted.

Gerard coughed, wheezing. "Yeah." He stretched up, grimaced, and took a deep breath. "But friendship doesn't pay, does it? I owe a great debt to Magnus, crippling debt. For what it's worth, the choice wasn't easy, but it was either this or pay it off fully."

Gerard had no sword on him, but pulled out a second dagger.

"Just know it isn't personal."

"It is to me," George amended.

Taking the first jump, George knew he was at a disadvantage, the small space and the difference in weight and size making the whole thing more dangerous the longer it were to go on.

They tested each other, prodding, jumping in and back. Small knicks and cuts on each other as they striped each other in blood.

George intentionally let himself get cut—he knew he would lose eventually anyway—but he made himself seem more at a loss than he truly was. Deception was one of the greatest lessons taught by Kristen.

But his choices were numbered, a motionless Kristen meant he could not leave her defenceless.

There was only one hand he could play that he knew Gerard wouldn't expect, but he knew he couldn't reveal Simantiar. Simantiar had every chance to reveal himself and make short work of Gerard and anyone else. But Kristen wasn't healed yet, and they still needed their help.

"Play dead," George murmured, sliding a hand into his bag.

"What?" Gerard asked.

In one seamless motion, strained by pure focus, George whipped Simantiar's still skull with such force that it knocked the man's head back with a trickle of blood, giving George enough time to return the knife in Gerard's exposed neck.

No words were exchanged, just Gerard's kind eyes looking up blankly till he collapsed. Blood pooled in his mouth and soon puddled around him. His death was suddenly so silent, so inconsequential, the coughs of the sick surrounding them all.

What transpired was already such a typical event that it didn't warrant anything more than a glance. The torture of death's embrace had made them numb to their surroundings.

"George..." A feeble voice spoke. George turned around to see the weak but conscious body of Kristen looking at him, a desperate hand outstretched as she tried to reach for him.

"Kristen!" George ran over, taking her hand.

"George..."

"Shh, don't talk."

"Behind…you."

George noticed too late, as Kristen watched helplessly with such listless eyes.

A needle pricked his neck, and the boy grasped it in panic as he stumbled back, falling over the chair and onto the floor.

George pressed a hand to the spot, his vision becoming fuzzy.

The boy could see Simantiar, lifeless there on the floor. George shook his head at the skull as a shadow cast itself over his vision.

"Well, well, well. Seems like you are finally awake. The boss is dying to see you in person, Kristen."

Kendrith took the rear, allowing the more experienced hunters to lead the way.

He hoped George and Kristen would be fine. Kendrith reassured himself that the boy was more capable than he gave him credit for and hoped that Gerard could be trusted. And if ever in a pinch, they did have a portable wizard.

Kendrith followed Logan's instructions, observing the two suspicious hunters closely.

The woman, Betty, was strange; every now and then giving an unnerving chuckle as she scuttled over to some tree and touched it tenderly. Kendrith almost felt sorry for the bark of wood.

Every now and then, giving off strange sounds of fascination, licking her lips with a devilishly long and thin tongue as she gathered strange leaves and plants that Kendrith didn't recognise.

Kasim was more stoic, controlled, and precise, never losing any focus as he strolled with acute grace. He was a man of the blade—Kendrith had no doubt about it. The man revealed nothing, even his steps were short and meticulous displaying control.

The sun was beginning to set.

"This is good—we can make camp here," Logan said.

"Yes, we have come quite a long way from the settlement," Kasim spoke with his thick foreign accent, like the sound of sand which grazed sediment.

Something was off in the way he spoke those words.

He was a storm in flight, his scimitars singing as they left their scabbards, his brown cowl whirling like a small storm devil.

The blade connected with Logan's hammer.

"I knew it. How much is Magnus paying you?"

"Magnus? Paying?" laughed Betty.

Kendrith sprang forward, but didn't expect the eccentric snap of Betty's wrists. She squatted down, wrist raised diagonally from her as some hidden contraption fired forward a thread-thin needle which met its mark in Kendrith's hand.

"Well, enough to pay off our debts to him. That is all."

Kendrith started to feel light-headed.

"What was that?" he asked, his speech slurred. He pulled the needle from his knuckle, a tiny puncture wound left in its wake as if from a cactus.

"Moria poison. It attacks the nervous system and makes you lose control of your motor functions."

Kendrith wondered why she hadn't used something more potent or lethal. But then he understood as she brandished her short sword and he peered into those crazed brown eyes like a bottomless pit of sadism. She wanted to enjoy her time with Kendrith.

"You are quite the pretty boy, you know that? Just my type." Her fiendish chuckle sent chills down Kendrith's bones, the same bones that suddenly felt alien to him, heavy as if turned into rubber as he fell to his knees.

"Kendrith!" screamed Logan.

"I am your opponent, Logan Van Dungen," spoke Kasim, his aura stoic and unperturbed by the deceit as his scimitars sang their tune.

Kendrith swung back and forth with his sword in hand, his vision doubling, his legs refusing to listen to him as he stumbled back.

"The toxin doesn't take long to take effect. It comes from a creature which roams these parts. It devours poisonous flowers and infuses the poison into its thorned back. It is very reminiscent of a hedgehog, you know?" Betty lectured casually while Kendrith's legs felt disconnected from his own body. Betty snapped a branch, breaking it even further and removing all the stray twigs, swinging it under Kendrith's leg and knocking him to his back.

"You don't seem to be looking so good, pretty boy. How about you lie down, and let me help you with that."

Kendrith fumbled around, for the first time feeling true fear seep down into his bones. Every other encounter, with beasts and monsters several times more foreboding than anything Betty could offer, had not shaken his iron will. Yet, as Betty swung the branch in front of her, blade presumably in her other hand—Kendrith wasn't sure, he couldn't even tell if he was standing or knocked down—he felt a cold fear blanket him.

It felt as if his limbs, his body, his eyes, and brain and head had all become independent of each other. None able to communicate, none able to tell his brain where they were. He thought that perhaps Logan was calling for him, but he wasn't sure. Perhaps from some far-off distant place.

It was true—Kendrith had never felt such fear as that which came with facing his own helplessness, and whatever vile thing Betty had planned in that mad mind of hers.

Kendrith reached above himself, hands fumbling—it felt as if his arm was rolling away from his body.

The tingling touch of stone. Adrenaline and fear gave his body a single moment of lucidity, as all Kendrith could do was hoist his arm up and fling.

"Ah, fuck!" Kendrith heard the thud, and even more so heard the curses. It connected.

Come on, Kendrith. Kendrith tried to force whatever competent functions he had to work together.

He got up, running away to a tree.

"Thank you for the gash, honey. How about I give you a matching one?" The words coming from Betty felt like they were from a feverous nightmare. Slurred and distant like swirling colours or the parting of oil from water.

Kendrith fumbled for his belt, fingertips tingling, unable to find purchase. Each attempt to grab one of the vials from his bandolier failed, fingers unable to wrap around them. The world was a swirl of colours. It felt as if the vials had flattened, turning into pressed objects printed onto his belt.

Fear crept up his boots.

Or not fear, Kendrith felt the creeping of vines which wrapped his feet, grazing him longingly, seductively, climbing to claim that which nature deemed its own. Was it magic? Was he hallucinating? Or worse, had Kendrith truly stayed for so long that vines saw him as nothing more than rubble?

Kendrith screamed, stumbling away from the grasping vines. "Logan!" Kendrith cried in desperation. But there was no reply, yet perhaps he just couldn't hear it. He couldn't hear anything.

Kendrith gripped his hands, feeling how one was still wrapped around his sword, fear freezing it stiff.

Kendrith cut the bandolier from himself. Hands trembling, the shadow of death came to claim him. He felt the hot warmth of liquid running down his alien chest—he cut himself while releasing the bandolier, but he could worry about that later.

Kendrith struggled to release the bottles, numb and trembling hands proving useless.

So he swung, the bandolier slamming against the tree before him.

The sounds of glass shattering came to him.

And so Kendrith leaned forward, tongue outstretched in desperation as he feebly leaned into the tree, allowing whatever cocktail of potions he had made to flow into his system.

He really hoped he was going to survive this.

The rest of the world turned to blood, the swirl of colours now just a stark red, a mind-pounding vermilion of raging blood in Kendrith's vision. Sudden flashes of reality sparked through that visor.

Darting in between trees, drooling across the floor, dirt under fingernails.

Breaking branches, pounding strides, hunting—a predator lost in the forest. Kendrith's senses had been a detached swirl of hazy instincts, limbs and senses all intoxicated and useless, but now they were almost overwhelming. Senses overran his mind, his thoughts, every single scent smelt from distances apart, eyes taking it all in, fear on his nose as moments of lucidity had him breathe out mist from overheated organs.

He was an animal, and whatever cocktail mixed within him made Kendrith nothing more than a raging beast. He couldn't feel his own heartbeat, but he could feel a numbing burn in his chest. Blood raced through veins, muscles tore and bulged. Every single sense so overcome that none of it seemed to function.

Kendrith ran; he sprinted; he hunted. He heard screams. He thought his own at first, but then knew they came from his prey. A distant thought. Who was he hunting? Where was he? He didn't know.

How she pleaded, how she screamed, now the one being hunted by a mindless creature that became as free as the wind through trees, as corporeal as the forest itself, as unrelenting as the cruel indifference of nature that grasped the world with ever-reaching tendrils.

When Kendrith came to again, he hung from a tree, bloodstained nails dripping to the floor, one hand holding himself aloft, legs squatted like a predatory gargoyle on a hunt.

Eyes bloodstained and frantically wide.

Panting, with something between his teeth. Kendrith looked down and saw Betty hanging motionless, held with her neck between Kendrith's teeth.

The cocktail burnt through his system, his body fighting, lucidity returning. A horror-filled state where numbness and adrenaline made him unaware of what he was doing. He was a passenger to the beast he had become.

So he hung there from the bloodstained branch, red marking him like warpaint. He hung there like some monstrous bat that stalked the trees to grab unwilling prey.

Perhaps it was the nature of the magical-soaked forest, or the cocktail of the vials alone, but his heart felt like it was tearing in two.

He opened his jaw, mist forming, Betty's lifeless body dropped to the floor like a sack of potatoes. Kendrith turned, eyes frantic—he didn't feel in control.

A step for him was a lunge in reality.

Kendrith turned and heard the skitter of a spider through a hollowed tree trunk, the tender touch of a leaf to the floor, the bristle of canopies, and then, like a loving whisper, the clank of metal, and the shuffle of dancing feet fighting for superiority.

Kendrith leapt, the world still a blur to him as he zoomed through it, the world still red as the trees melded into one and it all rushed past him. He cut through the standing trees like a blade, already right beside Logan's and Kasim's square off, neither giving any ground to their opposition.

Logan's hammer swings cracked and humbled the trees that bent and bowed to his might, Kasim swayed back and forth like a breeze—he was truly a sandstorm, bending to the weight of Logan's hammer that tried to hammer against the single grain. Kendrith saw it all as the fight of a boulder versus a sandstorm. Each swing of Logan's mighty hammer only had Kasim dancing to the momentum, bending through the strike. Each strike of Kasim's blade was like the colliding pressure of grains of sand against the side of a mountain. Neither would relent.

Kendrith jumped in, his sword left behind somewhere.

"Kendrith?" Logan spoke his name in stunned disbelief.

"I see you escaped Betty's poison. Though however you achieved this didn't seem to be without its price," Kasim said. His scimitars remained by his side, while his brown cloak billowed. His breath was controlled.

Kendrith charged. With a dagger unsheathed from his side, Kendrith struck at Kasim. The warrior breathed, calling air into his lungs that would be the breeze which lifted his sandstorm.

The two leapt, a strike of metal upon metal in blinding speeds. Kendrith's strike hit with a beast's ferocity, and Kasim's parried and returned with a leaf's graceful pirouette.

Logan used the chance, jumping forward to hit the elusive storm. Kasim leapt back, doing a backflip as if truly weighing no more than a few grains.

The man jumped again, landing atop a branch.

"I see this fight is no longer in my favour, but no matter. My job is done." The man vanished into the cover of branches.

Kendrith saw his prey, blood rushing to him. To give chase. That was what his mind raced for him to do.

He readied his jump; a hand grasped him from behind. Kendrith turned with pounding frenzy. He saw Logan's worried gaze.

"Don't. Let him leave."

Kendrith calmed himself, clutching at his heart. The cocktail vanished, the adrenaline fading into a ubiquitous hum so that he could feel all the pain and hurt that came with the sudden mix of potions.

He gasped, heart beating against his chest as if it were to tear through withered skin.

Kendrith fell to the floor, going fetal, a pained cry escaping him that pierced through the canopy of trees and took the shape of a crow's caw.

Chapter 34

When George next awoke, he did so with a start. He couldn't see. Was he blindfolded? No. It was dark. He strained his arms, finding them bound behind him, the rope chafing on skin.

George looked all around him; the ground was rough. His shoes had been taken from him. He heard the sound of water dripping from the ceiling. The darkness wasn't alien to George, so many times before he would sit with his sister as they buried themselves under rubble and let the wandering patrols of the city step over them. George found himself surprised that he wasn't more alarmed with the situation he found himself in.

He remembered the sting of a needle, the darkness that followed, and the desperate reach of a wounded woman who had fought for her life in the past week.

A week? How long had George been in his suffocating prison? He had no window to grant him a sense of time.

George forced himself to his feet, blood returning to sleeping limbs, his shoulders aching from the restraints and a drowsy fugue clouding his thoughts.

The bard walked the pace of the prison, the dripping of water echoing to the rhythm of his pacing. He murmured as he walked around, counting, measuring the distance, soft little whispers like the inedible gratings of chalk.

"Forty." George counted forty steps around the little prison, ten steps per each wall. There was a bucket left for his needs, and George placed it so that it would catch the drop of water. George heard the dull clunk of each drop against wood, soon turning into the sound of water into basin.

The first three walls were made of rough stone, but the fourth one was of wood, with a door locking him inside.

"Simantiar," George whispered softly. The boy went through the place to find no remnants of his bag or any of his weapons.

George weighed his options, sitting cross-legged as the bucket continued to fill, one drop at a time.

He felt his toes wiggle, felt the stretch of his bones and body, the tingling of his skin even without his sight. Then he noticed the ache behind heavy eyes, the rough stone against callused soles, and the shallow sense of hunger working its way up.

He considered charging against the door, trying to break the splintered wood with the force of his weight.

But what if there was someone on the other side? George rose to his feet again, and pressed his ear to the door. Focusing, concentrating, straining his ear. Only darkness in which George couldn't hear anything.

He slammed his head against the door, metal hinges rattled, a hollow thud escaping. George waited. One drop. Two drops. Three drops. After the second dozen, George stepped back, running back into the door with all his might. The door shook, the hinges echoed, the tunnels carrying the sound like the whisper of a whisper.

George hammered and hammered, the door rattling with each strike, each one a thunderous strike in the umbral black that was his prison.

The hours passed, or perhaps they were minutes; his shoulder ached regardless.

George gave in, the door still holding strong in defiance, barring him from his freedom.

Kneeling down, he sipped water from the bucket. His thoughts receded to memories of playing bob for apples with his sister, laughing as water rushed through his nose as his teeth failed to find purchase on the apples.

Those were better days. The present promised far darker ones.

Time passed, the world gone and distant, a light pierced through that darkness, swaying back and forth as it cleared the way through brambles of shadow.

A key clanked, a lock opened, and metal creaked—the door opened.

George flew across the air, his knee raised high in front of him as he took to the skies.

It connected—no, it didn't. George was weak, muscles aching, still in a daze. His body was caught during the flight and thrown back. George landed on his rear, his plate of food tossed into the room, bread and baked beans splattering across the floor, the bucket of water thrown over him. George gasped in shock—the water was freezing cold as it soaked him. The boy hyperventilated, breathing in and out deeply as he shivered. Water dripped from his nose, and matting greasy hair.

"That's what I get for bringing your food? Here." The stout and laboured body of a rough man laughed. "Maybe you will be a little more respectful tomorrow and I won't have to throw your food at you." The door closed, the lock clicked. The man and the woman were already turning to leave.

"No!" George cursed. What happened to him? The boy ran against the door again.

"No!" he screamed, fear returning to him much like the shadows as the lantern's refuge dulled.

"Please let me go!" George was soaked, water dripping from his chin— no, it wasn't the bucket of freezing water, it was his tears. The boy cried. He was terrified.

Again he was left to the company of darkness, abandoned with his thoughts. Each hammer of the boy's shoulder against the door grew more feeble, and George felt hopeless. His shoulders sagged as he cried openly. The cries of his tears were a relief, at least that kept the shadow away. Kendrith, Logan, Kristen, Simantiar, even Pecky. He wondered where they were. He felt so weak begging for their help. He needed them. But they also needed him. He cursed his helplessness. Each strike against the door left a more hollow rattle than the last, the last of his resistance breaking.

It was supposed to go differently, he was supposed to fly out of there, cut himself out, escape. He was supposed to go find Kristen, help her escape. Instead he wept, there on the rock floor, trembling, shoulder spasming from the cold water and weeping tears. He was a kid. He was helpless. The truth finally showed itself. He wanted to matter, he wanted to be as confident as Logan, as reliable as Kendrith, as competent as Kristen.

The boy's foot slipped, something giving way underneath his bare feet. The beans. With a wet splurch he slipped to the floor. Crying openly, he leaned against the wooden door of his prison. The boy wailed out into the darkness in defiance, as if trying to defy the veil of shadows.

Kendrith shuddered in the hell crafted of his own mind, fading in and out of consciousness. Mere moments of awareness as he watched Logan sit next to him, a ragged wet cloth pressing against Kendrith's forehead. "Fight it," said a far-off voice. "Fight it."

Kendrith writhed in pain, usually flitting between wakefulness and drifting into a retreating slumber that drowned out the suffering. His heart fought against the strange concoction of potions that pumped through his system, and ate away at his skin and innards. His heart squeezed blood with such agony that it lanced through his bones as a burning hot presence. The effects of whatever tranquilizer was injected into him was probably still doing its work.

Kendrith's mind retreated, and fell back into some daze of a memory from long ago, abandoning his current body to preserve itself, escaping into a place far from his hurt so that the pain he experienced could be a distant throbbing afterthought.

Kendrith awoke. His eyes blinked open, the hulking body of Logan was in his vision, but then the thought of Logan was gone, and instead Haggen was beside him.

Kendrith could smell the comforting aroma of beef stew and potatoes in the air, the scent of cinnamon reminding him he was safe. "Easy now," Haggen instructed as Kendrith propped himself up with a wince. He was bandaged up, the cuts sealed, but the aching of bone and muscle were still present.

"Pretty stupid, what you did there." Haggen seemed awkward seated on the stool that groaned under his weight. The large man emptied out the soaking rag and dunked another in fresh load of warm water to press against Kendrith's forehead.

Kendrith smiled, giving off a satisfied sigh as he felt the warmth of the soaked rag, the same kind he used when he would sink into a steaming hot bath and feel the hairs on his neck stand up.

"You have a fever, boy…" Haggen paused. "Your heart could have burst."

"Yeah, but it didn't."

Haggen continued to tend him quietly, his lips pursed as if withholding a scowl.

Kendrith felt as if he was forgetting something…something important.

"The girl!" Kendrith propped up immediately to a seated position, his body screamed at him in agony, as a myriad of pain and lancing through torn muscle and bone. The boy doubled over, grasping his stomach.

"Easy now," Haggen said.

"The girl, what happened with the girl?" Kendrith asked, looking up to Haggen.

Haggen remained silent, instead pushing away with the stool to reveal the other bed which carried the unconscious body of his combatant. How unusually genteel she seemed in sleep, so warm and at peace.

"Who is she?" Haggen asked. "I found the two of you like this."

Kendrith returned his gaze to his grandfather. "I don't know."

"Tell me what you do know."

Kendrith bit his lip, but nodded. He told his grandfather everything he had witnessed at that camp—the fire, the laughs, and the conversation.

"They are planning to assassinate someone?"

"I don't know for sure, but it seemed that way—that girl was going to do it."

The two turned their heads, staring at the girl's still sleeping body, her chest rising softly with each breath. The two looked to each other again. She didn't seem like a ferocious killer.

"We should hand her over to the authorities," Haggen said, his voice in an even deeper whisper.

"No, she's just a girl." Kendrith lowered his own voice to match.

A pause. "You like her?" Haggen realised, white teeth appearing from his smile.

Kendrith's cheeks turn red. "No," he retorted.

Haggen's smile grew even wider. "You like the girl." He leaned in, his words stretched and mocking as he purred his claim.

"She's my age, and I didn't think she was a bad person, so we shouldn't turn her in till we know the full story." Kendrith averted his gaze as if to give nothing away in his eyes.

"But who is the person at the head of their group?" Haggen asked.

"Verron."

Haggen and Kendrith turned to the girl, her eyes awake as she propped herself up.

"His name is Verron."

Kendrith and Haggen looked to each other shortly, then Haggen began to ask the questions.

"And who is this Verron to you?"

"The person who took me in when my uncle died."

"To turn you into an assassin?" Kendrith jumped in, asking before Haggen could get out another word.

"Why else would he kill my uncle?"

The girl was called Kristen. Her hair was a fair auburn of soft waves, her features long and lithe with a coldness to her eyes that was hidden when she slept, and that single vertical scar that marked her cheek.

Her uncle had escaped with her from the Gullian Empire over the seas to the west, a continent of its own with little liberty granted to the people.

Over perilous seas and a vicious storm, their boat was taken by the waves, but they made it, stranded not far off the coast of Bedal. If one were to take the western path along the narrow shores, one would avoid the northern trail of the unmapped regions entirely, and reach the fishing ports and trade towns of Bedal to the west of Adna. They are simple folk with no interest in the peculiar remnants of a lost magic.

Kristen retold the story, a story that she would repeat as a whisper in the back of her mind, over and over like a ripple of images that repeated themselves endlessly until she could see only the shadow of the memory played upon rocky walls.

She and her uncle survived. Stranded, they walked the sandy beach and tried to find shelter. But fate was cruel in its guise. They escaped the patrols of the empire, smuggled their way into a port, and took their chances with the sea. Survived. Only to be left at the mercy of mercenaries once they felt like they had made it.

"It was something they ate that day, or maybe we just pissed them off. Maybe they were swindled, or a contract had gone bad—I don't know what it was. But they were in a sour mood and we came along, a target for their frustration." Kristen recalled it all, recalling the events with a coldness that told of how often she had replayed the events till they formed calluses.

"Verron took me in. I don't know why he spared me, but he did. Taught me how to kill, how to wield a blade, and how to hunt."

"You care for him," Haggen said with a sense of realisation.

The campfire crackled. It had been three days since Haggen had found Kendrith and Kristen unconscious side by side like sleeping lovers. It was only now at night, under a campfire in the night of forest that Kristen finally opened up. Kendrith wondered if it was her way of saying thank you. Though she didn't yet run, her bag of belongings rested beside her as if she were always ready to depart, though her weapons were one thing that she wasn't getting back.

Kristen shrugged. "He raised me. Sure, he killed my uncle. But he is not always cruel."

"Be with a viper long enough and even then you convince yourself that it is good," Haggen said. It wasn't an accusation, but rather concern that lined his words.

"I don't expect you to understand," Kristen finally replied, her eyes to the floor.

Kendrith thought her beautiful. Not a conventional kind of beauty, but a remarkable one nonetheless. Her features were sharp like a hawk's— slender eyes, pointed nose, thin lips, and cheekbones seemingly carved in marble. Even her scar carried some tragic beauty to it. She reminded Kendrith of a single snowflake falling into a still lake, lonely, but resolute in its silence.

"That scar." Haggen pointed with the bladed tip of his dagger, a bit of rabbit meat stuck to his white beard. "Did Verron do that to you?"

Kristen took a strand of hair and pulled it over the scar, as if it confirmed his suspicions.

Haggen sighed, taking the knife and stuffing his mouth with another chunk of meat. He rose to his feet, his white tunic lightly unbuttoned to reveal the first of many scars that striped his body. Taking one gigantic bearlike hand he patted Kendrith's shoulder and lumbered back inside the thatched hut with only the shine of a soft candle's glow.

Silence and the crackle of the campfire filled the remaining space.

"Why are you still here?" Kendrith asked, and Kristen remained quiet.

He tried a different question. "Are you feeling better?"

Kristen nodded.

"Are Verron and the other men searching for you?"

She shook her head. "I do as I am told, complete my task. They trust me to do the scouting, and return when I see fit."

Kendrith leaned in. "So, why don't you run away?"

"I have nowhere to go," her response was as cold and featureless as stone, like an answer not wholly her own, spoken blankly and empty.

"But what about—"

A furious gaze shot at Kendrith. "But what? Where do I go? Hmm? Where am I to go? With what skills? What family? Who will take me in when I have only blood on my hands?" She wore her anger plainly for all to see, her eyes wide with fervor, hot blood pumping through her veins—but Kendrith thought that behind that frenzied stare was fear.

"I'm sorry I don't have some aureate father to coddle me."

Kendrith's eyes widened.

"How do you know about my father?"

Kristen's eyes widened in realisation. She had made a mistake.

Kendrith's eyes narrowed.

"Who is your target?" he asked.

No response.

"Kristen, tell me now, who is it you're supposed to kill?"

She looked up to Kendrith, tears in her eyes, biting her lower lip. That snowflake upon the lake now dissolved into water.

Yet she stared on, resolute. She had made her peace and she looked Kendrith in the eye as she felt there was something she owed him as she uttered her next words with grating spite. "*Jaylen Feller.*"

Chapter 35

Silence wafted between the two, the name of Kendrith's father filling the gap between, the crackle of burning firewood distant.

No words were exchanged, but both knew what was to happen next.

Kristen leaned forward, and Kendrith reached to his side to feel the empty space where his sword should have been. He cursed himself; he had become too lax.

The girl grabbed the untouched end of a piece of burning wood and tossed the burning embers at Kendrith. He leaned to the side, letting gravity quicken his fall as he fell from the stool.

Kristen grabbed her bag of belongings and sprinted.

"Haggen!" Kendrith called out from the top of his lungs.

The giant burst open his door just moments later, but it was too late—Kristen was already gone.

"Where is she?" he asked Kendrith.

"She plans to kill my father!" he warned.

Haggen cursed.

"Which way did she go?"

Kendrith pointed to the dark cut of woods where the girl had vanished.

Haggen sighed, his shoulders slumped. "It's not good, she's already gone."

He turned to the door, going back into the hut.

"Are you just going to let my father die?" Kendrith asked, still stranded on his rear. "We need to go after her."

"Nobody said anything about that…and stand up." The tenor of a serious instructor returned to Haggen.

Kendrith obeyed instantly, rising to his feet. His cheeks flushed just a little.

"We are hunters. So, that is what we will do. Hunt."

Three days had passed since then.

Jaylen Feller had business to the southeast of Bedal in Okoria—an obscure and rather unwarrantedly loud neighbour with little to show for it. His private troop of hunters and security detail provided guard as they wandered through unbidden by any problems from the forest. Jaylen himself sat inside a carriage pulled by two white mares, one as white as snow while the other seemed mottled by dirt.

It was the first time Kendrith was out in the forest. Haggen had told him several times that he was not yet ready, but the situation had changed.

Kendrith and Haggen talked stratagem two nights before—it was mostly just Haggen telling Kendrith what to do.

Haggen had described the concept of battle like a roiling storm in the middle of a sea: waves rising all about as tall spires clashed into each other with dark clouds above spewing thunder and lightning. He was the stone cliff in the middle of all of that, unmoving, silent, stoic. The waves crashed and the thunder hammered, but yet he would not move, just observe it all in silent contemplation. Kendrith tried to understand it, emulate it, but knew he was not yet ready.

"Why aren't we getting the town's guard involved? Or even telling my father about it?" Kendrith had asked a night before the plan went into fruition. Haggen was packing supplies, his back muscles tensed with the weight and rumination of tactic.

The bearded man turned around, heaving a sigh of contemplation as he considered his words. The large man licked his lips.

"Because I wouldn't want to break a young man's heart." The words were teasing, but the tone was anything but humoured…the giant sounded tired.

Kendrith blushed regardless, trying to compose himself. "I know you, that's not your only reason."

Haggen turned to him, the large man went down to a knee so they could be face-to-face. A large giant paw fell onto Kendrith's shoulder. And though the man stood fearsomely tall and could sow fear into the most intrepid of men, in that moment, he seemed fragile. The eyes of an old and tired man, laced with love and worry looked back into Kendrith's. Haggen's rough and chiselled face belonging to a warrior was filled with two soft and loving blue eyes that seemed to carry the stillness of a calm sea.

"The girl…she is being used. I have seen enough children being recruited by evil men to know that that is not who she wants to be. She feels like she has no choice, trapped and forced to love a man because the alternative would be to love no one. If we were to get the guards involved, she may end up being killed as well as part of their band."

Kendrith nodded—he was grateful and relieved to see that his grandfather was on his side.

The large old man reached behind Kendrith's neck and pulled the boy close, their foreheads bumping. It was like a stone in the palm of one's hand being pressed against a boulder.

"And the reason we don't tell your father is because if he and his personal security detail knew the truth, they would advise him to not travel, meaning Kristen and the killers would be lost. Or he might tell the town's guard. He won't tell Kristen the truth."

A hand slapped against Kendrith's head. "Stay with me boy, this forest brings death to the unwary."

Kendrith nodded.

The two crept far enough behind, trailing the path up towards Jaylen's entourage which escorted him through the forest.

Most of the creatures avoided them, leaving their path clear and unperturbed as other beings went for easier kills. The swamp to the east of the forest was avoided completely, instead the trail through the fairy lands was taken. The wood nymphs and pixies and other sylvan avoided the troop. A treaty stated that as long as the woods were respected and undamaged safe passage would be promised.

Next came the path between the wailing of haunted ghosts in the woods where the trees looked like silent mourners of their own birth until finally they reached the less filled part of roaming husks.

Kendrith's nerves stood on end. The boy looked to the canopies and back, staring at shadows thinking that if he stared long enough whatever hid underneath would show itself. Haggen had explained to him already that if they stood too close Jaylen's men would discover them, and that if they trod ahead Kristen's partners would discover them.

"What if we will be too late?" Kendrith asked.

Haggen shook his head. "Give those men some credit. They won't fall so easily. I know those hunters personally, and they are some of the best men your father recruited for his personal detail." Kendrith took note of the spite in Haggen's tone—he didn't like the fact that good hunters were being taken away from the guild.

"But even they wouldn't be able to handle an ambush. We will trail behind them. Wait for the first sign of combat."

"Men will die," Kendrith protested.

"Aye, they will. But this is what they signed up for. It is better to get into this risk and catch the men rather than let them escape."

"And what if Kristen informed Verron? What if the ambush is off?"

"Then we can head home. Once they are out of the forest, they are safe."

But Kristen will be lost, Kendrith thought, surely one that also crossed Haggen's mind. One could only hope that the ambush was still on.

Kendrith nodded. The whole thing sat uneasy in his stomach. Could he really allow people to die? To use them as bait. More so than anything, he hoped his father wouldn't be among them. And that made him even more nervous.

He looked to Haggen, the stone cliff at a roiling sea. He also had men out there, comrades that he knew from the guild. Kendrith couldn't imagine how hard it must have been for him to use his own friends as bait.

The patrol entered the forest where the husks lingered.

"Get ready," Haggen said resolutely, his stare forward.

Kendrith gulped. His grandfather informed him that if the ambush was happening anywhere, it would be where the husks were.

Kendrith wondered if maybe the ambush really was called off. That perhaps nothing would happen. Maybe Kristen warned them that Kendrith and Haggen would tell the authorities, that it was too much of a risk. All those thoughts and hopes were shattered when the first of the screams began. "Ambush!" Kendrith heard in the distance.

Kendrith and Haggen sprinted. The first of the bolts loosened from their crossbows.

It was a slaughter, one by one Kendrith and Haggen watched the arrows bury themselves into the necks of men and pierce the hood of Jaylen's carriage.

"Find the girl," Haggen said.

Kendrith nodded. He unsheathed his sword and for the first time since training with it, it felt heavy and awkward.

His heart drummed against his chest and thrummed in his ears, his instincts begged that he run away. The sight of spewing blood was like a painter's first brushstroke.

But the true artistry came when Haggen bore his double-sided axe.

What a force he was! Kendrith had never seen his grandfather in actual combat, and almost wished he never had. Just the thought that he wasn't standing at the other side of his blade was all that kept his own bladder from relieving itself.

Kendrith ran forward, running on the outer edges of the fight. "Let me distract them, while you find the girl," Haggen had instructed two nights earlier. He was more than just a distraction; Haggen was a goddamn storm, a force of nature as he mauled down the enemy men one after the other. The man roared like a god of war, his white beard speckled with the blood of his enemies, the calm blue eyes Kendrith saw earlier now that of a crazed man out for blood.

Haggen's axe cleaved like a scythe through wheat. One man tried to stand in Haggen's way, hefting a sword swing, but managed to fall to his rear as Haggen simply charged through him—it was like watching a man trying to block a boulder rolling down a hill.

Haggen took an arrow to his shoulder, but the behemoth didn't stop; he gritted his teeth and strengthened his charge. A berserker's roar bellowed from his mighty lungs as a splash of red striped him in his warpaint.

The distraction gave Jaylen's men enough time to regroup and reorganise. "Protect the charge!" the hunters ordered.

One of them crossed his hands over his stomach and unsheathed his swords. No, not swords—*whips*. Each inch of steel broke loose from the last to reveal a thread of strengthened metal running through its centre that held each cut of blade together.

The man danced like a tornado of blades, each strike of the whip clearing and cutting into men. The whips pulled back, deepening each cut.

Another hunter pulled forth a normal halberd, holding the enemy at length and cleaving through them at each opportunity.

Another pulled forth a crossbow, but not a normal one—it was custom-made. With a built-in rotary magazine, the man fired several arrows in a stream of steam-powered projectiles.

There was Kendrith's window.

The men were distracted by the steaming bull that was Haggen, breaking their defences, the storm of blades that came from the dancing steel whips, the torrent of bolts fired from a crossbow, and finally the cleave of a halberd blade that chipped away at the enemies' options.

There, in the field, shrouded by a hood, Kendrith saw the sway of familiar autumn hair and drawn daggers.

The boy ran, his feet guiding him, blood pumping.

The tidal waves of battle crashed against the shore and pulled him into its call.

The roar of Haggen was heard, his blood-splattered beard swaying with each move like the foam of a tempestuous wave of the sea; cries bellowed from both sides that abandoned any form of speech.

Each person, each combatant was a wave. Haggen was the stone cliff anchored within the turmoil, weathering the crash and breaking the waves. But Kendrith wasn't the stone, the cliff that remained unmoving with each lightning strike and tidal wave—he couldn't be. So instead, he was the boat, the single small boat of wood that allowed the waters to sweep it away to its flow.

Kendrith stared out from locked blades, as Kristen already snapped her wrist to unveil the telling gleam of three hidden daggers. Three puffs to strengthen his resolve, and the boy charged forward into the storm.

The occasional sword swung at his head. Kendrith ducked, returning a blow or two. He felt his blade cut, the feeling of resistance as the sharp end pulled through, though he didn't wait to see what he had sliced.

He couldn't stop, he couldn't turn back. Kendrith braved the storm and continued forward, for if he stopped riding the waves they would pull him under.

An arrow narrowly missed him, and the boy stopped to follow the arrow's path, and instead saw the swinging sword coming down at him.

Kendrith ducked at the last second, and the blade embedded itself into the bark of a tree.

The boy stabbed his blade through the opening in the assailant's armpit, and the blood splattered his face causing him to grimace and shudder.

But he couldn't stop.

Kendrith pulled out the sword, wishing he had more alchemical potions to use, but Haggen took them off him, telling him it would put too much of a strain on his heart trying to expel the toxins he had taken almost a week before.

Kendrith barely survived against Kristen with the potions. He wondered how well he could hold up without them.

Kristen walked up to three guardsmen who stood around the carriage. Coming towards the girl, he failed to see what happened as the men all instantly collapsed, daggers protruding from their exposed necks.

Kendrith ducked down, going into a roll, with the sound of dying men and steel on steel all around him. He could smell the thick scent of blood masking the forest air. The boy rolled back to his feet, a stone in his hand as he chucked it with all his might. It crashed into Kristen's head. The girl lost her footing as she stumbled to the side.

Dropping his sword, Kendrith leapt forward to where Kristen was only a couple of feet away from his father. He tackled Kristen off her feet.

The two rolled, their arms interlocked, falling off a steep slope, tumbling over dry leaves and littered twigs that snapped under their weight.

The sound of battle grew distant, the cries of frantic and dying men like an echo as Kendrith and Kristen fell out of the storm.

A tree halted their momentum, and the two cried out as they felt their bodies hit against it.

Kendrith's grip loosened, and he grimaced at the lancing pain.

But there was something else, a burning pain in his side. Kendrith felt for the source till he grasped the protruding hilt of a dagger and felt the warmth of his own blood at his fingers.

Adrenaline pushed him through, ears thumping, blood pumping.

Kendrith rolled away just in time to dodge the first stab of Kristen's dagger as she mounted him, the second stab impeded as Kendrith caught Kristen's wrist, panic giving him strength.

With a loose roar, their hands trembled at each other's strength. Kendrith pushed the blade to the side, cutting into the dirt. He threw an elbow to Kristen's head, and she grunted with the blunt attack, stumbling off him. Her hood came loose, her auburn hair was frazzled with dry leaves clumped in it. Her eyes were focused, sharp—she was ready to kill. Yet a single tear lined her cheek.

Kendrith clambered to his feet, his tunic already coloured red.

He pressed a hand to the wound around the embedded dagger twisting in his side. "You don't have to do this," he said with a pained wheeze, his lungs aching and cold.

"We both know I do," she said. With no trace of doubt in her voice, her conviction held back the dam which was guilt, which was the good she had to lock up to survive in a world where she was forced to kill.

Kendrith did not resist—he knew he could not win against her, and the sound of battle still resounded from atop the hill. He stood there, arms to his side, no weapon to his name, just a blade that drew blood from him bit by bit like a leech sucking him dry.

"Just walk away," she said. "You're not the mission."

"No. But my father is."

She remained silent. Kristen bit her lip, a second and then a third tear slid down her cheeks. The dam of her conviction was showing its first cracks.

"Please, don't make me kill you." Her blade trembled.

"Why? Because it would make it better if you don't kill someone who isn't your target?" Kendrith mulled over his next words, knowing that it would either break Kristen or make the situation even worse. He said them anyway. "The same way Verron killed your uncle?"

The girl's attention snapped and all composure that clung to her like a maleficent shadow vanished—just a scared girl now stood before Kendrith. Her chin quivered as tears blurred and morphed her eyes, her hands trembling as the blade remained outstretched.

"You want to take my father's life?" Kendrith asked. "Or do you want to take back your own?" Kendrith stepped forward, grabbed the knife in his side, and pulled it out with a grunt. A woozy feeling fell over him. He stepped forward, the red spreading across his tunic like an infection. Blood dripped down his pants sides and coloured his heavy steps.

Kristen gasped. "You will bleed out!" she warned.

The boy felt lightheaded already. He stepped up to Kristen, and her eyes went wide, unsure of what to do. The boy ignored her comment.

He took her other free hand. "The choice is yours," he said, handing the scarlet blade to her.

She looked down at it with such horror, as if up till then she never understood what it meant to see blood, of what it meant to take a life.

Kendrith tightened her trembling fingers around the hilt of the blade, how lithe and gentle they seemed, made to create rather than destroy, yet callused and covered in little cuts. Kendrith could never imagine what life the girl had lived through, but smiled at the story each cut told. They couldn't have all been bad tallies, right?

Without a word, Kendrith lifted the bladed hand, his vision already becoming blurry. Bringing the dagger to his heart, he spoke, "Kill me," he instructed.

Kristen wept freely under the weight of the request. She reached out to touch Kendrith's wound, his chest, but never fully touched it, as if she was afraid all she would bring was death. Both her hands carried daggers and she looked up to him pleadingly, begging to make him stop.

"Stop it," she whispered, beseeching.

"Only you can make it stop," Kendrith said. His vision was failing.

Finally he collapsed, his hand's grip fading from Kristen's.

The distant sound of battle seemed so far away. He could smell the cinnamon, hear the hum of Haggen as he brewed a stew in the back with his mountainous, protective back. No, it wasn't Haggen. There she sat, Mona Brosnorth, Kendrith's mother, rocking back and forth with a babe in her hands and a blanket wrapped around them as she so lovingly, tenderly, stared into her son's eyes.

The last thing Kendrith noticed was Kristen bending over him, her tears falling to his face, running down his cheeks as if to cry for him when he could not. "Kendrith!" How distant it sounded when she called out his name.

Like the shadow of an echo, Kendrith's name continued to resound silently in his mind. The word long lost, the vibrations no longer clear, but the name lingered like the words of a page drained of ink.

Kendrith's eyes fluttered opened. It was night. It was so long ago since that day. The crackle of a campfire came from his right.

The mercenary turned his head, and the lancing pain came to him all at once. His entire body screamed at him—he could feel the torn muscle fibres, aching bones, and throbbing headache.

He tried to swallow, but his dried-out throat screamed at the task.

"Here." Kendrith turned to the voice. For a second, he thought the giant sitting there was Haggen, but it was only Logan.

Kendrith reached over, grimacing with the effort, the consequences of his desperate act came with a vengeance, the pain lingering and stagnant. He grabbed for the waterskin that Logan had offered. Need overcame pain, as Kendrith's body ignored the screaming agony of limbs and greedily took down the contents of the waterskin.

It was bliss, like drowning in a lake after wandering in the desert. A sweet and pleasurable agony unlike anything else.

Finally, Kendrith pulled the waterskin from his lips, and relished the trickling drops of water that ran down his chin.

He passed the waterskin back to Logan, falling back onto the bed made of leaves and twigs. Bandages covered him. He could still taste the bitter berry and licorice that stuck to his tongue—Logan must have given him a recovery potion.

"You were having a fevered dream, your temperature went down…which is good. You kept mentioning Kristen's name in your dream."

Kendrith nodded. "I dreamt of when we met, when she still was working with the bandits. She could have killed me back then, you know? But she never did. She chose a different life, one that Haggen and I offered her." Kendrith smiled at the memory.

"You really loved her since the beginning, huh?"

Kendrith nodded once more. "Since the beginning."

Silence before Kendrith continued, "She helped save me, and Haggen vouched for her. She helped bring in and capture the rest of her comrades, but Verron escaped."

Logan nodded. "I remember."

"How long have I been out?" Kendrith asked, changing the subject.

"Two nights," Logan said, stoking the flames.

Kendrith rested his hand to his forehead. "I messed up, didn't I?" A tear streaked down his cheek—the memory that he had relived in his dreams seemed so fresh. The tear shed back then by Kristen now traversing time to be shed by him.

"You did what you had to do," Logan said. "It was careless of you to lower your guard and get stung like that, but you found a way out of it…even if it was a gamble."

"Damn it all." Kendrith's tears flowed freely.

"There is no point in worrying about the past, boy. We need to focus on what we can do now. I tracked the boundaries, we aren't being followed. Kasim already left, probably went back to report to Magnus."

"Do you think the others are dead?"

Logan went quiet. "I doubt it. There is a reason they were treating Kristen. They wanted her to get better. Why they would attack me, I don't know."

"And George?"

Logan didn't reply.

"Get some sleep. We need you recovered so we can go to the settlement and get back Kristen and George."

And Simantiar, Kendrith thought silently. He wondered if Simantiar was able to save them, to take them out of the camp, but there was no way of knowing for sure. And then there was Gerard. Could he be trusted?

"Logan, how are we going to save the others? There is a practical army waiting for us, knowing we are coming. You struggled against Kasim alone. How could we hope to beat the others?"

"I don't know," said Logan.

Kendrith pondered. The memory of George flickered in his mind. The young boy, fifteen winters passed, his sun-kissed skin, his frizzled hair, his white teeth as he laughed, and his eyes creased, Simantiar cackling on his shoulder. How perfect that image seemed. And then there was Kristen, a dark hollowness filled Kendrith's mind like a cloud. Was she even alive still?

One truth that had been learnt from Simantiar and George was that thinking outside the box helped, that there were always more options in that crazed and scarred world.

"Maybe we don't have to fight the camp alone," Kendrith finally said.

"What do you mean?"

"I mean that there is another option."

The third day Kendrith spent resting, recuperating, and meditating. He took a recovery potion repeatedly to expel the toxins of the previous fight. His fever came and went. That following night, his dreams continued to be haunted. By the third morning, he was ready. Not completely, but prepared enough to continue.

He couldn't continue to take any elixirs—his heart burned on occasion—and even if he could, he had made sure to shatter them all upon that tree trunk when Betty stalked him. The memory made Kendrith shudder—she would surely haunt his dreams.

The path took them northwest. "Are you sure the beast is that way?"

Logan nodded. "If my calculation is right, the beast will be patrolling down that path this time of year."

Kendrith wondered. "If the beast has a patrol route, and it is known to stick to that patrol route, how is it possible that my mother failed to recognise it?"

Logan shrugged. "Perhaps she made an error."

Kendrith turned to the man, irritated at the assumption that his mother would make such a mistake.

Logan must have noticed it, for he corrected himself after. "Or perhaps the beast came again from another trail. It does sometimes happen that the monster's attention is directed elsewhere."

Kendrith nodded. "How likely is it that it is going to kill us?"

"Very."

Their pace remained steady, dictated by Logan. Even with his massive war hammer slung upon his back and splint armour covering his body, the two mercenaries were goaded on by a sense of urgency—they couldn't afford to waste any time.

Kendrith felt his heart beat against his chest, and Logan took large strides across sloped forest floors, grabbing on to a tree to heave himself up.

Sweat beaded his temple, a light pant as he shrugged his shoulders, trying to loosen the surely sore muscles.

"We should be close," Logan said.

"Great, I have always wanted to rush into my death," Kendrith retorted. The burn that spread through his torso would not fade. More than once Kendrith clutched at his chest, feeling the strain that fell upon his heart. Yet he couldn't afford any pause.

Logan's arm stretched out, and Kendrith froze on the spot, his instincts and sense standing at attention.

"It's here," Logan said. The man bent to a knee, his armour clanking at the movement. Kendrith then saw it. The broken branches, leaning trees that looked as if they were pushed to the side. A few paces out they identified the present paw prints that Logan could have curled up into.

"It's here," Logan repeated, his voice going to a softer whisper this time.

Kendrith scanned the perimeter, eyes on the lookout.

"What does it look like?" Kendrith asked.

"I already told you, a large beast with a man's face and the body of a lion."

"Any other features?"

"How should I know? I've never seen it before."

Kendrith's eyes went wide. "What do you mean you've never seen it? So, how do we know how to deal with it?" His retort was a loud incredulous whisper.

Logan scoffed. "With a little bit of luck. Just keep your eyes peeled for it."

A hundred thoughts raced through Kendrith's mind. He felt their chances plummet. Neither of them knew how to deal with the creature, and there was no precedent or any reliable source of information about the beast. It reminded Kendrith of the aberration, the tall mass of dark force that roamed the forest like a tainted stain upon the world. Back then, the advice was not to engage, for a hunter always need know what the course of action is, what things to take advantage of. Movement, size, blind spot, numbers, environment—the beast, on the other hand, was an enigma, and Kendrith found himself scared when all the options thinned themselves into a strand of obscurity.

Kendrith looked out in frightened focus, the anxiety instilled by the elixir making him scan every point of vision twice and then thrice, but nothing could be found. Still trees stood as silent watchers, Logan and Kendrith shuffled their feet and blew frantic breaths, a swaying branch was touched by the wind—Kendrith froze; there was no wind…

"Run!" The words escaped his lips before he had a chance to process the information.

Kendrith's feet carried him towards the camp, Logan's collar in his grasp as he pulled the large man with him, the force of the pull and the slanted drop down the slope pushed their legs to higher speeds.

Then it happened.

A burst of trees, the tremor of the ground as paws punched craters against the forest floor and charged towards Kendrith and Logan. A granular roar like the sound of stones being gurgled.

Kendrith dared a look upon the moving beast. Vines and moss and weed had grown all over its stone body, short stout legs moving a colossal structure with the grace of a siege engine as it mowed over trees that groaned and snapped helplessly.

The creature had a man's face chiseled to it, a mane of leaves, and forestry that hung from its neck. Depressed eye slits peered outwards and years of corrosive rain caused streaked lines to run down its cheeks and give the impression of indelible tears. It had a small squashed nose, thin and delicate lips parted to reveal the razor-filled trap in its maw. The beast had no neck, no rotational power as it charged forward, its head and face pressed into its squat and forest-pauldroned shoulders.

The guardian of the forest took the bait—Kendrith just hoped that they would last till the settlement.

Chapter 36

Darkness is eternal, darkness is nascent, darkness is the all-encompassing nothingness that provided isolated company with George. His mind went back to when he was just a child, tucked away under floorboards in a run-down, dilapidated building, the comforting embrace of Lily in his arms, the squeeze of gaunt arms, soft flesh pressing in to feel the embrace of bones.

The closest George had to that memory was a bucket full of his fluids. He had stopped smelling it a while ago.

It was a retreat, an escape from the present darkness to far-off memories so that he could escape his imprisonment, in mind if not in body.

George had no way of knowing how much time had passed, time had come to a stop as far as he was concerned. The darkness talked to him, spoke from the shadows, judging George for wanting company.

Death loomed over him, a cold breath of ever-present paranoia that leeched at George's suffering, his hope, his strength.

That was how his story would end, in darkness, a black page to fill the book he and his sister had shared countless times, a tale not worthy to be shared.

Footsteps, sounds, shadows, light—the outside world didn't forget him. The ferry of light brought with it a spark from the outside, a spark of life to take George out of the darkness.

George let go of the bucket, the feeling of flesh and bone fading like the illusion it was. George ran to the door. He held his tongue, gasps escaping him as the chance for freedom showed itself one more. How desperate he was at the thought of it, how pitiful he found himself to relish just a soft stroke of lantern light to bathe in as if it were the most novel of items.

George held on to the hope that it was Kendrith who had come to free him, Logan in tow, and Simantiar back in his humanoid vessel with no secrets to hide. He held an ear out for Pecky's reassuring chirp.

The hope was dashed from him, a cruel ploy of the darkness to give him false comfort. He could almost hear the cackle—George knew he was losing his mind.

The same man and woman who had visited him before came to open the door.

"Go tryin' somethin' funn' and I'll break your arms, understood?" said the man, a familiar key clinking in the man's hand—they sounded like the knell of absolution.

George nodded.

"Do you understand?" the man repeated. George realised the man couldn't see him.

"Ye-yes." How alien George's voice sounded to him, his response a stranger's croak. Was it the darkness that spoke to him before? Or his own words rebounding upon those walls. His throat was sore. Had he been screaming? He couldn't remember.

"Yes," George said more clearly, feeling defeated and willing to comply in exchange for freedom.

"That's a good boy," the man said.

"Stop being such an ass, Fratchet, and let's get the kid to the boss," the woman said.

"Why you always gotta ruin mah fu', Isi?"

"It's Isabelle, you illiterate. Now hurry up and let's go."

The man opened the door, tying George's hands in front of him. George looked down peculiarly. Were they untied? When did the man untie it? The world must have blurred and faded into itself while George was locked in there. There was once a dark side to George, a ferocious beast born out of his need to survive, but somewhere in that darkness George must have lost it, his other half finding a better home in the crevices of black. The two made some comment about the stench in the little stall, something about a bet they had regarding spoilt food—George didn't quite listen.

These are my hands, thought George as he looked down at the ropes which wrapped themselves about his wrists.

The man called Fratchet went down on one knee, his face marked with scars, a cruel snarl forming on his upper lip from a cut that never healed properly to reveal receding gums and uneven teeth. "You try anymo' o' tha' funny business, and we's gonna have a lo' o' trouble. Understood, boy'o?"

George nodded feebly; where did all that strength and confidence go?

"Good," said Fratchet, another slap across the head.

"Let's not keep the boss waiting," said Isabelle.

George found comfort within the lantern's light, a spark from the outside. George huddled close to Fratchet, the end of the rope in the man's arm.

George stared out onto the borders of darkness—he could hear it, the abyss wanting the boy back. He did not care for the threats of the man or whatever cruel efficiency lingered behind the predatorily gaunt woman. He just stared out towards the dark as if looking away for just a second would cause it to grab for him.

"I think he likes you." Isabelle chuckled.

"Th' fuck you wan'?" Fratchet shoved George away from him, the boy fell to his knees. "I look lik' your dada or somethin'?" George's hands fell beyond the border. A primal, livid fear awoke in him as he scuttled backwards on hands and feet into the safety of light.

"Move it." Fratchet tugged at the rope, pulling George to his feet.

It couldn't have been more than a few minutes, but in a place where time didn't exist it felt like an eternity.

Light peered in from the end of the tunnel. George trembled with the elusive promise of escape, and the gaping maw of darkness behind him seemed to groan in silence at the loss of its companion.

What George heard next pulled him from one hell to the next.

They reached a wooden scaffold, the sounds of industry all around him. The sight before the young bard filled him with nauseating dread as his eyes widened to the machinations unfolding before him, towards the workings of something foul and curious.

George leaned closer to the railing and looked down.

Assorted long rows of work tables were stacked next to each other, and blood splattered the hall like long brushstrokes of strangely coloured ichor.

Men carried the carcasses of beasts harvested from the forest, belts and tables filled with appendages and curious tools, vapid and dismembered husks of transmogrified monsters were left lifeless where they continued to bleed from wounds.

George watched as pliers ripped out teeth and creatures were bled dry of their blood in wooden vats. How cuts of lean muscle were sliced to reveal disfigured bones bent like waves underneath.

The clanks and rummaging of tools were occasionally overhauled by shouts and calls, asking for men to hurry up certain procedures or divert manpower to other tasks.

The place stunk—a nauseatingly sweet, yet metallic smell filled the humid air. Sweat, iron-tinged blood, and all manner of things came together to result in something truly repugnant.

There were wooden stairs leading down from the rafter which George looked down from, lines and lines of industrial workers rummaging through assortments of beast as if at a flea market.

George watched as one ripped off the stinger of one such beast, pressing out the venom and containing the alarmingly purple mixture into a vial.

"Move it, kid. Not som' sightseein' tour." Fratchet pulled on the rope, and George stumbled along the path, following down the wooden steps.

The noise of industry rattled in George's ears. Hammers nailed limbs to tables, and men grunted as they tried to ply fingernails or teeth, or skin flesh for whatever property the beast's leather would provide.

Another slap across George's head. He could feel his senses return. He remained rattled, feeling the exhaustion finally set in and a previously unknown hunger ravage his stomach. But he was glad that he was no longer in that hell.

They stepped out into the settlement.

The sun was blinding, birds chirped along canopies, and the world suddenly seemed in order once more. Men walk to and fro from their tasks, from building to building.

George wondered where the man was taking him. At first he thought it to the hospice—having been taken out of his own nightmare he hoped that Kristen had escaped hers or that she was still alive, at the very least.

The hospice came and went, and the only other building that George was being taken to was the one that Logan had entered with Kristen's unconscious body on the very first day.

There was chatter inside. The soft murmurs of those submissive to a leader, talking with quiescent fear, something that was seen as respect among the callous hunters of the settlement.

Fratchet knocked on the door. A moment of silence, and the murmurs stopped like whispers of a ghost that suddenly realised it was being listened to.

"Come in," said a voice. It was not a malicious one; it was not gruff or harsh. It was calm, like the voice of a magnate or businessman in the company of civilised men. For some reason, that terrified George all the more.

George looked up to the man and Isabelle, and he took notice of the bead of sweat which trailed Fratchet's temple, the trepidation and stiffened body of Isabella. Their throats seized up, now in the company of wolves.

The door squealed on its hinges, swinging open with a light shove.

At the end of the hall sat a man on a makeshift throne of polished wood and worn velvet cushions, and three hunters stood around the man. A rug fashioned from the dried body of a forest beast covered the floor. It seemed to be some form of bear with dirty white fur. Its taxidermic head was filled with three white pupils on each side of its snout, running down towards the nose. With large pointed ears, two pairs of front legs, and two pairs of hind ones, the beast must have been massive based on the size of the rug itself that took up the space of the room. Its head had its multirowed teeth bared for any who entered the room.

More trophies of antlered creatures and squash-nosed bats the size of reindeer mounted the walls.

The whole room's interior was tacky and ostentatious.

"Please, come in. You are a guest in my town—in my house," the man said with parodied poise as he sat on his throne.

The sudden change from eternal darkness to blazing daylight and now back to the shadows of the man's hut made George's eyes ache; he blinked several times. He couldn't make out the features of the man who hid within the shadows of his own tasteless throne.

"Leave us." The man waved a dismissive hand.

Fratchet unfastened George's hands, severing the binds with a dagger.

George's escort and the three residing hunters exited the hut.

"Fratchet, you can also bring me the other guest."

"Yes, boss."

"And Fratchet?"

Fratchet froze, standing to attention. "Yes?"

"The next time you take too long, I will take your tongue. Understood?" The words were spoken as a threat, but didn't sound like one. Magnus may have just as well said that he wished Fratchet a good day considering the casualness of his tone.

"Y-yes, boss," Fratchet stuttered, turning to leave the hut. The man closed the door.

George could hear Isabelle slapping Fratchet across the head. "I told you, idiot."

The room was stuffy and stank of tobacco which had worked its way into the wood. A single circular table with four wooden chairs were to the right of George, filled with a steaming whole chicken cooked a leathery brown. The odor made George's mouth water.

George blinked again, his eyes adjusting. He then noticed another figure standing behind Magnus, a statuesque form, unmoving.

Something was underneath Magnus's hand. George's eyes strained at the task, his vision spotted from the blaring sunlight outside.

His eyes widened.

Simantiar, his skull, rested underneath Magnus's hand, the man's fingers tapped against the enamel surface rhythmically.

George forced himself to calm down, if Simantiar was so still and unmoving, then Magnus still didn't know of Simantiar's identity.

Next he noticed the rattling cage and the familiar flapping wings. Pecky was trapped in a hanging white birdcage.

Magnus seemed to notice for his smile grew insidiously devilish. "I believe this little guy belongs to you."

Magnus tapped the cage as Pecky flew into the bars as if trying to escape a predator.

The door opened again behind George, and he turned.

Stumbling into the room, drained and weak but alive, was Kristen.

"Oh, thank Vrania. You're alive!" George went to embrace her. Fratchet closed the door behind them.

Kristen returned the embrace. "George! Are you okay? Did they hurt you?" Kristen returned the worry, and she pushed George away to arm's length to inspect him.

"I am fine."

"Yes, the boy had some fight in him, but I thought it was worth keeping him alive for our reunion."

George and Kristen turned to face Magnus, and her eyes widened at the sight.

"Do you know this man?" George turned to Kristen.

Her eyes were filled with horror, her lip quivered, and her hands trembled like a child frozen in fear.

"I am also quite delighted that you are okay," said the man with such a tender and affectionate tone that it made a shiver run down George's spine.

The man was handsome, with a cold calculating stare in one eye, and the other milky white and blind, but still seemed as if it looked into one's soul. A fringe of greasy black hair hung over his forehead. A chiselled and sharp-jawed look. And he would have truly been handsome if the other half of his face wasn't left in ruin by grafted skin and pink flesh that was burnt long ago by some form of tragedy or other. Thick wormlike scars slithered across his ruined half.

"Verron..." the words left Kristen's lips like a haunted memory that had expunged itself, a phantom given life once more.

"No, no." Magnus chuckled, wagging a finger, his handsome side forming an insidious grin. "I gave up that name long ago; call me Magnus."

Chapter 37

"Verron?" Kristen repeated the query.

"Well, I guess for you I would always be your uncle Verron."

How pernicious Magnus's words sounded to George, like a writhing snake taunting its prey with festered truths. Only the sound of Pecky's occasional frantic movements filled the unnerving quiet.

"You are not my uncle! You killed him!" Kristen accused, what grace and composure George usually witnessed in her was entirely replaced by undulating fervor.

Kristen pointed a stabbing finger at the man. "You took my life from me! Made me your tool!"

Kristen stepped forward. Magnus didn't move from the spot—his posture languid, half slipping down his seat, legs splayed forward. One hand was placed upon Simantiar's skull, fingers rapping in waves. His other hand supported the weight of his slanted head, the elbow propped on the wooden armrest.

The man in the shadows stepped forward. Darkness bled into the man's flesh—his skin was darker than a starless sky, as dark as the prison George had resided in. His posture was large, bulging muscles and a broad chest leaving little to the imagination with his dirty grey-brown tunic, the upper buttons left loose to reveal the tale of scars which marked his chest, more of them evident on his bald head. Thick lips, sharp and unforgiving eyes; the man was even taller than Logan.

Kristen froze in place. Magnus's smile widened. "Prime specimen, isn't he? After you betrayed me and had most of my men killed, I travelled around to rebuild. Travelled to the east. Some land called Cronata. Poor wretched lot. But what potential there is in their squalid communities!" Magnus clapped his hands, leaning forward with elbows on his knees as if to share some audacious gossip.

"Picked him up when he was but a wee kid. Changed my approach a bit with him. Also changed my business." Magnus leaned back, arms outstretched as if to suggest the settlement and operations that were ongoing were akin to an empire of his own making.

"You mean the men who are harvesting monster parts in that cave of yours?" George asked.

Kristen's eyes darted to him, eyes questioning what he meant.

"Exactly, boy! Assassination is so yesterday, don't you think?" He seemed satisfied with George's remark, nodding agreeably. "All that wandering and work hazard and lodging. I am too old for any of that. Now I am in the business of dealing arms; plus, the pay is much better." The fleshy mass of burnt-and-pink flesh seemed to writhe in his own self-satisfaction.

"How could you follow this man? He sees you as nothing but a weapon," Kristen said to the dark-skinned man. The bulging mass of muscles that was staring out into the distance now turned his gaze slowly, dark eyes with the lightest of red hues meeting Kristen's. There was nothing in there, no life, no will of his own—just nothingness filled with the pernicious wants and dreams of an ambitiously insane man.

"You see, my little one, I changed my approach. Joma over here"— Magnus pointed up at the empty vessel of a man—"had nothing before me. He was a starving young boy on the streets of a rotten, dying town. I offered him a way out, a life outside of an arid wasteland where the rising sun would do nothing but glare down at them and watch them die in its heat. Strip them of rain and turn barely fertile land into dry clay.

"I gave him food, water, girls—I gave him more than he could ever ask for and he needed only to give me his will in return."

George put together the pieces of the story, the man who Kristen had served so long ago was the man who sat upon his throne and caressed Simantiar's unmoving skull. Kristen rebelled because somewhere in her heart, she knew there was a better life away from the smothering perversion of what Magnus saw as love. But the towering empty vessel before George had never witnessed any such thing, the man who had never seen water before was convinced that a drop was the same as the ocean.

Magnus did seem to care for Joma, but not with unconditional love. He cared for him the same way a businessman cared for his assets.

"Let me show you...come." Magnus motioned them closer, a wide friendly smile on his face as if he was about to show a magic trick.

Kristen and George hesitated. There was not a hint of menace in Magnus's voice, but rather affable curiosity.

Magnus drew a dagger from Joma's belt, and Kristen and George were compelled to come closer.

The tall man with his thick fingers faced his palm upwards in front of him. It sickened George when he realised that Magnus had done this many times before for others, to the point that Joma already knew the motions, the scars which marked his palms tallies of the performances.

The dagger drew a deep red line into the palm of the giant's hand—he didn't even flinch, his face unmoving in all that transpired.

"Ta-da!" Magnus's grin was almost cherubic, like that of a young and innocent child filled with wonder. The blood trickled from Joma's hand.

Kristen and George stared unmoving, terror filling George. Magnus's smile faded; he seemed almost hurt as he cleaned the blood off on Joma's tunic and turned the dagger into its leather holder. "Tough crowd," he said, leaning back onto his throne.

"Are you going to kill us?" Kristen finally said.

A moment of silence. "Eventually," Magnus replied. There was no surprise in the casualness of the words. George gulped—he already knew the truth himself.

"Why haven't you done so yet?" George asked, Kristen glared at him with eyes warning to let her do the talking.

"Well, Gerard was supposed to kill you. But he failed. Quite stubborn that man. Eventually the promise of getting rid of his debt made him see reason." Magnus sighed. "So, when Gary, our 'healer'"—Magnus made air quotes when he said the word, his face making a bit of an apologetic grimace at the term. The man leaned forward, the back of his hand hiding his moving lips for no one. "Between you and me, he isn't very good at his job," he whispered loudly.

"Anywho, when Gary knocked you unconscious, I realised you weren't some ordinary boy. And the fact that you employed Logan to take you this far out started becoming curious. Not to mention, I didn't think you were coming this far out into the woods anyway, Kristen. Something seems different about this venture."

"I was promoted," Kristen blurted out.

"Please, Kristen, we both know you were never as good a liar as you were a killer. Now, I do wonder..." Magnus reached to his side and pulled out George's lute. "Why would a bard hire a highly wanted member of Vrania's guild to travel the most dangerous and volatile place in all of Lenaren?"

George and Kristen remained quiet.

"See, I think that there is something of great value out there. Something that could be worth a lot to the right buyer, or perhaps something that I would take as an..." he paused thinking of his next word, "asset," he said.

"Plus, Kendrith and Logan seemed to have escaped my little ambush, so I need to keep you here till they arrive to save you. So, after you tell me about where you were heading, I will lure in your little boyfriend and Logan and kill them both, and then you." Magnus pointed at George. "I hope you understand, it's just business."

Kristen stepped forward, Joma tensed. Kristen stepped back again. Her words came from trembling lips. "You know about Kendrith? You were spying on me?"

Magnus smiled knowingly at the question. "In great detail, though my assassination attempts were less successful, I decided to cut my losses and all that. But you know what they say—good things come to all those who wait."

He spat on the floor. "Well, I guess fate is a funny thing. What irony that you came to love Kendrith." Magnus spoke with a suspicious familiarity.

"What do you mean?" Kristen asked.

"I guess this was after you betrayed us, so you wouldn't know. Kendrith's full name is Kendrith Feller, correct? Son of Jaylen Feller, your last and least successful mission. But also the son of Mona Brosnorth, daughter of Haggen Brosnorth."

George dreaded the next words.

"Who do you think had Mona killed? Who do you think fed her to the beast?" Out of all the terrors that George had witnessed, from the husks to the three men that hunted him in the forest and the beasts strewn on work benches, Magnus was the most terrifying. To George, he looked like a monster with human skin pulled over rotten bones—he was evil walking among men.

"But, when?"

"Before we ever met of course, when your love was still just such a young sprite with such wonder in his eyes. Mona and her expedition team came across our camp." Magnus shrugged. "When she found that our vocation was of a rather…lacking quality, she threatened to take us captive and hand us over to the judicial system." Magnus shook his head in disapproval as he reached over to a fruit basket and took a casual bite from a nectarine, the juices splurting and dripping down his tunic sleeve and dark-haired forearms, dribbling down the end up his marred chin.

"There is no way someone like you could have bested Mona," Kristen retorted.

Magnus gave a mirthful laugh from wet lips, seemingly amused. "How would you know? You never even met the woman."

Kristen didn't respond, her stare simply that of flame.

Magnus eventually gave an agreeing nod and returned the nectarine to its basket, half-eaten.

"You're right. There is no way we could," he admitted. "But we played dirty—poisoned her and her men, and left them paralysed along the stone lion's route."

Kristen's eyes widened as she began to tremble. "There is no way."

Magnus shrugged. "I didn't expect there to be loose ends when the patrol came looking for their remains, but it was convenient that it was all pinned on the lion."

"How could you?!" Kristen made to get up, only reconsidering the notion when Joma stepped forward like a looming shadow.

Magnus guffawed, barely able to contain his wits at the ostensible joke.

"Kristen, please. You have killed so many people when you worked under me, and you were good at it too. We have travelled to distant lands and covered many contracts in that time. It never was an issue before." Magnus's smile widened. "I can see with what murderous intent your eyes trail me, tell me something, Kristen: if you were the one who was there with me and I asked you to kill her, would you have hesitated?"

Kristen went incredibly still and speechless.

A soft chuckle from the languid Magnus as his upper lip swelled from the tongue which cleaned the hanging bits of nectarine between his teeth. "I didn't think so," he declared.

Sheer silence, as Kristen's fingers clenched into fists until her skin turned bone white.

"So, you will keep me alive, till you no longer need me?" she queried, a rage simmering beneath her words.

"That is correct," replied Magnus.

"So, you had your healer save my life and remove the venom, just to kill me?"

"I thought it appropriate that we meet again and have a little chat, catch up for old times' sake, before I rip your heart out and serve it at my dinner table for betraying me."

"So, you're saying I am healed?" Kristen looked up, no more trepidation, no more terror, no more doubt or shock in her gaze, just determination.

"Simantiar, now!" Blue light appeared like wisps trailing around Simantiar's motionless skull, the empty darkness of his sockets now giving off a light glimmer, like the explosive birth of a star far off in the sky, a blue shine twinkling into existence, before brightening into the aura of life that George knew to be his friend.

It was a gamble, but George hoped Simantiar had been saving his magic, concentrating on a spell and preparing it for when he was ready—now was that time.

Now was the time for them to escape.

The bear rug lifted off the floor, rising as if a gust of air snuck itself underneath and raised it, the fringes fluttered—the rug jumped up and flew to where Simantiar remained hiding him from sight as Magnus and Joma covered their eyes.

The rug flew like a standard torn into the grips of the wind, flying up, then returning to George and Kristen. As the rug descended, it filled itself to the same thickness it must have carried in life as empty limbs brimmed with magic, its body widening, claws striking out as Simantiar mounted himself inside the jaws of the dead beast and used its form as his mould.

"Yeah, baby! Weren't expecting that, were you?" The jaws of the fiendish bear closed on Simantiar's skull, the three pairs of eyes that ran down each side of the bear's snout shone red instead of their usual white.

The mounted head of an antlered beast rattled from an unseen force as the antlers tore off and mounted themselves onto Simantiar's form.

"I'm a bear! What you gonna do now?" The two pairs of arms rose by Simantiar's side and the snout opened. Simantiar was no longer seen and the roar that bellowed from his magical lungs was anything but human—a mix of a shrill eagle's cry and a bear's low growl.

Joma charged forward, a hefty scimitar unsheathed—the man moved faster than one would expect from his size. His blade was a blur as it cut into Simantiar, each cut however slid right through with no resistance as the white fur sewed itself back together as a swipe from two mighty paws sent Joma flying back.

Magnus was next. He used the distraction, the one time that one's eyes diverted to the exchange of two brutes, to close the distance, the sword struck out, piercing in one fell move as if done by a piercing arrow into the head of the beast.

"The skull is the sweet spot, isn't it?" Magnus asked, a frightening and sharp intellect in his eyes.

"That's right," Simantiar said.

Magnus looked down, seeing a gaping hole from Joma's previous onslaught where Simantiar peeked through. "But knowing that isn't much help, is it?" A spark shuddered from Simantiar's socket as if blinking mockingly to Magnus before the tear closed itself back up.

Magnus's didn't like being mocked—the sudden scowl he showed was evidence of that—and his usually handsome side now showed a terrifying grimace to match the rotten core he had within.

Cuts upon cuts shredded into the bear's body, trying to find Simantiar.

Simantiar did not resist, yawning as the man continued, all four bear arms on his hips, his two right hind legs tapping on the floor impatiently.

"Will this take long?" Simantiar's bear voice was like a deep echo from a cave.

Magnus turned red, his slashing blade a blur as he bellowed a roar.

Joma stood up, charging forward, his blade strewn aside as he tried to reach for Kristen and George to little avail, being catapulted back with a hefty swipe of Simantiar's paw which left large red gashes.

Joma didn't relent, seemingly unfazed by the display he tried anew, charging straight for Simantiar.

George's and Kristen's eyes widened at the display of pure might shown by that man.

The bear form skidded across the floor. It took all four hind legs of the body to dig its claws into the wooden floorboards to come to a halt.

Simantiar wrapped his arms around Joma, and let out a hungry bear roar as Joma's mighty body was flung into the ceiling, the wooden rafters snapping where his body hit. The man collapsed back to the floor, grunting.

"Let's get this over with." Simantiar raised his mighty bear paws, ready to stomp onto Magnus.

"Are you sure about that?" The man smiled.

George didn't understand why. "Simantiar! Something's wrong."

A brush of air, a breeze like a whisper's cold kiss tickled George's nape.

The boy clapped at the spot, and feeling the chill, he turned around to see a third man. He recognised him as one of the individuals that had travelled with Logan out into the forest. Dark-skinned, a tanned cloak draped around him, sharp hollow-cheeked features and eagle eyes. A scimitar was held to Kristen's throat.

"Drop your..." the man seemed to consider the right words, his accent thick and eastern, "weapon." He settled for the only word that could describe what Simantiar donned.

Simantiar turned around, his giant bear shoulders sagged all the more pronounced.

"Just please, don't hurt them." The bear jaws opened to reveal Simantiar.

"I won't have to as long as you comply." The blade pressed against Kristen's throat, but she raised her chin higher and backed into the man, as blood trickled.

The rug fell to the floor as if filled with nothing but air. Joma stepped forward, but Magnus raised his blade to bar his path. Joma halted, Magnus stepped forward to the unmoving pile of bear fur, prodding it with his sword. Nothing.

The tip of the sword lifted the rug, revealing Simantiar there as just a skull.

"Well, well, well. You guys are full of surprises," said Magnus, pleased at what he had found.

Logan and Kendrith ran for their lives, and the beast of the forest rammed through trees, cutting across overgrown paths where its paws of stone and moss hadn't trod since long ago. That was how it was; it would patrol across the borders to the path beyond, finding those that were either too ignorant, foolish or brave to wander into its path—perhaps all three.

Kendrith wasn't sure which of the three he and Logan were.

The path down was steep, and they allowed gravity to help their descent.

Kendrith slipped, his heart jumped to his throat, and he dared not look behind.

Instead, he willingly fell into the roll, using the steep slope to roll down, dragging dry leaves and forestry that clung to him. The forest was a blur to

Kendrith and so was the beast. A sudden white marble flash of weathered stone—he couldn't tell if the creature was close or far, but the looming sound of its huge body and the gravel roar it let loose made it feel as if the beast was close enough to take a bite out of him.

A tree braced Kendrith's descent as his back knocked into it. Kendrith coughed, the air leaving his lungs.

There the beast was, a path of destruction left in its wake as the trees were ploughed through, snapping in half or ripped clean from their roots.

The sad carved face of a mourning man leapt for the final bite.

Kendrith couldn't move in time.

The beast's path shifted midflight, the head turned direction, and the body followed suit. Its mane of vines and greenery swayed with the move. Kendrith barely survived, seeing Logan pant, the muscles of his arms filled with blood and tensed to their limit, his golden war hammer raised.

"Move!" Logan ordered.

Kendrith didn't need to be told twice.

He stumbled to his feet, dry leaves playing with his footing.

A roar from behind, a snapping tree trunk—the chase resumed.

"We are almost there!" Logan called out, as Kendrith and Logan continued to pull the beast free from its path, baiting it, leading a force of twisted and unknown magic into the heart of a settlement made up of cutthroat hunters.

Chapter 38

Ever since the journey from Haven, Simantiar had remained hidden within George's bag; how the events of the world change when all one sees is darkness.

Simantiar found himself sometimes drifting between reality and the world past. Simantiar didn't dream, didn't live—he was but a skull, and the skull nothing more than a vessel that anchored his spirit in the world of the living. But there was a thread, a faint blue one given light in utter darkness as it traversed hundreds of years to bind him to the man he once was.

His consciousness, his very being, wavered between the past and the present, that expansive bridge nothing more than a blue thread to balance on as he walked across his abyssal chasm. One slip-up, one wrong move, and he would fall into the void, the darkness, with nobody there to hear his cries. He would forget who he was, linger forever on that line between the present and the world that felt too real the longer he revisited it.

Torn from that thread, his forced trance broken, Simantiar found himself wrenched into conflict.

Being unable to intervene as Gerard and George stared off. The betrayal, the sudden stab of an injection forced into George's throat. Simantiar could only watch as George shook his head, instructing Simantiar against taking any action. Kristen was still fever struck in bed, conscious as she reached out feebly. Simantiar's own being went numb with the advice. And so Simantiar returned to the tightrope, balancing, waiting for a chance to strike.

He watched as George's limp body was taken away, he watched as Magnus collected Simantiar like a trophy, petted his naked enamel cranium as if it were a submissive and coy pet tamed by fear and starved of its master's love.

Yet still Simantiar waited, waited, the thread holding the spirit, stuck in a limbo of his own making.

Kristen appeared, George appeared—the time was right, they would escape, emerge victorious, somehow, like all the times before, find Logan and Kendrith and all would be okay. Even Pecky would return.

It didn't end that way.

Kristen and George were taken hostage, Magnus with malicious greed in his eyes, and now Kasim carrying Simantiar away to the cavern where his magic would be inspected. Simantiar had no choice—he could do nothing other than comply as his friends were held as an insurance policy.

Another opportunity, another chance, and Simantiar would seize it. Logan and Kendrith were on their way back, Simantiar was sure, and he needed to help them when the time came.

How he cursed his limited power, only capable of forming bodies as static spells which held form over time and used up less magic than conjured spells. The world was starved of its ether, and were he in his prime, all would be as he wished with just a wave and no incantation.

Simantiar eyed the many rows of workers bustling away in their workshops, the pile of butchered and drained bodies stacked on top of each other, listless eyes staring out, their souls now churning in the machine called war.

Simantiar was carried to a door at the side of the many workshops. It opened to show an enclosed workshop.

"Bayra, you've got a new toy to play with," said Kasim.

The room was filled with halves of papers and journals scribbled with the abstract and curious anatomy of the jungle beasts and unintelligible scribbles. The rest of the room was filled with discarded limbs and curious organs or digits, tools strewn about without any noticeable organisation.

Once the chaos of the room filled the workstations located in the centre and against the sides to the brim, it continued to scale the walls. Shelves were filled with jars containing removed organs that floated inside. One eye seemed to float aimlessly till it turned to stare at Kasim who entered the room. A dagger stabbed into the splintered wood of the table was mounted by the head of a purple-skinned beast with three rows of crooked yellow teeth and a barbed tongue which unrolled itself to the floor.

The room itself stank; Simantiar obviously had no nose to smell with, but also had no eyes to see with, yet still he held on to these senses by some magical feat and recoiled at the stench that filled him. The workroom had no ventilation or way of processing air, so the scent of exposed mutated organs, spread ichor, months of sweat, and other things Simantiar couldn't quite place assaulted him. There was an oily and lingering scent that had been allowed to fester—it wasn't quite fish, but perhaps it was athlete's foot or some other foul fungal spore that took residence there.

It was perhaps the one and only time that Simantiar cursed the fact that his senses worked.

"Put it to the side," the man called Bayra said with his wide sweat-stained back obscuring his work. He seemed to have some surgical tools as he cut into the cadaver of some beast spread on his work table. There was an audible crunch of breaking bone. Hooks and pliers and scalpels worked their way into the body of the beast as a burst of indigo ichor spurted out. Bayra dodged out of the way, the contents colliding against the dagger-mounted head and eating away at the smoking ruin of bubbling flesh until the tongue came loose and coiled itself on the floor.

"The boss wants you to inspect it now," Kasim said.

Bayra stopped working and put the tools aside with notable irritation. Sweat stained his armpits and back, what was supposedly once a white woollen shirt was now grey and discoloured. He lifted the layered magnifying goggles with stacked lenses that suddenly made his eyes look diminutively tiny in respect to his full cheeks and wide nose.

The man turned around, a groomed and otherwise courted moustache with an accompanying goatee covered his lips and chin, the moustache ends curled upwards with fine attention and the overalls suggested him a man of culture if it weren't for his brutish appearance.

Kasim tossed Simantiar over, and the man caught the skull.

"What is it?"

"A magical skull."

Bayra flipped Simantiar over and donned his goggles again. He peered inside, then shook him up and down as if expecting something to happen.

"Looks like an ordinary skull to me," Bayra said.

"It can talk."

"No shit?" Bayra shook Simantiar again, nothing.

"That's not all. We believe it cast magic."

Bayra's eyes widened like a child receiving their first gift. "Is there like a button I need to press?" Bayra asked, one eye closed as he closely inspected every inch of Simantiar.

"Talk or I will send you the jaw of one of your friends to talk for you," Kasim threatened, his voice calm and undulating.

"Oh, I am sorry…was lost in thought. Mostly just about how massive your nose is. Not like I was ignoring you or anything."

"By the gods," said Bayra. "It can talk!"

"I can do more than just talk, you sweaty excuse for a furball," countered Simantiar.

"Indeed he can," Kasim agreed. "The boss wants you to find out how he works. He can talk, and he will comply, so try to get as much information from him as you can." Kasim reached into a pocket within his drab cloak and tossed a few of Simantiar's bones onto the work table.

"These are some more plain bones. See if you can get anything from that as well."

Bayra nodded.

"Oh, and Bayra." Kasim tossed a third item to Bayra. "Wear it."

Bayra caught it, opening his fist to reveal a scintillating blue gem that seemed almost turquoise.

Bayra opened the buttons to his shirt, placing the gem next to his heart. The thing ate away at the skin, parting it like some magnetic force pushing a small dented nest, and Bayra groaned at the sensation. The gem brightened, light filling its core as it leeched upon Bayra's energy. Smoke sizzled and the scent of burnt flesh added to the noisome suffocating odor that violated Simantiar's nonexistent nostrils as the gem nestled itself a cosy home and soft signs of damaged skin circled it.

"That gem is called a life gem. It is connected with a counterpart. If one carrier of the gem dies, the other fades in light. So remember that. If we find that its counterpart is for some reason not shining anymore, then your friends won't be either."

Kasim then proceeded to call over two idle men. "Watch Bayra, if anything happens, you run to me."

The two men nodded before stepping inside Bayra's workshop.

"What do you want me to do with it?" Bayra asked.

"What you do best: experiment." Kasim closed the door behind him, the relentless sound of industry barely muffled by the door.

"You two, stand outside," Bayra ordered.

"But Kasim said—"

"I don't care what he said, stand outside the door, if anything happens, you can hear it. But until then, this is my sanctum, my domain. And I cannot unravel the secrets of these marvellous beings with the two of you oafs, especially when you have as much grace and dexterity as an intoxicated boar. Now take those log-fingered hands only good for destroying out of here and let me get to my artistry." The two men seemed to glower at Bayra, but finally complied, leaving the room and closing the door behind them. The frustration that radiated from Bayra seemed oddly placed, considering how his own composition seemed to hardly differ from the other men.

Bayra and Simantiar exchanged an awkward glance. Bayra scratched at his stubbled cheek.

"Sorry you had to see me like that," Bayra apologised.

"Don't worry about it."

"Never met a talking skull before. Are there many of you?"

Simantiar considered the exchange, not sure of how to respond either. It seemed even Bayra wasn't used to such a situation, perhaps more comfortable locked behind a door with his toys rather than skilled at conversation. Simantiar didn't blame him. He would also lock himself inside if he looked the way Bayra did.

"Not that I know of. Doubt you'll ever meet another one like me."

"Right, right," Bayra commented, looking down and away from Simantiar's socketless stare and instead looking to his shoes.

More silence.

"Listen…Bayra, was it? Right, I doubt there is any chance that you'd let me be on my way? My friends must be worried sick."

Bayra rubbed the nape of his neck. "Sorry, no can do, the boss will have me hung by the balls."

"Oh, come on—" Simantiar began, but was cut off by Bayra.

"That's not a figure of speech, Magnus *literally* had another man hung by the balls for trying to swindle him out of some money. You don't lead a pack of cutthroat men and turn them into an organised work force without standing above the rest. That's the glue that holds everyone together and loyal: fear."

Simantiar would have gulped if he could.

"Plus, I really am quite curious about how you work." Bayra did another round of flipping and turning as if the instructions were written somewhere else.

"I don't suppose you could tell me a bit about yourself? The process would be so much easier."

"I don't know enough about myself to tell you anything. And I hope you understand, what I do know probably isn't worth telling you since it puts my friends in danger."

Bayra nodded understandingly, as if he didn't fault Simantiar for his refusal. "That's quite all right. It would have obviously expedited the process, but to be honest, I quite prefer to earn my results." Bayra had a quite unsettling smile.

Simantiar remained on the table as Bayra turned around to rummage through old tools.

"Where is it?"

"Maybe I can help?" Simantiar said.

"No, no. It's fine. There is just this gem that detects magic. I can't seem to find it. Where did I put my ether gem?"

Finally Bayra gave up with a defeated sigh and came with something that was entirely not a gem. He held some form of rod—the wood was polished and dark. Some form of bendy appendage was stuck into a small hole at the tip of the rod. Dangling at the very end of the appendage, to give the impression of a fishing rod, was a fine barely noticeable thread as thin as spider silk ending in a slight blue teardrop.

Bayra carried the miniature fishing rod and dangled the bead over Simantiar.

"This will have to do."

Simantiar could have sworn that for a moment, the bead sparkled with a slight glow, but it could have also just been his imagination as the light faded completely.

Bayra held the teardrop over Simantiar's head. Nothing happened. Frustration glossed over him.

"Come on," he commanded, waving the rod as the thread waved around in the air fruitlessly.

"Everything okay?" Simantiar asked.

"Everything is fine." Irritation showed in Bayra's words as his cheeks flushed bright red from frustration.

Bayra went back, more clattering sounds. Simantiar found himself perplexed by the situation as the odd man returned with a second identical rod, but again nothing.

"If you are trying to go fishing, might I suggest seeking professional help? Maybe take a break and go and see the sun?"

"The appendage you see at the end belongs to a blindskitter. They are many-legged centipede-like creatures that use feelers atop their heads to track trace amounts of magic and suck them from the roots of tree trunks. The rods should still be able to detect magic."

Simantiar wondered if the tears fizzled out from the magic that he gave off?

Bayra waved his hand towards another wayward object in the room and scowled as he noticed they weren't working.

"Useless, all of it." He tossed away the rod which clattered to the floor and murmured something under his breath.

"Right, so maybe I am just an ordinary talking skull…not a magical one. Boy, I am sure your boss must be pretty disappointed at that."

Bayra gave Simantiar a look of annoyance before returning to his toolbox.

"Where was the ether stone?"

Simantiar's hands were tied. There was nothing stopping him from casting a slow incantation and killing the man, but the moment the gem upon his chest died, so too would Kristen and George. He thought about removing the gem, but surmised that would have the same result as killing Bayra. Perhaps an incantation to freeze him still and make him unmoving? Simantiar prepared the incantation silently, having it ready for when it was needed.

Bayra gave out a long and drained sigh.

"Well, looks like I'd have to do this the old-fashioned way." A long hatchet revealed itself in his grasp, and Bayra turned around with a steel-hardened expression that broke off Simantiar's concentration.

"Hey, hey, hey. We were just getting to know each other."

No response, the lingering gleam of light shining off the edge of the blade made Simantiar fumble to return to his incantation.

"I could just tell you what you need to know—just ask me anything. No reason to cut through hollow bones."

"I prefer taking them for myself." The hatchet lifted itself into the air, waiting to fall like an executioner's blade.

Simantiar's instincts kicked in. The chant of his whispers summoned discarded fingers, six in total from an assortment of bodies, anchoring themselves to the base, the six fingers flinching out of reflex, Simantiar slid to the side, the hatchet splintering wood rather than bone as it cut into the table.

"Come here, you little—" Bayra pulled, but the blade didn't release, with puffed cheeks, wild eyes, and a shoe to the table, the blade finally freed itself with Bayra's help as the pursuit commenced. Simantiar crawled over discarded limbs, rusted pliers and chisels, blades and spilt black oil— or perhaps it was blood.

"We can talk about this!" Simantiar protested, the fingers worked nimbly as if they were a shadow of his own. They carried Simantiar like scuttling feet working in unison to create waves of undulating movement.

"I will cut you!" Bayra called out.

Glass shattered, contraptions clattered to the floor, and the room was pulled into the turbulent chaos as Bayra's hatchet blade swung and aimed for Simantiar. A finger was cut off, the last trickle of dried blood oozing out as another dismembered appendage flew across the floor and took the finger's place. This one was the exoskeletal limb of some insectoid.

The door to the workshop flung open as the two guardsmen entered. "What is going on?" one of them asked as they beheld the chaos of the chase, Simantiar leaping from one pile of discarded junk to the next.

Bayra threw the hatchet, but a small gust of reflexive wind shoved Simantiar away from the blade's path, the limbs all claimed by the blade's edge.

Thump. Simantiar stared out in disbelief, clattering to the table. Bayra's own stare of fuelled rage subsided as he realised what just happened.

The hatchet found purchase, and dug into the forehead of one of the men, his eyes glazed over, blood trickling. The man collapsed back to the floor.

Silence, but for the sound of industry.

Stunned and shocked silence. "He did it." Simantiar looked up to Bayra.

Before the other two could say a word, the earth trembled. Frantic shouts came from outside, and in the sudden tremble of shifted currents, something happened.

Another man rushed to the door, his eyes looked down to the fallen man, blood pooling around him. Then to the others. "What are you waiting for? Come on!"

"What's happening?" asked the second guardsman.

"The beast of the forest! It's here." The man turned to flee, his duty done by warning the others.

Bayra's face turned pale as he turned around, packing his things.

"Come on, let's go!" said the guardsman.

"Not yet, my research, I need my research." Folded and pieces of stained paper are crumpled into a bag. The guard hesitated, before cutting his ties and running outside.

Bang, clank, swinge, fush. More and more parts came together in marriage; limbs twisting, contraptions joining, wood splintering.

Bayra turned around to witness the horror that Simantiar now embodied.

"My turn," said the mounted skull, his new form a mesh of organs, guts squeezed together, steel-spiked shoulder on one side and the barbed whip attached to his other like a tentacle arm with hooked thorns to pierce and shred; a leg of metal coiled and dented with the strength of rope to make it a more responsive appendage, the other leg made of bone and sinew from the poor purple-skinned creature splayed on the surgery table.

His final hand soared to him from the remains of a glass jar that shattered from the inside, the liquid inside causing the ink from the papers to run. The final arm was gaunt, slender, and long, scales ran across its skin as Simantiar could feel the ever-moving bone structure inside. He twisted it, manipulated it, and a blade suddenly grew out of the palm of Simantiar's hand made of reinforced bone.

The fear that was present on Bayra's blanched face tasted like vindication to Simantiar.

Chapter 39

Magnus and Joma exited the room while George and Kristen were left on their knees. The cries of terror filled the world outside, a sound which followed the rumbling as if a low growl came from deep within the earth.

"What is going on?" asked George, the sound of wood splintering and the trudging of large feet colliding with the ground sent soft vibrations through the boy.

A sudden roar like deep earth exploded from outside.

Kristen rose to her feet, her hands bound, but lifting herself to look through the window at whatever horror was taking place outside.

"By the wings of Vrania," she said, sharing the sudden surge of terror that filled all those outside.

"What is it?" George asked again.

"The beast of the forest—it's here."

George's own eyes widened and a sudden curiosity overwhelmed him as he too worked his way to stand and glance out towards the ensuing destruction and cacophony of terror.

The beast was large.

Its body like that of grey stone, vines and moss and weeds clung to its body, its lion's mane made of foliage and brambles, its deep-set face that of a squished and sad man, its eyes regretful as it tossed men up into the air, legs kicking helplessly at empty air, before disappearing into the gullet of the monstrous body of stone.

"We have to get out of here—this is our chance!" Kristen said.

Among the many items strewn all over the musty and nauseating abode, weapons were the most abundant with tasteless abandon.

Kristen scanned the place, the house suddenly felt like a child's blanket to protect them from the wrath of the beast without.

In a corner of the room, Kristen found her belongings as well as her weapons. She fastened them to her belt and body, strapping on the throwing knives.

She looked around, seemingly searching for something while George unlocked Pecky's cage and the bird flew out the window.

"What is it?" George asked.

"That's not all my knives."

Kristen then turned to a nailed image of a wanted poster from long ago depicting Magnus' likeness, several of her daggers were nailed onto it.

With a grunt, she ripped the knives off and pocketed them in their sleeves, the final knife she pried free, glanced at the image, and slashed down the middle, before pocketing the blade. A rancid spit worked into her throat before ejecting onto the image for good measure.

George looked disgusted.

Kristen shrugged. "I've got some things to work out." She smiled at George before the two grabbed the rest of their belongings and fled.

George was relieved to find the rest of his stuff haphazardly left in his burlap sack including his lute case in the corner of the room, though his golden coins were missing and his heart dropped.

A few more turns and he found a chest with a padlock that hindered him.

"Kristen!" he called.

She hesitated, but was swift and picked the lock in under a minute to reveal the stacked silver and gold talents inside.

George took what was his and whatever else he could comfortably hold.

"Why are you so rich again?" Kristen asked.

"Loads of adventures in tombs unearthed a few treasures up for grabs." Pocketing the coins in his purse they absconded as quickly as they could.

The hut proved a poor veil to protect them from the horror that took place outside, but the sudden rush of terror and pandemonium painted on the faces of the men and women swept them into the hysteria.

"Let's move!" Kristen told George.

"We need to get Simantiar!"

"Where is he?"

George pointed towards the cavernous maw from where men spewed out, curious machinations and contraptions carried in their hands.

"What is in there?" Kristen asked.

"Weapons."

George looked back to the ensuing chaos, already several men and structures lay in ruin.

Men with harpoons notched into crossbows fired at the beast, while others threw rope over the creature's head for others to catch. It clawed and stepped and roared at them, leaving behind splatters of viscera and gore.

The harpoons pierced the beast's stony skin, wrapped itself into the coils of its vines, and flew over its body for others to nail the pitons and weigh the beast down.

It roared its stony roar, flinging screaming bodies away with a heave of its stout and bulky limbs.

George caught a glimpse of Magnus shouting orders. Joma's muscles strained, his face in a grimace as he tried to hold down the weight of the beast with his bulging biceps as his heels ploughed the floor.

Magnus stopped calling orders, his head turning to George and Kristen as he dropped his waving hand and turned his entire attention to the two.

"We have to go," Kristen urged, all bravado from when she slashed his sketching gone.

Another gravelly roar as the beast charged forward and pulled several men off the ground. They screamed as they were flung into the air.

"Kristen!" George pulled her to the side, as the beast trampled over Magnus's hut while men were flung around like lice shaken off a mutt.

Magnus ordered something over the shouting and agonized screams of the injured, pointing frantically as Joma's eyes fixed themselves on George and Kristen. The impending sight of the man charging them with such focus terrified George more than the beast made of stone.

George and Kristen turned to escape as the cavernous maw of the sad-faced stone lion loomed over them—Kristen shielded George as the stench of death neared.

Bumph.

George looked up to see the sudden crack which spread across the beast's cheek, the familiar golden hammer of the tallest man he had ever seen, save Joma.

"Bad beast!" said Logan defiantly with his usual boisterous candour as he readied his weapon for another strike.

But not before a shadowy black blur rammed into Logan's side, lifting the man off his feet as his brutishly heavy hammer abandoned his grip.

Logan planted his feet as it became clear it was Joma pushing Logan back. Logan's rooted toes leaned against the weight, digging long divots into the dirt.

With a challenging roar, Logan wrapped his fists together and hammered down at Joma's back to no avail; like oxen whipped into pulling its hinged weight, Joma strained even harder.

Pushed against a tree, Joma broke his grapple, rising in the moment of Logan's distraction to land several surprise haymakers through Logan's broken stance. The black fists came back bloody with torn skin as Logan's head rocked back with each impact.

At the sound of brittle cracking like the surface of dry clay clattering to the floor, George and Kristen looked from the battle of the titans to stare at the sorrowful slitted stone eyes of the stone beast that bore down upon the two.

The settlement of indulgent enterprise and perilous occupational hazard toppled upon its rotten foundations. Those who took part fled with no loyalty to bind them as bodies littered the field. Many men tried to organise their forces, gathering obscure weapons from their workshops to aim at the beast, perhaps only those who were truly bound by something more than just the promise of stained wealth.

Kendrith slashed through the field, his body low, his centre of gravity a constant moving force. His vision closed in as he let the wind carry his body and jump upon the man he saw in command. Their eyes met and their blades clashed as Kendrith took note of his ruinous face.

Yet there was something more, something hidden underneath that malicious glare in his eyes, a sense of familiarity half revealed behind the ruined scar, a scratch at the back of Kendrith's mind. The blades sang as their edges ran across each other, a high-pitched ring as they parted, how gorgeous a sound as the choir of the panicking folk around ran to and fro—Kendrith and the man he presumed to be Magnus circled each other.

Kendrith's conditioning had caught up enough so that he recovered from the strain of his body—it proved more than enough to equal Magnus, but Magnus's work with the blade wasn't without skill. There was a cruel grace to how the man swung his sword—an efficient and calculated strike that aimed not for great broad strokes to carve, but rather tender, surgical attacks that nipped at vitals and arteries.

The attacks unnerved Kendrith, but the world beyond Haven had hardened him. He had learnt much during his time, not about the monsters which prowled the forest itself, but rather the conniving and foul soul of man. He stared down at Magnus, who attacked and feinted and pierced with a precision designed to cut loose the threads that bound man together and watch the layers unravel—just to see what would happen. But Kendrith grew numb to that foulness, watching from behind a veil as he struck down all attempts of Magnus to cut through.

"You wanted to have us killed," Kendrith said.

Magnus chuckled, a hoarse-throated thing, but fear rose in his throat like bile as he started to realise how unmatched he truly was. "I hope you understand, it's nothing personal, it's just business."

That voice, that face—the itch strengthened, and Kendrith knew the man before him like how one knows the outline of a shadow.

"Kendrith!"

Kendrith turned to see Kristen and George sprinting towards him, no Simantiar in sight. The beast trampled around as it tried to loosen the tangled ropes which ensnared it, and a dark-skinned man as large as Kendrith's own grandfather wrestled with Logan against a tree.

The beast roared, its stout body coiling together before it leapt forward, and a loud snap came from the hapless tree as it broke down its trunk and sent both Logan and his assailant flying.

A sudden snare wrapped itself around Kendrith's throat, the strangling force pulling him back as his sword absconded from his grasp. Kendrith watched helplessly as Magnus rose and fled.

Kendrith dug his fingers to loosen the rope, the woven hemp burning and chafing and crushing his throat—he tried to gasp for air to no avail.

Kicking feet were pulled off the ground as he hung suspended from a tree branch, the sword of Vrania strapped around his shoulder taken from him on the ascent.

Down below he watched as Kasim stared up at him. "Usually, I would have already killed you, but you humiliated the boss, and I know he'd pay a substantial fee to do the same to you." Kasim tossed the relic to the floor, not realising its worth.

"Kendrith!" Kristen called out from beyond. Kendrith tried to signal for her to stay away—Kasim was no man she could take on, but the flailing of his arms looked like a struggle against gravity rather than a warning.

"But first, I guess I will have you watch as I murder your girlfriend."

It all happened in a flash for George. He saw the rope which suddenly wrapped itself around Kendrith's throat and pulled him across the floor like livestock hung to bleed.

"We can't take him," George said.

"No, not in a direct confrontation. What did I teach you?" Kristen queried.

"We are smaller, weaker, so we need to use everything at our disposal to level the playing field."

Kristen nodded, pleased with the answer. "I have a plan," she said.

Kasim drew his two scimitars out from within his dusty sand-coloured cowl.

The man paced forward, an aura of confidence raising him above the bedlam. Men and women were reduced to primal instincts which promised survival—but not Kasim, he prepared himself for a dance.

Kristen unsheathed her own short swords, closing the gap.

George knew that two of the primary lessons he was taught to claim advantage were stealth to gain the element of surprise, or feigning innocence or friendship to have the enemy lower their guard. Her only other word of advice if both those failed was to flee.

But, George remembered Kristen's words, *Sometimes, running is not an option, in which case, it is time to improvise.*

Suddenly, Kristen changed direction, running diagonally through men and women who charged towards the great beast or away from it, but Kristen's gaze never left Kasim.

George ran the opposite direction, catching how Kasim's eyes tried to follow both.

Kristen lowered herself to the floor to pick up loose rocks as she turned to throw.

Kasim stepped aside each one, his head bobbing and weaving with each toss, others parried by his blades as he stood there unperturbed.

George joined in, cradling a pile of his own that he would throw as hard as he could, disorientating Kasim with two ranged assaults from both flanks. But it mattered little, like a blade of grass dancing in the wind, Kasim's body bent and swayed and occasionally swatted the loose rocks from the air.

George could feel the panic rise and wondered how Kristen managed to keep at bay that call for urgency as they watched Kendrith's feet kick the air with less and less fervour, his face reddening in the distance—they were running out of time.

Kasim veered away, an angry grunt coming from him. The man raised his face as blood trickled down his cheek.

It worked! The hail of stones distracted Kasim enough so that Kristen's blade hidden within could find its mark. Easy and simple stones thrown to dictate the pace gave her the opening she needed.

Now was George's only chance. The boy sprinted forward, that moment of shattered pride taking place exactly as Kasim turned towards Kristen.

Only moments ago, Kristen had asked what George thought Kasim's most notable trait was. "His pride," he said. And that was exactly what Kristen and George confidently attacked, almost mocked him with what was a simple attack.

"Warriors have pride," Kristen had said. "Especially a warrior with a cock between his legs."

George sprinted—he was never as much of a force to be reckoned with as Logan who wrestled with another giant, nor as swift as Kendrith who pounced with such feline grace, nor as nimble as Kristen as she weaved her way to victory—but the one thing George did have was instinct, and his instincts timed the exact moment he charged forward.

George's blade still remained in his scabbard, Kasim's attention and rage focused on the woman who harmed him, his side fully open.

George rolled across the floor, his strapped bag and lute case lost in the stunt, his feet returning to plant themselves firmly on the rise as the axe his hand had found left his grasp.

Thump.

There was no wet sound of steel reaching flesh, nor the sound of steel meeting steel, but rather the sound of an axe chopping wood, the sudden sound of a snap, a sack falling to the floor. Kristen charged forward on cue.

Kasim turned around to find Kendrith choking and gasping for air, a knee to the floor as he tried to stand.

The sudden realisation that his hubris cost him a victory was seen plainly on Kasim's livid grimace. With a fuelled roar of her own, Kristen jumped with her two blades, bearing down with all her weight. The sound of steel rang like chimes dully through the battlefield with an audience of none.

Kasim never had a chance to recover. Kendrith matched with a roar of his own as he unsheathed his blade with a flourish that revealed the intricate design of Vrania's blade—the sigils on it alone demanded veneration and awe.

Kasim was on the defensive, stumbling back and trying to regain his footing.

As a pair, like ribbons twined in lasting struggle and love, as many dances before be it in the bed they shared or on the field, the two lovers matched their strikes like coiled venomous snakes.

Kendrith's throat strained with agony, the burn of the rope marks and the tightened airway pleading for a chance to relax, but Kendrith could not give up the opportunity granted by Kristen and George. In tandem, Kendrith and Kristen matched each other, striking forward, one blade prodding as another covered.

Kasim buckled under the weight of the sudden attack. Kendrith had heard about his empire, the Gursan of the eastern lands. They had developed a breathing method where their mind entered a trancelike state, taking in only what mattered, relinquishing all thoughts that did not matter to the present.

If Kendrith strained his ears, he could hear it—how Kasim gave in to the trance, trusted in it, his body moving so fluidly, so purposefully as two puffs of air escaped his lips and a long drag entered through his nose. Yet, there were moments that the pattern buckled, the rhythm broke, the exchange of exhales and inhales were disharmonious like the tip of a needle balancing on a thread that swayed too far on either side.

Kendrith couldn't allow Kasim to recover his breathing.

George simply watched their blades clashing. He wanted to help, but he had to trust that Kristen and Kendrith had things under control.

He looked to Logan—the man had made no attempt to raise his hammer, and Joma was without a sword at his hip as the two faced each other with strength alone. George rolled his eyes, finding there to be more truth to Kristen's comment about men than he'd like to admit: just two men in a fight of pure strength on which their vain pride hung as a prize.

Most of the huts and all the tents lay in waste as the settlement residents ran for their lives.

One defiant man raised some form of projectile weapon that spewed flame from its maw, its metallic body grafted with the remains of a beast. The flames ate away at the vines of the stone lion, sizzling the greenery before the man disappeared into a stony gullet; a ruin of blood stained the stone beast's teeth, limbs and human flesh finding itself a new home inside as the sound of crunching bone and grinding stone was audible over the pandemonium.

George's eyes grew wide as he watched a familiar figure step out, and by familiar he meant unfamiliar—Simantiar donned a new form, one made of discarded beast appendages as a sudden tentacle arm whipped out from his shoulder and straddled the beast's neck before it could gobble down another victim.

The beast strained, pulling against Simantiar's own strength.

Simantiar had stepped out to behold the carnage that took place, the farce of a militaristic empire toppled. Simantiar called upon simple arcana to locate the struggling members of his band, and looking up to the towering beast, Simantiar decided to stretch his new body.

Limbs wrapped themselves around the gigantic beast, pulling. "Come on, beast! Magical being versus magical being!"

The monster rushed forward, Simantiar's coiled tentacle arm still wrapped around the monster's neck as Simantiar roared, dragging the beast down to the floor. With its head lowered, its centre of gravity buckled, and the monster fell, ploughing up fine earth as it dragged itself across the dirt.

Simantiar's tentacle appendage tightened like a taut spring as the beast tried again and again to chomp down on him, its chin grazing farther into the floor and digging trenches.

Simantiar pulled on the makeshift reins and mounted the beast.

The creature struggled to its feet with great difficulty as Simantiar's new bone-blade protruded from his other arm, trying to break into the stone with little success.

The creature rampaged, paws pounding prints into the floor with every pounce to shake Simantiar loose. Simantiar stabbed again and again, the blade snapped with his final strike.

The creature charged forward, ramming through a house and turning into splinters as if it was made of loose branches.

It reared into the air, monstrous jaws snapping at Simantiar tucked into its neck.

Think, think, dammit. Simantiar pressed his enamel forehead to the writhing beast, but there was no response. Was it not made of magic?

Come on. Simantiar's eyes drifted to its body. A thought came to him. A crazy and insane thought.

Simantiar abandoned his body of scavenged beast appendages and returned to his skull form. The limbs and body parts fell like a sheet of snow from a tiled roof.

And then he vanished, his consciousness first melding with the vines coiled around the creature. The mane of foliage moved towards Simantiar, caressing him, holding him, cradling him. The discarded body parts were trampled underneath the feet of the rampaging and frantic beast that wailed such a sorrowful sound of gravel.

And then Simantiar vanished, becoming one with the stone and greenery within the body of the beast itself.

George's gaze dashed between the clash of blades and the stomping rampage of the beast.

Truly everyone had either left or died fighting.

George could do nothing but stand there and helplessly watch the exchange of blows between Joma and Logan, and the struggle of Simantiar as he tried to pull the beast under his control.

George turned to the fringes of the forest as his eyes widened in anxious worry.

Creatures emerged, great beasts that blossomed thanks to the horrid alchemy of the forest. They stepped forward with snarling tongues and grotesque forms.

They must have been drawn in by the sounds of battle, and it was then that George noticed the sounds of screaming men and women echoing from within the forest like a choir of the damned lost at sea.

George watched with unbridled horror as a lithe impish creature of purple grey jumped upon a man's shoulders and dug its piercing fingers into his shoulders—the man screamed, a sound cut short when the impish being with its long mosquito-like proboscis pierced the man's forehead and George wondered if he just imagined the slurping sound over the ensuing carnage.

A thought crossed George's mind. At a sprint, he prayed that Kendrith and Kristen could survive long enough till he returned.

Simantiar opened his eyes. *Wake up,* he thought he had heard.

His eyes blinked open, his vision blurred, but focus blended in until the world that was showed to him was warm and colourful, not the bleak, dour world he remembered where everything was a little more grey and the clouds seemed to promise rain.

He looked to his hands, they were made of flesh and bone. He recognised that green-hued vein which ran down his right one.

A dog jumped up to him, his friend. This new world was bright, an orange-hued warmth to it that filled him with love and life.

A bark from Timmy. Simantiar looked down to him and took note of his bristling brown fur rubbing against him, the loving deep brown eyes and the hanging tongue.

The dog licked his face. It jumped down and ran in a circle before sitting. His tail wagged, his tongue panted.

"It's okay, boy, I'm here. I'm not going anywhere." Timmy barked and Simantiar knew it was a lie, but Timmy barked anyway.

Simantiar looked out—he remembered the hill. It was a spot he would come to often with his mother and Timmy, but over the years, it was just Timmy and him. They would sit beside an old oak tree with a swing hanging from a branch, and stare out towards a setting sun as the wind brushed against the foliage and made the tree leaves rustle with its passing. The scent of spring was thick in the air and promise of new beginnings filled Simantiar's heart.

But he knew this world wasn't real. Simantiar didn't remember the tree, nor the swing. But he did remember Timmy. Turning to Timmy, Simantiar slowly understood. The beast of the forest. The entity of stone. After the fall of it all, Timmy must have succumbed to the bleeding forest.

That was why he waited, that was why the beast of the forest prowled and guarded—he was waiting for Simantiar to return as the forest changed his body into that of an eternal sentinel.

A tear, or perhaps the memory of a tear, graced Simantiar's cheek within the make-believe world that Timmy had created. The loyal dog barked, and Simantiar realised how dearly he missed his furry friend. It was an imagined glow, but it was filled with so much love, so much hope for Simantiar's world that all that despairs must have leaked out of his pores and turned his physical form into that primal monstrosity. But inside, where he was, the tenderness was like a painting of a sorrowed soul daring to hope for brighter days.

Simantiar was back, even if for just a moment. Summer came into full bloom, butterflies and bees fluttering and buzzing about. The clouds softened ever more above as rays of sunshine pierced the sky like pillars of light.

The sombre cold of autumn came next. Simantiar watched as his old friend, Timmy, aged, but there was only love and contentment in the dog's eyes.

Timmy barked, happy to see Simantiar again. Simantiar shed another tear, and then another.

Timmy hobbled over to Simantiar, old and slow, resting his head upon Simantiar's lap with soft resignation. Simantiar was grateful for this reunion, grateful for the gift Timmy had provided by returning the lost soul of what it meant to be alive to Simantiar as he cried like a human would; as he remembered how it felt to form a lump in one's throat; as he remembered the feeling of trembling fingers that petted Timmy's fur.

The chill came, rust-coloured leaves shed from the branches of the oak tree.

Timmy's fur fell out in clumps.

Winter came next, and the cold blanket of snow formed around the two of them as Timmy's eyes grew weary. Another bark. More feeble this time, but still happy.

Before the end of winter came and the cycle ended, a vision appeared— a lake atop a mountain, a view across the canopy of dark green towards the lands beyond.

The world died away, the blanket of snow covering the tired soul of Timmy who died in Simantiar's lap, as the realm in which they lay now fell to ash.

George ran back into the hospice centre that was surprisingly still intact. The men and women that remained in their deathbeds coughed and panted and moaned in resigned pain as the world around them fell to pieces; they seemed to care little for any of it. The putrid stench of the dying lingered. It was a certain sweet-scented musk that George braved through.

George quickly did away with the doctor who was huddled up in his office, downing some strong odorous alcohol, his pleading words fell upon deaf ears as mercy was worth little in the situation.

George rummaged through the belongings of the cabinets, cursing why he didn't ask Gary first about where to find something that could help. At least everything was labelled.

George found what he was looking for, a labelled pouch with powdered remains of what could have been harvested from a moth.

"Hope this works."

His apparent haste was halted by an odd sight as he left the building. The great beast of stone suddenly stood very, very still. It had seated itself, like a dog would sit when expecting something. It was then that he noticed Simantiar was missing.

The urgency at hand pulled George back to the present—he had no time to waste.

On the double, George sprinted back towards the fight between Kendrith, Kristen, and Kasim.

The beasts were edging closer, already some of them preying on the fleeing masses who ran from one danger into another.

George had no time to lose.

He arrived just as Kristen and Kendrith were losing momentum. Kristen received a broad kick to her stomach and went reeling to the ground; Kendrith was all that faced Kasim now—but he kept his momentum while meeting Kasim's strikes. Whatever dance Kasim had lost himself in, Kendrith matched him with ferocity and grit and pure willpower. If Kasim were balancing on a tightrope, then Kendrith balanced over a cliff's edge.

George tossed the bag, moments of tact and strategy a luxury that he couldn't afford—they were pressed on time. All George could do now as the beasts closed in further was hope that Lady Luck was on his side.

Be it due to reflex, or some sort of tunnel vision or because of pure luck, the powdered bag exploded upon the edge of Kasim's scimitar. George watched as the nimble hands slashed the blurred leather pouch, its contents spraying him. Kendrith lunged back in surprise.

The fluff covered Kasim, and the man coughed as the shimmering stuff glistened with iridescent patterns.

Kendrith panted, pointing with his glowing sword at the eastern warrior. "What is that?" he asked.

"Magic pheromone," George said as Kasim's coughing continued, the ravenous sounds of the closing-in monsters became more and more audible. "Must have come from some type of moth." George gasped for air, his arms propped on bent knees to hold his weight.

There was a sudden sound of a smack, a wet cracking sound. George, Kendrith, and Kristen turned to see a ruinous and frazzled Logan mounted atop an unmoving Joma, his usually midnight-dark face now painted red—the man lay motionless.

Logan dismounted, gasping for air, with a slight limp in his walk as he waddled over to his hammer. The giant man spat a loose tooth laden in blood to the floor, his tongue inspecting the gap in some recess of his mouth as he waddled over to them all.

"You done showing who the bigger man is?" Kristen mocked.

"Absolutely." It sounded like Logan wanted to say something clever, but between the rasping of air, the blood that came from his ear, and the bruises which marked his expression, he couldn't seem to find his wit. The large man just fell to his rear, his hammer at his side as more beasts came closer and closer to them all.

Kasim finally finished his coughing fit. "It was unwise to not take that opportunity when you still had it," he said.

Kendrith shrugged. "I don't seem to care very much all of a sudden."

Kasim shook the fluff off himself, but the glistening stuff was surprisingly stubborn. "What is this?" he asked.

"Magic pheromone, like I said."

Kasim's eyes went wide as he considered what was being said. "You mean?"

George simply pointed out towards the monsters that were coming in. All of them closing in…or rather just closing on Kasim.

The man stepped back, only to look down to see the chalk-white caterpillar-looking thing that crawled up his leg, then two, then three.

The man panicked, his usual composure now gone as the vile hairy slugs wormed their way up, a slime trail in their paths, circular mouths filled with rows of teeth eating away at the powdered fluff.

Kasim jumped back, flailing, panicking, as his scimitar tried to slash away at them with great urgency. The slugs then bit into his flesh, drawing blood. It didn't take long for them to disappear inside. The man screamed with such dismay at the pain, not realising that he had cornered and stumbled right into the monsters that smelled the pheromones leaking from him.

"Nice sword." Logan nodded at Kendrith, one eye already swelling up.

The sounds of Kasim's agonised cries went unheard in the background, followed by the sound of teeth biting into flesh and crunching bone.

Kendrith looked down, looking just as defeated. "Thanks. You knew, didn't you?"

Logan nodded. "I had my suspicions. You used only your steel sword in the woods, never the supposed silver one. And who wraps their weapon like that unless they have something to hide?"

"We better get out of here," George said.

The others simply nodded in approval, but George couldn't help but feel bad for the way Kasim died.

It was only then that Pecky returned to sit on George's shoulder. "Thanks for showing up," George said in mock admonishment.

Kristen, Logan, George, and Kendrith walked over to the unmoving body of the beast. Its body was remarkably still.

"Is it still alive?" asked Kristen.

"I don't know," answered Kendrith.

"Look at its face," added George. The four of them looked up at the beast's expression to see where there was usually a sorrowful man with slitted eyes and sorrowful brows, there now was a smiling man, eyes slightly open to reveal the stony complexion of fulfilment and gratitude. "Still bloody scary if you ask me."

"I did see that vile skeletal being I saw before in the forest—must be behind all this," said Logan in contemplation.

George, Kristen, and Kendrith all exchanged curious and awkward looks.

"Logan, there is something we need to tell you," said Kendrith.

Logan's face donned a look of determination again, curling his fingers around the haft of his war hammer and looking up at the moving body of the beast. "Hold that thought," he said.

The band turned to the beast to see the creature move, its mane rustling as if returning to life. But the beast itself remained statuesquely still, as the mane and others vines coalesced like slithering snakes into one mass of foliage and brambles and vines which then slid off the stone body to leave it bare and naked.

The mound curled in upon itself, weaving from inside until it began to straighten and take form, standing to the full height of a man made of nothing but greenery with Simantiar's skull mounted on top.

"Ha! I knew it!" Logan charged with his hammer aloft, his limp and fatigue suddenly gone.

"Wait, wait, wait, wait!" Kristen, George, and Kendrith jumped in front of Logan, arms waving in panic.

"He is with us!" George explained.

Logan lowered his hammer. "What do you mean?" he asked, eying Simantiar suspiciously.

That was when George, with some comments from Kendrith and Kristen, explained the entire story.

"That was quite a tale."

They all nodded, though Logan still didn't seem to trust Simantiar.

"How did you manage to stop the beast?" asked Kendrith. "Was it your antimagical properties?"

Simantiar shook his head. "The beast was called Timmy—he was my dog some long time ago."

Everyone's jaws dropped. "He must have wandered into the forest after whatever magic took hold here. It must have changed him, turned him into a stone sentinel waiting for my return. When I did return, he must have finally fulfilled his purpose, and the magic faded."

He went silent for a moment. "'Let the man of stone be your guide'," Simantiar said absent-mindedly.

"What was that?" Kendrith asked.

"When I was inside his mind, I could see it—the path to a grand lake like from the poem. It got me thinking." Simantiar turned around. "Is this the man of stone from the poem?"

Everyone seemed speechless and bewildered, except for Logan who was more than just confused.

Kendrith knitted his brows together in deep consideration. "That would make sense."

As Logan started to ask Kendrith what was meant, Kristen stepped forward with sorry eyes. "Timmy must have been very happy to see you."

"Yes, he was. I'm sorry it ate your mother, Kendrith," Simantiar said, interrupting his explanation to Logan.

"That's all right," Kendrith said, and he seemed to truly mean it; it was a thing of the past.

Kristen and George looked to Kendrith in unison, something important lost in all that chaos.

"Magnus!" They blurted out simultaneously.

"It's fine, we'll find him."

"You don't understand! *He* killed your mother!"

The band followed the tracks which led away from the settlement. Simantiar used some form of light magic to detect the trail left by Magnus. The musk or scent he gave turned into a wafting trail of smoke.

Kendrith dictated the pace by extension of the fact that he ran ahead of everyone else. The man had gone incredibly quiet, a seething wrath ignited inside him after learning Magnus's true identity and his mother's death.

His grip hardened around the hilt. Magnus had killed his mother. The sword felt like a cudgel in his hand, a makeshift weapon, foreign. Was this really what he wanted the sword for?

At the end of the trail, Kendrith froze in his tracks, mouth wide open as he panted. Sweat trailed his cheeks. Or was it tears? He wasn't sure.

He fell to his knees, a mixture of exhaustion and being robbed of his vindication just leaving him with roiling emotions with nowhere to go.

The rest of the band arrived soon after, first Simantiar and then the others.

Logan started, "Isn't that...?" His words drifting off as he simply observed the unspoken spectacle.

Kendrith just began to laugh, his rage turning into hysteria and confusion as he couldn't help but laugh at the whole absurdity of it all.

He fell to his rear, his laugh turning into sobs.

What fucking irony, he thought as the sword fell from limp fingers and clattered to the floor.

There it was, the monster with the hideous creature built like a skittering totem pole with branches of arms, large vertical maws, and four uninterested expressions on four encompassing faces. Whatever remained of Magnus, or Verron as Kendrith remembered him, was now being gobbled up by the monster, as the last of Magnus's naked feet vanished and just a lobbed shoe remained of the cruel, pitiful Magnus, the Magnus who tried to create his own Tower of Babel made from balanced sticks rather than stacked stone.

Chapter 40

The slumbering snore of the dark voiced itself as crickets chirped and bushes rustled and the campfire cracked.

The band was silent, recuperating from the onslaught. Since Simantiar no longer needed to hide he took on his humanoid body and planted roots into the ground, drawing energy from the reserves he had lost.

Kendrith tried hard to tend to Kristen, his worry plain for all to see, but Kristen's reassurances fell on deaf ears.

Kendrith was more distant than usual, reserved and brooding. The discovery of Magnus's remains left him feeling hollow, and not even the beast that devoured the monster was dealt with.

More often than not, George found Kendrith's head hanging low, his shoulders slumped, and his thoughts somewhere far away. The sword of Vrania removed from its wrapping seemed even dimmer than before as it lumbered around uncomfortably upon Kendrith's back, swinging and knocking into him.

"So, what's the story with the skull?" Logan nodded to where Simantiar meditated away from the campfire's glow. It drew George's attention away from Kendrith—he suddenly noticed he must have been staring.

George stayed silent, his hands looped around his knees. The soft glow of the campfire tried to bring life to him; George acutely noticed how he watched the rays of light and eyed the shadows beyond.

"He is…umm, he's Simantiar, an ancient wizard from the old world."

Logan sat silently. "Oh."

George looked up to him, frowning. "Oh? That's all you can say."

"Well, I suppose this isn't the first time someone has heard that and seemed shocked. And after all that happened, I don't really care."

George nodded, grateful that it wasn't to become a whole exchange—he didn't have the energy for it.

"You were brave today, far braver than most," Logan said looking down. "But no one, especially under my watch, should have to put themselves into harm's way like that."

"It's fine," George muttered. "I'm not a child."

Logan considered his words. "Perhaps not. To be fair, when we first met at the bar, all I saw was a young boy coming to terms with growing up. But you proved yourself capable today." Logan's words slowly fell quiet.

"Say what you like, but I know that look—I've seen it countless times before. Children forced to grow up before it is their time; good children, children that cared for others, but never got cared for. You may be grown up, but you never had a chance to be a child. I don't want you to feel as if the world rests on your shoulders. Confide in me and those two vile lovebirds." Logan nodded towards Kristen and Kendrith's soft bickering. Pecky cocked his head curiously.

Something began to touch George's soul, a feeling within. It watered the desolate soil of his emotions that were made to dry out and wither. He was grateful to Logan. He may have been called a child, but it wasn't without acknowledgement of who George truly was.

Logan rose, coming to sit next to George. "I failed you today, let you get captured, and put you in harm's way. I can't promise that I won't let it happen again, just know that I will try my best."

The days went by slowly, the band camping and tending their wounds. George had taken his lute from his case, battered and blemished from the demanding trek.

Simantiar hovered beside him and saw the sorry state of the instrument. With a wave of his hand, the forest answered his call, vines coming down to break pieces of bark from trees to mend the broken wood, a second wave bending the instrument and restoring it to its former appearance.

George looked up to the old wizard. "Thanks," he said, but his appreciation seemed hollow, and so did his smile. Something was happening in George, a toiling war where he realised what the world demanded of him, of what it meant to be alive, the feeling of never knowing what tomorrow will bring, and what choices might bear consequences. He felt the prison of darkness so acutely, and his fear as vividly as if it were a living thing.

"Play it," Logan said, biting off a leg of chicken that was abandoned from the camp. Kristen was already up, her fever now gone, but a languid aura still surrounded her. She sipped from the tin bowl of soup in her hands, bits of rabbit floating to the top. The pot itself rested in the centre of the band's camp, equipment thrown about, showing how they had stayed for several days.

George looked to Logan, unsure of himself. When was the last time he even played the lute? When was the last time he picked it from his case? At the time, before he had even met Kendrith, the lute was a way to give voice to his sorrow, a companion so he didn't feel so lonely.

Now he looked down at the thing and it seemed alien to him, awkward in his hands. His digits had grown stiff, with dirt under his nails and callused palms. What had been smooth, lithe fingers before now seemed like hands that knew of pain, hands that had lost too much innocence to nurture the lute's sound. Since meeting Kendrith, getting to know Simantiar, and meeting Kristen, and now Logan, he no longer needed the lute's sound to console him. Suddenly, George came to realise he wasn't alone anymore. Kendrith had stayed even though he had no need to, even though his contract was done, Kristen had accompanied them of her own accord, and he knew for a fact that Simantiar had become close to him in the same way he had become close to Simantiar.

George looked back down to the lute, and suddenly the instrument didn't seem so alien to him anymore—the boy smiled as he plucked its strings.

The sound coursed through the air and filled the others. A comforting thing that first pluck was, and every second and third and fourth vibrating pluck twisted and mended itself into a tapestry of music: waves that washed over the band.

George didn't recognise the sound. It was new, unburdened by the weight of loneliness, yet also void of innocence. It was a sombre, yet beautiful melody which seemed accepting of the world's hardships, and yet grateful for all its beauty—beauty that in spite of everything else seemed charitable.

The stiffness in his fingers absconded with each concord of strings, blooming into beautiful sounds which gave a new voice to George, an emotion that gave a glimpse to the true nature of maturity—contentment. The sound melded together, as if the very strings of the lute unravelled and spread to the others, tugging at the threads which moved their emotions, tugging at doors which opened memories.

Kristen looked up from her bowl, a blanket over her shoulders as she rested her head upon Kendrith's shoulder.

And perhaps, just for a second, perhaps George allowed himself to see an image of Lily before him, and his circle of companions seemed complete. A shadow that always lurked in some corner of his mind began to fade; a shadow that constantly promised to protect George and shield him from danger; a shadow born from the need to survive. It was the mantis in the recess of his mind; the Other at the bottom of the well. It faded, and soothed, with each passing tune until what George saw in the corner was not some obscene presence of death, but a crying little boy with tousled hair.

The performance came to an end, and George's spirit seemed all the lighter for it. The band clapped for George, gentle, appreciative claps.

"You've got a gift," Logan said, his voice stern and sincere.

George simply nodded.

Night befell the camp and Simantiar took watch, after the battle against Magnus and the magically transfigured form of Timmy, most of his reserves had been depleted, and his connection to magic and nature was broken. Now, he had fixed that connection, and found that as he put himself back together, his body seemed lighter. That night, Simantiar's body unravelled and spread around the camp, fencing the others within as they slept, his skull lost within the tangled web of vines and foliage somewhere in that network as his consciousness rode its currents. The vines were the same that wrapped themselves around Timmy, his dog. Now Simantiar carried the greenery like an old scarf that one wears for the scent that lingers; he could sense the soft shadow of warmth, the feeling of fur that touches the skin long after it's gone.

The pieces fused, the parted memories divided like oil with water started to meld once more as the healing of Simantiar's broken mind took fruit. His consciousness pulsated along the swaying border of vines around the perimeter as darkness lingered, and the monsters were kept at bay. His mind planted its roots into the past as Simantiar's consciousness drifted again to a previous life.

Simantiar travelled as a hermit, covered in a cowl and with staff in hand as he traversed the long distances to his old home. A playful lilt appeared to his lips, the thought of finding his mother, and seeing how much she must have grown.

With a snap of his fingers, his beard lengthened, turning ash-coloured. The wizard stroked it, feeling the ragged bristle on his fingertips like the prick of a horse's brush.

"Hmm, and what about?" With another snap of his fingers, the white of snow seeped into his hair, spreading out from his roots, and with another snap, a few of his teeth sucked themselves back into his gums, crow's feet formed as deep wrinkles about haggard eyes, and a few liver spots to finish the touch.

Simantiar laughed at the form he had taken, remembering how gods of old would don similar disguises when they walked among their subjects. The smile faded as soon as it had appeared, and Simantiar shook the thought from his head. He was not a god, and it was a dangerous idea to entertain. For all his power, he could never allow hubris to turn him into a creature of entitlement and pride.

As Simantiar trod through his old city, still as lavish and shamelessly opulent as when he had left it, he couldn't help but find his previous mood returning. The man trod through the crowds of well-tailored folk, their garments made of the newest and most extravagant of materials, wearing their status on their sleeves, and yet Simantiar walked upon that sea like jetsam in the ocean—he didn't belong and the stares proved it.

Simantiar smiled at the absurdity of it all. He tried often to explain to Cernunnos the customs of man, and even he sometimes could not fault the ancient avatar of the forest for his confusion.

As Simantiar continued on his trek, he came to stand before his old home.

Often he would have seen his home through the eyes of familiars, sensed that his family was still doing well, yet this was the first time that he would return to his mother. And that was a long time ago. Over the past several years, he did it less and less as the more it felt like he was invading his mother's privacy…or perhaps it was her deteriorating health that was the true reason.

As Simantiar pushed the door open, a servant came to greet him.

"Good afternoon, sir. This is private property, what business do you have with Madam Giselle?"

With the most feeble of voices and rickety of holds upon his staff, Simantiar spoke as a withered hermit would. "I am but a weary hermit passing through. I was told that your lady would be gracious enough to offer me succour in return for tales of my travels."

The man who met Simantiar at the door was Sebastian, always a well-postured individual who knew his place and duty, a man who saw not worth in the title of the task, but the diligence. His age had begun to show however, tired eyes with the wrinkles beginning to manifest. And even though the man hid his reply out of professionalism, Simantiar could tell there was a certain gregarious nature to Sebastian, who was gladly willing to offer refuge for those seeking it.

"I am sure the lady of the house would gladly permit you entry, with room and food for the night. Please, do come in."

As Simantiar followed Sebastian into his old home, looking around at the expansive garden, he recognised a lot of it. The aesthetic of a babbling brook, the stone walkways, the bamboo beam which rocked back and forth every time it filled with enough water from the stream. It was a certain aesthetic brought from a culture in the east.

Several other servants seemed to tend the garden or rush about the house.

As he continued, Simantiar recognised the familiar pond which he had played at since he was a child. When no one was looking, Simantiar flicked a finger towards the pond, making a small fish made of water break the surface. The long-forgotten nostalgia made Simantiar smile at the memory.

As he continued into the home, Simantiar was brought through the front gates and around a side entrance to a flower garden which his mother was tending.

"Please, if you could wait here for a moment," Sebastian said, entering the glasshouse and speaking to Simantiar's mother.

Simantiar couldn't hear the words that were spoken; well, he could, but didn't want to. Certain things were not meant for his ears, and he could very well imagine what words were being exchanged anyway.

Giselle Trufin looked through the glass and at Simantiar's haggard form, smiling with warmth and hospitality as she nodded. Age had only served Giselle, like a fine-aged wine that accentuated her beauty—what used to be a lean strength was now a wizened regality. Simantiar could tell with what deference Sebastian approached his mother.

She had sun-kissed and slender hands like the delicate stems of tulips; wrinkles revealed themselves as Giselle smiled with those same lips that would kiss Simantiar good-night, those tender eyes that offered Simantiar strength when he had doubts, that same dress Simantiar would fall asleep on as his mother stroked his hair. The only thing that struck Simantiar with pain was to see her limp legs as she sat upon her wheelchair of polished dark wood and carved filigree patterns.

When one proved to be as powerful as Simantiar, it was easy to forget the things that made one human, that cause people to return to a time when all they knew was a mother's love and the strength that bound them—it took much to repress the tears and uphold the farce.

Sebastian returned. "We will gladly be accommodating you," he said guiding Simantiar to his room.

The act of struggling to climb the stairs was far more annoying than the climb itself. Eventually, Simantiar was brought to a guest room larger than any room offered at an inn and far more luxurious. Floating orbs of light held on hourglass-shaped vases with blotchy patterns, the beds a rampant pattern of motley colours. The duvet was a deep magenta, the pillows a soft blue, a sheet was an even softer yellow, and a canopy with a mesh of different bright colours that did not accost one's sight with such ostentatious display, but rather seemed to work in harmony to deliver a soft concession of marriage between colours that usually opposed one another.

The room's rug showed a woven image of a road going through a forest and a castle nestled at the far end of the path through rising hills and open fields.

From the image itself, vines had sprouted, emerging from the rug into the guest room which purposefully crawled across the floor, climbing up walls and spiralling up the bedposts.

"When you are ready, there will be a hot bath waiting for you." Sebastian excused himself, closing the door behind him.

Looking closer, Simantiar appreciated the sheer effort that went into the design of the room, filled with further ornaments crafted by the most skilled artisans—a polished desk at the corner by the high-ceilinged window, and a wardrobe expertly crafted with detailed carvings of curled sprigs.

But this wasn't the home Simantiar remembered, his own room from when he was a child was only a few doors down. Simantiar's beard returned to its previous form, his teeth out of hiding, his skin back to its invigorated youth.

With another snap of his fingers, Simantiar turned into a cloud of dust, vanishing under the door of the guest room and over into his old room. His room was much like he left it. The large bed always felt like it could fit several more of him, which it often did, as he made clones of himself just to have the warmth of someone to cuddle.

Shelves were filled with all kinds of books on magic which he would only read sporadically. A table of his own where he would doodle creatures and have them come to life.

What Simantiar did not expect was to see his dog, Timmy, curled up in his old bed.

Timmy's eyes wandered towards Simantiar.

"Uh," Simantiar said, his mind turning blank as Timmy rose from his spot, tongue hanging loose and excitement in his eyes.

A bark.

"Shh!" Simantiar shushed Timmy.

Another bark as Timmy circled the spot in uncontainable excitement before jumping down and pawing at Simantiar's drab clothing.

Despite the dog's discernible age and sagging fur, none of the energy or excitement seemed to have dulled in him.

"Shh!"

Again another bark as Timmy panted with pure joy.

"For crying out loud." Simantiar snapped his fingers, the sound now unable to escape his room.

Giving out a defeated sigh, Simantiar knelt down to his old friend and started to pet him. The dog acted in kind and showed his love by licking Simantiar's face.

"Stop it." Simantiar chuckled, turning away wet cheeks only to be slobbered elsewhere.

"I said stop." Another more joyous laugh as he leaned away only for Timmy to lean farther in.

Simantiar collapsed backwards, Timmy now running to and fro as his joyous limbs had nowhere to place their excitement.

The door opened, Simantiar's eyes grew wide as he watched his mother wheel into the room with sombre and loving eyes. "I knew it was you," was all she said.

Simantiar took his bath, a long drawn-out thing, partially due to the warmth it provided, but also partially because he avoided his mother.

Come nightfall, Simantiar entered a tea room, fashioned as a type of lounge.

The sofas were a mix of short and stout dry red like the auburn of autumn, while another longer sofa was a light and inviting turquoise which seemed like it struggled to decide between a green or blue shade. Several handwoven rugs filled the room. Ornaments and glass-inserted cupboards lined the walls. A floor-to-ceiling window gave a view out into the streets of Yumia. Lavish spires with pointed colourful domes rotated with slow purpose, balconies radiated sunlight captured in jars that lit up neighbouring streets, the joyful cry of those who wished to party against the setting night, and plazas waiting in still obeisance until they would be opened again.

Giselle took a sip from her tea. "I was hoping you would join me," she said, the crow's feet as she smiled were soft, the wrinkles seemed as if they were caressing the white sclera of her blue eyes.

"This is my favourite spot in the house—it gives you a clear look at the city and the moon," she said, but of course Simantiar knew that, it was the precise reason she built the home on that space and had the room face the direction it did.

As Simantiar took a seat, Sebastian poured him some tea and excused himself from the room. The moon's glow shone through the high-ceilinged window, illuminating them both in its glow.

Simantiar had stayed with a group of druids during his travels, not only learning about the power of nature from Cernunnos, but also the power hidden behind the filtered rays of a moon's glow.

A power that was gentle, nurturing, and lulled you through its radiance while others tried to play pretend-god with their bottled rays of sunshine.

Simantiar told her about the lands hailing far to the east, of northern tribes, of the conflicts to the west where strife still continued. Sharing stories of creatures made of pure celestial life, of fairies, of runes left behind from civilisations long lost—an adventure worth a lifetime.

Madame Giselle did not speak once during the entire exchange, soaking in all that Simantiar had to share and watching him with great interest...and love.

"I am happy to see my boy has had such an adventurous journey."

"How did you know it was me?" Simantiar almost blushed as he wondered how he ever thought he could deceive his mother.

"Oh please, do you really think you could fool your mother?" she asked, bare feet poking out of a long modest dress as they lay propped upon the footrest attached to the wheelchair.

"Was it that obvious?"

"For somebody so good at magic you understand little of humanity."

"Did Sebastian know?"

"He had his suspicions, but I knew from the moment I saw you. Even knew when you would watch me through your familiars."

"But how?"

"Come now, you are my son, I still have some talent with magic."

"That's not an answer," Simantiar retorted.

Giselle giggled, leaning in to brush away Simantiar's golden locks and look her boy in the eyes. "Magic is nothing short of amazing, it creates and provides, but the one thing it was never able to solve is the enigma of life itself."

Simantiar nodded, smiling, he was a fool to think he could fool his mother. There were some things that just went beyond the power of magic. A mother's love was one of them, and her touch was another. How it felt to have the touch of skin graze his cheek with such brittle love that one had no choice but to want to cherish it and protect it from all who may harm it. Warmth and cold simultaneously ran up Simantiar's spine—he just wanted to fall into her arms and sleep like days of old.

"I'm sorry I never said goodbye," Simantiar began.

Giselle shrugged. "I admit, I was angry to begin with, hurt even. Waited day and night for my son to return to me."

The words made Simantiar's heart ache.

"But I knew you had your reasons to leave, only a fool would try to grab the wind."

"They did." Simantiar pointed out towards the people, the soft echo of laughter coming from a party a few streets down as dancing shadows played upon neighbouring walls.

Giselle shook her head. "No, the thing they grasp isn't actually sunlight—it's pretend. Sunlight is that which is scarce, that which one cannot grasp, that which comes from above and you enjoy under the shade of rustling tree branches. Sunlight is sunlight because it is fleeting, what they have is just a glorified light bulb."

Simantiar nodded.

Giselle seemed suddenly so distant. "Your father taught me that."

"I know." Simantiar didn't mention the fact that his mother would bring up the same words of wisdom whenever she could.

"So remember, son. Look all around you and you will see what life has to offer past the magic, past the trails of hubris where people lose themselves in their obsession. There is something to life if you take the time to notice it, like the love in another person's eyes, there is something to tending a garden and watching it take fruit rather than snapping your finger and numbly watching the seed explode with tampered life."

"One of the first lessons you taught me." Simantiar nodded his head in reminiscence.

"Life is about taking time, having patience with hope and watching the chick break free from its shell rather than ripping it open because of our own inability to appreciate the calm of nature."

A sudden loud bang radiated from outside as a red dragon wormed its way across the sea of darkness with a fanged snarl and ravenous eyes, before the evoked being burst into blinding lights that filled the sky with fireworks.

One could barely hear the awe of the people from the party.

After what Simantiar's mother had said, the display seemed so hollow, so pitiful. Life was life, it was eternal, be it the magic that flowed uncontested or the patient trunk of a tree that grew into a sentinel with strong roots. The fireworks didn't seem like festivities anymore, but rather a pitiful challenge towards the starry sky that went unheard.

Simantiar looked down to her legs.

"Why don't you have it healed?" he finally asked. He had watched countless times before when his familiars would visit, watched as his mother's health deteriorated and her legs failed her.

"It's magic sickness—the constant strain as a consort to the Bernham family is catching up to me." Her smile was a bitter, sombre thing.

"I could try to—"

"No." Giselle cut him off. She looked over to him with rheumy eyes as her lips quivered, but her smile never faded. She put a hand to Simantiar's cheek who watched her with concern.

"I want to be human, I want to live that way to the best of my ability, to honour your father."

That night, Simantiar heard his mother's wails and thought it the wail of a banshee.

She could pretend it was her desire to be human that truly stopped her from seeking help, but Simantiar knew better. She had been that way since the beginning, living within the ghost of her husband's death. Perhaps she had made her peace with death a long time ago, and if she truly wanted to fade away with this last act as her own, then Simantiar respected that. Part of him wished he could change things, go back in time and redo it all. And he could, he had the power. But the words of his mother rang in the back of his mind and he deferred to them.

That night Simantiar returned to his own room, tucked into the covers where he drew in the lingering scent—a scent of a past time, one that felt real, one that tugged at his heart because he lived that life, was patient with it, and was now reminiscent about in bittersweet nostalgia as he drifted to sleep; sinking deeper and deeper into the weight of his mattress, deeper and deeper into the sweet embrace of slumber.

Chapter 41

Morning came as it always did, and Simantiar awoke—not from sleep, but from trance, half expecting the touch of soft bedsheets and the nostalgic smell of home, lingering only as a faint memory to tie the past and the present together.

The vines that Simantiar fed with magic over the past night now unravelled to his call, coming together once more to create a body. This time, there was something new—a faint understanding of an idea as natural as any, but which had eluded him thus far.

Most of the vines fell to the earth, where they would return to the soil, or return to the trees where still they had time to serve nature—though Timmy had no body to bury, his essence had seeped into the forestry where it would return to Tiria.

What remained were thin strands coiled together, forming skeletal impression-like shoots from a coppiced tree. The shoots curled and braced till they held Simantiar's skull in place as water rose from root and soil into the air, coalescing around the merged vines to form the impression of a winged falcon.

The shoots now seemed like a spreading network of nerves, with Simantiar's skull nestled within where the simulacrum of the falcon's head would be.

"Whoa." George gasped, bewildered by Simantiar's new form, a strange ancient and natural beauty to the guise he took.

"Cool, right?" Simantiar joked, turning around in his bird form to show off every contour of his fashioned vessel. "I will fly ahead and make sure there are no nasty surprises."

Simantiar took flight, breaking through the canopy.

A few hours had passed, and Simantiar only had to redirect the path of the band occasionally to avoid the few gatherings of husks and a stray group of the Withered—vacant beings with dark and deathly-looking skin stretched over bone. The few transmogrified monsters on their path were either avoided or dealt with swiftly.

Logan began to share of the Withered. "They used to be people—at least that's what we believe—barred forever from the gates of the afterlife, neither dead nor alive, a broken shadow of what they used to be. Evidence suggests that they are people of the old world, hollowed out after the Great Cataclysm of Magic that spread through the lands and scorched the poor sods close enough," Logan said.

Simantiar couldn't help but feel pained, remembering bits and pieces of his final battle. Was it that which sundered the land? Were these pained shadows who also could no longer find peace in life after death? He wondered…were there any among them that he knew?

During his flight, Simantiar dared visits towards old homes, that of Yumia, but saw no trace of his old life, just jagged rising hills.

Simantiar returned from another patrol, and his avian body of water broke apart, sending his skull careening, as his plummet was arrested by the forestry all around where he took upon a humanoid body and landed with barely a sound.

"Is something wrong?" Kendrith asked.

"Not at all. I think I found the lake."

The band continued on their path. Logan and Kendrith made sure that it was in line with the sketched map that Kendrith had drawn. They travelled up the steep mountainside, through the trees which clambered at the incline.

What awaited them at the top was the rising mountain peaks which closed them in, the highest standing of the uncharted lands. Night had already fallen and brought with it a slumbering beauty. Like a mistress, there was a brazen charm to the world, bearing a confidence of daring vices, but tempting passion: a night of beauty and danger, given free rein without the sun to make their proclivities known to the world.

The mountain path allowed them passage only so that they may gaze upon the hollowed crater which was nooked to the mountainside, filled to the brim with rainwater.

"Where to now?" Logan asked.

The group pondered.

"Under the dipping mountain…" George whispered the words as he wondered. It didn't make any sense. The mountain before them rose high, how can a mountain dip?

"Over the rising lake." The lake itself seemed stagnant, and as far as their eyes could see, no opening seemed to present itself above.

"Let's get some sleep—we can mull it over in the morning," Logan said, already setting up camp in front of the lake.

Kendrith observed the area, the high vantage point and limited accessibility made it perfect to keep watch.

George struggled to find sleep that night, so close to the finish, so close to the promise. In truth, a part of him never thought he'd make it, that he would just keep chasing the apparent ghosts of a fabled story. George opened the book before him and reread the passage over and over, running his fingers over the fabled volume.

And perhaps that was still the case—there was no evidence that the golden vault existed. Let alone the dead end that they reached, looking for a dipping mountain. *What does it mean?* the young bard wondered.

"Can't sleep, huh?"

George veered his head from the sparkling stars, stars that seemed to almost be having a conversation with him, a quiet one of glint and shine. There he saw Kristen, a playful smile on her face as she watched the young boy. Logan had taken first watch with Kendrith at the campsite.

George simply shook his head.

"What do you think is inside it?" Kristen asked. George wasn't sure if she believed in the tale—he wasn't quite sure if he himself did either—but still he humoured her, appreciating the distraction.

"Don't know. Lily used to think it might be an angel." George allowed himself a wistful smile. "Or our parents, waiting there for us. But, if the legend is true, I would expect to find my sister in there."

Kristen seemed taken aback. "Do you wish to have your sister back?"

George shrugged and fidgeted with a smooth flat rock in front of his folded feet.

"Come on, your secret is safe with me, softie." Kristen nudged George and earned herself a smile.

He nodded gingerly. "Yes. I know it is silly to wish for things which are a fairy tale. But if I can get my sister back, I would. She was all I ever had as a child."

"It isn't silly at all. One should always be allowed to hope for things—it gives us the courage to dream and perhaps sometimes, we are given what we want."

George was comforted by the words.

"You loved her very much," Kristen said after a moment. "I'm sure she loved you too."

"Thank you."

"What are you going to do after you find the vault?"

George wondered for a second. It was a good question, what was he going to do?

"I hadn't thought of that yet."

Silence filled the gap—Kristen wanted to say something, the sound of crickets like that of encouragement.

"How is Kendrith?" George asked, looking over Kristen's shoulder to the man as he seemed to sharpen his blades absent-mindedly.

Kristen sighed in exhaustion. "He will be all right. It's difficult for him."

"I'm sure it is. To have learnt that his mother's killer was hiding in the woods all this time, making money off the guild without him knowing...couldn't even avenge her in the end."

Kristen hesitated for only a moment. "That's not the only reason. Kendrith grew up hearing stories of adventurers and quests. His own mother and his grandfather were renowned for their feats. Everyone knew the name of Brosnorth, and he is trying to follow their shoes...unfortunately they are mighty shoes to fill. He is having some doubt. Wondering if his father was right to question his dreams."

George nodded, though he could never begin to understand what Kendrith went through; Kendrith's pain was his alone.

Kristen continued, "He thinks he isn't worthy of the sword. When he returns home, he wants to give it to the guild."

"What?" George questioned.

"What?" Another voice rose, it was Logan's. He was eavesdropping. The man suddenly flushed red, redder than George thought possible as he tried to shrink under George's and Kristen's gazes.

Kendrith rose with a defeated sigh. "I am going to stick to the escort route through the Forest of the Dead and light escort missions. I won't be needing the sword. If someone else at the guild can make proper use of it then all the better."

"But—" George began.

"And that's the end of it. I am going to sleep. You should do the same." Kendrith trudged away from the group, finding a spot for himself to brood in.

Kristen sighed again. "Don't let him get to you. He is just upset. I think he just needs time."

George said nothing.

Kristen went quiet for a while. "You are very free to come stay with us."

George turned in confusion. "What?"

"After this is all over—come stay with Kendrith and me. He is sulking a little now, but I am sure he would love to have you."

George simply looked at her, unsure of what to say. He learnt the lute by himself. Learnt to read by hiding away in school rafters and taking notes in what little light was provided. Travelled perilous lands and came close to death on several occasions. He never had a place to stay for longer periods of times. Now that he thought about it, he didn't recall ever spending as much time with the same group of people since Lily.

"You don't have to make up your mind now, but just know that both Kendrith and I would love to take you in. You could find work at the guild. Maybe even become a minstrel."

George simply nodded, saying his good-night and trying to find sleep. Though now his thoughts were occupied with something else. He wondered, with no small amount of fear, what *would* he do after he found the vault?

Simantiar scoured the edges of the lake, heard crickets chirping at the base of the mountain, and saw the treetops spreading across the land like a blanket of lichen green. He gazed at the world beyond as it grew tranquil in the darkness of night, it was familiar—not the sight, but the sensation.

Kendrith had become sullenly quiet since the truth of his mother was discovered. Simantiar dare not mention that he noticed how dull the sword's gleam had become, that which was supposed to embody Kendrith's dream now nothing but a blunt instrument.

There was a sense of kinship between the band, the odd and strange ways in which they met, the confusing state of Simantiar's own existence. He wished he could help Kendrith, he really did. But there was nothing he could do.

Then there was George…they were so close to the vault. But what if it didn't exist? What if it was just another fairy tale? Simantiar had joked about that since the beginning, but now he truly wished the vault existed. After all they had gone through, he couldn't bear the thought of disappointing George.

And after all things are said and done…what about Simantiar himself? He lived as a being of energy outside of his own time. Perhaps he would try to find out what happened with Eindeheid?

The thought nagged him, a creeping uneasy feeling of something that he wanted to forget, but now the truth was too close to ignore.

Simantiar turned, no vines to connect him with the roots of nature and all that was, but rather a lake before him, as the serene and unmoving surface was disturbed by a light breeze which sounded like the mountain's snore.

One foot after the other, Simantiar dipped his leg into the lake until he was completely submerged. Ripples spread, the stillness simply grazed rather than broken.

The world above disappeared, only the rumbling of the mountain remained and the distortion of the water—as time itself cocooned around him.

Simantiar's head burst from the surface of the water, taking in a deep breath, a breath so sweet and decadent that he appreciated every bit of it. He could have easily cast magic to breathe underwater, make gills appear on his neck.

Simantiar quite often let his mind wander to moments lived in the past, memories relived as his body pilgrimaged in the present. And quite often, it was the story of Hubys that visited him.

He recalled the tale of how Hubys was said to have been a powerful sorcerer, bending the will of the universe to his very own beck and call and reshaping it as a god might.

He twisted forests and trees to make himself a temple of coiled bark and leaves, created cities that floated on solid clouds, erected mighty mountains, and cut spanning rivers through continents at the flick of a wrist. And eventually, Hubys would merge with the trees of forests, become a fish to swim in a pond, and soar so high as an eagle atop of clouds to look down upon the specks of land as a god might look upon his own design.

But soon, Hubys forgot what it meant to be human, merging with the world and becoming one with all that was. The story goes that Hubys at some point turned into a gust of wind and never turned back. He became one with the babbling brook of clear water, one with the cloud above, and one with the trees of the world. Thus, the human with the power of a god eventually shed his mortal coil and became one with all that was—lost to nature and perhaps reclaimed by it, to become life itself, ever-present and immortalised as all that could be and all that will be.

Simantiar contemplated the story often like a cloud hanging over him as his powers became manifest and his limits seemed ever harder to grasp.

Once, he even dreamt that he had become Hubys himself, wild fervorous dreams where he would awake in a cold sweat, relieved to find that he was not an unmoving tree stuck in the middle of a forest, struggling to remember who he was and forced to watch the world move past him.

Some viewed the tale as a means to celebrate the union of man and god, but Simantiar always heeded it as a warning just as his mother intended him to. *To forget one's true self is to lose oneself to that which tempts.*

And so, Simantiar kept that story close to his heart. He tried to remember the feeling of dirt between his toes to anchor him on this plane and within his mortal coil.

That was enough contemplation for Simantiar. The wizard rose from the water and dressed himself, finally ascending the mountainous terrain. Through the sentinel-like peaks and the ever-vigilant clouds, the curly-haired man came to fall upon the raised plateau which held the arena of Magus Tha.

Simantiar entered the place with his staff of oak, bent and twirled like a wizened sage tree, the sagging hood of his cowl draped over his head much like a hermit, but he did nothing to hide his appearance this time. Here, he would greet new students and old teachers alike—with deference.

There weren't many familiar faces on campus, and Simantiar had drawn more than one curious stare or whisper. He ran into the occasional person, those who became teachers at the academy or those who were still teaching. He was sure there was one person who refused to croak, and surely Ciro was somewhere to be found, and Moran must have toiled in some room.

He knocked on an open door, and inside sat a very familiar face from a nostalgic past belonging to a boy who had grown.

Miss Clarisse wore her age with stoic pride. She had also moved to teach at the academy before the boys themselves were of ripe age. Her wrinkles were more pronounced, heavy bags showed under her eyes, and her spectacles rested on the bridge of a thin, yet pronounced nose.

"What is it? My class is over, and no you may not try to retake the test." As callous and stern as ever, Miss Clarisse didn't even veer her head to the door, simply packed away her folders and books as she finished up for the day.

"I think I am a couple of years too late anyway on that retest."

That was when she turned, looking at a bearded and rugged-looking man leaning against her door.

The teacher squinted, fixing her spectacles as she came face-to-face with Simantiar, trying to discern any features which might help her solve the mystery. Her gaze was riddled with confusion as she tried to draw upon a folder of truly hundreds of students which came and went in her lifetime.

"You are going to have to be more specific than that, most of my students are no good," she said, a surprising tease to her comment rather than distaste as Simantiar was so often used to.

"It is good to see you are still terrorising the students, Miss Clarisse."

A sudden spark of recognition came to her widening eyes.

"Simantiar?" she asked, taken aback to a long-forgotten time which floats upon the surface of one's thoughts like tattered ships lost in ocean fog.

"It is so good to see you, child!"

Simantiar almost stepped away from the teacher's embrace, still remembering how terrifying she was and a stubborn fear ingrained to his past self made him tense in response.

Simantiar hesitated for a second, startled before returning the embrace. Truth be told, Miss Clarisse cared, and she cared a lot, would even protect the children with her own life if it came down to it.

Miss Clarisse took Simantiar's head with her hands and rose to her toes, kissing him on either cheek.

"My, how you've grown!"

"That usually happens with time."

Miss Clarisse smacked him across the head.

"Yet I see your troubling wit hasn't abandoned you," she said, back to her austere self.

"Nor your backhand." Simantiar stroked the point of impact.

She laughed, truly overjoyed to see how much he had grown. The creases and furrows of her face suddenly vanished in the faint lines as never-before-seen wrinkles of laughter formed at her lips and eyes.

Miss Clarisse invited him inside, offering a drink and more.

"And how is Usellyes?" Simantiar finally asked. He tried to keep it casual, but there was a tenseness to the faculty, a worrisome aura which Simantiar took note of since Emilie's and Zaros's words.

His old teacher suddenly became very quiet, a sullen look to her gaze. "Simantiar, I think you should know that this is my final year—I am retiring in a month."

"How come?"

"Usellyes was always a bright boy, and my most promising student. So much potential in him, I always knew that. But it seemed he became more potential than person. Ever since he took the seat of headmaster, Usellyes has had…plans; 'great things,' he says. I can't help but worry that the boy has gained too much confidence for his own good, making questionable choices with little concern."

"What do you mean?"

Miss Clarisse seemed to hesitate for a moment before deciding to confide in Simantiar. "He wants to harness the magic of the world, bend it, and concentrate it to a focal point. He hopes the amount of arcane power would allow him to perform miracles that could further humanitarian goals."

"But, that kind of power…"

"Aye. The boy means well. I can see it in his heart, and the hearts of those he's captured. But there are risks that are associated with what he has planned, unpredictable things that come from trying to force nature into a way it wasn't meant to be. I think he knew that once. Used to recite the theories of old, but now I wonder if he spoke those words without knowing what they truly meant. Perhaps they were just sounds to him." Miss Clarisse seemed to contemplate it, thinking back to a simpler time when it was just about scolding children in a classroom.

"Usellyes is upstairs in the grandmaster's study," Miss Clarisse stated before packing up. Her mood suddenly seemed so distant. "Perhaps you can talk some sense into him." She didn't sound hopeful.

As Simantiar walked up the spiralling stairs to the grandmaster's study, located at the top of one of the minarets, he wondered what he would say to Usellyes. Was it a bad idea? Was there any reason to question what he was trying to do? Perhaps it was just silly worrying on their part, but all of it seemed rash.

To drain the mantle of magic from the world and stuff the blanket down a well—who could tell what would happen from having that much concentrated magic in one location? There were some working thought experiments regarding the concept, propagating words such as *leakage* or *bottlenecks*.

What would happen to the balance of the world? Would it fall apart? Would creatures of all kinds starve? There was still too much that was unknown about the enigmatic force known as magic.

Simantiar reached the top, where animated armour stood to the sides as sentinels.

"The Archmage and Grandmaster Usellyes Von Avernan is expecting no visitors at this time," spoke one of the sentinel's voices, a metallic and static tone to it.

"I am sure he will be willing to see me."

"The Archmage and Grandmaster Usellyes—" the sentinel continued to repeat itself.

The recording cut off midsentence, as Simantiar snapped his fingers with a sigh, the armour rattling to the ground as it was robbed of its magic.

As Simantiar swung the mighty double doors open, he was greeted by an opulent and richly fashioned square-walled study with not a speck of disorganisation present. Simantiar recalled the chaos of Mylor's old work room with its own personality, yet the study before him held no such charm, just meticulous organisation as nothing seemed remotely out of place.

The end of the room had a bracketed window swung open, and a raven perched beside it on a horizontal cut of wood that Simantiar wouldn't have given a second thought to if it weren't for the misty black sheen which radiated from it and the third vertical eye upon its forehead that betrayed it as a familiar. Just below the window was a richly fashioned rosewood table stacked with organised pens, paper, and more books.

Scribbling away with calm focus was a familiar face grown wise and handsome. Usellyes's dark shoulder-length hair came down in luscious locks. His headmaster robe was a blue deeper than any that Simantiar remembered that it was almost black. His features remained as sharp as ever with dainty fingers made to hold quill toiling diligently. There certainly was an austere humbleness to the poise expected of Usellyes's spirit.

Without turning away from the table, Simantiar's old friend spoke, "If you are planning to assassinate me, let's get this over with."

"What is with the lot of you and not looking up at your potential guests? It's rude, you know, even if I were an assassin."

At that, Usellyes looked up, recognition in his eyes almost immediate.

"Simantiar?" A statement that questioned Simantiar's appearance, not his identity. "My god! Where have you been, old friend? I have missed you!" What a smile Usellyes sported, a smile like that of an innocent child seeing his best friend again after a long week, no sign of work or tribulations to his domineer as he rose to his feet and came to embrace Simantiar in a hug that lifted him from the floor.

"Got lost on the way here." Simantiar wheezed through squeezed lungs, his face turning red.

Usellyes released Simantiar and replied, "Well, a good thing you finally made it! Was getting worried. Twenty years! Was about to send a search party to find you."

Simantiar chuckled. "Aye, it is good to see you again."

Simantiar and Usellyes spoke the entire night away, servants bringing meals and drinks for them, the two even getting drunk and having laughs of their own. Simantiar shared tales of his travels.

"What a marvellous creature this Cernunnos sounds to be!"

"Yes, he is a great teacher, and an even greater friend." Simantiar's speech was slight slurred.

"I would have loved to meet him. I heard of the treaty you formed and the infrastructure you built."

Simantiar found it odd how even after so much drinking Usellyes managed to be so articulate and dignified.

"Yeah, well. Sorr', Cernunnos doss'n rearly like other humans."

"Toast to that!"

They laughed.

As the alcohol came to get the better of them, the night was livened by pranks played on the staff of the castle.

It started off harmlessly, having an animated broom clean the dust from the floor, only to conjure a gust of wind to have it start all over.

Of course it did not really bother the broom, but the act itself was hilarious to the inebriated two.

Eventually, they moved up the ladder, having faculty float in their beds and rise to the ceiling, to awake the next morning and blame the students for their tricks.

Or turning a whole room upside down as the early rising servants went to prepare themselves for the day, only to find their classrooms flipped.

Of course, no one even considered accusing the headmaster, for he wore the stern look that a headmaster should, and oh so well did he play the role of the disappointed teacher that no one dared even consider him to be so devious.

Come morning, Simantiar went about the academy while Usellyes buried himself in work. "After hours, I would like to show you something." An air of excitement surrounded Usellyes as he said those words, like a child looking forward to showing their parents what they made in hopes of encouragement and appreciation.

Of course, Simantiar had a good idea of what it was that Usellyes intended to show him, but still he smiled, feigning ignorance. He appreciated the time, walking through the long winding halls with the rare sign of life striding through to get to some place or another. When the students retreated to their classrooms, the academy's towering vaulted halls and looming pillars seemed so obsolete, echoing Simantiar's footsteps as if trying to fill the grand hall with anything else other than the absence of students.

Most of his exploration involved old halls: the laboratory for potion mixing and alchemy had expanded, with new passages and better equipment since his years of research; the large extracurricular hall which involved magic-heavy games or arcane fencing; the zoological centre which featured the most peculiar and bizarre of mystical creatures, all the way from your typical tamed griffin to a caged imp, pulled from its crevice in the world's underbelly for them to study or the odd little pixie or changeling, a small family of rabbits with antenna and large azure eyes.

Another shop for woodworking as well as to find the perfect material with the magical properties needed to create a wand or magical staff, always used for those who wanted a more efficient method to channel their arcane might.

Simantiar finally permitted himself into the library, not so much to read great volumes of things, but to find books that may shed some light on what he had discovered from his years of travelling.

How little there was to read; over the years, Simantiar believed it a shame that the heights of magical education came down to being locked in a classroom and learning of things that they never got to experience or see for themselves, how it was only a game of pretend to grasp the true stretch of the outside world. He remembered what Miss Clarisse had said just the night before about Usellyes never truly understanding the breadth of the words he spoke.

Simantiar did find books on the fey and sylvan creatures of nature which incorrectly professed their powers and abilities as another form of sorcery. It wasn't wrong necessarily, but the lack of explanation made it seem as if the arcane magic taught at the academy was the same as the gentle nudging of guiding nature's hand, and that was not the case at all. Simantiar had found his soul in the magic of Tiria, and he experienced a sense of transcendental love at submitting himself to that power: it felt like the only thing he had earned and not been handed.

Along with that, Simantiar found little to no mention of magic from the eastern lands, their equation of balance, using the gentle equilibrium of the world to shift everything they wanted into fields of positive or negative energy—to create or destroy.

Simantiar rubbed the bridge of his nose, returning the third book he'd picked up.

Simantiar stared out the window and suddenly noticed a little too late how dark the sky had gotten. He had no way to tell the time and it was of little importance on his pilgrimage.

Hurrying back to Usellyes's study, he did not turn to dust or travel back in time or teleport—he simply merged with the walls of the castle and traversed as one with the masonry—in a matter of a single second he emerged from the top of the tower's staircase and stood in front of Usellyes's study. The wizard fixed his hair and pulled on his attire, a more fitting set of clothes given to the alumni of the academy that displayed opulent sashes of gold mixed with blue and purple and green as Simantiar opened the doors to the headmaster's study.

Usellyes scribbled away at his desk.

"Hope I am not intruding," Simantiar said.

Usellyes looked up, startled. "Oh my, is it that time already?"

Simantiar just smiled, not admitting that he too lost track of time.

Usellyes rubbed his eyes with the back of his hands, then stretched and blinked out his strained eyes.

"Good time to take a break, anyway." Usellyes rose, closing the study doors behind him and heading down the stairs.

The path that Usellyes guided them through led down to the depths of the academy which burrowed through stone and winding paths; the chambers were off-limits to students and Simantiar never knew they even existed.

It was built like a maze, and imbued with magic of confusion. Turning left meant that Simantiar faced right, staring at a path which originally wasn't even there, walking into a pit meant suddenly walking up against a wall with gravity working against you.

Disoriented and frazzled, Simantiar simply followed Usellyes until finally they came upon metal double doors that towered as if made for giants. One by one they opened as soon as Usellyes stepped forward.

Finally, Usellyes and Simantiar came upon the final door which swung wide open to reveal a grand hall of mages running to and from stations, lively in their exchanges and pace.

"What is this?" Simantiar asked, taking in the vast construction before him. Arcanum runes were carved into the walls and pillars that held the place aloft. The opening before them was a long walkway which led to a well with three steps leading to its brim. The path was filled with runes which circled the well itself, a clear crystal gem the size of a boulder held atop of it using forged gold clasps which held it in place.

"The future, my friend." As Usellyes was about to explain, another voice interrupted them.

"Well, isn't that a familiar face?" Moran strode to the two. He had managed to lose some of his paunch belly, but that hefty affable look to him still positively gleamed with that placid smile.

Grease covered his hands and face, and his sleeves were rolled up. Simantiar remembered Moran used to be gifted when it came to creating autonomous machinations and engineering bold artifacts. Usellyes had shared of how Moran had spent several years abroad at Usellyes's behest when he had no clue where to go since graduation. Moran was reluctantly taken as an understudy by the great craftsmen to the north.

"Come, I want to show you my plans."

Moran returned to his work as Usellyes took Simantiar aside to show the blueprints and scrolls of magic fused with ancient texts.

"Usellyes, what is all this?"

Usellyes turned to Simantiar, a playful and excited smile. "It's 'you.'"

"Me?"

"In some shape or form," Usellyes amended as he pulled away from the work table to wave at the well. "We plan to gather the magical arcana from the world into one focal point, creating a well.

"Let's see how much you remember from our alchemy classes with Miss Clarisse. Why does water change shape, but rock is hard to break?"

"Because of the chemical bonds, of course. Water has weaker bonds which makes it so easy to separate."

"Yes!" Usellyes seemed excited that Simantiar answered so perfectly, if only to further explain what he was doing; Simantiar became increasingly concerned with the truth of the moment.

"So, by concentrating all that magic into one focal point, we force the bonds to react to one another and—"

"Become dense…" Simantiar surmised. "You want to create a pool of concentrated magic to multiply whatever spell it is you are doing." Suddenly, as most of the words that were spoken were addressed to himself rather than to Usellyes, the truth of it all was coming together.

"Usellyes…have you considered the implications of what you are trying to achieve here?" Simantiar asked, and on cue, Usellyes rolled his eyes.

"Not you too—if anyone, I would have thought you'd understand. You with your limitless potential, imagine what could be done here! Children wouldn't need to suffer, just as I had. Nobody would need to starve, or suffer diseases, or go through war, or even be sad. This is *the* well of wishes. A simple coin toss, and all that one could hope for—nay, no longer hope, hope will become obsolete because things will just *be."*

"That is not the way of the universe—there is balance to things, Usellyes." Their conversation was now becoming elated, their voices rising as Simantiar dreaded the passion and confidence which with Usellyes addressed the project—this would only end in a fight.

"Bah! To hell with precious 'balance.' We can control it, cheat the scale and make it heavier, and maintain balance through standards. We have the power to solve all the problems of the world and yet we sit here, in our mighty towers, and strive for enlightenment while the rest of the world suffers. We go, 'Ah! Eureka!' and pretend to be higher beings while the rest of the world suffers for it. What's the point of all this enlightened knowledge if we can't use it to do good?"

Simantiar did not respond, at least not in words. He stood there seething, heavy and laborious breaths.

He extended an arm as from the shadows of his sleeve pounced a black matted adder, one of the most venomous creatures to slither the sands.

Usellyes leapt back, an expression of primal terror on his face.

The adder's fangs never did reach Usellyes as Simantiar simply grabbed the serpent by its head and slammed it to the work table, conjuring a hatchet to part the snake's head; then both hatchet and limp adder turned to dust in the wind.

"There is a cycle to things, equilibrium. A delicate balance of give and take which puts all things in their place, for if one turns tyrant, nature will at least eventually turn them into dust so that we may move forward."

Usellyes became enraged, the perfectly trimmed beard with a silver soul patch did little to hide the tremors of fury that bubbled to the surface. "Don't dare lecture me on Ouroboros. I learnt of the wisest philosophers and scholars while you flirted away with your loves, never putting in an ounce of effort. Born with the talent, the looks—a life of love. How could you ever begin to understand what children like me went through?"

Simantiar suddenly went quiet, his fear realised. He always knew that Usellyes would bring that up in conversation, and he was right to do so. Perhaps Simantiar was wrong, but even if he wasn't, and the world would split apart, what right did he have to tell his old friend, who suffered so, not to at least try, that his suffering gave his madness credence?

Usellyes, in all his rage, spat in his friend's face. The same friend who was like a brother to him ever since they were just children, the same friend who had been by his side and urged him on to make friends, to realise how he brought people together, how they would come to find purpose in his passion and drive—the same friend who drank and reminisced just the night before until the sun rose to burn the fantasy away.

"You have all that power at your fingertips. I know that you won that duel between us out at the ring when we were children. I know all too well what might you must have at your fingertips to simply forfeit the Magus Tha. I could see it in your eyes." Usellyes's words turned even more venomous than the conjured adder. "I saw with what disgusting pity you looked at me, like you were sorry." Usellyes went up to Simantiar's face, his breath was hot with rage upon Simantiar's sullen face as spittle struck.

"You have all this power." Usellyes chuckled. "Yet, you do nothing with it, simply travel from world to world without a care, without a sense of duty, without a sense of responsibility to help those that truly need it.

"Well, fine. I never asked you to; born with this power and not even a clue in the world of what to do with it except merrily travel. Fine, I will get that well of magic, I will use it since you refuse to, and I will give all those who wish it the end of suffering, the greatest desire of their hearts without anyone needing to beg or fear."

Usellyes stood there, huffing and puffing the last of his rage. The grand hall of people all stood silently, all entranced by what had just taken place and none daring to say a word.

"Get out." They were Usellyes's final words to Simantiar. A final, cold command, meant only for his ears.

Chapter 42

George awoke to see Simantiar standing over the ledge overlooking the uncharted land forest—there was still a soft, telling pillar of smoke which rose from the abandoned settlement.

Simantiar looked like an art piece, so still and effigy-like with his knotted roots and other forestry. His shoulders pauldroned and still, his coiled back seemed heavy and tense, and his calves of wood taut as if he were ready to spring forth.

Simantiar had grown more quiet and brooding to George's memory, sometimes seeming to be still lost in whatever realm he had fashioned within his mind's eye.

The wizard would only ever share bits and pieces, never enough to truly reflect on what kind of thoughts he ruminated.

George rose from bed and consumed a light breakfast of stale bread with bitter butter, the last remaining jerky, and some morsels of dried nuts.

Simantiar wasn't the only one who was quiet, though he alone stood looking over the edge as the light leaves upon his form rustled from the passing wind which whistled through gaps in his form.

Kendrith too seemed lost in thought, staring out occasionally or staring upon a loose piece of bread in his hand as melted butter dripped to the stone floor.

His sword barely ever left his side and his eyes seemed just as distant as Simantiar's nightly travels.

After breakfast was had, George hesitantly joined in on the search for an entrance—probing walls and feeling paths, his feet overturning rocks as the group split into twos while Simantiar explored alone for a side entrance or movable wall.

Perhaps the entrance was magical? But even then Simantiar could find nothing along the path that would assume there was an entrance.

As the sun began to reach its zenith, a horrible and looming truth settled like a heavy stone at the bottom of a lake in George's heart: the vault didn't exist.

But the map, and the vision granted by Timmy…there was so much effort put into it all. It had to exist, didn't it?

George felt the stone scrape and scratch against his fingers, blisters would surely form as he rummaged harder and more desperate. He had gotten so far. The vault had to exist.

Soon enough, at the rise of noon, the band gathered together and Pecky nestled himself away from the sullen lot into a nest he had built within Simantiar's chest.

"I'm sorry I wasted your time," George said.

"No, George. You didn't waste our time. This…this entire experience has been…" Kristen's attempt at placating George fell flat as she put a hand to his shoulder. He didn't move, but he also didn't lean in.

There was a coldness to the moment.

"Kendrith, say something," Kristen said turning to him.

"What's there to say? There is no vault. We all already knew that."

"Kendrith!" Kristen admonished.

"No, he's right," George said, and his chest felt hollow. How horrid it was to grow up, for those who dared to hope only faced disappointment.

"It is what it is, George. You travelled the length like planned. There aren't many who can say the same. I know not the reason for your travel, but find solace in the travel made and failed, rather than in the venture never dared," said Logan.

The words were poor comfort in the face of it all. George thought he had steeled his heart and walked the path knowing full well it was all a fairy tale, though it seemed they all dared to dream and were left with nothing.

"Get some rest. We will pack and leave come daylight. Take a bath while you are here."

Kristen rose with her irritation plain to see as she pulled Kendrith to the side and harsh whispers battered him.

George looked to where Kendrith had sat and noticed the sword of Vrania abandoned.

The sun was uncharacteristically bright and the full white clouds passed over a blue sky. It irked George that the world seemed so merry despite his sobering circumstances.

Birds could be heard chirping in the distance and the wind's howl never rested.

Hesitantly, George reached into his sack and withdrew his book. The leather surface seemed more faded than he remembered, the edges tattered and flaky, and the bindings were coming loose.

Whatever shine it once carried in his mind now seemed tattered and dull.

Regardless, George opened its pages in search of any bit of hope still left to offer.

He scanned the poem over and over, and eyed the image of the doors as if in search of some secret.

"Under the dipping mountains." It didn't make sense, how could mountains dip?

"Over the rising lake." His lips moved by themselves.

The boy stretched stiff limbs and groaned at the fleeting satisfaction as he collapsed recumbent and the book fell over his head.

"Under the dipping mountains," he repeated to himself in a soft murmur. Something about the phrasing wouldn't let him be. "Dipping…"

He strained his neck to peer at the discarded book, but instead found Pecky a mere breath's length away.

George smiled, the shadowed company of the bird a constant soft presence which brought with it little moments of joy.

The bird with its dark, matted feathers rotated its head and chirped, hopping even further.

"You know, Pecky, this is a good angle for you," George joked. "You look quite different upside down."

George's eyes widened in an instant as his body jumped up with a start.

His smile went from ear to ear, his heart beat once more with life as the heavy stone faded and he felt like he could breathe again.

"What is it?" Kristen asked.

"I found it!" George declared.

The group turned at the sound and converged on George's location.

"The entrance?" Kendrith asked sceptically.

George nodded, before running forward towards the lake.

He skitted to a stop as loose pebbles rolled down into the water.

Turning around, George stared up at the sun and shielded his eyes, yet his smile would not relent.

Turning back to the pool, George pointed.

"What do you mean? It's just the lake," Kristen said.

George shook his head. "Look again, look at the reflection."

The band changed position, moving back and forth until realisation seemed to dawn on them also.

"The dipping mountains," Kendrith said.

"Over the rising lake," added Simantiar.

Life returned to George's beating heart—he was right to hope.

Simantiar had scouted ahead to confirm a submerged hole leading into the mountain.

All their equipment was packed up, and Pecky landed on Simantiar's shoulder as the wizard parted the water, creating a path for them to walk into.

As the band descended inside, the water wrapped itself around them creating a spherical ball.

George looked about in awe as they drifted beneath the water in their bubble. The light above the surface shimmered with shifting rays of sunlight, creating a glittering and mesmerising surface.

Pecky chirped nervously, crawling deeper into a shelter of twigs and leaves which protruded from Simantiar's shoulder.

The mountain cavern finally showed itself as Simantiar guided the bubble through a long, tunnelled path. Eventually, they rose back up and exited the other side. Rather than undo the bubble on the surface, Simantiar lifted their cocoon up from the water as it drifted across to dry land.

The cavern which they now traversed stood wide, with no light to mark their passing, but Simantiar created globules of conjured illumination to float around them.

"I admit, though I question your intentions, fiend, you have proven yourself to be quite resourceful," Logan said, taking the rear of the group as Simantiar took the front.

"I am glad my skills are proving to be so useful. Please, perhaps I can rub your feet next? Or maybe, you would like it if I were to rub you—"

"Did you hear that?" Kendrith suddenly said.

The winding tunnel seemed still, unmoving, vast in its size that even a whole caravan could fit through. Yet, that very passage seemed undisturbed for years, abandoned, and lost to the annals of time.

Yet, when straining their ears, a howl swept through the passage, a groan as if coming from the mountain itself, aching old bones stretching themselves.

And then quiet. The caverns continued to slumber, the light chasing the darkness away to illuminate the path in front of them.

"Probably just the wind," said Kristen, and perhaps they all just hoped that was the case.

How hollow those winding tunnels seemed, lost veins of a mountain now feeling the trudge of life wandering through them once more. Derelict pathways that fell apart with each step forward.

Simantiar's light seemed almost to act autonomously, splitting between each other, one going on ahead to a curve to light the path and scout while others preemptively sought out dark corners where threats lay. But no matter what, the three globules orbited the band of travellers protectively.

The howls still swept through the tunnels, frightening things that echoed like ghosts of the past, peeling away at the bravery of the group.

"Are you sure it's just the wind?" George asked.

No one answered.

The group broke through the tunnel's end, now giving way to intricate walkways and bridges, interlinked and locked across a wide yawning chasm which gave way to the depths below. It was only darkness, the fall showing a sea of black waiting to devour unfortunate souls.

"Whoa," the words slipped through Kristen's lips, her sense of awe evident as the words echoed far and wide, carrying through the slanted bridges of the chasm and filling the stifling quiet.

The light which swarmed around them seemed tiny, their island unimportant within the ocean of darkness.

"This is incredible," Logan began, looking all around at the architecture. "What a find! I need to make sketches to bring back to the guild."

The chasm spanned a hundred meters across—platforms made of stone attempted to sew the mountain's flesh together.

How precariously they loomed, seeming to be on the precipice of collapsing one by one for what had been millennia though still they held strong and probably would for another age.

Logan riffled through his belonging, presenting a notebook and piece of granite as he began sketching what he could from the little light that was available to him.

"Stay close. This place is old. We don't know how structurally sound it is," Logan said in between gasps of astonishment.

Simantiar led the way, the lights now all centred around them turning in opposite directions.

The steps they took up those slanted platforms held their weight, strong despite their falling out of use.

Simantiar suddenly stopped in his tracks.

"What is it? Do you see something?" Kendrith asked, hand already at the pommel of his sword, looking around for anything that might be a threat.

George followed his gaze, his own eventually trailing up towards the never-ending rising chasm walls.

"I know this place," Simantiar murmured to himself, remembering, words spoken as a soft thing, but the quiet of that chasm demanded it be heard.

"What do you mean?" George asked.

Simantiar knelt down onto his knee of bark, running his fingers of vines and roots over the filigree patterns shrouded by the dust of time upon the platform. The patterns were clear, even though faded and rent of their origins, it was undeniable to him.

"What is this place?" now asked Kendrith.

"Home," Simantiar provided.

"What do you mean?" asked Kristen.

"It's Eindeheid: my academy."

Simantiar remained quiet as they continued to climb the rickety platforms which served as bridges, ledges on the sides of the chasms allowing a path to new areas. How distant it all seemed as they climbed, watching pebbles fall to be swallowed by the shadows below. What things might they find in that darkness?

Simantiar didn't explain much about what he meant, but he recognised the symbols and figures on the stone bridges. He recalled the artistic shaping of the academy, the magical drawings, the faces of progress and arcana, with some lifting their hands with the sun in their palms, regal robes worn by bearded men who held the gaze of destiny in their eyes.

"Simantiar." Kristen spoke his name with caution, there was something that happened, something that stilled Simantiar's voice as if dragging him down to the chasmic depths and swearing him to secrecy as all things from its time were.

The wizard stopped in his tracks, turning back, the globules of light made the arcana of his eyes gleam with sullen, silent reminiscence.

"You know something, don't you? If this was once your academy, what happened to it? This path we walk...it will take us to the golden vault? What even is that place?"

Simantiar finally turned around fully. "I don't know."

"You must know something," Kendrith added.

"Maybe." The word was broken, a silent thing as if Simantiar dreaded to wake up the past with his voice.

"I believe that lake, the mountains, they were all part of the academy...the world has changed so much." His words distant and unsure.

"I don't know how...those mountains, they rose so high. They challenged the clouds just as the hubris of my teachers challenged the gods. We would peer down the edge of the academy to the clouds which drifted by us as if it were our domain...but now"—he looked back up. "It's all gone, the mountain range brought down to a simple ridge and the academy blown to ashes, just a pool of water remains trying to reflect the ghost of the past so we may see into the nothingness we brought." How low the ancient wizard sounded as his shoulders of leaves sagged.

This was not the man the band knew; a man lost in contemplation, no humour or mirth to his voice, just sadness.

"Woe are we who once stood atop the clouds," he said absent-mindedly, the words spoken out into the darkness as if they could carry past to the spirits of friends and teachers who once lived above the chasm.

They all remained silent atop the platform, not even the howling wind to be heard.

"I know not who you are," Logan began, "nor can I say that I trust you. But I know the weight that rests heavy upon your soul and know that you are not alone." Logan exchanged a knowing glance of his own with Kendrith. "You wish you'd done things differently, that you were there for whatever had happened—believe that we all share in your pain. But perhaps you can tell us what you know about this place? For the past is done, but the future still lives." Logan rested one of his large bear-sized paws on George's shoulder, the boy slightly kipping from the weight of it. "George still lives and we need to be prepared for what awaits us. Do you know what this vault contains?"

Simantiar didn't respond immediately. "No."

"Is it even real?" Kendrith asked.

"I don't know."

Silence again. George looked left and right, staring at the ascending tilted platforms of stone and the encumbering darkness that their light couldn't reach.

"But I can find out…" His words were spoken with a sense of inevitable dread. "But I will need to meditate, return to my memories, and find out the truth."

The others nodded.

George shifted where he stood, a pebble knocked off from the edge of the platform and plummeted into the abyss. "Look, this is great and all, but could we *please* get off this platform first?" he pleaded.

As the band continued on their path, finding the ledges along the way too narrow for any meditation and the platforms too steep and inviting of death, they eventually came across another small cave along another ledge.

"In here," George called, as Simantiar came forward, the light of his globules stretching in to make sure nothing hid within the darkness.

The band settled inside, setting up camp as Simantiar went to meditate in a corner.

The air was thick and heavy, no doubt Simantiar knew that breathing must have not been easy for the others as a stale air filled the valley of shadow.

The group produced what little firewood they had left, stacking it together and making Logan's flint obsolete as a pointed finger from Simantiar lit the fire instantly.

"If something happens, just wake me."

The group nodded, the globules of light now shrinking, turning into simple motes that drifted up for a second like sparks before fading into nothing.

Cross-legged, the roots of Simantiar's body dug into the mountain, breaking loose gravel and piercing rough rock to connect with it all, taking him back in time to a past where his home was radiant and encompassed all of what could be and all that was accomplished. He tasted the cleansed fresh air of the hallways, felt the shine of polished white marble, and heard the chatter of classmates more acutely than ever before.

The mountain spoke to him, embraced him, and took him in, as for the first time since meeting George, he felt like he had found a place he could call familiar.

The roots dug deep, penetrating the carcass of a world lost and finding the spirit which would guide him.

He was home.

Chapter 43

Simantiar returned to the depths of his soul—and such depths they were. How easily he entered that trance, easier than ever before; the world of ragged chasms and precarious stone bridges was left behind.

Yet Simantiar did not tread through his memories—however he was scared.

That one emotion crept to the forefront as the pieces of his past drifted past the murky depths to float on the surface of his pool.

Even if Simantiar fought with his very being, he could not ignore the inevitable truth piecing itself together, a truth he was rightfully afraid of, rightfully tried to drown.

In the recesses of his mind where a twilight dwelt, Simantiar lay upon the water's surface. The sun was setting over the horizon and the ocean coloured a faded black pool waiting to submerge him in his past for evermore.

Simantiar lay there, not human as his past left, but rather the body he had donned during his time in the future, one of bark and leaves and vines and roots. A body to anchor him to the realms as he remained reluctant to return to the depths of those dreams out of fear of what he may find. *Dreams*. What a word, one that connived and robbed and betrayed— seductive in its allure. A dream that started comforting and blessed could quickly transform vile and nightmarish.

And now, on the endless waters which spanned the horizon all around, Simantiar continued to drift, his arms splayed open, adrift on the water, its surface rippling. Hesitating, he looked upon the sky of his mind and saw the merged colours of a setting sun's orange bleeding into the tranquil dark of a night sky.

The wizard waved his hands and stars appeared to quench his need to look upon the twinkling sight, to ask it for guidance as he was stuck under the mountain's belly in the real world.

Finally, Simantiar submitted himself, his hesitation droning on as the wizard closed his eyes and began to sink—sinking slowly into the water which held him, devouring him as slowly as quicksand might until it finally swallowed him whole, only bubbles escaping to the surface, taking him below the depths and into the darkness below where his memories awaited him.

What turmoil swept through Simantiar as he left the underbelly of the academy, the construction place where old friends and familiar faces had built a place which to them carried hope. Their brows laden with sweat and grease and fatigue—the true signs of labour, but equally so, they smiled at one another, given strength by their camaraderie.

What things roiled within him, being kicked out by a man who was not only his best friend since his fingers barely understood the power they wielded, but also a brother, another part of him that he did not know how to live without.

The labyrinthine dive of the place still proved marvellous—the way the walls and paths constricted and changed, with infinitely looped stairwells and walls closing in while others opened like a living vessel, like a throat constricting to control the passage of unwanted debris.

Yet in a daze—as Simantiar's mind went a million miles away, lost in conflicted doubt and thought, drowned in guilty sorrow—he was not able to appreciate the construction of the place, only drag his feet along the stone floor, up the dividing paths and back out of the academy.

There were few people in the hallways now, all either gone for extra work, or extracurricular activities or faculty running to and from classrooms.

And so, with a bowed head and heavy heart, Simantiar left the academy.

Simantiar stood at the precipice of the academy's platform, past the stage of Magus Tha and staring off towards the world. The wind tugged at his loose robes, played with his beard, and rode his wavy hair.

He looked down, clouds strafing by over forest lands, and beyond that in the distance somewhere on a mountain ridge was the home in which he grew up.

What world awaited them when the well was finished and the hopefuls completed their task. Would a dream without conflict come to fruition? Or a calamity based on paradox?

Simantiar knew which of the two was the future that awaited them, but still he considered—nay, hoped to be wrong—that a world of dreams was possible, if only to quench the pain in his heart that tried to tell him of what may come.

And so, just as he wasn't wanted, Simantiar turned to dust in the air and vanished without a trace.

Simantiar's travels took him far, back across the paths to old teachers.

Cernunnos was the first on his path.

"I don't know what to do," Simantiar said. For the first time in his life, he was truly lost. All those years of travel and enlightenment now seemed like simple fancies when it came to a situation like his. For the first time, Simantiar felt what it was like to be truly helpless, to find that magic could not solve his problems. If only he had taken his mother's words more seriously.

Cernunnos nodded, the bark and branches of his body groaning at the movement. "If what you say is true, your friend is truly delving into things he doesn't understand." Even the old guardian of the forest sounded concerned, even if it was all hidden behind the guise of wisdom.

"Tell me, Cernunnos, what would you do in my stead?"

The ancient force shook his head. "That is not for me to decide. Usellyes is your friend and this is your choice. Though you and I both know that if it comes to it, you may have to do that which you most fear."

"But how?" Simantiar hung his head, gripping his scalp as if to shake the answer to the surface. "To fight my best friend? The one who has been like a brother to me? How could I ever do such a thing alone?" Simantiar looked up at his mentor, tears in his eyes, wishing for someone, anyone, to rob him of his choice.

Cernunnos trudged closer to Simantiar, towering over the boy that sat on the rock and cried helplessly, hands shaking, lost.

Cernunnos lowered himself, his front equine legs folding as the centaur-like creature that he was, his humanoid half leaning forward. The creature of bark and vines and root took Simantiar's head and pulled it in, their foreheads, one of flesh and one wood, touching with a grunt from Cernunnos.

Simantiar could hear the constant writhing of forestry inside Cernunnos's body.

"Whoever said that you would be alone in this? I am the guardian of the forest, it is my duty to protect it even from your friend. But you are also my friend, and believe me, Simantiar, I will fight and stand alongside you when the day comes, for this is a burden not solely your own."

Simantiar crossed the world once more. A sense of purpose instilled in him for what may come, a purpose that drowned the sorrow of lost friends. He remembered that pledge given to him by Cernunnos, a promise to protect the forest and nature at all costs, even if it meant facing Usellyes alone. And that sent a chill through Simantiar, the thought of a mentor and friend fighting to the death. But that was irrelevant, for the truth of the matter was that no matter how much Simantiar detested the idea, he would face Usellyes regardless of what may come.

Though, when Simantiar would sit and rest, or awake from slumber, he would find his sorrows returned. A part of him was split—a duty bound conscience ready to do what needed to be done and a regretful spirit, dreading what was to come.

Over desert lands to the east with waves of flowing sand, Simantiar returned to opulent, domed palaces with powerful and reverent kings who flashed their avarice proudly. Handwoven carpets filled the walkways, and albino tigers were kept as pets that yawned beside their paunch-bellied owners and their turban crowns.

Other lands where the rulers sat on thrones atop of pyramids, awaiting their visitors.

Others lived in kingdoms with simple sashes for clothes as they walked cobblestoned floors in sandals, with statues of legends filling the promenade as if to state that all who visit must look upon their past and acknowledge their history.

Each channel crossed, every part of a new world visited, Simantiar revered their cultures, but more than that, he saw how all their perspectives on the world differed, all their theories on magic contradicted each other—yet they all held truth.

Old mentors welcomed Simantiar with open arms, listened to his plight, and, with faces of stoic stone, gave their verdicts. For they were scholars, messiahs of magic meant to bridge the living world with the fringes of the outer. They took strands of the loose fabric which swayed in the ethereal winds to provide wisdom.

They listened to Simantiar's story, and each gave their comment, all of them similar—that Simantiar needed to stop it. Yet the way the answers were given, monochrome and vapid, as if it was just something theoretical brought to them, showed how the mages distanced themselves.

And with each one reaffirming what Simantiar already knew, his heart grew heavier and his resolve stronger. One to be the cliffs upon a mountainside at sea and the other to be the storm that darkened the distant waters, coming ever closer to grind upon each other and chip away until there was nothing left but Simantiar's past in tatters.

Simantiar sat there upon the large, spanning river, the last of his pilgrimage done, now realising that every mentor revisited was for every piece of will gathered.

He came to them all to ask permission. Theirs and his own.

He tossed a rock, trying to skip across the surface, but he always managed two at most. No magic to aid him—he was sick of it. Eventually, he just tossed the rock, watching it sink into the depths below as if pieces of himself discarded.

"I've always had a weak throwing arm," Simantiar said out loud, hearing familiar footsteps coming behind him. Those of limp, dragging feet came closer. Yet as always, they were the controlled, disciplined steps of respect, of patience, voicing their approach and as if carrying a promise of wisdom, one could sense the strain with which the feet were dragged.

"Keep throwing enough stones and you may awaken the river from its sleep." The voice that spoke and limp that followed belonged to Ahmaku-ta. A sage to the king and keeper of scrolls.

Simantiar turned to the man, a tall and lithe being, age carried proudly upon his haggard bones. A staff of prized ash wood as his third leg, humble but austere green robes like shrubs of a desert draped his body, and a white beard hung to his midsection. With bags under his eyes and the wrinkles forming granules upon his weary liver-spotted skin, Ahmaku-ta looked down on Simantiar with kindness and love for a student and friend.

"Good—perhaps the river could eat me whole," Simantiar said sullenly, tossing another stone, a part of him humouring the idea of a rising river coming with the head of a snake to devour him.

"It is a weight of burden on your shoulders, my friend, one that no one should carry, but that you do regardless."

Silence for a time, as Ahmaku-ta stood there in solidarity, giving the peace that Simantiar's mind needed, but also the presence which his soul required. A kindred spirit standing, as if to say that he was there to hold Simantiar up.

"I feel so weak," Simantiar finally said. A truth he hesitated to tell anyone, be it his mother, Cernunnos, or even Usellyes, for he knew they all expected him to stand strong and tall. That it was his duty with what power he held at his beck and call.

But Ahmaku-ta's presence knew otherwise—they all knew otherwise—but he was one of the few that braved to break that illusion, not through force, but through patience. Waiting for when Simantiar was ready to confide.

"I am nothing without this magic." Simantiar tossed another stone in the river, as if it proved his point. "All I have to offer is that which was given to me, not that which was earned." A dark memory surfaced, a time when he had envied Usellyes with all his being the diligence and talent that had proved his worth.

"And now, I am supposed to kill my friend? My brother? Couldn't even stop him. I feel useless. Should never have gotten this power—it always should have gone to someone more deserving."

"You are right," Ahmaku-ta said, his voice callous, harsh in its statement.

Simantiar buried his head between his legs and shuddered at the truth of it. It's one thing to believe such things yourself, but another to hear it from those you respect.

"Or not." The austerity gone, the kindness back; Ahmaku-ta chuckled to himself as if it was a joke. "Did you expect some wise words about you being the chosen one? About you being the only one who can stop your friend? Please. I respect you too much to feed you such nonsense."

It was quiet for a time more, just the winds blowing past and an ibis drinking from the river before them.

"But that is irrelevant. What matters is the gift you have been given, the path you have followed, and what you believe in. I do not question the intentions of your friend Usellyes.

"Is he a bad man?" he questions.

"No," Simantiar responded almost instantly.

"Of course not. Perhaps he is misguided...or we are...no one ever knows. But here is what I can say, my dear friend.

"You have this power and you have a task. It matters not if you deserve it or not. What matters is that you choose to do what needs to be done. No legend is ever born one, no king is ever born a king, they rise to the occasion in a moment of truth. No person should bear the weight that you do—and yet you bear it, what matters now is what that means for you."

The words provided by Ahmaku-ta did not quell the toiling doubt in Simantiar's soul. They gave no clear-cut answer as to what must be done, but rather provided a simple truth that removed the barriers and had Simantiar carry his doubts with confidence. It's not about if he can or can't do, if he should or not, if he deserves it or not—but rather what he will do now that he can.

Simantiar considered returning to Eindeheid and settling things for a final time with a heavy heart.

But there was one more place that persisted in his mind, a final person he felt compelled to visit before he left.

Shorta was a disparaged land of humid swamps and screaming crickets.

A river ran through its belly which carried alligators like driftwood.

At the heart of the forest, buried beneath leaning rubber trees and rising thick palms was a hut that filled its surrounding with the wafting scent of bubbling soup and the soft contemplative hum of its inhabitant.

Simantiar knocked on its door.

The humming stopped. Silence for a while. Simantiar was sure that Noima must have certainly been startled at the casualness of the strange knock upon his door as if he were still living within a bustling town.

"Who is it?" Noima asked.

"An old friend!" Simantiar supplied.

The door opened to reveal the incredulous expression plastered on Noima's face. After a second where disbelief turned into utter joy Noima embraced Simantiar.

"Nice to see you too," Simantiar said, trying to ignore the pungent stink of sweat that radiated from Noima's armpits—he finally understood why Zaros was so repulsed.

Noima distanced himself and Simantiar repressed the urge to gag.

Noima must have noticed, for he froze to then smell his own armpits, the colour of his cheeks reddening even further despite the high humid temperatures underneath his ragged patches of ginger facial hair—he looked obviously ashamed.

"Sorry, I don't get many visitors out here and some daily habits suffer because of that."

"Don't worry. I get it," Simantiar chuckled heartily.

Noima had grown into a spectacle-eyed man built like a bent willow switch. His fingers were thin and long, his spectacles magnified the bags under his eyes, and a premature receding hairline ran his scalp.

Noima had been a naturally observant student and only fell out of notice when he didn't share Usellyes drive. But his own humble intellect allowed him a modestly impressive grade in every class, even those that preached combat.

It was rather a shock to everyone when he decided to drop out.

"Please, take a seat."

Simantiar entered the hut and the gamy scent of the roiling pot immediately made his stomach grumble.

"Smells fantastic," Simantiar said.

"Thank you." Noima took a ladle and sipped from the contents, licking his lips to clean up the few drops of darkened meat water which clung to his beard.

Simantiar gave Noima a quick rundown of where he had been the past several years, they shared their encounters with mystical beasts of lesser-known origins, and exchanged detailed notes of where they could encounter some of these celestial creatures.

"A phoenix of water?" Noima asked incredulous. "You must be joking."

Simantiar shook his head. "I saw it with my own eyes. It lives in a vast lake built within the endless caverns of a mountain. It would rise and fly across its dome above and lightly spray drops of its winged body onto its pool. I discovered a single drop could heal any wound."

Noima's eyes widened. "Any wound? But the implications!"

Simantiar shook his head. "It only works at the pool."

Noima's excitement seemed to momentarily still itself, but he seemed no less excited at the prospect of seeing such a mesmerising creature with his own eyes.

"What are you doing here?" Noima finally asked.

Simantiar answered with a question of his own. "When was the last time you saw Usellyes?"

"When I worked for him."

Simantiar frowned. "You were working for him?"

Noima served two bowls of soup with some floating potatoes and bits of frog before taking a seat at an adjacent crate and using a larger crate as a table. There was a cloth pulled over the crates, as Noima regrettably managed to spill food one time which seeped through the cracks and damaged his research.

Noima took a sip from his soup and nodded with his head bowed to the bowl. "Yes. He knew I was quite adept with crystals and asked me to join him for a project." There was a dismissive, yet knowing tone to Noima's remark, perhaps also a hint of hesitation.

Simantiar shared it. "And what did you create for him?" Simantiar tried his best to not sound inquisitive or accusatory, but he must have failed for Noima placed his bowl before him and turned a serious glance to Simantiar.

"A crystal which wound focus and harnessed magic, a conduit if you will."

Simantiar nodded ruefully.

"Considering my candid response, I expect you to act in kind—what is he doing?" Noima asked determinedly.

"Usellyes is trying to build a conduit to amplify magical power. It would allow a great deal of constricted Arcanum to be focused and used as fuel to compensate for the magical drain it requires."

Noima nodded. "I was the one who created the crystal—within its shell lays a centipede frozen in space."

"Omukade," Simantiar said with chilling realisation.

Noima nodded. "He used the symbolic nature of it to absorb the power and concentrate it. The crystal is just an amplifier. After I realised what he was doing, I left. Told Zaros and Emilie." Noima showed his remorse openly. "Ciro and Moran didn't want to hear it."

Simantiar and Noima were quiet for a while, the mouth-watering scent of their bowls left forgotten till they went cold.

"What will you do?" Noima asked.

"Stop Usellyes, of course."

Noima considered his next words. "Can you?"

"I have to."

"Even when you love him so?"

Simantiar's surprise betrayed him as he looked to Noima with an open mouth.

"Come now, it's not a secret. I knew there was some affection between you two. Everyone did. We just all wondered why you never acted on it."

Simantiar looked to the past. Why didn't he? Why didn't Usellyes?

Before an age could come where they would become led by primitive urges, Simantiar surely felt a certain love for Usellyes; and he knew that Usellyes, though quiet, had a love burning just as fiercely.

"Things changed," Simantiar said, though he knew it was a substitute for an answer he didn't truly have. There was love between them, always, but he also couldn't help but notice the growing competitiveness and jealousy in Usellyes…especially after their Magus Tha.

"How did you find out?"

Noima stared on with a look of hurt as he leaned forward and tenderly caressed Simantiar's hand.

"You notice things about the people you love."

Simantiar went hot red and felt his heart skip a single painful cold beat.

He stumbled over his words and struggled to find the right words in his frantic shock.

"I…I didn't know."

Noima shook his head. "You had your eyes on another."

Simantiar suddenly lowered his head, feeling a pang of shame he couldn't quite place.

"Do you still feel that way?" Simantiar asked, the words forced through hesitant lips. He felt his jaw stiffen and his palms go cold with sweat at the notion.

"We were children, Simantiar. That was long ago and I haven't seen you in many years. I have moved on."

Simantiar wasn't sure what came over him, but a burning sense of desperate determination filled him.

"I never got the chance to." Springing up from his crate, he paced over to Noima and placed his lips upon Noima's in a trembling act of compassion.

Simantiar's kiss was fierce. He noticed he was holding on, scared that if he were to let go, he would be denied. A fear that melted away when he noticed Noima relax and return a passionate, wordless kiss.

They shared a bed that night, a bed that they filled with regrets and warring doubt, a moment of love married with their dared vulnerabilities.

When Simantiar left the next morning, it was with a promise that he would return to Noima when his business was dealt with—though Simantiar felt it in his very soul like a dark foreboding secret that he never would return.

And so, Simantiar returned, no longer as a wandering soul finding the pieces he needed to summon his conviction and gain the confidence necessary to do what was right, but rather as a crashing wave, a blazing storm at sea, rushing with the conviction it lacked before.

Nothing would stop Simantiar as he stood at the bottom of the mountain, how it towered over the world like the realm of gods.

Beside Simantiar stood the elk-horned Cernunnos.

Chapter 44

As one, Simantiar conjured the winds, raising his palms up to the sky as the air obeyed, and lifted himself and Cernunnos from the ground. With swiftness they were elevated and brought up through the clouds. The domineering spires of the mountains which rose like pillars loomed challengingly as Simantiar elevated himself to the realm of the gods—no realm was off-limits to him.

As they landed on the platform, the first of the guards showed themselves. No students walked the premise but arcane fighters.

The helmets they wore seemed slim and elegant, filigree almost in nature. The garments draped around them strengthened with arcana to act just as armour would without weighing down their finesse.

One of the guards stepped forward, seemingly surprised at the sudden presence of Simantiar and his companion. "Apologies, but the academy is currently off-limits. Students are asked to vacate the area as the academy will be closed until further notice."

There were thirteen guards in place, each one capable of handling a platoon of soldiers single-handedly with the stretch of a blade which extended magic as part of themselves. Where most of the mages used wands or staffs, the elite arcane warriors used weapons of magic. Their reputation was without compare in terms of their mastery and competence.

They were taken apart instantly.

Not with the might of Simantiar but that of his elk-horned friend, who unravelled and abandoned the equine form he had donned as a centaur and instead took that of a forest.

From him burst nature as if he were a walking forest of trees and roots.

A tree grew where he had stood, grass spreading through the landing pad of the academy and claiming all which stood in its way, spreading like a wave, as if time had sped up and nature reclaimed the forest as its own.

Vines swatted the guardsmen aside with branches, dragging them by their feet with tangled roots and wrapping them in vines as in an instant the entrance was seized.

The two ventured farther inside, Simantiar walking with conviction in his stride.

Cernunnos trailed right behind him as a morphing mass that spread endless growing vines and moss that ravaged the academy, cracking the cement floor to embed its roots, and trailing behind Simantiar as if his herald; just a forest effigy of writhing vines and wooden antlers focused at the centre of it all.

"Usellyes said you would be back, that you would try to stop us," an arcane warrior said, guarding the path deeper into the academy.

This one Simantiar recognised as well. Joselyn. She was a prime and talented classmate of his when they were still young, timid and distant, even more so when a talented Simantiar embarrassed her.

The moment the light broke through her abyss and dragged her out from the darkness was when Usellyes offered his hand to her, smiling without pity, just reassurance. And it was the moment when Simantiar fell even further out of grace.

Another that Usellyes had saved, another that saw the good in Usellyes's intentions—another Simantiar would have to strike down in order to save everything.

"Joselyn, I'll only ask you once. Stand down. You have no idea how dangerous Usellyes's plan is."

"How. Dare. You?" Venom dripped from her pursed lips. "You dare tell me what Usellyes can do? It wasn't him who quailed me as children. It wasn't he who used his magic to embarrass me."

"I didn't mean to, we were just chil—"

"'We were just children.' I've heard that excuse enough times. Usellyes wishes to use his talent for the betterment of others. And I see the truth behind that."

A truth donned on Simantiar. "You love him." The words were spoken unintentionally, but Joselyn's reddening cheeks betrayed her secret.

"You're not getting past me." The determination in her voice didn't falter. "Ciro taught me all of your tricks."

Simantiar's heart skipped a beat. Another friend to face in the kiln of disastrous ambition.

"Perhaps it's that easy for you to forget, to simply tell yourself we were kids, but it meant so much more to me. The embarrassment that would follow me for the rest of my life. People calling me your practise ball." Joselyn brought forward her spear.

Simantiar narrowed his gaze...did people really call her that? Was he really so clueless?

"Ciro taught me the arcane fighting art. How to defend myself, my honour. She gave me the tools to quell their mocking. But what did you do in all your awe-inspiring power?

"I will imprison you just as I did Mylor and Miss Clarisse and all others who stood in the way of Usellyes."

Her weapon stretched out before her as she leaned back into a lowered side stance. Her centre of gravity was low, with corded muscles protruding from defined forearms and tensed like metal chains wrapped around her spear.

Simantiar's heart skipped a beat.

"They are imprisoned?" he asked worriedly.

"Don't worry, you will join them soon enough."

"Ready yourself, Joselyn. Just know that I'm sorry." Simantiar spoke the words sorrowfully.

Yet Joselyn offered no such honour in return.

She vanished, her image faded as she moved forward impossibly quickly.

The spear thrusted true, Simantiar sidestepping it only just as the blade pricked his cheek, a small trail of blood ushering forth.

"So you do bleed," she said, smiling victoriously as the cage created by writhing, encrusted vines closed them in.

Simantiar blasted force energy towards her, never striking her as the masonry of the walls crumbled at the impact. Again and again, Joselyn flashed back and forth, appearing and vanishing before Simantiar had a chance to strike her again.

Cernunnos grabbed her, the vines now covering too much space for her to constantly elude them.

Joselyn spat at Simantiar when her arms wouldn't move, the bracers she wore heating, trying to burn the restraints off.

"Get your lapdog off me, or does the mighty Simantiar really need help?"

Simantiar waved his hand, and Cernunnos released Joselyn.

"You will regret that," she said, as she charged the wizard once more.

And that was all. Simantiar returned to the present, as Joselyn stood there with a dazed look. A tear ran down Simantiar's face as he stepped up to her dreaming body, her spear arm falling to her side, but never letting go. She never even got to use it.

All that had just happened played along into her fantasy. Simantiar felt how important it was for her to break free of her childhood, to grow past herself. It was something that Simantiar understood all too well.

"How I hurt you. I'm sorry for not knowing better, I am sorry for not noticing how much you must have loved Usellyes, to see him be with the person you despised so much."

Now, the fantasy of battling Simantiar would play out, and she would believe herself to be close to victory, only to fall due to misfortune and pass out. She would never know the truth of Simantiar's overwhelming victory, that she never even got to lift a finger. He saw this as mercy, a vile form of magic to instil false memories into someone. But perhaps that was one act of pity he allowed himself and hoped it would be enough to release her from her own torment.

"Why did you do that?" Cernunnos voice spoke deep through Simantiar, an echo that rattled his mind as if spoken deep within a mountain.

"Because I had wronged her when we were children. I hope that this at least would quell some of her rage."

Cernunnos remained silent. Simantiar remembered the story—the story of a man who forgot what it meant to be human and faded into the wind.

"Please find the others and free them," Simantiar requested and Cernunnos agreed.

Yet, they had more pressing matters, as Simantiar descended into the academy grounds.

"Good luck, old friend." Cernunnos's voice echoed behind as Simantiar would have to complete the rest of the journey alone.

The tunnels were built with carved runes of confusion, to elude the human senses and disorient the unwanted. It wasn't weak magic by any means albeit simple—what made it masterful was the purpose with which the runes were placed, each simple in nature, but as a network of interlaid pieces, they webbed together in masterful architecture to create a network unlike any other.

It wasn't that Simantiar unravelled that magic simply—it would take him hours to understand its intricacies. Instead, he just looked past the veil, morphed his own human understanding to look only at what stood before him and disappear under its current. Splitting his own consciousness into several pieces and sending them forward through time, creating alternate realities which his future self knew would only get him lost, letting his past know the way he needed to take.

His power frightened him. Within those tunnels meant to confuse and disorient, within the dark path lit only by the ominous flame of torches on walls, he felt closed in. To control such power frightened Simantiar unlike anything else, to break something that was so craftily made, like a sandcastle beneath his feet.

The man walked the halls, though the trail could not elude him, try as it might. His own thoughts roiled in confusion instead. Absent-mindedly, the man trod his way through the path, one foot after the other guiding him, while he wrestled with thoughts of the battle that would come. He would see old friends, and they would greet him as an enemy. He would see Usellyes, a brother, and would be deemed a threat, to be killed for the greater good the same way Simantiar deemed them.

What power had they already summoned at the well? Part of him wished they had summoned enough power to fight for their convictions, as was their due. If Simantiar's power proved too great, there would be no justice, no argument that the fight was won because their cause was just. It would just be a merciless beating.

Would he have to kill the people in the room? Would he have to kill Usellyes?

And then he stood before the final doors. Even the guards that had tried to stop him had been dealt with without even noticing, his mind too busy with his dark thoughts. How easily Simantiar dealt with a human life. His power terrified him, for no man should have such power to deal with things without consideration.

All those emotions, all the fugue which filled his mind with fog as he found his way across the most elusive labyrinth ever built, all the emotions which battled against him...finally they quieted, leaving behind a remorseful sorrow, a numb resonance of duty as he simply faced forward with a sigh, and gave in to his power, to what was asked of him.

One by one the towering double doors with filigree markings and magical history toppled, falling one after the other as weightless dominos that broke the mason floor under its weight and raised powdered stone.

The man walked on heavy feet, guiding himself through the raised dust towards the end of the hall where friends waited for him, expecting him, and the first of the spells were fired.

Chapter 45

A numbness worked its way through Kendrith, a sobering darkness which convinced him of how foolish his fancies truly were.

He looked over to the sword that leaned beside him, limp and awkward. The sword had felt clumsy ever since he had come across what was left of Magnus, and emotions toiled and warred within.

This was not how he imagined the tale of his heroism would go.

Perhaps his father was right. First his mom, the greatest of all, was not felled by the seductive allure of adventure, but deceived by humans to die a cruel death.

Logan had explained that it was in fact Magnus's men which found Mona's remains and returned them in good faith.

His fists tensed at the thought—Magnus must have relished in the deception, laughing with such malignance while offering his greatest sympathies.

Had he been there when Kendrith sobbed over her body?

Perhaps she was the target of an assassination?

Kendrith shook the thoughts, they only sowed more darkness into his chest that grew into thorned brambles squeezing his pained heart.

He knew there was hate, doubt, and so much more clouding his mind.

But there was one thought within all that which became undisputable. He was just playing with fancies of his own making.

Becoming a hero? Saving lives? A woman nearly killed him in the woods because of his own carelessness…he even let himself be devoured by his own seething need for vengeance that his feet moved before he even realised.

What shame clouded over him when he found the totem pole monster eating away at Magnus.

Was that really what the inheritor of Vrania's blade was meant for? To cut down a man for something as hollow as vengeance?

That was not who he wanted to be, that is not what his mother, or Haggen had wanted for him.

And it showed.

The blade became heavier than before, its light completely faded—it was now just a blunt instrument to wave around like a club in the hands of a troll.

He hadn't mentioned this to Kristen, but he thought of hanging up the mantle for good. A life of adventuring was not his to have, and perhaps his father would still be willing to train him to take over the business.

Chapter 46

The great walls of the mountain held stories, whispers of a time long lost, whispers spoken in eternal slumber as its past told of conflict, of strife. The evidence was all around the band of travellers—a testament to lost time.

Logan stepped out from the cave where Simantiar lay cross-legged in his slumber, the others sat inside, waiting around the still light of fire which burnt the stale air around them.

George could hear the whispers and he wished nothing more than to let the past sleep.

The light of the campfire danced, illuminating Simantiar in his cross-legged trance and the knots formed by his vined body. A worried Pecky crawled farther into the spots in between the vines, only the barest black feather or shade of red at its skull peeking through.

"What do you think this place is?" George spoke, a silent thing devoid of life, but not quite a whisper. It showed caution, that they were all keeping their voices low, yet not sure why.

"We will find out soon enough—Simantiar will tell us all about it," Kendrith said in turn as he sat leaning against a stone wall deep in dark rumination.

Kristen leaned on the opposite side, right by the entrance to the cave, a throwing knife dancing between her fingers.

The fire continued to crackle, smoke rising, a dwindling flame forced to be tame as Kendrith rose to go to the entrance—a light cough at the escaping ribbon of smoke.

George rose to follow.

The merc looked left and right in search of anything suspicious—if he had noticed George following behind, he didn't show it.

George felt nauseous from the encumbering darkness that waited to swallow them whole with the rest of its lost history.

Logan emerged from the right, his golden hammer illuminating his path.

"Find anything?" Kendrith asked.

Logan shook his head. "The whole place seems abandoned, no sign of life, like it's ready to collapse. It is quite a find, Kendrith. The guild will be happy with this one."

"First, we will have to make it out alive."

Logan nodded his agreement.

A sound, the drop of a pebble.

"Did you hear that?" Logan asked. Yet, only the silence of darkness persisted.

George looked around, the dull sound of sediment echoing in his mind.

"We're not alone," Kendrith said.

Kendrith unsheathed his sword, though the previous flourish was lost, the skill and confidence with which Kendrith stood spoke for itself.

Logan followed suit, hafting his hammer.

Kristen came to them. "Is something wrong?" she asked.

"Be ready."

Deafening silence.

She drew her own short sword.

A moment of thumping rhythmic quiet.

George drew his daggers.

The thump of a heartbeat heard over a held breath in the darkness.

Another moment as they all peered into the surrounding dark.

A shadowed hand grabbed the ledge in front of them as George kicked it loose, and a shrill, gravelled scream plummeted into the depths.

One, two, three, four.

More quiet as the body thudded against a stone bridge below and the muffled sound echoed the chasm walls.

Logan and Kendrith leaned over the edge, to make sure the creature was truly gone.

Logan raised his hammer to the abyss so that its light might shine bright, and what they found was the shambling army of the Withered which scaled the mountains walls, lured in by the light of life.

"Group together!" Logan called, no longer a quiet voice, for the mountain was awoken, the Withered grouped together like obsidian ants from their burrows.

"Above us!" Kristen called.

George turned to see they were surrounded, with more of the humanoid remnants clambering above them.

Their skin was like dark leather pulled over gaunt bones, a dwindling hole where their heart used to be from where pulsing orange light spread to feed their forgotten bodies.

"Wake up, Simantiar!" Kendrith called.

Nothing from within.

"Get him!" Logan ordered as Kendrith ran inside.

Kendrith ran into the tunnel, the black shade of the Withered grouping together, coalescing like an umbral mantle to swallow them whole.

Kendrith ran beside Simantiar with George following. "Wake up!" Kendrith said, shaking the serene cross-legged Simantiar oblivious to the chaos all around them.

"Shit." Kendrith squirmed, trying to raise Simantiar from his rooted spot. Pecky now flew from its recluse and stuck with George.

"He's stuck," Kendrith groaned through gritted teeth.

"Hurry it up!" Logan called, his voice barely noticeable from the hordes forming outside.

As George watched the entrance, one of the dark monsters clung above as it scuttled with inhuman movements.

"Kendrith! Hurry!" George disposed of the creature with one of the throwing knives Kristen had shown him how to use, allowing a relieved sigh as it met its mark.

"Fuck it," Kendrith said, taking one of George's daggers from his hip and cutting away at Simantiar's neck, grinding down the vines one by one, as with one final twist, Kendrith ripped the mage's skeletal head from its body and tossed it to George.

"Protect him."

"But his body!" George called out.

"We don't have time!"

Kendrith broke through the cave entrance to find the horde of the Withered which came upon them like a rising wave.

"We need to go higher!" Kendrith called out, hoping to control their numbers on the bridge.

"Where is Simantiar?" Kristen asked.

George flashed the severed skull of Simantiar, the life in the mage's eye's still present, but dwindled.

"What's wrong with him?"

"He must still be dreaming!"

The group moved, forming a tight ring as they pushed back the horde drawn to life as if longing for a lost past.

The group fought their way through onto the next stone bridge which rose to the other side. More of the Withered came from both sides, their overflowing numbers causing many of their fiendish kind to fall off the edges.

Their numbers were controlled and easy enough to fend off. The band protected their flank as Logan led the way.

One bridge led to two, and then to three.

"We can do it! Just stay together," Logan called, but fatigue had already begun to set into Kendrith's bones, and he knew he couldn't be the only one.

A hollow explosion. "Did you hear that?" Kristen asked.

Even the Withered gave a moment's pause, caution now in their gazes despite their mindless fervor.

"Move! We need to move!" Kendrith called out. Whatever it was that could give the mindless doubt was certainly nothing trivial.

A dust cloud formed above, another explosion, and from there, a being of horror dove for the band.

Its body was that of a massive centipede stretching out eternally as the cloud of debris seemed to spit out more and more of the monstrous creature.

"Look out!" Logan said, batting away the first of the pincers that came to devour the group, with a gnarled and inhuman face as if carved in stone staring through the pincers. The large centipede creature spanned several meters, crashing onto the back line of the Withered who now were either crushed beneath its weight or falling to their doom.

"Kendrith!" George called out.

"I know! From the forest!" Kendrith called back, though this one seemed different. It seemed physical, more powerful, more...definitive.

As the band scaled the bridge, the centipede dove into the dark below, came back up and knocked through the stone platform, shattering it.

The two stone halves lifted into the air, shards of stone strewn about.

Pieces of rubble and a deluge of the Withered vanished into the darkness as the resulting force sent Kendrith careening through the air.

When next he opened his eyes, he felt the relief of ground below him and turned to see Logan by his side.

He blinked, trying to orient himself as he noticed Kristen and George were left behind on the platform they had just escaped—stranded.

The centipede ran down the walls, its pincers in full show, spread wide as it dove for Kendrith and Logan.

"Oh, ancestors of mine, cast our light in this lost realm." Logan's hammer flared bright with holy power as it caused the centipede to screech and recoil. The scream it let loose sounded almost human as it crashed into more of the stone platforms that rained down. Kendrith had to tackle Logan out of the way of a large chunk of stone.

More and more of the Withered fell from the cascade, like ants washed down by a stream. They all fled, retreating to their crypts, as the true lord of the mountain appeared. Or perhaps something even more ghastly hid away in the shadows, yet to chase the centipede away.

"Kendrith!" George called across the span, his voice straining to make himself heard.

"Keep going! We will find another way across!" Kendrith called back.

"Prepare yourself," Logan said, tightening his stance, as the centipede rose again, a cry of fury escaping its fiendish self.

Kendrith held his sword, sweat-clumped strands of hair stuck to his forehead as he readied himself.

"Wait…" Kendrith realised that the beast wasn't coming towards them.

He looked up to George and Kristen. "Run!"

The two looked down to see the beast scuttling straight for them.

George and Kristen rose to flee.

"They're not gonna make it," Logan said.

"Run!" Kendrith cried louder, as if the urgency would give them speed.

But he knew his desperation would make no difference.

He glanced down at his blade, holding it in both hands and concentrating in wild desperation.

"Come on," he pleaded. "Please." His voice trembled at the urgency as a looming sense of helplessness seeped into his bones and pried his eyes to stay open.

Already the beast rose into the air to suddenly dive back down.

"Please!" he begged the dim sword.

Suddenly, George turned around to face the creature.

"What are you doing?" cried Kendrith, but that was when he noticed that George held something in his clenched fist.

A sharp flash brightened before the beast, the thing veering off course and rising once more, its tail barely missing George as he ducked under it.

"It's not enough! Use more!" Kendrith shouted, abandoning the blade.

George lifted more of Simantiar's bones out of the bag as the creature returned for a second attempt, this time an even brighter flash of blue light filled the cavern. The beast's body smashed into George, sending him flying into a neighbouring wall as it veered away.

"It's not working!" Logan bellowed, but George had no time to rise, as the creature circled around again, flying through the sky, its legs skittering through air as it turned, going straight for George, its pincers opening wide.

"George! Use them all!" Kendrith shouted.

George lifted the bag of bones at the last second and threw them at the face of the beast, all of them exploding at contact with a volatile blue bang. The beast writhed in pain, the remains now crumbling to ash from the reaction.

Kristen ran to George and saw him to salvage as many as possible of the charred remains of bones strewn across the floor.

"We have to go!" Kristen called out in desperation, as the beast returned for another attempt, smoke rising from its chitinous skeleton.

How helpless Kendrith felt. He lifted the sword again. "Please." He noticed he was crying, tears streaking his cheeks, his hands trembling, his voice breaking.

Kristen reached under George's armpit and pulled Simantiar out of his grasp.

"No!" George called out with a soft echo, but it was too late. They could only watch as Kristen raised Simantiar's skull to the beast in one final desperate attempt.

There was a moment of brief silence, the type of silence that comes when a fragile cup flips from one's fingers or a sudden arrow pierces the heart, a moment of stillness that makes the whole world go quiet before the ruin…and then there was the deafening explosion.

Chapter 47

It could be heard before it was seen, the pained wail of a wounded monster, a long, thrashing body pounding against the mountain walls that quaked in turn.

A massive, unparalleled explosion travelled the entire course of the mountain walls, a stream of wind that plotted to tear and reap asunder any who stood at their plummet.

Whatever of the Withered that didn't cascade into the darkness below now completely fell back into their vile abodes. Kendrith had to blink several times and even then still spots blinded him from the chaos.

He had to blink one. Twice. Thrice.

Till finally his vision adjusted just barely to the darkness to make out the shapes of George and his love and the shadow of a great centipede scuttling into a crevice like a rigid worm into its home.

Kristen and George were knocked to the floor, whatever bones that could have been salvaged were gone with the aftermath. The bright light had now faded away completely, as only the pained groans of George and Kristen could be heard.

"Is it gone?" Kristen called out. "I can't see."

"Yeah, it's gone," Kendrith called back, a moment of silence as they all processed what had just happened.

And then laughter.

Delirious, incredulous laughter at their luck. To survive not just the beast, but a force so powerful that it shook the foundation of their surroundings…and then the first of the debris started to rain.

Kendrith gasped in understanding "Move!" he bellowed.

But it was too late, the ledge underneath their feet cracked and crumbled, giving way to the endless fall below.

Time seemed to slow down again. George. Kristen. Simantiar in some distant dream. They fell into the dark, gaping maw that hungered in silent patience.

Time returned to the present as George kicked Kristen in the side, just barely sending her sprawling onto a ledge where she held on for dear life while George continued to fall deeper and deeper to the unforgiving depths till the sea of silent darkness swallowed him and Simantiar whole.

Chapter 48

Arrows of beaming blue light whirred through the air before bursting into tatters, elemental strikes of fire and icicles, kinetic energy balled up and fired: all which failed to pierce the barrier that cocooned Simantiar.

"Now!" a voice called out, it sounded like Moran's.

As the cascade of attacks bore down on him, the ground below Simantiar's feet gave way, and a thick liquid swallowed him whole. Before the ground could solidify, Simantiar lifted himself into the air as easily as stepping out of a shallow hole. He did not need to cast anything anymore, to notify the world of his intent because he instilled his will on that which he wanted.

And so the murky ground parted—because Simantiar willed it.

And gravity no longer held him—because he willed it.

And no attacks reached him—because he willed it.

As Simantiar came to stand before old friends he did not attempt to hide his pained expression. He wore his guilt as plain as day, not for facing those who he should have seen as friends nor for letting this get so far— but because he knew their intent was not enough to ever reach him.

"Stop this." The dust settled as Simantiar walked on air. "You can't beat me," he assured them.

"Perhaps not with your current power," Moran spoke with his thick accent. Even then, when they stood as enemies, the humour in his gaze was just how Simantiar remembered him. "But what if we levelled the playing field?"

"Please, Simantiar. Stop. We are supposed to be your friends."

Simantiar turned with a heavy heart to the familiar voice—he had wondered when it would be that their paths would cross.

There she stood, Ciro. She had truly grown into a testament of will and dedication. Her muscles corded like tightly wound steel over a strongly rooted tree. The sides of her black shoulder-length hair was shaved short and light scars marked her body as tallies for her progress.

"Please reconsider. You don't have to join us. Just walk away."

"I can't." Simantiar's brave front began to shatter. He thought he was prepared—how foolish he was.

Ciro's expression matched his own. He wanted nothing more than to run over and embrace her lovingly, but an invisible wall not born of some spell, but rather by the barriers of their inner conflict held them apart.

"Don't do this." She stepped forward, tears were in her strong, willful eyes. Her whisper was meant for his ears alone as she pleaded desperately.

"I can't." Simantiar's own voice broke.

She sighed and turned away, her moment of vulnerability already gone. If it weren't for the rheumy eyes and slight trail of tears Simantiar would have questioned if she truly had suffered at the thought of facing him.

Her attire was not that of the moon-silver silk draping her shoulders expected of arcane fighters, but rather a leathery matte black that strapped her figure and left her arms bare, daggers and swords hung all over her form ready to be used.

Other than the rubble and scorched walls, much of the hall seemed the same, except for the magical crystal held above the pool at the end of the hall and the cords which stretched down from it, disappearing behind Usellyes who stood there waiting, contention in his gaze.

The man turned around to reveal the cords plugged into his emancipated and minute back, running down his ridged spine. Several more cords ran down the back of each arm, and one final cord attached to Usellyes's heart, infusing him with magic.

"Soon Usellyes will be able to stand face-to-face with you. Soon you won't be the only one with incomprehensible power," Ciro said, her back still turned; her voice was that of stone.

"I won't ask again—reconsider this madness," Simantiar spoke out to the entire room.

Their responses came hardened as they all took their stances, wands at the ready, magic already being welled to their fingers in the form of crackling electricity and incantations on their lips.

"Know that I take no joy in this," Simantiar said as he moved forward. No longer could he be a wandering scholar, because the world demanded otherwise. No longer could he pretend to just be friends, for duty called upon him. Usellyes's words echoed: *What's the point of all this power if you won't do anything with it?* What irony that the power would be used to kill his friends.

There was no contest of strength, nothing to prove as mice tried to face a lion, for they all froze in place, unmoving.

Simantiar returned his feet to the floor: the mighty to walk among men.

"This is between us, Usellyes," Simantiar said, trying hard to make the pain in his voice sound like conviction.

Usellyes stood waist deep within the shimmering pool at the end of the hall, the light of the crystal reflecting off its surface and dancing across Usellyes's visage like shifting iridescent scales. His chest was bare, no muscles on his sleek figure for he was a student of the arcana. His usually groomed shoulder-length hair was now free and untamed, framing driven eyes. The light of the pool made the hate he bore even clearer.

"You think this is over?" Usellyes asked, no mirth in his query. "You shall know what it is like to walk as a mortal, to walk beside your peers and struggle as they struggled—you shall know that you can't just show up from missing for years and undo all that we have built."

Simantiar was unsure of what Usellyes meant as he walked past his comrades of old. And then he saw it, in the corner of his eye, a single twitch.

Reflex saved him. Reflex learned from his training among monks upon mountaintops with no walls to keep the elements out, battered endlessly by harsh cold winds that stiffened his muscles as he mastered his body and felt the slightest change in his surroundings.

A swift clean cut that slashed through the air, rending just strands of gold instead of a head. Simantiar's body bowed deep, hands to the floor as his instincts took over. Legs wrapped around the swinging arm, twisting the body to the floor as a resounding *snap* and pained scream told Simantiar of a clean break to the claimed limb.

Simantiar was clueless. Was the assailant hiding? Were there more? How come he didn't notice?

That was when Simantiar saw those he had frozen circling him, unbound from their invisible yokes.

An icicle pierced the wizard's shoulder, blood flowed, and Simantiar cried out in pain.

Sharp cuts of wind slashed at him, and his shield failed as barrage upon barrage of spells cut at him with little tact or strategy—his attackers had no need to hold back.

Simantiar rolled off the man whose arm he had broken, only to see the hue which emanated from it. Broken cartilage and bone fused back together in grotesque fashion as if reversing through time; the man screamed his pain.

Simantiar looked over to Usellyes, the crystal above him shimmering iridescently, switching between green and blue and yellow and purple; Usellyes's eyes burned bright with unimaginable power.

Is that how people see me? A short thought flashed in Simantiar's mind, a notion of fear as he saw Usellyes's likeness within the shimmering pool, and for a moment could have sworn he saw a god.

The attacks continued.

Two mages synchronised their incantations, a flawless merriment of words as they motioned for the ground to rise and so it did. Two stone golems emerged, leaving behind a crater as they trudged towards Simantiar.

At the back of the room, more sentinel bodies of animated armour came to life as they donned their carved armour and power cores of arcane. Empty, crow-like helmets sat upon their heads and their long spears pointed forward.

It was no longer a matter of thought—Simantiar had to strain, think about his spells, his incantations, and lessen the power of Usellyes that constricted his own abilities.

The numbers swelled as barrages of attacks came forward, Simantiar's own mind fugued as the magic eluded him much the same way a word eludes the tongue.

Ciro raised her hands as the shimmering incandescent blades at her side rose of their own accord and slowly pointed their ends at Simantiar.

Ciro waved the blades forward as they swayed like wafts of air, singing as they parted their surroundings.

It was all Simantiar could do to evade the concord of barrages—bobbing and weaving, split-second barriers that shattered upon impact, scorched clothing, and the scent of burnt flesh filling the stale air.

A sash of cloth wrapped itself around Simantiar's arm before transforming into the head of a yawning serpent ready to strike—Simantiar turned his flattened palm into a blade and cut himself loose.

The blades danced all around like a whirling storm till Simantiar conjured shards of ice that deflected the coming strikes.

As swift as her own blades, Ciro pounced into the storm and claimed one of her swords from the air in a downward curve. It was all Simantiar could do to hold her at bay with stacking ice broken to splinters.

Her blade pounded and pounded, chipping away at Simantiar's defences as she abandoned the blade in exchange for an axe that formed in her grip.

In his moment of distraction, Simantiar's arms were suddenly bound by sashes that spread his arms apart. He turned to see the floating hilts shifting their bladed ends into harmless sashes made to restrain.

"Surrender!" Ciro demanded.

"No!" Simantiar was surprised at his own conviction, at the purpose that burnt inside him.

From beyond the whirling storm of blades the others watched in anticipation.

Simantiar's breast fogged, his eyes turned a misty white, and his hair went suddenly stiff and rigid as his olive skin turned a crystal white.

A coldness worked its way up the bindings till they shattered into broken shards.

Ciro retreated as the storm of blades followed, but in their place came the vortex of flame.

A rising fire took form as a circle of mages chanted incantations of Igni, creating a bottled inferno constricting around Simantiar and melting his body of ice.

He couldn't breathe.

Gasping breaths escaped his withering and pained lungs as his body temperature changed too rapidly.

With a resounding bestial roar that tore his lungs into agonizing shreds, Simantiar transformed once more.

He would not be overcome.

His body hardened, his skin crystallised, and his breath cracked like strained ice till it snapped and fell to the floor.

One.

Two.

A dull third.

Simantiar's heartbeat came to a hollow stop.

The vortex of flame fell away to reveal the raggedly armoured Simantiar and his body of stone that clumsily trudged unharmed.

One step led to two, before the first crack spread along his stone chest—the crack spread, growing larger and larger.

The armour broke apart and Simantiar fell from it like a snake sheds its skin.

The two large gorilla-like golems stepped forward to face Simantiar's own skeletal creation, but not before his own work balled itself up to the floor and an outer carapace shelled itself around it, forming into an even greater machination.

As the gorilla-like beings approached, Simantiar's own came to tower over them, hammering down with its weighted fists to flatten the first with the dull rough sound of stone hammering stone and a cloud of ground dust rising into the air before the giant creation grabbed its pummelled foe by its arm and knocked it into the second.

The two animated armours charged within that window of time, piercing Simantiar's slower golem and retreating before it had a chance to retaliate, chipping away at the form one by one.

Simantiar focused on his own issues.

Ciro stepped forward, her floating arsenal of shifting and transforming blades suddenly fell apart, shattering, turning into wind.

No.

Simantiar looked closer, and tiny little blades of dust shimmered with scintillating beauty as each speck of sand was powdered steel.

The storm came carried upon the winds of death as Simantiar conjured his barrier—now holding strong as the dust worked its way around.

Ciro charged forward, a blade forming from the storm in her hand before she blinked out of existence and appeared before Simantiar, her blade already midswing as it cut through his chest.

Again she blinked outside, her blade leaving her hand and two backhand-gripped daggers filled her fists as she returned for another strike.

Then an axe.

Then a knife.

Then a sword.

A chakram.

A spear.

A mace.

Bit by bit Simantiar was brought down to his knees, his hands covered in bleeding cuts as they trembled to hold the shimmering dust of blades without.

Ciro appeared, a great axe in hand waiting to sever Simantiar's skull.

"Do you give up?" she asked.

"Never."

Simantiar blew from his mouth and caught Ciro off her guard.

She coughed incessantly.

"What did you do?"

The storm died away, and Simantiar lowered his arms in defeat, conjuring what little power he could through the open hem of Usellyes's magic to heal and revitalise.

Ciro continued to cough endlessly.

"I devoured pieces of your dust with each of your strikes, using it as a conduit for a powdered sleep spell." Simantiar spat blood to his side.

Ciro's eyes widened before narrowing languidly, as a drowsiness seemed to waft over her.

"But…the damage to your body." Ciro's speech slurred.

Simantiar nodded. He could already feel the piercing needlelike pain that coursed through him as he had forced specks of razored dust to tunnel through him.

Ciro collapsed, the dust of steel falling to the floor.

Returning to the balance of his own magic with a centred breath, Simantiar evoked the touch of life, of nature where he still held power.

Perhaps his power had been dulled, but he could still thread it like a needle. Find the seam. And unravel the enemy within the chink of it all—it was only a matter of time till he found the single loose thread that would have it all fall apart.

Simantiar wouldn't hold back anymore—he couldn't afford to anymore. But Ciro…he couldn't bring himself to kill her.

There was no time to ready himself, as a charged blast of kinetic energy worked its way towards Simantiar. He recognised the ability from when he lived among the monks, and it was no coincidence that his bald-headed assailant seemed to also have studied among them.

The golem of his making had already pummelled its smaller contemporaries and swift-animated armour and now kept at bay as many of the others as it could.

Simantiar elbowed, nudged, and redirected the coming forces with wrapped kinetic energy gloves of his own. Keeping his right leg in front as he took a defensive stance, he returned blasts to the attacker and others to keep them at bay while ignoring the screaming ache of his body.

Many were dazed and stunned from the onslaught—they were scholars, students, the best of their kind. But very few present could be called warriors.

Soon the monk bunched his palms together and drove his arms back, collecting energy before releasing it for one big attack. He released the coiled power, each transfer invisible except for the refracted light which would barely tell of its position.

Simantiar acted in kind, firing a blast which mirrored the monk's precisely, summoning the stone floor to clamp down his feet as the two blasts connected, sending a shock wave that knocked everyone off their feet. Simantiar's large golem fell apart by the ensuing rubble that crushed the two animated bodies of armour and three more mages.

Simantiar charged the monk before the others could return to consciousness.

Each blow was given with the intent to kill, to destroy, as Simantiar struck first. His palm redirected so that the blast hit the top of a pillar instead, cracking it. The monk struck with kinetic energy concentrated around his fingers, aiming for Simantiar's kidney which he deflected with a knee.

Each force given was redirected, given back in kind with another blow, rending the stone floor of the chamber apart at each deflection that dug invisible divots into the surrounding area.

More and more exchanges with shorter intervals, each block telling with a slight iridescent shimmer and a blurred pocket of air.

They shuffled closer and closer, till the force of an elbow met that of another, till stacked knees sent waves of energy to topple the other off balance.

Fists with concentration of force were deflected by forearms, the resulting blasts dispersing more tattered spectrums as each strike made the air tremble with their explosive match.

It seemed to continue as a stalemate, until Simantiar was on the retreat, falling back to the experience of the monk who battered against him.

Simantiar diverted one more attack—the blast burst through the body of someone rising to their feet, completely obliterating their upper half and leaving a crescent of blood.

More and more of the attacks struck at the other mages, cleaving limbs or taking heads. One unfortunate duo became flattened by a battered pillar which collapsed on top of them.

Simantiar was on the retreat and he used the opportunity to redirect an attack so the force went straight for Usellyes, but it just dispersed upon a barrier, the iridescent light shimmering.

Simantiar struck one more time, not to the monk, but rather to his right, an attack that seemed to be nowhere near his opponent as a blast of force took the head off another mage readying to attack.

The monk saw an opening, readying to blast a hole through Simantiar's chest. Yet, he stopped short.

The monk looked down to his side, seeing a gaping hole as blood dripped down from it.

There stood a second Simantiar, a conjured double that brimmed with equal threat.

The curled fist pulled out of the gaping wound as the monk dropped to the floor.

Only three mages remained, one of them being Moran.

Simantiar's conjured soul-warrior floated like a giant beside him, its form barely discernible as it vanished completely.

Simantiar was bruised and bleeding, panting as blood ran down his arm, dripping to the floor.

Moran rose alone, and no words were spoken.

"No hard feelings," Moran said, a wound at the side of his head trailing blood.

"No hard feelings," Simantiar parroted, surprised at how resolute and cold he sounded.

Moran's own machinations clattered and rose to life, gemstone eyes of blue filling the framed sockets of a metal wolf, and another beast like a sabre-toothed panther made of gold frames and clanking dark cogwheels that could be seen whirring inside. From its back whirred two stinging tails like that of a scorpion as a hiss of steam blew out from its clenched metal teeth.

Rising from behind them was an owl—a low metallic hoot escaped its working body as its wings spread open and continued to stretch further, layers of feathers spreading out until its body was like a giant veil of metal.

"I will be just a moment, Usellyes."

Another hoot signalled the attack as razor feathers perched from their wings and shot out like projectile daggers.

A single breath of tranquillity anchored Simantiar who danced upon the winged assault. His flicking wrist parried and redirected the onslaught as the daggers piled in his free hand to be cradled.

The wolf and stinger-tailed beasts charged forward with their teeth bared as Simantiar held the bladed feathers together and spread them out before him as if opening an accordion, only to release the blades a moment later.

All in all, the wolf, the beast, and the owl powered down and the crack of electricity told of their damage before they plummeted to the floor.

Moran panicked with his paunch belly as he stepped back in trepidation.

Simantiar reached down and grabbed a loosened piece of stone and whispered to it tenderly. The object unravelled into a pudgy substance like runny clay before slowly sheathing the final feather left in Simantiar's possession.

When the feather was covered in the stony sheath, he released it in flight and buried it in Moran's thigh.

Moran gave a pained groan as he stumbled to his rear. Already the stony sheath released itself from the dagger and spread along his wounded limb.

"What is this?" Moran asked.

"Something to protect you."

"Stop. Stop it, Simantiar. We are friends!" His panicked cries fell on deaf ears as the remainder of the stuff consumed Moran and turned him into a statue, freezing him in his state of pure terror and fear.

The shimmering man within the pool didn't respond, as Simantiar appeared before the other remaining mages and in an instant teleported them to a harsh land far, far away from the academy. Blizzards blazed across the realm, snowy hills reaching for the skies like icy thorns.

"Goodbye," was all that Simantiar said, as he vanished back the way he came. The last thing he saw in their eyes was fear, terror. Watching Simantiar in a way that he now finally understood, watching helplessly the same way he saw Usellyes. They scrambled up towards the god, begging for mercy.

And there he was, watching the determined eyes of Usellyes back in the chamber.

"You may have taken me by surprise before, but I am prepared now, Usellyes."

Simantiar's stare matched that of his old friend's. Determination. Power. Magic. The lock which held the wizard's power at bay was now released, with no limitations to worry about. Usellyes's eyes glowed, giving off an iridescent gleam that shifted and changed like ink floating on the water's surface. Simantiar's eyes glowed blue, burning brightly with might, as the mage stepped towards the pool and powers collided.

The blast of energy tore the room asunder, and a wave of power caused the water of the pool to thrash like roiling waves at sea. The very fabric of reality shook upon their staring competition. The mountain trembled all around them. Pebbles and rubble arose as if in veneration. Each step taken towards each other greatened the tear, made the mountain, and even caused Tiria to quake, trembling at the toil of keeping existence itself together as their bubbles of opposing might ground against each other to release occasional sparks of arcane friction.

Simantiar stepped onto the rim of the well, removing the robes from his body and had them float like rippling manta rays instead of falling to the floor, for the robes of a god would not dirty themselves so. Followed by his tunic, which he did not remove, for a god need not worry about such trivial acts as the tunic removed itself from Simantiar's touch, gliding incorporeal through him.

As Simantiar stepped to the pool, the surrounding air seemed to thicken, a murky palpable atmosphere uninhabitable by mere men as all the air that would have been able to sustain life vanished, making space for the squeeze of magic permeating through it all, contained within that one instance.

The place was now a vacuum, not a place for mortals, but a fitting space for gods to meet.

As Simantiar took the first step to the shimmering water of the pool, staring down at Usellyes with the gaze of the mighty, its water parted, not touching a single spot on Simantiar's skin as he descended, the water bending around him so that it would never touch him.

For a god needeth no power that hath been borrowed.

Chapter 49

The bellow of the mountain whispered of darkness, to despair for it would become the crypt of the travellers, and that they would be lost to oblivion just like those who came before, just as the last light of their hammer dwindled and faded. The whispers it spoke weren't told with malice, weren't promised with delight or passion—it spoke of sobering truth, of what had happened to those who came before, of the task the mountain bore time and time again and of what it saw would come to pass: that Kendrith and the others would be no different, and the secret of the vault would be coveted for evermore.

Kendrith wandered on, his mind a haze. Simantiar was gone. George was gone. What were they even doing there anymore? He looked to Logan who seemed as stoic as ever, unshaken by the events that had passed.

Kendrith turned to the opposite path. He could still make out the telling outline of his love as she trudged aimlessly through the darkness. The plan was to find a connecting bridge, to have Kristen walk the path to them and then work from there. Though Kendrith was unsure if there would be a way out. The bridges below were broken apart and there was still the question of the monster and the Withered.

They wandered in silence, an invisible thread binding them together, knotting their pace as Logan's light seemed to fend off the creatures that lurked beyond its reach—a desperate shine of light to give the false comfort of day as its dimming seemed indicative of the troop's own rising despair.

Every sound, every drop of stone put them on edge. Kristen tried to blend in with the surroundings or to find a crevice to hide under, while Kendrith and Logan stood back-to-back at the ready. Yet, all that haunted them was their own descent into madness, their constant vigilance creating specters of their own making that nicked at their heels. Already their bodies stank of sweat and dirt; Kendrith tried desperately not to humour the idea that soon they'd stink of rot.

Only insidious silence came as they waited—a haunting and filled quiet as specks of dust barely visible trailed the dark chasm which made them all distinctly aware of their own inevitable doom.

After an age, a measurement in time based on their own frazzled composure rather than a clear sky, the troop finally found a way across.

It was a corner in the chasm that seemed to have been abandoned midconstruction. They saw haphazard-looking rope bridges rather than those of stone spanned the chasm, discarded picks eaten by rust, and carts with unstable wheels standing on rusted tracks, loaded some time ago with rock never used.

Kendrith looked over, but noticed that Kristen didn't seem to have seen the bridge, her head hanging low and feet dragging behind her. It pained Kendrith to see her so, surely it must have been the fall of George that made her feel that way.

"Kristen!" Kendrith risked calling out her name—the sound echoed through the mountain, the voice of life in a place of death. Kendrith pointed at the rope bridge which spanned the chasm, wooden boards gone or hanging by a thread. One could only describe the sight akin to that of an old man who trembled upon the support of their cane as they rose to stand on feeble knees.

Kristen worked her way across.

Some of the wooden planks groaned from years of rot—each of Kristen's steps was careful and delicate. Others simply gave off a hollow echo as she advanced with caution.

Logan lifted his hammer higher and willed its light brighter for Kristen.

"Ancestors have mercy," the titan of a man murmured, trepidation clear in his trembling voice.

He tapped on Kendrith's shoulder, who turned to see what had Logan so frazzled.

Kendrith followed Logan's gaze upwards and looked in dismay at the winding mass that slumbered on a net of rope upon its cradle of bones. There the centipede rested. Its body tightened and coiled in moving concentric circles. It was impossible to tell where its body ended and where its head began. Kendrith could now hear the chittering of its skittering feet.

Kendrith and Logan both looked back down to Kristen, trying to still their distress lest their panic distract her as she paced right below the slumbering monster.

Kendrith's eyes darted between the beast and Kristen, motioning for her to move faster.

All their tact seemed to be for naught as a bone must have slipped through the net to drum against the wooden plank right in front of Kristen.

Kendrith's heart stopped. The white enamel blur of bone clattered with a dull echo.

She cried out in surprise as the bone continued its descent, the sound of its fall reverberating through the walls of the dark chasm. Each drop resounded with an even quieter, but longer lasting echo; it told Kendrith volumes about the fate that probably met George and Simantiar.

Kristen turned to look above her, if the sight fazed her she didn't show it as her cry from before turned into stark, petrified silence.

Kendrith simply motioned for Kristen to hurry.

She nodded, advancing forward with half of the way cleared, leaning over missing planks and testing her weight before continuing.

Kristen tested her weight, the soft groan of a plank like the decrepit sound of an old organ key betrayed its nefarious plot. Kristen slowly lifted her feet and leaned back.

Kendrith let loose a sigh of relief—he didn't even notice he was holding his breath.

Crunch.

The sound of snapping wood bounced off the walls, a loud break in the old wizened bones of the bridge.

A terrible screech from above made Kendrith's blood go cold.

"Run!" Kendrith shouted, watching as caution was blown to the wind and Kristen sprinted to the end, leaping over planks and daring to hope that luck was on her side.

One plank snapped, and her entire leg disappeared into the gap. "Get up!" Logan called out, and Kristen strained to free her leg.

The centipede rose, more and more of the bones now raining from above to present a most unpleasant omen.

The centipede crawled onto a nearby wall, a crack now on its face from when it clashed with Simantiar's skull.

It screeched, charging for Kristen trapped on the haggard bridge.

Kristen gave a last desperate look at both Kendrith and Logan, one of apology, one of regret, one of goodbye.

She raised her elbow, breaking the next plank in front of her as she vanished down the gap. The beast broke into the rickety bridge, snapping it in half.

"No!" Kendrith called out.

"Kristen!" Logan echoed.

The two peered over the ledge only to be knocked back onto their rears as the massive body of the centipede shot up before them like a rising pillar.

"We have to move!" Logan ordered.

He tried to grab Kendrith, but the man saw only despair as he shook himself free and vaguely felt his hand wrap around his sword hilt. The sound of majestic steel being drawn was like a soprano's glass-shattering solo at an opera.

Kendrith dove underneath the charging beast and raised his blade to pierce the monster's belly.

There was just a moment's spark before the sword recoiled, avulsed from his grip.

A mere heart-pounding moment of lucidity flooded over Kendrith as his doused blade rattled across the floor, and he turned to witness the mere second in which Logan saved it from the precipice.

He turned with startling efficiency and ran towards Kendrith. "Move!" His command was not a request.

He grabbed Kendrith by the collar of his jacket and dragged him into a triangular opening in the mountain.

Logan pulled Kendrith inside with him as the mountain shook, the head of the centipede hammering against the opening just a second too late as it failed to get its prey.

Yet Kendrith knew, as they slumped against the rocky wall, the mountain would become their tomb.

The two heaved heavy, panicked breaths. Breaths of despair, as they inhaled the hopelessness of the situation. The centipede was already long gone, probably in search of other prey within its den.

Many in their field were taught that in dire moments, the best course of action was to remain calm and assess the situation. Yet, at that moment, no clear path presented itself.

Logan started to chuckle, laugh even, his usual sanctimonious presence, one of purpose and righteous cause was now gone to reveal the terrified human beneath. A hand covered his eyes as his laugh turned into something bordering on delirium.

"What's so funny?" Kendrith asked, the strength sapped from him, leaning against the wall as his legs spread themselves before them. The true weight of mental and physical exhaustion finally showed itself.

"Nothing," the large man said, wiping tears from red eyes; if they were tears of laughter, or fear, or both, Kendrith couldn't tell. The man was now giving off light chuckles, the fumes of his macabre humour running dry.

"It's just...how typical that all who follow the Brosnorth line die. How noble, how splendid, how heroic they seem until the weight of their legend crushes them."

"Don't you say another word," Kendrith murmured, energy returning to his bones through gritted teeth.

"How your mother and your grandfather went on to only die meaningless deaths."

"My grandfather asked you to join him! You left your teacher, your friend, your brother, to go alone and die! And you *dare* insult his memory!"

"Aye! I did! You saw what perilous path we had set upon. I reject no duty set upon me, but that mission of his was not sanctioned by the guild, nor was there any pay. Why risk my life? For nobility? Pah! I act upon a creed of honour, not stupidity."

"So, that's it, huh? The great Logan Van Dungen. A man who acts out of greed rather than purpose."

"What purpose? The same one that buried your mother? That had her devoured for trying to capture Magnus and his men? That had your grandfather be lost to whatever godforsaken place he went? The same purpose that will have us die in this tomb from a lost age?"

"So, why did you come?"

"Because it was my duty to do so! Because the guild saw me bound and I honour that compact! But know this, if it weren't for that boy wishing to venture out into these godforsaken lands because of a child's fancy, there is nothing that could drag me out here to die the same death your grandfather did." He guffawed and flailed his arms in exasperation. "Serves me right for humouring a child's fairy tale!"

"Don't you dare speak about George that way..." A burning hot flame ignited inside Kendrith. He was surprised to find how much he cared about George's dream...perhaps it had become his dream too.

"Oh, come on, the great Haggen Brosnorth, the walking mountain! Invincible and without equal! Well, guess what? He did meet his match, as did we, dead under an *actual* mountain.

"That is what happens to the Brosnorths, Kendrith. You may have your father's name, but you are a Brosnorth through and through." Kendrith was unsure if he felt insulted or proud of that comment. "And all those who follow them."

"Don't you dare say it," Kendrith snarled.

"I would have died if I had followed your grandfather out here, especially as I was back then."

"Don't you dare…"

"As did George and Kristen!"

Kendrith saw red, not realising how quickly he had sprung to his feet, how quickly his legs flashed forward, anger filling his fatigued muscles with a blazing burn, but the man didn't care. The sword of Vrania collided against the shaft of Logan's hammer to ignite a short spark of blue.

Logan grunted at the strain, fatigued arms trembling as they held Kendrith's sword at bay. Kendrith himself leaned in with his entire weight, teeth clenching so tight he feared they might crack.

Only the soft sound of grunts and rattling weapons filled the air between the two.

The hammer tilted, sending Kendrith's blade to the floor as Logan grabbed Kendrith's collar and pulled him into a head-butt.

Blood spurted through the air, Kendrith's nose bloody and broken as Logan used the chance to kick Kendrith in the stomach with his tree-trunk legs.

The giant rose to his feet as Kendrith slammed against the wall, Logan's hammer at the ready.

Usually, their fight would be a game of tact, feints and light blows to judge the enemy with admirable acuity, learning from each other before the real fight. But neither side had the mental fortitude or energy for such a thing as reckless and brazen strikes were all that their exhaustion could muster.

Logan swung his hammer wildly. Kendrith only narrowly dodged the reckless swings with legs that struggled to obey him as one grazed his rib and sent him flying. Kendrith winced, hoping it was a bruise rather than a break.

Logan panted, the head of his hammer dragging on the floor, his usually groomed hair now wild, sweat-matted strands sticking to his forehead and his moustache a frazzled mess.

Kendrith charged with sword at the ready.

Logan groaned, raising the hammer for another clumsy exchange.

The hammer swung forward expecting to meet a forward attack as Kendrith tossed his sword through the air. The hammer liberated itself from Logan's grip as the giant stumbled forward to narrowly escape the blade's edge, escaping with only a cut to his cheek.

The sword planted itself into the wall behind as Kendrith leapt onto Logan who fell helplessly to his back, left defenceless to the onslaught of fists that met him.

Logan fell recumbent, submitting to Kendrith's fury as bleeding fists pummelled away at him and Logan's blood mixed with Kendrith's own.

Kendrith panted, wheezed, groaned, and cried. He couldn't will himself to stop even though his body begged him to do so.

His punches became softer, weaker, his arms refused to listen to him.

"Better?" Logan finally asked after an eternity of quiet, his voice a raspy wheeze as his own broken nose whistled with each breath.

Kendrith rolled off Logan, falling beside him.

Kendrith spat to his side, blood and saliva flying. "Better," he said in between breaths.

Logan grasped at his nose and a loud crack and grunt told that he returned his septum to its original spot. Logan spat too, a loose tooth was his reward.

"You could have killed me, you know?" Logan said nonchalantly, his breath still haggard.

"Yeah, but I didn't. You could have killed me too."

"Yeah, but I didn't," Logan parroted.

They chuckled, both of them beginning to laugh together at the absurdity of it all with hysteria. One of Logan's eyes was swollen, and his lip cut. Kendrith's nose was also broken and crooked.

"Ow, ow, ow." Kendrith wheezed, a hand to his bruish hip, his laugh whistling through a broken nose.

They started to laugh harder at that, Logan's nose whistling, and both of them laughing hysterically at it all.

Finally, through pain-filled groans and dying laughter, chuckles left behind like the final embers of a dimming fire, silence returned.

"I'm sorry for what I said, Kendrith. You didn't kill the others. We don't even know if they are dead yet."

Kendrith remained silent for a while. "What are the chances they survived? And let's face it, you're right. My family has always welcomed death—we crave it. You were smart to not go with my grandfather...and it's unfair that I blamed you for his death."

"Aye, perhaps it is unfair, but you're wrong. I regret that decision every day."

The silence which filled the two seemed to fill with the endless possibilities of what Logan considered saying next.

"You try so hard to chase after Mona's and Haggen's footsteps that you still remain in their shadows."

There was a sinking feeling in Kendrith's stomach.

"That's why I didn't follow him. That's why I stepped out of the shadow of a legend to make my own. I knew my light would never reach his, but I achieved great things, regardless. And I am proud of that.

"Haggen was the strongest man I had ever known. If he didn't make it, I wouldn't have either—not now, not when I was still only a second-rate hunter."

"Logan. Why do you do this? There are other jobs. Other positions. You don't have to work for the guild if you really fear travelling here."

Logan stayed quiet for a time. "I don't hate it. I take pride in my work. And I am experienced and cautious enough to guarantee my safety." The words almost sounded like a tasteless joke given their situation.

"But that's the difference between Haggen and me. He did it for the thrill. To discover, to battle, to explore. I did it because of honour, for my family, and the background we have cultivated. Plus, where else would I find work? No. I do what I do and I take pride in it." The words rang with a truth that Kendrith had never considered before then.

Tears now came from Logan. Kendrith didn't have to wonder if they were tears of laughter or fear because he knew they were tears of regret, harboured for years.

"I'm sorry."

"It's okay, it was never your fault...talk about a bad time for regrets though, huh?" Kendrith joked half-heartedly which earned him a hoarse laugh.

When Logan didn't reply, the two just laid there, surrendering themselves to their fate.

All of that was ruined at the sound of a familiar voice.

"What happened to the two of you? Are you okay?"

Kendrith and Logan opened their eyes to see Kristen towering over them with Pecky perched upon her shoulder.

"Kristen?" Kendrith muttered the words in disbelief. The man wondered for a moment if he was losing his sanity.

"Who did this to you?" Kristen asked.

"I thought you died!" Kendrith jumped to his feet, ignoring Kristen's question.

"Did…did the two of you beat each other up?" Kristen looked around at the scenery, her eyes lingering at the wall where the sword of Vrania jutted from.

"Something like that," Kendrith replied, exchanging glances with Logan as blood poured down his face and one of his eyes was swollen shut.

"The two of you are unbelievable," Kristen stated, obviously angered.

"How about you? How did you get away? We saw you fall."

"I didn't." Her tone was filled with incredulous anger. "I dropped down to the face of a rock and clung to it, then climbed my way up to find you two idiots beating each other up."

Logan sat on a rock, his back to the wall, arms stretched out over his knees as his hammer leaned against his shoulder. Blood splattered the wall as he spat. On the other side of the room, Kendrith was bandaging Kristen's hands. Her skin was blistered and torn from where she grabbed at the rocks.

"Are you okay?" Kendrith asked.

Kristen simply nodded, not looking Kendrith in the eye, and the man continued in silence.

"What did you two fight about?" Kristen's query was quiet and though her rage didn't subside, there was an undeniable placated curiosity that lined the stern question.

"Some grievances concerning Haggen and Mother…the usual," Kendrith explained.

"So, you finally talked it out?" Kristen asked.

"I guess we did."

"I'm sorry," Kristen said softly, her gaze falling to the floor. The words were spoken fearfully, to address that which needed to be addressed.

"I'm sorry about George," she said.

"Hey, look at me." Kendrith nudged Kristen by the chin, making her look him in the eye with those piercing eyes of hers which concealed her kind soul. "It's not your fault," Kendrith said, as confidently as he could.

"This is the second time he saved me, you know? The first time was when he killed that creature in the forest...where you took to get me help...and now he did it again," Kristen confided.

"He doesn't see it that way, you know?"

Kristen looked up at that.

"George believes it was his fault you got injured in the first place. That he should have paid more attention back then."

It was true though, if it weren't for George, Kendrith would have been left in an even deeper pit of despair. In many ways, George proved himself more capable of saving them than the professionals did. Kendrith allowed himself a smirk and hoped against hope that George and Simantiar had survived.

But he needed to find a way out of there and return to Haven first, with or without the sword of Vrania.

Kristen was silent for a moment. "He was so close...so close to reaching his goal." The words she spoke echoed the truth that everyone had been avoiding thus far. That all of it was for naught. And as Kendrith bandaged Kristen's hands, he couldn't help but feel sad at the thought. How George had smiled. The adventures they had through the Forest of the Dead. How he had forced himself into Kendrith's life and that he was all the better for it. There was no telling what happened to Simantiar. Was he also dead? Or did they both survive by some miracle?

Kendrith shook the thought away. "We need to find a way out of here," he said.

Finally, Kendrith finished bandaging Kristen's hands.

The cavern was silent, except for a drop of water somewhere resounding like a phantom from someplace distant, and the soft, occasional chittering that could be heard beyond the entrance, like that of an insect scuttling in the back of his mind, evoking an itch that couldn't be reached.

And so, the group sat in the dark, the dim light of Logan's hammer offering soft succour while they waited, eating what rations they had left.

The sword of Vrania lay discarded and forgotten in a corner of its own.

The band walked deeper into the cavern filled with echoing drops as Logan's hammer lit the way.

More and more of the darkness retreated from the winding path. Until finally, the hammer revealed a truth better left hidden.

Kendrith's eyes widened. "It can't be," the words fell from trembling, incredulous lips.

"That's impossible," Logan echoed.

They stared down upon the despairingly familiar figure of Haggen Brosnorth, his body now nothing but bone.

Kendrith fell to his knees. Whatever little strength of conviction he had vanished into a puff of smoke. His hero, his champion, proven mortal, after all.

Kristen walked forward absent-mindedly, her hand reaching for the skeletal and unmoving skull as if it to tenderly cup its cheek as tears flowed freely down her own.

"You were like a father to me," Kristen voiced, kissing his forehead with such tender love.

It was undeniable to Kendrith—that axe that he'd seen countless times lying by his mentor's side. The stature of the body, and even what remained of his clothing.

"He must have come here and discovered it during his travels," Logan said numbly.

Kendrith nodded. "Sought refuge after what happened with the centipede, probably." Kendrith balled his fist—this was not the hero's end he was promised to immortalise Haggen as the spirit of a hero. His image of the once great Haggen was shattered. No longer some great beacon of heroism. He was human. Just like the rest of them. And he had received a very human death.

Logan stepped forward and took Haggen's axe from the ground. Rust had eaten away at it, but its heft seemed just as foreboding as Kendrith remembered.

"If we ever make it out of here, we should return what remains of him to Haven where he belongs." The deep contemplative deference in Logan's voice was obvious to all present.

Kristen and Kendrith made sure to pack up what little else remained of Haggen, including his bones.

The three stood there to mourn the fallen friend and hero before continuing on the path which soon too would become their resting ground.

"What is this place?" Kristen asked, as the rough natural construction of the caves gave way to smooth man-made walls.

The two glanced up to see the etchings carved as murals into the walls.

"Some form of inscription?" Logan queried, lifting the light of his hammer to unveil the hidden text.

Kendrith looked to the wall, humbled by the knowledge that they had remained hidden for a countless age. How small they felt, insignificant in the presence of those who lived during a time when Simantiar was not just a legend.

The carved murals showed a battle, a mage facing a gathering of sorcerers alone.

The mural showed the lone mage drifting along the ground with robes floating behind, equally so there was a well upon which the mage drifted onto and came face-to-face with their advisory.

One bore the sigil of the sun, while the other that of the moon.

"Is that supposed to be...?" Kristen caught herself before she could say his name.

"Simantiar?" Kendrith inferred, looking at the engraved grooves of a boned figure destined to rise again.

Further and further the images revealed a tale, one that could be discerned with the few writings of an ancient text that Logan and Kendrith could only decipher in parts, while the rest they gathered from the images.

"Simantiar seemed to have a friend, a close one," Kendrith said.

"One depicted by the moon," Logan added.

"But they had a falling out of some sort...must have been pretty serious to earn such portent murals. Did they perish?"

"No...not perished. Otherwise Simantiar wouldn't be here now."

"While his friend was swallowed by some sort of pool." Kendrith cupped his chin in thought, both of them lost in the meaning of the murals.

"So, the academy, or more so the mountain, was blown apart from that power," Logan continued.

"And through the rubble, wizards came, learnt of the truth from Simantiar's half-living body."

"And so a pact was made."

"What kind of pact?" Kristen asked as the two grew silent. Both Kendrith and Logan carried concern in their eyes.

"To seal Simantiar away, and create trials for those who wanted to retrieve his remains." The words were spoken and the group knew fully well of the implications.

"Simantiar was supposed to be found, supposed to live for thousands of years, trapped, so that George could find him...so that he could return Simantiar here...to finish what was started."

"Finish? Finish what?"

Kendrith hesitated. "To finish what was started with his friend, the one from his stories...Usellyes. There is no vault, this was what it was all about."

Chapter 50

Like colour running from canvas reality fell apart. The outlines of the painting still remained, but the details were washed away by the river of power which coursed from Usellyes and Simantiar.

Shapes bending, stretching, losing their permanence.

And so too did the shimmering waters of the arcane pool continue to part as Simantiar willed. Usellyes stepped back, disdain clear on his face, refusing to accept that even then, even with all his newfound power, that Simantiar still stood above him.

Usellyes summoned even more strength to himself—the arcane magic that usually lay spread across the world, invisible, now concentrated to such a degree that it condensed into a pool of heavy iridescent liquid, diluted and harnessed by the crystal above to pump even more of it into Usellyes.

The mountain shuddered, the ground trembled, and rubble continued to fall from atop the chamber as the world literally fell apart.

But it wasn't to match Simantiar's magic, for he must have known it would never be enough, and instead Usellyes conjured an antimagic field.

The world returned to normal, the academy and the mountain upon which it lay stopped rattling, stopped being torn apart by the seismic pressure of magical poles grinding with sparks that threatened to unravel everything.

The condensed arcane pool rushed together, the clashing waves overlapping one another—it was as if two giants played upon the world's oceans.

Simantiar panted, the strain of his magical power didn't come without effort, and even then, he stood there shocked that someone was able to smother his will; grateful of the possibility that there were powers that could hold him in check, and yet terrified of it all the same.

"What will you do now, Simantiar? Without your glorious magic to aid you? Do you feel as helpless as we all do?" Usellyes mocked, but there was an earnest curiosity to his query.

Something about Usellyes seemed different. His aggression was brash rather than tempered, his flame unbridled, with a certain delirious and rabid look to his eyes that made him seem wholly unlike himself.

"You think I'm helpless?" Simantiar questioned. He could see Usellyes standing at the ready, expecting Simantiar's inexplicable power to still manifest itself through the antimagic field.

But no such magic came, instead, a fist—the last thing Usellyes seemed to expect—landed straight between the archmage's eyes.

Usellyes stumbled through the pool as blood ran down the man's nose.

"Look at your crooked nose! Look at what drips down your lips!" Simantiar compelled, straightening his fist out before him so that all could see. "Look at what marks my fist! You bleed! And so do I! Don't forget who you are, Usellyes!"

"No. With this much potential I am so much more. I can finally bring an end to suffering!"

Simantiar waded through the thick arcane water and punched Usellyes once more, sending him down to the ground where he gripped the lip of the pool.

"Do you really believe that I would always fall to rely on my magic? That I would never strive to learn things beyond just that? There is more to being alive than fists. My mother taught me that. It was my hubris to believe myself special, to use my magic on the unwilling in hopes of bringing them joy—it only made things worse. Joselyn's hate for me saved me—why can't her love save you?" Another punch and blood flowed down the broken nose.

Simantiar grabbed Usellyes and raised him from the floor, wrapping his arms around the thin man from behind. He lifted Usellyes off his feet as the cords which connected him thrashed and the arcane water splashed all over the rim. Simantiar grabbed Usellyes in a headlock till his wild resistance quelled and the waters stilled to reveal their shimmering reflections.

"Look at yourself!" Simantiar said, anger in his voice, disappointment. He didn't expect to find his own reflection so alien. He could almost see the young boys they used to be, the bond they had so long ago, and how there was once a time when they could have even been lovers.

How far they had drifted since then, how estranged they had become. Noima's tender love resounded in the back of Simantiar's mind. A part of Noima had finally reached Simantiar, and he could only hope that his own persistent love could reach Usellyes.

"Do you like what you see? What you've become? A mere shadow of the man I once knew, that I loved."

Usellyes did not respond as he attempted to escape Simantiar's grip. Simantiar searched for a single hint of regret, looked for disgust in what Usellyes saw in his own reflection. Usellyes grunted, his grimace one of loathing, his eyes seemingly avoiding their own reflection.

"I admired you, you know," Simantiar began, a placating promise whispered into Usellyes's ear. "How you worked so earnestly, how you earned that which you wanted. And perhaps if our roles were reversed as children, it would be me plugged into a crystallised Omukade."

"Stop it with your lies," Usellyes said in return. "You had everything from the start. It was me who admired you, who wanted to *be* like you. For if I had such power, I would have never known such suffering. Do you know what it was like? To beg? To have to steal? To have people's eyes gloss over you like the stain beneath their shoe?"

Usellyes drew even more power from the well, his eyes glowing a fierce orange as his body became a vessel for the arcane. His body shuddered, cracks forming in the container he had become, the magic overflowing too quickly.

"Stop it!" Simantiar called out, but Usellyes was already too far gone. The antimagic barrier started to break from within.

"I can see it…" Usellyes began.

"A future where we will meet again." Usellyes began to shed his human shell, the glowing light breaking forth until he shone as bright as a bottled sun with flaring radiance.

And so, the pool of arcane magic began to swallow him, as the overflowing magic within Usellyes began to become a part of him, and the arcane took him on as a being of pure magic.

"Will you be there to try to stop me again, Simantiar?" Before Usellyes was swallowed up entirely, the antimagic field was torn down, the culmination of that spell welled and pulled into Usellyes's hand that suddenly grabbed Simantiar's arm.

Light burnt and sizzled through flesh, and Simantiar cried out in pain as smoke rose from the touch, the hand of pure arcane light searing him as his hold broke.

"But before that, a key, and a curse. For when the time comes, it will be only you who can unlock that door." Usellyes released his grip, his face now barely over water as he spoke the last of his words. "Yet, I am curious to see if your words match your conviction. Are you still Simantiar, if I take away that which defines you most? Your love for magic. Time is of no consequence now, and I will gladly wait millennia until the starry-eyed hopeful with a suffering past comes to me in hopes of their wish—and I will grant it."

And so it happened that Usellyes disappeared under the waters, and no matter how much Simantiar waded through the arcane pool, still he found no traces of his old friend, just the hard stone floor beneath.

The magic infused into Simantiar's arm took hold, branding into muscle and bone, and the pain was agonizing. The pool of arcana, torn from its delicate shape and forced together, once an intricate and complex pattern, but was now bundled into a chaotic knot thrashed its waves.

The power of Usellyes and Simantiar faded, removing the force which had defiled the magical weave that covered all living things; it unravelled with terrible force, trying to return to its natural state. An explosion happened, the sound wave thrumming through the mountain like a deep grumble, the rubble now raining down in greater clumps. The sound reverberated through Simantiar's very bones.

"The academy," he said. A sudden realisation of what must have happened, that the very place he used to call home was now sundered on the surface. Cernunnos, all the other students and faculty... Simantiar could only pray that they got away in time.

He turned to see the one remaining ally of his unconscious on the floor.

"Ciro!" He remembered.

He raised a hand to cast his magic.

Nothing.

He flicked his wrist, but found that no sorcery beckoned to his will.

Even in his moment of contemplative disgust he called upon the pool of magic at his feet, but found that even that would not heed his wishes.

He imagined Usellyes watching and laughing with such mocking glee, to see himself proven right, to see how helpless Simantiar was in the face of his mortality, to even draw upon the pools power which didn't heed his call to save someone.

"Hypocrite." He could hear Usellyes berating him.

Disgust and panic filled him as the rest of the mountain collapsed, its foundations toppling over.

He tried to get out of the pool, but it seemed that even fate mocked Simantiar as a giant boulder collapsed onto Ciro.

Before his attention could turn to Moran he was already broken into several pieces.

"No!" What a great and despairing wail escaped Simantiar's lungs as his cries turned into weeping sorrow.

How helpless he felt.

Simantiar fell to his knees as the rest of the rubble collapsed all around him. He tried to beckon the weave to him, to command it, but that connection was lost, severed by whatever searing pain was branded into him.

Usellyes's final words continued to ring in his head. That his link to magic was taken away, that his very being pulled from him as if to challenge him.

The touch of that concentrated arcane water made Simantiar sick to his stomach—how the liquid clung to his skin, demanding to be used.

For a moment, he saw Usellyes looking back in the pool, not the monster he had become, but the kind boy he used to be, full of wonder and hope.

Simantiar cursed himself, that perhaps he had truly shared wisdom and platitudes without ever truly understanding what it was like to be the downtrodden, to judge all from his throne and pretend as if he knew their suffering.

The reflection in the water smiled lovingly and with forgiveness.

A smile that turned into a vile, insidious grin which taunted Simantiar. Childlike Usellyes watched with a Cheshire cat smile till his gum showed and it seemed like the corners of his mouth would tear.

Such a maddening frenzy in those restless eyes.

"How does it feel to be helpless, Simantiar? I could bring Ciro back. All you need to do is ask. Moran. Everyone who now dies because of your selfishness."

"You're killing them!" Simantiar managed.

"No. I'm not. You are. I can bring them all back to life whenever I wish. All you need to do is ask."

Simantiar's mind pounded, his hands trembled. His breath quickened and he realised he was having a panic attack. His mind returned to a long time ago, after he had rescued Usellyes and was driven mad with the Omukade which lurked in his mind.

He seriously considered the offer, but his lips wouldn't obey.

"Pl-please." Tears streaked Simantiar's cheeks as he tried to will himself to say the words. Usellyes's mouth opened even wider until like a leather sack it pulled back to reveal the Omukade's reflection.

"Yeeees?" The query was soft and drawn-out like a pernicious whisper that taunted.

The roof rained down now in even greater clumps, the waters of the pool clashing against the rim.

"All you need to say is 'Please return them to me.'"

Was Simantiar going to die? Would he ever see Noima again?

"Pleeeease."

Fear motivated him, fear of loneliness, fear of helplessness. His mind felt like it was being torn apart from the inside.

"Plea—" Simantiar's final plea was never heard as a block of stone came crashing from above, breaking upon the surface of the crystal.

Simantiar watched powerlessly as the reflection of the broken rubble drew nearer and buried him.

Simantiar wasn't dead, not fully. Usellyes made a promise to him and Usellyes kept his promises. The years passed by, turning into decades, and then into centuries. Simantiar's consciousness stilled, wafting through the eternal waters of his soul, a candle of life snuffed out, sailing the abyssal sea on a wooden board until something would light the candle again.

And thus it happened, that the first of the rubble was cleared from Simantiar's tomb, a sound filling the place, Simantiar's consciousness returning into all that was left of him, just bones atop of bones. The empty pits within Simantiar's skull were lifeless and dark, as a sudden blue light twinkled to life, like a single star in a black sky.

Simantiar returned, finding that death would not claim him yet.

Chapter 51

Simantiar awoke, the dream finally over, and his memories returned to the man who had lived far past his lifespan.

Yet, he awoke in darkness, not surrounded by his friends in a cavern, and as he commanded his fingers to move they did not, as he wiggled his toes they did not—the wizard felt naked in that emptiness.

He could feel a hand, a hand that cradled him protectively, a hand that held him within the pits of an abyss that seemed to be the valley of death itself, where no light could reach, and where no life could flourish.

Simantiar remained silent, ensuring himself of the void that surrounded him, and then summoned magic to himself—magic that now disgusted him. He could feel the power he was drawing, power from the very pool of arcana Usellyes had infused within him to sever his link to magic, and yet grant him immortality. A silent insult it was, for if Simantiar wanted to cast magic he had to use the same means which Usellyes had. Still that maleficent grin that stared from the pool followed him, a taunting laughter at the back of his cranium that he only then noticed.

The twinkling blue glow of his eyes brightened, and a mote of blue light formed above Simantiar's skull to illuminate the surrounding area. How he regretted it—as the mote of light uncovered a most rueful sight.

Simantiar felt as if he had committed an atrocious act, a sin unlike any other to defile the laws of that very abyss he found himself in. All around, he found that he was but one unremarkable skull among a sea of them. Littered all around him was death, skulls stacked upon countless bones as far as the mote of light could reach and continuing ever after. He knew, then and there, the remains that filled that valley of death, were the remains of his brothers and sisters, mages of old, teachers, classmates, students that came long after he had left.

Ciro.

Moran.

Did Cernunnos get the others out in time?

Simantiar knew from the beginning that Ciro and all the others were already dead. A longing ache filled his figurative heart when he realised that Noima must have waited for him.

He knew that they had all been dead for a very long time...but watching it all end the way it did filled Simantiar with a profound sadness he couldn't place.

Simantiar turned his gaze to behold the worst visage of all which were the bloody remains of George cradling him in his grip.

Empty and vapid eyes stared to a place where no light shone. He was lost to the depths like a shadow, the blood that spilled from him baptising the remains of all the lost that came before.

His quest cut short, the promise he carried close to his heart now impossible to fulfil.

If Simantiar had the power he once did so long ago, he would have returned George to the living in a heartbeat...even if it was at the cost of that single beat.

"I'm sorry, I'm so sorry," Simantiar said, unsure of what had happened while he was gone, only to find that he had found himself in a dark crypt, a place he should have joined long ago. "I'm so sorry," he said again, words now spoken for all who rested there, dead because Simantiar could not stop Usellyes, dead because he was too naive.

Overwhelmed, Simantiar found himself lost. He wasn't special, not anymore—he was just like everyone else, even with incomprehensible power he couldn't save those that mattered to him most. "I'm sorry."

The blue mote of light descended slowly, the light dwindling, flickering. "Please, no." Simantiar wanted to cry, but had no eyes to cry from. "I'm sorry." Simantiar begged, but the light faded, and the wizard turned mortal sobbed at the bottom of the valley of bones, surrounded by George's bleeding body and the thousands of dead that would finally welcome him home. "Don't leave me to the darkness," Simantiar begged as the final bits of the mote vanished and his concentration broke. He was back in that umbral crypt where his mind had been eternally still till George discovered him.

He felt watched, the empty, shrouded sockets of the vapid skulls watching him with quiet judgment.

He wondered if it was worse to die with their unforgiving and haunting gaze, or to lament their stare for all of eternity.

"Please," Simantiar begged into the abyss, but nothing answered George's hand which cradled him felt so lifeless.

"Don't leave me here." Simantiar knew he had no right to ask of such things, no right to beg release from where he belonged. Yet still, he could not help but feel terror, he could only hope that it was just a horrifying dream.

"It's okay," a voice spoke. Was Simantiar losing his mind? Creating whispers and worlds to fill in the void?

"We have been expecting you." There it was again.

Simantiar saw the blue glow return, yet it wasn't his own, but rather something else entirely.

Simantiar watched as a familiar man stood before him. Mylor Hershaw, with his bald head and salt-and-pepper beard, the old headmaster who had scolded him oh so long ago looked on tenderly and with fond reminiscence. But there was something else in his spectral eyes, something that Simantiar didn't know he needed till just that very moment. There was forgiveness.

"It's okay, boy. You have nothing to apologise for. We are all with you."

And like that, the specters of a thousand other people ignited like sky lanterns being lit; their bodies translucent, blue auras enrapturing them as if halos as they floated upon the very bones that once carried their souls.

"What…what happened?" Simantiar began.

"When you had your bout with Usellyes, the rest of us who were still in the academy never survived the impact. What remains could be found from the calamity were brought down here, buried for the day when you would return."

"But how?"

"Cernunnos. He conjured the spirits, called us back, and bound only the willing. Those of us who were at the academy or in the vicinity rallied to the call." Mylor shook his head in regret. "That boy Usellyes, I told him he should stay away from all of this. I should have stopped him when I could."

"I am sorry, Simantiar." A familiar face stepped forward, it was Moran, regret in his eyes still despite years of reflection.

"Moran?" queried Simantiar.

"I should have never joined Usellyes. His promise of hope and dreams blinded me."

It all seemed too much for Simantiar to process. It seemed only minutes ago that he was battling the mage and his allies. Though Simantiar knew that the spirits before him had a millennium to reflect.

"Simantiar." Ciro stepped forward. Even as a translucent spectre she still seemed so strong, so reliable. A friend one could have truly relied on. "You have no idea how long I have waited to apologise." Even as a ghost the guilt she harboured in those tormented eyes spoke volumes.

It is one thing to do wrong by someone and move on to newer things, even if the relationship could not be mended. It was another thing entirely to partake in an error so grievous and be forced to face the consequences of your own actions for an eternity. Simantiar broke down just minutes after regaining his memories and, learning the truth, he couldn't begin to fathom what that meant for everyone else.

"I'm sorry, Simantiar. You were right. I was foolish to not consider the repercussions."

Simantiar cut in. "I'm the one who should apologise. After everything, I still let it happen." Simantiar considered the last of his memories. "Usellyes seemed…different. He wasn't himself."

"Usellyes blinded himself too," Mylor explained. "The nights leading up to his plan he showed a mania that I had never witnessed before. He was already training to connect with the crystal." Mylor hesitated for a second. "That day, when you traversed the biomes and removed your arm ring, it was Usellyes that stole the key, wasn't it?"

Simantiar confirmed it.

"You covered for him, didn't you? Because he brought back an Omukade."

Simantiar begrudgingly admitted the truth.

Mylor did not admonish Simantiar however, it was time to look to the future for those who still lived. "Usellyes must have been infected."

"Like how I was?" Simantiar asked.

Mylor shook his head. "No. Not with an actual Omukade, but by their essence, by their very denoting properties he must have been twisted to become a conduit for all things. His intentions never changed, the choice to do what he did was still his own. But that much power, that much arcane potential must have twisted his understanding of pain and consequence."

Simantiar recalled the events that passed and affirmed Mylor's theory. "When I last saw Usellyes, he saw no error in the lives he cost. He believed it was my fault for not wishing it all away. He believed that if he could make it all go back to how it was before, that it was of no consequence what he did in that moment."

Simantiar went quiet as the gazes of all those from his past looked on. There was no pain in their eyes. Just expectation. It was time for them to look forward, but Simantiar knew not what he could do.

"I'm sorry. After all this time, here I am and there is nothing I can do. You all put your faith in me and I let you down." Simantiar turned his gaze to George. "I let you all down," he repeated.

"We all carry our burdens." Mylor waved at the others, classmates of old, Miss Clarisse, her stern expression gone, now only showing one of warmth and compassion. One by one he could see those who stood with equal measures conviction and regret.

There were some among the sea of people who he didn't recognise, but they knew him. And there were other faces he searched for, but couldn't find. He wondered if he truly had hurt Joselyn so.

There was no Emilie, or Zaros...there was a part of him, a regretfully selfish part that hoped against hope that Noima was also there among the endless faces...nothing.

The thought that the man who he never saw a future with until it was too late lived his life without Simantiar was equally a comfort as well as a sorrow.

A sudden thought occurred to Simantiar. "My mother wouldn't happen to be among you?" He realised it was a far cry from being possible considering she was nowhere near the academy when it all happened.

"My boy," Simantiar now saw his mother standing before him. No wheelchair. No seat. Standing as a spectral visage of the strong, empowering mother she once was—she seemed more alive in death than she ever did among the living.

"How?" Simantiar asked.

"Ask Cernunnos," she said smiling. It was a sombre smile, one that belonged to a woman who had waited a long, long time for her son to return; a smile saved for the chance of one final meeting. Any amount of time passed would be worth it just for that one reunion.

Simantiar felt naked as just a skeleton to his mother who seemed so beautiful as a spectre, unmarred by any imperfection.

Simantiar realised something. "But! What about Father?" Simantiar knew the truth, knew her intent to die so she may return to her love.

"I have been waiting for so long among the living, what matters a few centuries more when I get to spend eternity with him? Plus, Cernunnos visited me when I was at death's door and told me the day would come when my son would need me again. What kind of mother would I be to refuse such a chance to see my son again?"

Simantiar wanted to cry and cursed his vacuous skull.

"Mother," Simantiar said, tears welling in his eyes. "I'm sorry, Mother, I am so sorry." His worst fear had been realised, his mother taken from the living because of his mistake.

"Don't be, for you have a burden on your shoulders nobody should have to carry."

"And you won't have to carry it alone, any longer," Miss Clarisse said.

"For we stand by you," Ciro added.

The thousands of gathered mages, familiar faces and not, raised their hands and clasped them together.

"For you will no longer need the promise of Usellyes, for we shall give you what arcane power we still have. We will do this together," Mylor finished, extending his hand to touch Simantiar.

"Wait," Simantiar halted him.

"What is it?"

"You should know…that I will use some of that power to bring George back." Simantiar nodded to the still lifeless corpse of his friend. None of the specters touched his lifeless body, instead gliding upon their own remains that filled the valley like a coursing stream of spirits.

"But you will need every last bit of magic to face Usellyes!" Moran began, yet a wave from Mylor's hand silenced him immediately.

"We entrust our magic to you—what you decide to do with it is up to you," Mylor granted.

"Just…when you're done, make sure to join us in the gates beyond," Giselle said with a mother's tender smile, a smile that still managed to tug at his transcendental heart.

"I plan to," Simantiar said, renewed conviction flowing through him, and with that, a heavy burden shared upon the shoulders of spirits long past.

His eyes drifted to his mother. "I know you disapprove, that life runs its course and—"

"And yet here we all are, in a time not our own, bound to a catacomb of calamity. This boy didn't have to die for our errors. I trust in you, my son. We all do."

Simantiar looked out towards the sea of smiling spirits that looked down to him and even though their touch filled the living with only the chilling cold of the afterlife, he felt their warmth overflowing. They trusted him. They had waited. Patiently awaited Simantiar's return for a thousand years.

Giselle bent over and the strong lithe hands of a mother raised Simantiar's skull so that she could grant a final transcending kiss on his enamel forehead, and the power flowed unyieldingly.

The power that rushed into him was exhilarating. A sensation as familiar as when he was still connected to the weave, a warmth that reminded him of love, of friendship and trust, of a time when Usellyes was everything to him. Yet within that stream, Simantiar also felt regret, hate, guilt, envy, and things that made everyone human, and he accepted it all wholeheartedly.

This was his chance to do things right.

The crowd of people disappeared, darkness returning momentarily and then gone once more.

Simantiar stood, no longer made of bones and bark and roots and vines, but now of flesh and skin. He looked much like his old human self; a full beard, long grown out hair, light bristles of arm hair upon sun-kissed skin. The man chuckled for a moment, finding himself lost in what had just happened. Laughing that he now had skin, teeth, eyes, a nose—all of the parts from when he was alive now returned to him. He looked to his hands and noticed his body surrounded by a blue halo that radiated from him, the blue light rising as wisps of smoke from his eyes, leaking out from his new vessel made of the powers of those that trusted and loved him.

This was not the same power he had from ages long past, but rather one entrusted to him by those who believed. It felt warm and snug—the kind of feeling one has on a cold winter day wrapped under a blanket with a warm drink in one's hand. It radiated from him and gave him hope. It was not the baseless, meaningless power he once had, but rather something greater.

Simantiar pulled on the strap of his trousers to look inside. He smiled, bellowing a loud laugh that echoed through the valley of death. "Still got it," he said.

He let go of the strap, a resounding snap to his waist as Simantiar could feel pain again. "God, that feels good."

Simantiar turned around, his smile now fading at the sight of George's still body.

"I'm sorry, George. Once more it is you who has saved me. Thank you."

Simantiar knelt before him, his ghostly cowl draped over the remains of old friends. He placed a thumb against George's forehead, bowing his head with eyes closed in concentration. "It is not yet your time," he said, as the magical aura that brimmed and surrounded him spilled from his fingers like an azure fog that settled over George, filling his cold body with the warmth of life.

George hadn't been dead for long, and his spirit had not yet passed on. But the task of reversing the pull, of denying death its due and tearing George's spirit back into its own broken body was no easy task. Already Simantiar could feel the gifted essence drain from him, already he felt his power dwindle. It did not matter. George lived to the end of his days as a human, had grown so much in the past few months, saved Simantiar, and brought him back to his tomb so that he could finish what was started. Simantiar knew that he would either finish things with George by his side or not at all.

A gasp. A beat of the heart. A cough. George returned to the land of the living. Broken bones and ruptured organs mended themselves with the suture that was Simantiar's magic.

"It's okay," Simantiar began, rubbing his back as he continued to cough, recently defunct lungs now filling with air once more and the pain that came with that.

George looked up to Simantiar once his coughing seized, and tears filled bloodshot eyes. George recoiled from Simantiar. "Who are you?" he demanded.

Simantiar seemed a little surprised, then remembered how he must have looked. He smiled idiotically. "What? Did I seem more normal to you as a bag of bones?"

"Simantiar?" he asked quizzically.

"In the flesh! Quite literally!"

George leapt towards Simantiar for a tight embrace.

"Careful!" Simantiar didn't see it coming as they both toppled over into bones that gave a rattling echo through the darkness.

They both laughed, the shadows didn't seem so scary anymore.

"You feel so human. What happened to you?" George asked.

"To me? What about you?"

George seemed to suddenly remember something as he patted himself down.

"I'm alive?" he asked.

"Wasn't easy, you know," Simantiar admitted, a great deal of his power drained. He couldn't help but wonder if he had enough strength for the battle that was to come.

George grew quiet. "Thank you."

"I should be the one thanking you," Simantiar replied.

"Where are we?" George asked, letting go of Simantiar and giving off an awkward cough.

"At the bottom of the mountain. We fell when some centipede monster attacked us."

"Like the one from the forest?"

"No, this one was different…this one had solid form, the one I told you about did not," Simantiar explained.

"My god, all these remains…so many people must have died."

"They did," Simantiar said ruefully.

Simantiar's gaze was suddenly caught by a curious item. It was George's lute, torn from its case that lay a few feet away. The lute was broken and in tatters with a broken neck hanging by a single string yet to snap.

"George…your lute." Simantiar was already beginning to cast a spell and fix it.

George seemed dismissive. "It's fine."

"But—"

"I don't need it. Not anymore. We are so close, Simantiar! We are almost at the vault."

Simantiar suddenly felt his heart beat a cold beat. Having no ostensible facial expressions made him lax as George seemed to read him like an open book.

"Something wrong?" George asked.

"When we find the vault…will you be making a wish?"

George seemed dumbfounded. "Are you saying it's real?"

Simantiar went incredibly quiet as George's face lit up with pernicious hope.

"Simantiar...do you remember?" George asked him.

"I remember everything." He nodded, unsure how to explain the truth of the vault. Simantiar remembered the book that George carried with him, the one inscribed with Usellyes's name. He must have set this all up, set it up for a reunion so that he could prove to Simantiar that people wished for such power.

"How do we get out of here?" George asked, looking up, but the light from Simantiar's body could only reach so far.

"George. There is something I need to tell you," Simantiar tried to explain.

"It's too dark. Can we climb?" If George had heard Simantiar he gave no such impression.

"George, the vault."

"Can you fly us out?"

"George!" The bellowing sound of Simantiar's renewed visceral throat sent resounding echoes through the endless chasm that cut through George's musings.

George looked to Simantiar in a new light—he must have never seen Simantiar so stern before.

"You hope to find your sister, don't you?"

George blinked. "I mean. Yeah, if I can get my sister back."

Simantiar bit his lip and instead swallowed his retort and waved a hand over the lute as it began to mend itself back together, a discordant pluck of strings that gradually rang out from a forming hollow base.

"Well then, it would be best you have something to play for your sister when she is back among the living."

George wrapped his fingers around the lute hesitantly and returned it to an equally restored case.

"Everything all right?" George asked.

Simantiar buried his dark thoughts and smiled a toothy smile once more. "Absolutely. Better than ever. You ready?"

George nodded. "But how do we get out?" George asked, changing the subject.

"Easily," Simantiar said, walking over and picking George up in his arms as mighty wings sprouted like a spring from his back, growing and growing until each wingspan ranged longer than Simantiar's own corporeal form.

"How did you do that?" George asked bewildered.

Simantiar simply smiled. "I am Simantiar, the greatest wizard to have ever lived!"

And with a great wing beat that lifted them off the sea of bones, the two rose, escaping the valley of old resting friends and soaring upwards. Simantiar's halo shining bright, challenging all the creatures of the dark.

Yet he couldn't help but wonder…when the time came, would George prove Usellyes right?

Chapter 52

"Do you think it is still out there?"

"Probably."

The silence between Logan, Kristen, and Kendrith was unnerving.

Kendrith and Logan did most of the talking. The information they gathered from the murals filled in much of the gaps.

"Slowly, on me," Logan whispered to the others, leaning on the wall, his golden hammer at the ready.

Kendrith could tell that Logan was on his last legs, the bout they had and the constant running in heavy armour had taken its toll. But the truth of the murals, and of who Simantiar was gave them hope. That perhaps at the very bottom of that eternal darkness which spanned the chasm was their salvation.

"Slowly." Logan beckoned them forward as the large centipede patiently scuttled above, waiting for more signs of life—of food.

"There is no way we can make it—it knows we are trapped here," Kendrith said.

"We have to try," Logan rebuffed, unable to hide the doubt and exhaustion in his own voice.

Suddenly, a blue pillar of streaking light shot up through the chasm like a searing ray.

"What was that?" Kristen asked.

A shrill, monstrous scream was followed by the sounds of thrashing bodies slamming against the chasm walls till the floor beneath Kendrith's feet trembled, and they were showered by dust.

The screaming stopped, silence, then the trio watched as the charred and smoking ruin of the centipede plummeted into the darkness. All that could be heard was a slowly fading echo of its chitinous body bouncing off walls and crumbling bridges and then nothing.

"What just happened?" Kendrith murmured to himself.

The trio ran to the edge and looked over the precipice, yet the darkness had already claimed the beast, just the destruction on its way down to confirm what had taken place.

The blue light brightened above as Kendrith, Logan, Kristen, and Pecky veered their gaze and looked up to see the blinding light which had them shield their eyes.

The light dimmed and their arms fell so that they may know their saviour. Cowled and hooded, with a full beard and lustrous blond hair floated a man with resplendent angel wings—and in his arms lay George fully alive with a wide teasing grin.

"Vrania." The words escaped Kendrith's lips as a whisper, his gaze filled with bewilderment and awe.

"Guess again!" The angel had a dumb smile on his face, one that took away from his divine presence.

Kendrith seemed confused, until he noticed George alive and well in his arms.

"You won't *believe* who this is," George said with barely restrained excitement.

"Simantiar?" Kendrith queried as Pecky flew from Kristen's shoulder and onto the man's as if knowing the answer.

"In the flesh!" spoke the floating, winged man.

"You love that joke, don't you?" George mused.

Simantiar pouted jokingly and tossed him from his arms.

Kendrith, Kristen, and Logan screamed a unanimous cry of panic as they leapt forward to catch George, his weight flattening them all to the ground. "By the heavens, George, are you all right?" Kristen asked concerned, clambering out of the pile to check George for any injuries.

"You guys are no fun." Simantiar crossed his arms and drifted to his feet.

"He could have fallen back down!" Kendrith shouted.

"Oh please, he's alive, isn't he?" Simantiar winked.

"Really, I'm fine," George explained, clambering down from the others.

Kristen embraced the boy. "Thank the heavens you're all right. I couldn't live with myself if you died."

"You are just full of surprises," Kendrith said, noticeably relieved.

Logan gave a grunt of agreement.

George looked the two of them up and down. "What happened to the two of you?"

Kendrith and Logan seemed to suddenly shy away from the conversation and redden—Kendrith had completely forgotten about his injuries.

George looked to Kristen. "They fought each other, didn't they?"

The two seemed to shrink even further.

"Well, they sorted some things out," Kristen left it at that, not chastising the two for their actions.

Logan went to his knee, his hammer placed standing by his side.

"Logan, what are you doing?" Kendrith asked.

"I am in the presence of a great lost mage, and thus I show reverence."

"Just a while ago you said I was a spawn of darkness and now you are bowing your head? Just get up," Simantiar replied in annoyance.

"Yes, Your Radiance."

"Oh blimey, I preferred it when you were trying to kill me."

They laughed, all of them. The light of his halo, of his aura, banished the bleak, suffocating darkness that permeated the realm, and life and hope returned once more. The shadows which spanned the chasm like festering roots of a dying tree and had once provided succour now showed a glimpse of how majestic and awe-inspiring a place it once was.

"What happened to you?" Kendrith asked, touching Simantiar's face as he landed, the wings retracting back.

"Hey, hands off the merchandise." Simantiar slapped Kendrith's arm aside. "What? You preferred it when I was just a bag of bones? This is my true form! I feel alive again!" His aura burned even brighter at the declaration.

"What is this all about, Simantiar?"

"I've regained all my memories."

"Yeah, and we learnt a thing or two as well," Kristen added.

Kristen led the way, showing the murals that told of the happenings within the mountain.

Simantiar turned to the back of the group past where Pecky pecked against Simantiar's shoulder, seemingly confused why he could no longer enter him.

George gazed at the murals, and with each passing block of stone another layer of darkness loomed over him and his mood grew sullen at the growing realisation.

Upon learning of the past, Simantiar realised a lot of the missing pieces were coming together. Like the explorers that had found him, the book that was left behind in Usellyes's name, and the plan that was put together.

Simantiar told the others of the truth, that he was cursed with an antimagic seal, that the powers he summoned were borrowed from the pool of arcana that was forced into him. Of what all this was meant to bring.

"So, the vault is real?" Kristen asked.

Simantiar confirmed with a nod—he still wasn't used to the feeling of itching skin or twitching nostrils. Or the taste of stale air in the caverns that suffocated him and pressed against his lungs or the blotches in his vision whenever his eyes glazed over the balls of light. Even if it was temporary, he was glad to feel alive again.

"But it's not that simple, is it? You are saying that Usellyes is waiting behind the vault at a well. To settle things once and for all?"

Simantiar nodded again. "But it's not that simple. The reason this all started was to prove a point."

"What point?" Logan asked, eyes narrowing.

Simantiar hung his head and licked his lips in consideration. "Should you enter, Usellyes will promise all of you the chance to fulfil your greatest desires."

Seven eyes in total, if one weren't to count the swelling mess that was one of Logan's eyes, widened in disbelief at the statement.

"*Any* wish?" Kristen accentuated.

Simantiar could only nod.

"...he could bring back my sister?" George questioned incredulous. "Lily, she could return to us?"

"George, I need you to understand. You don't want this." Simantiar lowered himself and stared straight into George's eyes with his own sea-blue pair.

"Why not?" George challenged, his fists balling up and his arms rigid and tense as he tried his best to hold back the tears. "It is my sister. She could come back to me. I could protect her." Like a cracking dam the first of the tears flowed from rheumy eyes.

"Why not?" Logan reiterated, but his question seemed to be for more stoic academic purposes.

Simantiar looked up to the giant. "Because the last time he promised such a thing the world was drained of its magic and monsters spewed from its maw. Something changed in Usellyes, something which gave him power at the cost of understanding what it means to be human. He stripped me of my connection to magic and had me imprisoned for a thousand years to prove a point while the rest of the world suffered for it. Simply because he believes he can undo it. He needs to be stopped. And magic needs to return to this realm."

The others stared on, unsure and dumbfounded. Simantiar didn't blame them. The concept of magic returning to the world of Tiria seemed so strange and alien. What did it matter to them if magic did or didn't return?

"Whatever." George brushed Simantiar away and walked back to the entrance of the hall.

Simantiar turned to the mural on his right, seeing the likeness of Usellyes represented by the sigil of the moon and him at the rim of his pool represented by the sun.

How much he'd give to return to the day they met and were nothing more than starry-eyed boys with so much wonder.

Chapter 53

The highest floor of the chasm held two golden gates. Vaults with whatever content inside barred from view.

The surface of the gates, though the occasional gold forced its way through, was marred with years of decay and dust.

Simantiar was suddenly filled with doubt, a sensation that coursed through him the higher they ascended.

His newly returned eyes constantly wandered to George who sulked with his eyes to the floor.

He couldn't allow them to enter—this was his fight after all, not theirs. He couldn't risk allowing George to be a liability.

"Ready?" Kendrith asked.

Simantiar just nodded. "It's strange…it seems like just yesterday that I was playing around with Usellyes at the academy…feels like I've just awoken from a very long sleep." Simantiar looked down at his hands, feeling the stretch of limbs he hadn't felt in millennia now shrouded in a soft blue glow.

Logan pumped his chest piece. "If there is anything you need, I stand by you."

"Just stop, Logan. Make sure you keep everyone safe."

Logan bowed, and Simantiar rolled his eyes, unsure if Logan was just messing with him or was serious about the reverence stuff.

"Are you going in alone?" Kristen asked with palpable concern.

Simantiar nodded feebly. "This is my fight, I shouldn't have brought you here." His eyes absently glossed over George and met his scornful gaze. Simantiar was the first to look away with painful regret—he could feel his newly fashioned heart squeeze with a warm guilt-ridden hurt.

Kristen refrained from following Simantiar's gaze—she seemed to understand and nodded supportively.

"Give that Usellyes a good thrashing," she said and came forward to hug the man. "I will never forget you, Simantiar. What an honour to have known you, and what a great man you turned out to be." She whispered the last words as they were meant for Simantiar's newly regrown ears.

Kendrith was next. "What an adventure it was, aye, Simantiar?"

"What an adventure," Simantiar echoed, a sombre truth becoming more and more real with each goodbye. He knew for sure that Kendrith too had a wish on his mind, the sword of Vrania strung on his back with repressed temptation. They too embraced one another with human warmth and flesh.

"George...I..." Simantiar couldn't find the right words. "Thank you for bringing me here." There was almost a pleading note to Simantiar's voice, the type of placating tenor that begged for forgiveness.

"Good luck with everything, Simantiar."

Simantiar had forgotten what it was like to feel a broken ache in one's heart. He all too quickly was reminded of the pain that came with life as George turned away with a cold and distant shoulder.

Kendrith must have noticed his hurt, for he stepped forward with a fond knowingness and understanding which placated Simantiar's wound. "He will be fine. I will take care of him," Kendrith promised.

"Are you sure you wish to go alone?" Logan asked.

Simantiar nodded begrudgingly. "It's my score to settle. Plus, I can't promise I'd be able to protect all of you.

"Once the doors close behind me, leave as quickly as you can. There is no telling what calamity might take place. Once the seal is gone, nothing can hold him back."

Simantiar snapped his fingers as loose rock came together to create a large nimble golem of brown to carry them to safety.

"My creation will get you there fast, just hold tight on the descent."

Pecky was the only one who unwillingly left Simantiar's side and had to forcibly be handed over to Kristen's delicate hands whose fingers closed around the frantic bird so that he wouldn't escape.

"Let's finish this." Simantiar raised a hand to the door, something deep within him awakening. The door pulled at the blue aura that surrounded him, turning into an iridescent glow that the door swallowed. Clumped dust and dirt shook and fell from its surface as the door began to return to its old shine and glamour.

The vaulted door suddenly seemed brand new and a close enough rendition to George's book. It was golden with filigree patterns coiling across its face and an image of Usellyes with splayed arms underneath a crystal.

The door budged, old machinations turning inside as aged and forgotten parts moved after falling out of use. It groaned with the effort of an old man forcing tired limbs to rise, and more dirt showered the entrance.

The path before him was dark, as one by one adjacent braziers burst to life and lit the path, revealing a high-roofed antechamber with a well at the end of it and a luminous crystal fastened just above.

The chamber felt almost venerating in its display, awaiting to become lit only at Simantiar's presence as he stepped barefoot into the room. He already felt himself greatly weakened since reviving George, his powers drained, and he already sensed his tether to the realm lighten. Could he face Usellyes? Would he win? Did he make the right call by reviving George?

Simantiar shook his head—there was no time for doubt. He made the right choice.

If the air outside the chamber was stale and suffocating, then the air within the chamber felt ancient and unwelcoming.

The sound of his footsteps echoed menacingly across the stone walls—they wanted to be heard.

A thought occurred to Simantiar then. He thought back to what a few days of being linked had done to Usellyes oh so long ago—how it had warped his sense of reality and right from wrong. Simantiar remembered then what it was like to break out in cold sweat. *What difference would a millennium make?* he wondered.

Much of the chamber was still in shambles, from broken pillars to broken tiles and roof, but the room itself was cleared out. Those who came long before must have seen the importance of this confrontation and followed whatever instructions were laid bare to ensure that this meeting would happen. Though if there were those who took Simantiar's side or that of Usellyes he didn't know, and whichever was their story was long forgotten to the annals of time.

Simantiar looked into the corners, the signs of an old fight still present, craters formed from the battle of golems or the exchange of force that came down to martial might.

Simantiar turned to the corner and remembered his battle with Ciro so vividly. He veered his attention and recoiled in fear as he for a brief moment mistook the broken rubble for what remained of Moran.

"Still yourself," Simantiar urged, placing a hand upon his beating chest and felt the thrum of trepidation seep into his bones. He gulped, feeling a thick lump fall down his throat. All his senses, all his returning emotions filled him with human dread and panic.

"So you finally came." A voice echoed through the chamber, the brazier lights flickering as the water of the pool rippled restlessly.

Simantiar started, flicked his gaze to the sound, and gasped.

"Finally, it is time." From the pool before him, Usellyes began to rise: a being of skin pulled over bones, inebriated, hunched over with limp arms, and, gaunt as he was, maleficent power dribbled from his every pore.

Simantiar vanished through the great golden gates as George and the others turned towards the animated golem which would lead them to safety.

"George, what are you doing?" Kristen asked as she was getting ready to climb aboard the creature. Logan had provided pistons and harnesses to ensure that they would be able to hold on.

George looked to his feet, the brown of his leather boots so faded due to the dust and residue and muck and dirt from his ventures that he couldn't discern its true colour anymore.

Was that it? All those years looking for Simantiar. All those years trying to fulfil a promise to Lily.

The vault was right there in front of him. Everything he had ever wanted, the only rhyme or reason that gave him purpose whenever he awoke. What would he do now? A part of George's heart broke, a part he never knew was there. It felt as if Lily was dying all over. Truly dying.

This quest of his, this venture to find the vault kept her memory alive, reminded him that he was doing it for her...but now that he had to turn away from it all...

He was so close to his promise, would he really let it slip from his fingers?

The vault was closing.

"Boy?" Logan called.

George tightened his fist.

With a look of apology that betrayed his intent, George turned and sprinted towards the closing gates.

"George! No!" Kendrith called out. But George didn't stop, his feet carrying him faster and faster with renewed energy though his calves burnt with exhaustion and fatigue.

"Damn it, boy!" Logan cursed.

George slid through the closing gates.

"Hurry!" George heard from behind as to his surprise he watched the sliver of an opening continue to close.

But not before Logan barred the way. His colossal hands strained as they tried hopelessly to hold the door open.

"What are you doing?" It was Simantiar's voice.

George turned to find his friend face-to-face with some gaunt, sickly creature inside a pool of shimmering colours, cords rising from his body to connect the strange man to a crystal above.

Kendrith slid through the gap and sleighted his grandfather's axe from Logan's hip before propping it against the closing doors.

"Hurry!" Kendrith bellowed.

With veins popping through skin and strained neck muscles pronouncing themselves, Logan cleared enough of an opening to slip his way through, Kristen following right behind him before the metal haft of Haggen's axe bent itself out of shape and was propelled outside the door.

Pecky just barely managed to work his way through the most narrow of openings before the telling thunderous sound came from the closing door.

"What are you doing?" Kendrith demanded, grabbing George by the shoulder readying to admonish him.

George shrugged off Kendrith's grip. "I am getting my sister back!" George challenged.

"Ah yes, my first hopeful. I have waited a thousand years for this very moment. A moment where my dream is to be realised. Come forward and make your wish, so that Simantiar can see how truly misguided he is."

George tore his gaze from the others and paced forward. The being did seem human in the most basic of terms, but off at the same time, like a crude imitation of life; there was a greasy, unnerving air about Usellyes.

Simantiar grabbed George's arm and seemed to want to urge George to reconsider. But something in George's gaze made Simantiar pause as his hardened expression turned into one of concern.

Simantiar loosened his grip. "Is this really what you want?"

George simply nodded. Something about Simantiar's tone weakened his resolve.

"And what about Lily?" Simantiar asked.

George's heart beat with a strange sharp pain at the query.

He didn't offer an answer and instead continued walking on in a sudden doubtful haze.

"Ask me for anything."

George was brought back from his musings and noticed that he had tears in his eyes. He stood dead centre between Simantiar and Usellyes, only a couple of meters away from the strange figure.

He wiped his eyes of their sorrow. "I used to have this sister. Lily. She was taken away from me because of an illness."

"Yes, I can see it. You loved your sister very much. She was killed by something very common. Would it have been a nobleman's daughter with that disease she may very well have survived given the right medication."

A seething hot rage worked its way up inside George at the idea.

"The world is unjust—it took from you what you cherished most, it took from you love while those born into privilege never dealt with such hardships. But I can bring her back."

George looked up, hope blossoming like flower petals bursting open within his chest and releasing all that pain. "You can bring her back?" George repeated.

Usellyes nodded. *"Just how you remember her. No more hardships, no more having to steal, no more having to live on scraps and go cold when it rains."*

"George! Don't do this!" Kristen bellowed from behind, but a simple wave from Simantiar's hand silenced her and the others.

George turned to look at Simantiar's stoic glare. He wasn't going to stop him. Guilt worked its way through George.

He was conflicted. He knew it was wrong. It felt wrong. But the promise of having his sister returned to him was everything he could have ever asked for.

He didn't want to be alone anymore.

"All you need to do is ask."

George was about to open his lips when the memory of his sister returned to him. Lithe, so diminutive. Sun-kissed cheeks and such a bright smile; always sickly, always so delicate. She reminded George of a sunflower.

The tears returned, but now they wrung through a pained heart.

His lips trembled. "I can't," he muttered the words brokenly.

"What was that?" Venom in Usellyes query.

"I can't do that to her. She would never forgive me," George admitted.

There were things that felt wrong to George simply because they did. The thought of robbing from neighbouring urchins was one of those things. The thought of allowing Kristen to plummet to her death after all the trust she offered was another.

The thought of giving in to the temptation of resurrecting a lost sister at the potential cost of warping life itself outweighed all the rest.

An incredulous and rising shrill roar escaped Usellyes's lungs like the radiating knell of a sonar beast.

The mountain rumbled all over and the waters of the iridescent pool thrashed against the rim.

George covered his ears and cowered to his knees at the deafening sound as a sudden pull from his back knocked him off his feet and tore him through the air until he landed next to Kendrith and the others.

"Bring him to safety!" Simantiar ordered.

Simantiar called upon the warmth of his newfound power which blanketed him like a shroud and marvelled at how easy the magic answered to his call. Other times it felt like he had to rip the weave from its place as if it were something stationary and hammered into place. But then, it felt like thousands of guiding hands pressed their warmth against Simantiar's own hand and that credence came with reassurance.

The first thing Simantiar did was call upon an invisible wall which blocked off the screaming shrill echo of Usellyes, the surface already vibrating with such force and cracking under the weight.

Next Simantiar summoned his spear of fire.

Something hammered against the back door of the chamber as finally, Simantiar's golem entered through the drained vault and strode as if an ape of stone which grabbed Simantiar's friends in its arms and anchored them in place.

"Ignis Ra Gungnar!" Millions of tiny little flames licked away the air from the mightily flaming shaft before Simantiar tossed the blazing inferno that flashed forward like lightning.

With a simple touch from the tip of his glowing ethereal hand, Simantiar granted a gust of wind as tiny as a pea, and watched the torrent and whirling force of the spear turn that minute puff of air into a ravenous vortex that pulled everything into itself.

It was all over in a second as the lightning strike of spear and wind burst apart like torn cloth and just tarps of flame and wind hung in the air.

They were pulled into Usellyes's call, demure in its beseechment as a hot blinding flash like molten iron formed into a sphere in Usellyes's grip.

Simantiar prepared himself for the coming strike as Usellyes raised the sphere up into the air like a physical simulacrum of the sun itself.

The shadows all around stretched until a linked chain of burning iron expelled itself from the miniature sun and worked its way towards Simantiar, binding his hand.

"What kind of sorcery is this?" Simantiar asked.

"You have no idea what power I have uncovered in my slumber, Simantiar. Despair, Simantiar, for I have ascended."

Simantiar felt the chains go taut and his flesh sizzle, the burning linked bars beginning to draw him in as he pulled against the force.

"It is over."

"Like hell it is," Simantiar called upon the dormant power of his trusted colleagues and felt the strength harden him.

"Ignis Ra..." the words turned into the sound of ash and ember igniting within a burning kiln, "Phoenix!"

Simantiar burst alight like an effigy of straw, his eyes blazed and his arms pulled and shattered the chains of molten iron. He could feel the fire coursing through him and felt how it burnt away at the offered souls entrusted to him. This was one of the most powerful spells Simantiar had ever mastered when he was among the living and even then he couldn't hold it very long.

"Impossible," Usellyes muttered in disbelief.

Blazing wings burst from his back as his own eyes were like burning hot coals within the sockets peering right at his foe.

With a mighty beat of his wings, a heat wave filled the room that could make any simple mortal go dizzy.

"Leave!" Simantiar bellowed like a burning god at George and the others who were being dragged away by the colossal golem.

When next Simantiar turned his gaze forward, he closed the gap in the simple blink of an eye and grabbed at Usellyes's throat. He himself was already standing at three times the size of any normal mortal and far outclassed even Logan in terms of height.

"You will never match me, Usellyes." The skin at Usellyes's neck burnt and a charred ruin of roasted flesh turning black was left at the edges of Simantiar's grip. Usellyes burnt his own hands trying to grab the mighty, blazing fingers, and his voice came out like a hoarse croak as kindled sparks of ember escaped his gasping sallow maw.

"This is...far from...o-over," Usellyes managed, his voice breaking into a strained malicious cackle as the skin and bones of his body peeled away and a great centipede worked its way out of the shell.

The thing wrapped itself around Simantiar in the blink of an eye and crushed him with its coiling strength.

Instead of getting burnt, the beast seemed to absorb the flames gratefully and increase its crushing strength.

The legs undulated rhythmically with ostensible delight as the head of the centipede loomed above and leaned in with expecting pincers spreading in anticipation.

"Simantiar!" George bellowed from the end of the room in desperation, as Simantiar's fiery form flickered and died and all that was left was Simantiar being crushed.

Logan took his hammer and swung it with all his might against the face of the giant golem which released its hold. The band fell to the floor and Kendrith brandished his blade.

He panted and barely kept the light-headedness which clouded his mind at bay.

"Kendrith," George called, drawing Kendrith's attention to the sweat-laden boy who then pointed to his sword.

Kendrith blinked momentarily in disbelief, did he just imagine the slight blue hue?

"We have no time to lose!" Logan returned their attention to the matter as they charged forward and he became their vanguard.

With inspired courage, Kendrith followed right behind with everyone else by his side.

Pecky zoomed through the air and chirped feverously against the centipede monster, its relentless pecking and calls nothing more than a buzzing nuisance, but it did enough to distract the monster which Usellyes had become.

With a winding swing and challenging roar, Logan raised the haft of his hammer and knocked aside the swiping tail of Usellyes.

Golden hammerhead and polished obsidian exoskeleton met in combat and pounded against each other with overwhelming strength.

Daggers soared through the air from Kristen's belt and simply bounced off the hardened shell.

Kendrith stood alongside Logan and felt his arms ring as his blade bounced off Usellyes's backhanded tail swipe.

Simantiar used the distraction and dispersed into an ethereal blue spectre fading and gliding through the viselike grip of Usellyes and joining the others.

"I told you to leave!" Simantiar stated.

"And let one of my charges die? Never!" Logan contested.

"Then we will all die!" Simantiar warned as his golem leapt over their mighty forms and wrestled with Usellyes.

"So be it!" George stated.

Simantiar looked to the others and found them all nod in solidarity.

"You are all mad." Simantiar smiled with fondness at the others, and indeed, they all were fools.

Kendrith knew it—they were broken people with broken dreams, each one of them either forgotten or a simple footnote in a tale that perhaps no one would ever know about. But what they would do that day would impact the entire world of Tiria.

"Stand strong!" Logan ordered.

Simantiar's golem quickly lost the fight as Usellyes snarled and hissed like grating metal as its body coiled and wrapped itself around the golem bit by bit until its large, constricting body could not be avulsed and a simple bone-shattering squeeze turned the golem into a pile of rubble, its pieces falling into the pool and sending its waters splashing.

A bone-chilling and deafening shrill scream escaped Usellyes as it charged forward.

Simantiar stepped forward and formed a triangle with his thumbs and pointer finger.

"Tauran Es Gaiant!" Simantiar bellowed as a mighty bull the size of a colossal elephant appeared in front of Simantiar with the same elusive radiant blue aura that made Simantiar. The bull charged and each weight of its mighty hooves reverberated through the halls and clashed headlong with Usellyes. A pained scream filled the room as Usellyes's progress was halted and the bull dispersed into fading wisps of arcana.

Logan roared and seized his chance through the cover of the moment to swing his hammer.

An audible crack filled the room like that of snapping bone.

Kendrith thought at first that it must have come from Logan, but then saw the exoskeleton of the monstrous beast break from its head and from its shell came another form.

It was like murky tar in the form of a coalesced form which rose, the umbral darkness of its amorphous body worming its way out.

Its centipede-like legs were now replaced with digited black arms and hands, its bulbous head appearing last with a single vertical eye nebulous in its shine and shifting iridescent sheens that glittered across the surface of the maddening oculus.

Chapter 54

Like a gelatinous worm squeezed from its tube, the dark inky body of Usellyes contorted and stretched itself as the others drew closer.

Simantiar tore Logan back as the large man landed on his feet and skidded to a halt.

"By Ivaldi's beard. What is that?" Terror trickled from Logan's lips.

"Don't touch him!" Simantiar bellowed as already Usellyes's long length coiled and stretched in search of its first target.

A loose spell speedcast from Simantiar's lips formed doubles and triples of the others as they divided into clones and confused Usellyes's senses.

They weren't just simple shoddy illusions—they were just as real as the original and again, Simantiar felt a sizable portion of his magic fade and his skin break into a cold sweat and his knees grow heavy.

His phoenix form had many variations, ranging all the different forms of the universe from flame to lightning to the celestial star-powered cosmos.

But he had no power remaining to conjure any of those forms anymore without depleting the rest of his reserves.

Instead, he pinpointed the retreating Pecky in the air distinguished by its crimson mohawk and brown-matted feathers and white belly.

With a few more incantations formed and feeling his fingers go numb, he evoked a trail of ethereal blue smoke that expelled from his dried lips and worked its way upwards towards Pecky, the dancing smoky ribbon clung to Pecky who seemed to panic at the strangeness of it all.

It enshrouded the bird, but Pecky seemed to then expel it like an aura and then grew.

Talons grew into the claws of tigers, wings spread exponentially with no end in sight, the woodpecker beak curved into a mighty bone-crushing weapon and the red of its scalp scaling rigid feathers and wings to give the impression of an infernal bird of prey.

Pecky's formerly diminutive size now matched its relentless energy as its wings spanned across Usellyes's entire length at thirty meters. A single beat of its wings sent gusts of wind that threatened to snuff out the braziers and everyone else flying as its shrill call went from a small chirp into a bone-chilling cry.

The blue layer provided protection as Pecky wrapped its gigantic claws around Usellyes and pushed it to the floor where they wrestled in stalemate.

Usellyes's serpentine body thrashed the columns, its tail's mere touch devouring the hapless copies that vanished into the form like being encased in viscous ink. The clones had but a moment to voice their despair before fading into the abyssal depths of that body, just the mere trail of smoky ribbons telling of their pitiful fate.

It eventually coiled its body around Pecky and slammed him against a pillar which toppled as if it were stacked hay.

Usellyes's one eye spun around in its gelatinous squirmy socket like a crazed gyroscope before the dazzling shimmer of its maddening glare settled on one of the clones. Its previously vacant face split to reveal the pointed rows of umbral teeth and the stringed tar-like substance that dripped from it.

As it shot forward, its movement was suddenly halted from the ethereal blue chains of ghostly aura which wrapped itself around its neck and held it in place. Simantiar's grip trembled at the effort of holding Usellyes back.

The creature turned its gaze and charged for Simantiar instead only to again be halted, as another set of chains bound to a distant pillar held firm.

Then another.

And another.

Until from all angles the chains bound Usellyes's movements and bought Simantiar what little time they could till he came up with a plan. The hope was short-lived as the pillar opposite Simantiar tore loose and Usellyes's blobulous body wormed its way with its reaching inky arms.

George watched helplessly as it was all that Simantiar could do to keep Usellyes at bay with compact force bursts of magic compounded from his fists as Pecky returned to fend off Usellyes's attacks.

George's counterparts dashed across the room with no sign of actual intent other than to distract from his real friends among the sea of copies which flittered everywhere.

Watching his copies being devoured by Usellyes's umbral body sent a cold, numbing fear through his bones that made him freeze in his trepidation.

How fear clouded the eyes of his clones as he watched himself vanish without consequence as if it were some portent look into his own waiting end.

Looking around the room, George tried to think of anything that could turn the tide.

He was certain their weapons would prove useless against the body of the creature and there was no telling what would happen if it managed to touch them.

His gaze fell upon the pool. Drain the water? It was impossible.

His eyes landed upon the iridescent and still crystal that remained latched in place above the pool.

"Kendrith!" From among the many versions of the stoic hunter, only one turned its gaze with knowing intent.

"Do you still have any bones?" George shouted.

Kendrith's gaze seemed to widen with understanding as he went through his belongings and withdrew just a single bone that was left from George's payments.

George pointed towards the crystal, and barely could one see the telling form of a large centipede trapped within its shell.

Kendrith simply looked to the crystal and back at George before nodding his agreement.

Simantiar tried his best to assist Pecky, but little by little their advance was being cornered as Pecky's light flickered and his size dwindled.

"Pecky!" Simantiar called out in desperation, but his little companion was too far gone in the ecstasy of his transformation, having a chance to match his own boisterous energy with his size and feel like an apex predator.

Usellyes's many arms stretched out, their tar-like forms dripping to the cobbled stone and mummifying Pecky who broke under the weight.

Simantiar reacted immediately, dispelling the form as Pecky's original form rushed out of the embrace and escaped the abyssal burrow reserved inside Usellyes.

The moment was all Usellyes needed and Simantiar cursed his foolishness as more umbral arms broke from the stone floor and captured Simantiar.

Simantiar found himself being lifted off the ground, struggling with the binds that restricted his magic.

When finally he looked ahead, he stared deep and straight into the endless peering eye of existence which was Usellyes's eye. A great dark sphere like a radiant black hole stared out as a pupil, and cosmic rays danced and flitted across its edges as if it were a great star pitted with a dark belly, while all around it floated specks of glittering stars as a meteor cut across the scene and nebulous galaxies drifted in the distance like the bloodshot veins of celestial eyes.

"Oh, Usellyes, what have you become?" Simantiar asked despairingly.

"Everything." The voice came from a deep and dormant place beyond the veil of reality as the sound echoed inside Simantiar's thoughts and he watched the great maw of Usellyes stretch wider and wider and wider as if it were planning to devour an elephant.

Something caught Simantiar's eye and a great gloating grin filled his face.

"Oh man, you really did get played."

Usellyes spun around as its maw returned to its normal form.

Its shriek before was one of hate and malice, now it was one of unbridled panic as Usellyes watched the dim sword of Vrania break into his crystal while George held the final bone of Simantiar, dangling it over the crevice with what was left of Usellyes's curse.

"Stop," Usellyes commanded, his voice reverberating across the entire chamber, a low incessant thing which sounded like it was low enough to stem from the pit of a dormant volcano.

Simantiar struggled against the tar-like fingers and grip of Usellyes, the substance dripping from him in big blotches.

The clones stopped their running and stood at attention, George and Kendrith looked on puzzled.

"I do not understand, I am not your enemy. I am your friend, the friend of all beings. What I offer you is your deepest, strongest desire. It is why you came here, isn't it?" Usellyes's tone sounded forgiving, lamentful, and hurt. Simantiar believed that there was truly a side to Usellyes, despite his corruption, that believed what he was doing was good.

"Kendrith," the name was spoken almost like a slithering whisper. Kendrith gave his attention to Usellyes who fully turned around to present Simantiar locked in his binding appendages.

"I see what you desire, I see it in your heart." The great nebulous eye blinked, not only staring at the present Kendrith, but beyond. Simantiar could feel how the eye peered into Kendrith's soul, into his very existence, peering into his very core and his link to the world.

"I see what you want."

"The sword does not matter to me." Kendrith cut in, declaring his acceptance as he took the bone from George and dangled it over the opening himself.

Usellyes gave an unnerving chuckle before slithering ever closer in self-assurance.

"The blade? Becoming a hero? Nay. You wish for your mother to return. For Haggen to return. That is what you truly desire. I see the truth, the fear you harbour within. You are no Brosnorth, yet you feel the weight of carrying on their legacy."

Kendrith's resolve visibly faded as he lowered his outstretched hand at what was being said.

Usellyes followed his momentum and urged Kendrith to fall into the leering seduction of his promise. *"Brosnorth would return."* Usellyes turned his great peering eye towards Logan. *"A wish shared by two."* Usellyes returned his attention to Kendrith. *"Your mother would come back, Haggen would return too. They would carry on the name and lessen your burden. They would give you the approval you so desperately seek.*

"You are no Brosnorth. You are a Feller, just like your father."

"Don't listen to him, Kendrith!" Simantiar called. He felt the last vestige of his power fading, felt his mind grow weary, and his thoughts felt scattered. It was the fleeting impression of death grinding away at the thread which tied him to the world.

"Silence!" The chamber quaked at Usellyes's order, the tar-like substance dripping on Simantiar as smoke rose from the reaction and his form corroded.

"What will it be, Kendrith?"

There Simantiar was again, watching the impossible choice that was being asked. It was always about bringing back loved ones, always it was about not being alone. Simantiar wondered if that was all that life was, the memories and connections of close loves that made the culmination of a good life lived.

Kendrith stared down at the bone in contemplation. "My mother was Mona Brosnorth. My grandfather was Haggen Brosnorth…and my father is Jaylen Feller. You are right, I may not be a Brosnorth." Kendrith sounded as if he were somewhere far, far away from everything.

His fist curled around the bone with rekindled resolve.

"But that doesn't mean that I am not a hero!" With an unwavering roar he lifted the bone and swung down.

Tendrils struck upwards from the ground and pushed Kendrith away, sending him as a flying blur that slammed into a wall and obscured him in a cloud of debris.

"Kendrith!" Kristen called out.

The bone had left Kendrith's hold and bounced off the crystal with a hollow knock before rolling onto the floor.

"George! Get the bone!" Logan ordered.

George hopped down from above, barely avoiding the grasping tendrils that reached for him.

Simantiar felt his body go from a numb coldness into a bleary fever. His concentration wavered. His vision blurred.

The clones flickered before slowly fading into nothingness.

"Get to cover!" Logan ordered.

"Pitiful." The tendrils released their hold and Simantiar plummeted to the ground, feeling for the first time in thousands of years how air escaped his lungs.

The man coughed incessantly, watching blurry-eyed as a black wormy body crashed into the surrounding architecture.

"Stop it." Simantiar reached out a feeble hand, his pleas an unheard croak coming from dying lungs.

"Stop it!" He tried again. There was the distant sound of more rubble breaking.

In the bedlam of chaos, a holy blue light shone through the destruction.

A great pained shriek bellowed across the chamber walls as the streak of blinding blue soared through the air.

"Get up, Simantiar. You have a fight to the end."

A hand grasped at Simantiar's back as he felt unending power rush into his soul.

His vision returned, the pain from his lungs vanished, and his knees regained the strength to stand as Simantiar found himself pulled to his feet.

He turned and saw Kendrith born anew, a similar aura of pure blue encasing him, his body radiating endless power and great resplendent wings spread across his back—the blade of Vrania shone a glorious colour like that of a clear sky at noon over the sea.

"Kendrith…" Simantiar spoke, for the first time at a loss for words.

Kendrith gave a knowing and comforting smile. "Celebrations come later. Finish what you started."

More power rushed into Simantiar.

"No!" Usellyes abandoned his other targets and rushed forward as Simantiar found enough energy to take on a new form.

"Atman Es Raijin."

Lightning speared through the mountain and pierced straight towards Simantiar, instilled with the power of static and infused with his Arcanum. A cloud of dust obscured him.

Usellyes blew the cloud away with his advance and struck upon the giant form of Simantiar with emblazoned long rod of lightning in hand and four arms in total.

A second body sprouted from Usellyes's back and rushed towards George.

Kendrith's wings soared right behind and cut away at Usellyes's second form like a torch through darkness.

Chapter 55

There were many ideas that had crossed Simantiar's mind over his unnaturally stretched lifespan.

One of which was the fact that the concept of god is powerful, for it instilled an infectious idea that clung to people and made them act without god ever having to get involved.

Love was also a powerful force, for it brought people together and created communities and promised legacies.

But after all that, he learnt during his fight against Usellyes that the concept of oblivion, of the abyss, was far more overwhelming than anything else.

His own power was gifted by friends of old who waited patiently in a forlorn valley for Simantiar to return—out of love and out of trust they waited. Kendrith had just infused the power of Vrania's own sword, the power of a true god, into Simantiar without hesitation. His friends that traversed hundreds of generations still bound themselves to Simantiar and a new kinship was born across time.

Yet, nothingness was nothingness. It was absence. Power could be limitless—Simantiar had seen that strength. But oblivion was inevitable—that was the truth he saw within Usellyes's eye.

Simantiar had taken on the avatar of lightning, a god of storms and still he could not match Usellyes; he had donned the blazing writhing inferno of a phoenix and still his light was smothered.

Why? Because Usellyes traversed the stars and beyond. Darkness would come eventually and the last star would fade into darkness, and oblivion would come.

That was the truth of how Simantiar felt as he struggled against Usellyes and felt himself pushed back.

That was the truth of how he felt as he watched Logan, Kristen, and George flee desperately for their lives as Kendrith snipped more and more of Usellyes's body only for it to regrow—a shadow can't be cut, after all.

It was all so fleeting, all so trying.

The encompassing tar of Usellyes's body threatened to devour him.

The centipede within the crystal had already infected Usellyes, had already twisted his mind and made him forget what it was like to walk among men.

Perhaps there was only one choice left to Simantiar, to end everything the way it began.

If he could not destroy the endless nothingness which Usellyes championed in the promise of dreams, then he had no choice but to pull Usellyes out of that darkness.

Just as he had with Timmy, trapped within his stone lion, Simantiar closed his eyes and the crackling lightning that armoured him vanished so that he could once again visit the true Usellyes, to let himself sink into the tarry depths.

Did his friends call out to him in the distance? He couldn't tell.

Chapter 56

Simantiar opened his eyes slowly. Flicking them open as if to double-check and ensure that what he was about to face was not going to tear him apart.

But he saw no black world. No inky sky. No vile contempt.

The place…felt lonely. Pure.

It was a white world, endless and empty. And within that white world sat a young boy with black hair who sobbed alone.

Simantiar walked forward. He was no skull. No body of roots and vines and foliage. No man. He was a boy once more.

"Why are you crying?" Simantiar asked the crying boy, his voice that of a young child's yet to break.

The crying boy did not reply, his head buried between knees drawn to his chest. His shoulders heaved with each sob.

Why was Simantiar there again? He couldn't quite recall.

"It's okay. You don't have to tell me," Simantiar said, as he went to sit by the crying boy.

"I will just sit here till you want to. My mother said that it is important to let people grieve—it's what makes us human."

The boy wailed, his sobs originally a leak in a dam now giving way to a flood.

The boy did not lift his head, though he clamoured and held and tugged on Simantiar's robes and buried his chest into Simantiar's neck and cried with such unbidden emotion that Simantiar could only imagine what torment had festered inside.

"Simantiar is gone!" Logan bellowed over the sound of battle as they all did their best to avoid the winding tendrils, while Kendrith did his best to hold them at bay.

George could barely hear him, as he had his hands already full with trying to grab the final bone that clattered across the floor. George rummaged through the broken terrain, tiles, and earth that now made uneven footing.

A clatter, and George turned to see the bone slide across the floor.

He scuttled on all fours, a massive tar body pounding in front of him and barring his way.

Logan jumped in front of George and swung his hammer into the body as it slowed the attack and seemed to be sucked into a bubbling mass as if it were quicksand.

"Let go of the hammer!" Kristen called from somewhere.

"I can't!" Logan responded.

George reared backwards as another mass closed in behind him.

Kendrith battled against the two heads of Usellyes, finding himself being drawn into a corner.

"Kendrith!" George called out in desperation.

Within a moment's window, Kendrith sent a slashing wave of razor-thin air that severed the body in front and freed Logan's hammer.

There was the opening.

George rushed forwards and dove as Logan collapsed backwards. The shadowed body mended itself instantly and George missed it by a hairbreath as he landed in the clearing where Simantiar's last bone lay.

"Gotcha!" he declared with bone in hand.

"George, hurry up!" Kendrith cried, as the beast gave off a shrill scream like a fork scratching tin. Kristen seemed at the end of her wits as she dodged the chaotic brawl of her love and Usellyes's twin bodies.

George rose up, and ran towards the crystal. He ducked and weaved over and under the sprouting tendrils until he slid under the body of the worm just before it crashed into the ground and Kendrith stood atop it with resplendent and spread wings of glorious blue.

Jumping up and around the well, George grabbed one of the beams that connected to the crystal, clambering up to the ring that held it aloft.

"George!" Kristen called out.

A spiked tendril shot towards the boy who shielded his eyes.

Nothing happened. It stood frozen in place. The thrashing forms of Usellyes stopped moving.

"George, now!" Kendrith called out as he worked his way out of their coiled bodies.

George returned to the present, raising the bone overhead and slamming it into the hole the blade of Vrania had made.

The crystal trembled, reverberating on the metal ring that held it.

What remained of the pillars crumbled apart.

Another point on the crystal shattered, the contents falling into the roiling pool of magic below.

More light bled through, the break now spreading like a fissure through a frozen lake.

The thing trembled upon its station as more of its pieces shattered.

A telling and portent crack of stone and rock filled the hall. The damaged chamber rattled and the first of the debris was shook loose.

The waters of the pool thrashed back and forth as its contents began to vanish—the liquid turned into mist.

Usellyes's shadowy form began to shrink like shortening shadows, the muck fading like tattered fabric of true black. All that was left behind was a gaunt and decrepit Usellyes in Simantiar's embrace.

One that did not emanate some foul nefarious magic that played at being human, but rather a truly piteous man with slumped shoulders and a defeated spirit who just looked tired and frail.

The fissure upon the crystal widened and a sound like thousands of shattering glasses filled the chamber as the Omukade within fell lifeless into the pool.

Simantiar looked up, tears in his eyes to match the black ones that streamed from Usellyes's eyes.

The chamber trembled.

"We have to go!" Kendrith shouted, running by Simantiar with George in tow.

Simantiar stood still, watching his old friend with a sense of hurt as the man simply stood there defeated.

"Usellyes?" Simantiar asked.

"Just go," was all that Usellyes managed. He sounded like his own self, uninfluenced by whatever vile power had taken his mind. Though now the guilt and defeat clung poignantly to his last words.

"Simantiar, now!" Simantiar turned, running to the broken entrance with the others as the place collapsed all around them.

The final view he saw of Usellyes was the tightening of his skin on old bones, a rapid process of aging, as suddenly the years came all at once. The man standing on rickety legs dragged himself to the well. Yet Simantiar never had a chance to see how it all ended for his friend as the rest of the passage filled with stone.

His mind returned to Moran, to Ciro, and again Simantiar watched as another one of his friends was claimed by the chamber for the last time.

"We have to keep going!" Logan shouted, the entire mountain now falling in on itself.

"Simantiar." George looked at him with worry, as the wizard's glow dimmed rapidly.

"We have to move!" Logan instructed.

The band ran, trying to work their way down.

"Not this way," Logan said as the others watched a torrent of the Withered scaling the walls, several peeled away from their grips by falling refuse.

"Then where?" Kendrith asked.

"Here," Simantiar said, trying to walk. He fell to a knee, looking down to see one of his ghostly legs had already vanished.

Kendrith, without saying a word, lifted Simantiar up, putting an arm under his shoulder. "Let's see if you still have room for one more miracle."

Kendrith's own reverent form was gone, and he was back to normal.

Simantiar hobbled forward with Kendrith's help. Then he waved an arm at the wall, and the wall broke down to open up a path leading out.

"This way! Hurry!" The band ran through, as the mountain continued to fall in on itself.

Chapter 57

As the band continued to run, the first sign of light shone through.

"Almost out!" Logan assured them.

The echo of the mountain began to grow more and more distant.

The light of Simantiar's glow vanished completely and his body with it, leaving just a skull behind.

"Gotcha!" Kendrith said, catching Simantiar on his fall.

"There is the Simantiar we know and love," Kristen teased.

Freedom, as they all broke through to the surface.

The final rumble of the mountain faded, quiet beginning to return like a promise, as birds broke free from the canopy and into the setting sun. Looking down, they saw the rising dust disperse to reveal the sloping landslide of rubble which buried the lake and everything else.

The band collapsed onto the ground, as Logan immediately took off his armour. "I need a vacation," he said, panting.

"You're telling me," Simantiar echoed.

They laughed, a soft thing at first through their exhausted limbs, and then full-on bellows of laughter, fuelled by the dawning realisation that they had survived the impossible.

All around them, grass started to grow atop the mountain, moss colouring the stone green and flowers blooming with a beautiful shine to them.

"What is all this?" Logan asked.

"Magic," Simantiar said, "It's returning to the world."

"What does that mean?" Kendrith asked

"I don't know…it could be good…it could be bad…time will tell."

They all grew silent.

"And what will happen to you, little skull?" Logan asked, now only respect and trust in his voice.

"Well, there are plenty of people waiting for me, and it's time I get going."

They all understood what those words meant, as Pecky came popping out of George's pocket.

"There you are!" George claimed in surprise, not even noticing that Pecky had sought refuge within.

The bird rushed towards Simantiar, pecking his skull. "Yes, I will miss you too," Simantiar tried to joke, but his tone sounded quite sombre. "As I had promised: things that you had never seen before."

The bird had its adventure, did experience what it came for, and so it flew off, out into where it would be at home once more.

"Hey, George."

"Yeah, Simantiar?" The boy tried to hold back his tears, smiling in return.

"That's a beautiful sunset, isn't it?"

"Yes, it is."

Kendrith placed Simantiar down on the ground. As the others decided to take a walk, George came to sit down next to the old wizard.

"There…at the end. Did Usellyes…?"

Simantiar was silent for a moment before answering. "Yeah. I think he had a chance to see what had happened. He was freed from the influence."

"Do you think he regrets doing what he did?"

"Maybe. I just know that finally being sober after all those years must have left him a horrid hangover."

They laughed.

The sunset was a beautiful yellow bleeding into orange, one that promised a new tomorrow with hope and life.

"It was fun, wasn't it?" Simantiar asked.

"Yeah, it really was."

"Thank you, George…for finding me in that darkness, for pulling me out. Thank you for helping me finish what I started. I am glad to have met you."

When George didn't respond, Simantiar spoke on. "I am sorry, George. That you couldn't see your sister."

"I am the one who is sorry. You were right, Lily was gone. Her time was over a long time ago. The best I can do is carry her memory and live on for tomorrow rather than looking at the past. Plus, I still fulfilled my promise: I did find the golden vault."

"I guess you did. I am sure she is smiling down on you right now."

George allowed himself a beaming smile.

There was a moment of knowing silence. "Make sure you visit," George continued.

Simantiar laughed. "Of course! Who would annoy you if not for me?"

George laughed, rubbing his runny nose as the tears came freely, yet George was at peace, finally.

"What will you do next?"

The sun continued to set.

George shrugged. "I don't know, maybe stay with Kristen and Kendrith, if they will have me."

"I'm sure they would be happy to."

"After that...well, I'm not sure, maybe some more adventuring. Find myself a new talking relic."

"Ha! Best of luck with that."

They stayed quiet.

"Wow, that sunset went quick. It's already dark, isn't it?" Simantiar asked, yet the sun was still setting, and its glow had not completely faded.

"Yeah, it is," George said through wet eyes, holding back tears. It was just moments ago that a great indomitable force such as Usellyes was defeated, and it was just hours ago where they were fighting for their lives—George didn't expect to be saying goodbye to a dear friend so soon after everything had happened.

"Hey, George."

"Yeah?"

"Could you play me a song?"

"Sure, Simantiar. Which one?"

"Any."

And so, George took out his old lute from its case and began to pluck the strings.

"I call this 'The Fantastically Underwhelming Epic of a dead wizard and an average bard.'"

Simantiar chuckled. "Sounds like a good one."

And so, George played the tune, a song about a clueless boy with a promise, about an ancient skull that only berated the boy who found him in the lonely darkness of a tomb. Of the deadly mercenary they found on their way, of all the Hobbers and thugs and husks found on their path.

When the song was over, tears ran freely down George's cheeks.

"Simantiar?" he asked.

Yet, no reply came as the skull simply looked out onto the horizon.

"Till we meet again." The boy struck a final chord on his lute, as the last of the sun vanished beyond the horizon.

Epilogue

The only quiet which thickened inside the room dissipated when the first child dared to speak—the sound of the breaking quiet was as audible as the breaking of ice on a frozen lake: it was deafening.

Everyone was enraptured by the tale, and the orange glow of twilight nestled itself into the room through the shuttered windows like an unexpected visitor that joined in on the tale.

George leaned back—finding himself taken with the story.

At each chance he regaled visitors with stories of what had happened.

It was truly an adventure unlike what others would hear—of great legends and their improbable feats. Of a wizard who was a shadow of his own true power compared to his living days. Of a perilous and grave battle that nobody ever knew about except of what came after—when magic returned to the world.

"What happened next?" the child repeated, a boy who had stood up and held on to the rim of a chair in eager anticipation.

George shrugged, brushing away his brown locks and stretching sore fingers.

He leaned back, retiring the lute to another chair and sliding down his own seat with arms stretched overhead and a languid and notable yawn.

"We climbed back down."

"But how?" asked a girl this time.

Another shrug from George.

"With great difficulty." He never had his chance to respond, but instead Kendrith did from the back of the room, his free hand thrown around Kristen who folded her arms and smirked happily. George smiled at their corner.

"And what about Logan?" one kid asked.

"He gave up the adventuring life." George pointed up to a corner of the room where Haggen's broken axe hung with its own plaque, though broken it still held a mighty weight of a story. "After hanging it up, he decided to live a more comfortable life. He now trains others within the guild." There were astounded murmurs from the audience.

"Brokk! I would like the buy this young bard of ours another round." It was Jaylen that spoke, the good mood and the surroundings persuaded Kendrith's father to indulge in a few drinks—though it was true that most who didn't consistently test the boundaries of their limits soon found themselves staring at the bottom of a barrel. Jaylen was undoubtedly retired and free and drunk.

Brokk still seemed strong and reliable, though age had worked its way in white streaks through his facial hair as he nodded. "On it."

"And a toast!" Jaylen struck his tankard up into the air as a man tried to hinder his fall.

"I'm fine, I'm fine," he drunkenly murmured. "A toast!" he continued.

"What for, Dad?" Kendrith asked, humouring him.

"To my son! And his beautiful partner." Jaylen stumbled over to their table. "I know you tried to kill me, but hey, let bygones be bygones. Am I right?"

Kristen blushed at the reminder and receded into Kendrith's hold, who laughed at the remark.

"It's fine, Dad. Thank you."

Jaylen explosively shot his arm up into the air again. "And to their unborn child!"

Kendrith's eyes widened and Kristen buried her reddening cheeks.

Kendrith's expression suddenly turned a lot more dour. "Dad! It was supposed to be a secret!"

"Oops." Jaylen plummeted to the floor, serenaded by the laughs of several entertained children.

George laughed and retreated for the night.

He had a room of his own at the inn where he retreated to each night. His earnings allowed him a modestly secure future and the few quests either as a performer or as an extra hand for the guild earned him a modest profit on top of that.

It was a moment he looked forward to, a mere second of reminiscence as he would open his room door and stare upon the familiar empty skull which looked back at him.

"Hello, Simantiar. How has your day been?"

Afterword

The first draft of my first book was thirty-five thousand words and took me nine days to write and another month to self-edit and publish (with a plethora of errors, but I hoped the story made up for that, which it supposedly did).

In comparison, *The Fantastically Underwhelming Epic* took me just over two years to finish and ended up being over a hundred and sixty-six thousand words.

The book is a part of me and surely a testament towards my growth as a writer and a person.

I had gone many months with barely a word added, had lamented and considered several times to scrap the project and start anew. But I knew I owed it to myself, and my readers, to persevere and struggle through and I am so glad I did, for I have come out the other side truly in love with the characters that fill these pages and, more than anything, they feel alive to me.

I hope that love and care came through for all of you as well.

Acknowledgement

I want to start by giving thanks to all the essential workers, during these trying times, who put themselves at risk on the front lines of this pandemic.

Thank you, Tina, for being such a supportive and wonderful friend. I don't know if I would be as ambitious regarding my dreams if it weren't for your constant encouragement and taking the time to read my work.

I would like to thank my love, Veronika, for being such a steadfast supporter of my work and being there for me not just on my buoyant days, but also my sullen ones.

And Paria, for loving my work and motivating me to be just as great as you believe me to be.

My parents who push and humour my love for writing.

To Scotty, for being such an adamant and responsive fan of this book and embodying the tale I wanted to share.

And finally, all my readers. If it weren't for the comments that so many of you leave me I am sure I wouldn't be quite so fulfilled as I am at this very moment.

About The Author

Kian N. Ardalan born in Germany to Iranian parents only to be brought up in Dubai. Kian from the very beginning was exposed to vast backgrounds and cultures of the world, never truly feeling like he belonged to any one place.

Along his journey, he discovered his love and passion for writing which started out as a hobby before the encouragement of online readers dared him to imagine a future where this could truly be his career.

Studying in Vienna, Austria, he looks forward to finishing his degree in sociology and looks forward to further challenges in his future as he begins to plan his next book.

Feel free to get in touch under:

Clubhouse: Kian Najmechi

kiannardalan@gmail.com

Insta @ardalan.writes

Facebook: Kian N. Ardalan

SubReddit: /r/KikiWrites

Reddit: /u/Kinpsychosis

Website: kiannardalan.com

Stay In Touch

Enjoyed the journey? Perhaps it was the sarcastic Simantiar or the reliable Kendrith, perhaps the more humble, but cunning George?

Whatever it may be, do you wish to read more by me or just follow my career?

Sign up to my newsletter on kiannardalan.com

What can you be expecting next?

An audiobook! *The Fantastically Underwhelming Epic* will be coming as an audiobook through the channels of Podium Audio.

New book:

The Mistland series is a Dark Fantasy world inspired by the incredibly beautiful and dark world of Dark Souls, as well as Hollow Knight, told in a cryptic and maddening world.

It will be a far darker journey, but also very real in terms of human suffering and enduring such woes.

It will also be a chance for me to represent the disabled community through the experiences of one such character you will get to meet.

Stick around and I hope you will continue to follow my journey!

About this edition

When I first wrote this book, it was supposed to be a stepping stone to jump off onto my first real book series. What I did not expect was the overwhelming support and words of encouragement I received from all of you readers.

The original version of this book was far from polished, and I wondered if it was worth sending it off to an editor to bring up to standard. Not just because it would cost money, but because I wondered if it was fair for those who read the original version to experience a different journey.

In the end, I decided that getting it edited was the right thing to do. All the money I received from my initial sales was reinvested into a website, editor and a few other things.

If you enjoyed this book, stay tuned for the AudioBook version narrated by Kevin Kemp, and coming out soon thanks to Podium Audio!

And if you did truly enjoy this book, consider leaving me a review letting others know!

Books By This Author

The Dragon's Heir

The kingdom of Varity has fallen. The princess is just a child, small and unaware of the plight that has befallen her home. A knight, charged with one final task, delivers the king's only daughter to the home of a fierce dragon, dwelling in the mountains. One rumoured to be impossibly tall, with a sea of treasures that dwarfed any kingdom's.

It was here where the princess spent her days. It was here where she grew into a young woman, a kindled fire blazing inside her.

And it is here where one day fate's hand will set her on the path to reclaim what is rightfully hers. But at what cost?

Made in the USA
Coppell, TX
16 March 2022

75069129R00288